# SWEAR

NINA MALKIN

SIMON PULSE

NEW YORK   LONDON   TORONTO   SYDNEY   NEW DELHI

SIMON PULSE

An imprint of Simon & Schuster Children's Publishing Division

1230 Avenue of the Americas, New York, NY 10020

First Simon Pulse paperback edition September 2012

Copyright © 2011 by Nina Malkin

All rights reserved, including the right of reproduction in whole or in part in any form.

SIMON PULSE and colophon are registered trademarks of Simon & Schuster, Inc.

Also available in a Simon Pulse hardcover edition.

For information about special discounts for bulk purchases, please contact Simon & Schuster Special Sales at 1-866-506-1949 or business@simonandschuster.com.

The Simon & Schuster Speakers Bureau can bring authors to your live event. For more information or to book an event contact the Simon & Schuster Speakers Bureau at 1-866-248-3049 or visit our website at www.simonspeakers.com.

The text of this book was set in Adobe Garamond.

Manufactured in the United States of America

2 4 6 8 10 9 7 5 3 1

The Library of Congress has cataloged the hardcover edition as follows:

Malkin, Nina.

Swear / Nina Malkin. — 1st Simon Pulse hardcover ed.

p. cm.

Sequel to: Swoon.

Summary: In Swoon, Connecticut, seventeen-year-old Dice's life is returning to normal after Sinclair stole her heart and disappeared, but when her best friend's boyfriend goes missing Dice finds that Sinclair and an old promise are involved and she must, reluctantly, use her special abilities again.

ISBN 978-1-4424-2110-3 (hc)

[1. Supernatural—Fiction. 2. Missing persons—Fiction. 3. Love—Fiction. 4. Psychic ability—Fiction. 5. Conduct of life—Fiction. 6. Connecticut—Fiction.] I. Title.

PZ7.M29352Swe 2011

[Fic]—dc22

2010050950

ISBN 978-1-4424-2111-0 (pbk)

ISBN 978-1-4424-2655-9 (eBook)

*For Hobo Joe*

—*You are so lovely in slumber.*

—*Ha! Why, because I'm silent?*

—*No, not at all. It's a certain vulnerability you rarely display when awake.*

—*Why did you wake me, then?*

—*I did not wake you.*

—*So I'm dreaming?*

—*Dreaming? Hardly. Dreams are for children.*

—*Huh . . . I've heard of people talking in their sleep, but not conversing.*

—*Ah, but you're often surprised by your own abilities, the things you can do.*

—*That's true. Especially where you're concerned.*

—*For instance, did you know you could do* this *in your sleep?*

—*No . . . no, I didn't.*

—*And what of this?*

—*Oh, no. Oh, no . . .*

—*And this . . . and this . . . and this . . .*

# PART I

# THE GARDEN

 I

LOVE IS BLUE. A CLEAR CERULEAN WHEN NEW. A BRIGHT, BOLD, TRUE
blue in its glorious throes. And when it hurts, as it inevitably
will, love turns deep, dark, the color of a bad bruise. I know all
about that deep, that dark—I've been dealing with it for a while
now. One night of true bliss with the boy I love, and then he
was gone. Had he found the peace eluding him for centuries? Or
was his destiny null, void, blank, nothing? Don't ask me. All I
know is that what we shared—tumultuous as it often was—went
beyond tangible presence. He left me, of his own accord or by
some immutable force, but he's with me. I feel him. On me. In
me. Through and through me. That's how I can handle it.

Even though it hurts like hell. Literally. Our night was
intense—naturally, he put his mark on me. There, along my
inner thigh, storm-colored, tear-shaped. Only why won't the
blue bruise fade? Stroking soapy fingers across it in the shower,

I fall back against the tile, his imprint still so tender and reaching all the way to my core.

Six months later—as in now—the blue bruise remains.

Like I said, I can deal. I've . . . adapted. Here it is, almost summer, and I'll wear a skirt or shorts without a thought to my tarnished skin. At night, I'll sleep, ignoring that stained aspect of my anatomy. Sure, sometimes, alone in bed I'll press my hand there, and the pain is still the pain, except not exactly. Oh, and the nocturnal trysts, dreams that aren't dreams, during which we chat . . . and stuff. Then there's the after blow—the selfish ache of his absence—which kills. Only I have no control over any of it, or him. Sinclair Youngblood Powers. Boy turned ghost turned golem turned . . . who knows. My Sin.

*"Di-i-i-i-ce!"*

That would be Marsh. Shrieking. Except Marsh doesn't shriek. So I dash from the backyard, where I'm tending tomato seedlings (crazy, I know, a city girl like me) to find a foot-high blaze snarling on the stove top and my best friend haplessly flailing a pot holder.

"Marsh!" I hip-check her out of the way. "Fan the flames, why don't you?" I find the lid to the pan, slam it over the orange plumes. Grease fires and such don't faze me much these days. But Marsh, her eyes wide and brimming, cringes against the sink.

"It's out," I state the obvious. Adding, soothingly, "No worries, Marsh. No harm done." No harm, unless you're the chicken cutlets she's torched beyond recognition.

She blinks back tears. Which is weird. I mean, the girl blew away her abusive father with his own Clint Eastwood special last fall, and having shouldered so much suffering at the hands of Daddy Demento, she doesn't easily freak. I yank off my gardening gloves and put an arm around her.

Instantly she crumples. "Oh, Dice . . ."

"Marsh, come on, hush, okay? Nothing happened."

She sniffs, hard, and gets it together. I let go and watch her as she leans rigidly against the counter.

"I must've got . . . distracted." She presses a knuckle to mauve-tinged half-moons under sleepless eyes. "I'm sorry, Dice. I ruined dinner."

I just shrug. Marsh and I have been housemates since right around New Year's. She'd moved with her kid sisters into the new place, twenty miles away in Torrington, but the whole situation— with them, their mother, and New Pop—proved too tense. Living here, Marsh can graduate from Swonowa with our friends, still tend her beloved horses, work all summer to earn cash for vet tech school, and of course be close to her boyfriend, Crane.

The deal works both ways, though—it's good for me having Marsh around. My parents rarely are. Daddy landed a role in a series that shoots in Toronto. (Ever see *Officer Demon*, that show about the vampire cop? Yeah, he's the grumpy, overworked coroner.) And when circulation tanked at Momster's magazine *In Star*, she got a new boss, this Brit who makes Simon Cowell look like the Dalai Lama; her hours are more insane than ever. Taking a four-hour train-then-cab ride or driving a rental from Manhattan to Swoon, C-T, is so not on her schedule these days. Marsh is my buttress against loneliness; and she really is—lapse into patricide aside—a regular girl: down-to-earth, no-nonsense, and so a healthy influence. Ordinary is my number one goal these days, normal my nirvana. So I say, "It's not like your chicken supreme is so hot anyway."

It's true. The division of labor here at 12 Daisy Lane is usually: cooking = me, cleaning = her. Guess I was lingering in the garden too long and she got hungry.

Marsh sniffs again and slides her lank blond bangs. "Oh, shut up," she says, and tries a smile.

I try one back, though both smiles are weak. Something's definitely up with her. Sitting at the table in the tiny dining area, I say, "You want to tell me what's going on?"

For a beat her eyes narrow, that look she gets when she thinks I'm playing psychic detective. The girl is still a little spooked by my so-called gift.

I cock my head, press my lips. "It's pretty obvious. You're not the type to space out over a sauté pan."

Marsh sits opposite me, toys with the edge of a flea-market doily. "It's Crane," she says, her voice so thin it needs to be fed intravenously. "He dumped me."

"No, no, no, no." This may be a crazy, unstable, screwed-up

world, but if anything's for sure in it, it's that Crane Williams loves Kristin Marshall.

"Well then, where is he?" she wants to know. "I haven't seen him or heard from him in two days!"

Two days? Impossible. Although . . . yeah, it was two days ago that Crane's brother Duck called to cancel practice. They have this band, the Williams boys and another guy, Tosh Peters— basically a cover band plus two originals Crane wrote—and I'm kinda-sorta in it. On impulse I sang with them last week, and they've been bugging me to make it official. Strange, then, after I said I'd come to the next rehearsal, that they blew it off. "Two days. Huh."

"That's right," Marsh says. "And I keep going over it—what I said, what I did or didn't do, to make him mad or . . ."

I hate when girls do that, assume that whatever went wonky with their romance is some fault or failing on their part. Of course, Marsh hardly had stellar role models in the relationship department so I cut her some slack. I stand up. "Let's go."

"Go—where?"

"Their house. We'll see if he's home, and if not, we'll get something out of Duck." We call him Duck but the boy's more magpie—you can't shut him up.

This seems to make sense to Marsh; she nods once, and we're out the door.

"Wait a sec." I touch her wrist. "I'll be right back."

A restored relic from the 1700s, our clapboard farmhouse could go up like tinder. I just want to double-check, make sure all the burners are off. Call me OCD—you dance with death enough times, you can't be too careful. In the kitchen, though, everything's cool. Very cool; too cool. You'd never know by the temperature that we'd just beat down a blaze. Or by the smell. Not burnt chicken but . . . roses?

There's not a single rosebush on the property, but the scent is unmistakable, and unwelcome, snapping me back to the first and only funeral I ever had to attend. The church a sea of flowers, as you'd expect when someone so young and so beautiful so tragically dies. I see her now, my best friend since fourth grade, laid out in an open casket, her high-necked, long-sleeved gown demure, like nothing she'd ever be caught dead in. Now I'm giggling aloud, just as I did then—oh, the irony!—the giggles going headlong toward hysteria. Convulsively I laugh, I can't help it—the smell of roses so powerful and the chill of the grave so close. Which makes no sense, no sense at all. Unless I'm about to—

*NO!*

I haul off and slap myself across the face so hard my eyeballs bounce. Effective. That slide into clairvoyant never-never land that I never-never want to experience again? Neatly avoided. Damn, who knew? One good self-inflicted blow can psych out a psychic episode. I'll have to remember that.

II

RUBBING MY JAW, I GO MEET MARSH ON THE PORCH TO FIND THE
redolence of roses replaced by that of French fries.

"I need to copy your civics homework." A "hello" would've
been nice, a "please," but my cousin Pen has forgotten such
niceties. "Like the last three weeks' worth. I seem to have fallen
behind."

I'll say. Considering how often Pen's shown to class, I'd be
surprised if she knew that civics is the study of citizenship and
not Japanese cars. Now, graduation close enough to kiss, she's
playing catch-up. "Sure," I say. "Just not right now."

"How come?" Pen pops three fries at a time. "Where are you
going?"

"Rehearsal," I lie. Glancing at Marsh, I figure she might
want to keep the Crane conundrum between us.

"Ooh. Rehearsal." Pen snorts, then juts her chin at Marsh.

"So you're in the band now? What do you play—skin flute?"

I don't want to smack her; I really don't. When it comes to Pen, I practice patience. She's been going through changes lately. The dedicated junk-food diet that's added considerable poundage to her former cheerleader physique. The self-mutilated spiky mop that was once her cascade of shampoo-commercial hair. The well-adjusted It Girl who graciously took me into her social strata when I moved here a year ago has segued into this pastiche of nihilist, slacker, and all-around brat.

Late-onset rebellion? Early-onset senility? No, Sinclair Youngblood Powers. There's not a citizen of Swoon who didn't fall under his sway in some way, Pen especially. What Sin did to Pen—the possession, the seduction—it wasn't pretty. Yet in her warped way, she probably misses him almost as much as I do.

Marsh, for the moment, ignores her.

"I'll drop the civics off when I get back." Pen only lives across the road.

Tilting her head lest one crispy remnant escape her greedy tube, Pen considers this. She chews, and swallows, and then says, "No."

"No? Yes: no. Look, I don't want to be late."

"Not the stupid civics. I don't care about the stupid civics." Pen employs the meaty expanse between thumb and forefinger to wipe her mouth. "I want to come," she says. "If Marsh can be in the band, so can I."

My cousin doesn't share any familial tendency toward ESP, but she senses me wavering. She hasn't hung out in a while. Deep down she might be jealous of how tight Marsh and I are now. Deeper down, she must be battling some demons—lost to the perky, naive person she used to be, at odds with the sullied femme-bot Sin turned her into, and completely clueless about how she might wind up.

Marsh can sense my indecision too and tips the scales. "Let's just go, okay?"

Pen turns on her heel, her now ample ass switching with some of its old saucy flair. After all, she's still Pen—just a pudgier, discontented version. "My car, if you please!" she says, and we take her rich-girl ride instead of Marsh's hooptie.

It's a short drive from Daisy Lane to the Swoon town center, but Pen's yammering makes it feel endless. "So tell me how you play the skin flute," she taunts, locking eyes with Marsh in the rearview mirror. "Like this, right?" She jabs the inside of her cheek with her tongue.

"Pen, just stop." I don't want to smack her. I don't . . .

"A real virtuoso!" She cackles, and leans on her horn to piss off the car she nearly smacks into.

Sotto voce, Marsh goes weepy in the backseat, but Pen and I both hear her.

"Nice, Pen," I comment.

"Don't cry, you turd," she says, though her face falls quickly from mischief to chagrin. "I was just teasing, Marsh, really! What the hell—"

"You're an idiot, that's what," I inform her.

"Just tell her!" Marsh blubbers. "I don't care! Call Channel 8 while you're at it!"

I swivel to check on her, slumped against the upholstery, then open Pen's console for tissues. "Here." I hand off a ball of drive-thru napkins.

"Tell me what?" Pen insists.

"Crane dumped me."

"Marsh, you don't know that—"

"He did! He did!" she moans.

"Oh my God!" Pen echoes in sincere harmony. "Marsh, I'm so sorry—I *am* an idiot. Oh, Marsh!"

The chorus of female dismay comes to an end at the Williamses' driveway. The rambling stone manor house looms above us, beautiful, imperious, and old. And right in front, Crane's Cutlass SS—not so old, but certainly vintage.

Looks like Bruise Blue's guitarist is home.

# III

ARGUMENT IN THREE ACCENTS: THE NASAL BOSTON BARK OF PAUL Williams; the clipped yet wispy London lilt of his wife, Lillian; and the far-flung tones of their younger son, raised all over the world and quite accustomed to speaking his mind.

"Hard work should make a man of him! Instead he gives up, runs away, the worthless, ungrateful—"

"Please! I will not have you call Crane worthless! Simply because he doesn't fit the mold you'd force him into. If he's gone to find himself, I champion such courage."

It's easy for us eavesdroppers to figure out the thrust of this fracas. The east wing of the house is under renovation, and Crane, having put off college, got pressed by his father into manual labor. As far as we knew, he was fine with it—at least he got to hang with Marsh and play music when he wasn't pounding nails or mixing mortar.

"Courage?! You—"

"Stop! Cease! Desist!" Duck, shrilly. "I can't stand your fighting, which doesn't make a shred of sense anyway. If Crane's gone off, why is his vehicle in the driveway?"

Excellent point, but weaned on procedural detective dramas like I was, I know Crane could have ditched his sweet ride and hitched his way out on the Frontage Road.

"And moreover"—Duck flings an arm in our direction—"why is his beloved in our foyer?" The Williams parents turn from the great hall to our trio of intruders.

"Marsh! Darling!" Lillian Williams wafts regally our way, paisley caftan—a gift from some maharaja—and prematurely silver hair streaming. She insinuates herself between Pen and me to clutch Marsh against her bead-bedecked bosom. A clumsy maneuver for them both, Marsh being fashion-model tall and having to stoop for the embrace. Lillian then holds Marsh at arm's length, peering into our girl's eyes. "You do know where Crane is, don't you? No! You needn't say." She hurls a look at her husband. "I know in my soul he's on a journey, a journey he needs to take." Back to Marsh now. "But if you could tell us something, anything, to set our minds at ease . . ."

"I . . . um . . . ," Marsh stammers desperately, then stops, settles for tears.

"That's it!" Paul Williams thunders. "I'm calling the police."

"Paul, don't!" The boys' mother flits toward him, feet bare, toe bells tinkling. "I'd know it, I'd *feel* it, if he'd come to harm, and you'll only alienate him further . . ."

Duck shoulders us out of the vaulted foyer and through a passage that leads to the music studio; then, rethinking it, ushers us outside instead. Tucking his arm through Marsh's, he steers us across the grounds. "Truly, you don't know where he is?"

"No," she says. "What a selfish ninny I am! I've been a basket case thinking this was his way of breaking up with me."

"Tut-tut!" Yes, Duck actually says that. Think Oscar Wilde trapped in a beefy linebacker's body. "That would never happen."

Marsh isn't listening. "When all this time, he's been . . . he's . . ." She trails off.

"When did you last see him?" I ask Duck.

"After brunch on—"

A piercing whistle—street-hustle, city-style—interrupts his reply. We stop in our tracks.

"Yo!" The whistler waves, trots up, his nimbus of hair like coffee cotton candy. Tosh Peters. "Damn, Duck, your father does *not* like me, man."

Duck swats air. "To him, anyone over eighteen who's not at university is an imbecile or a criminal and probably both."

This garners a consensus of sighs: parents and their unholy fixation with higher academia. Tosh's folks, same deal—all aghast when he announced he'd be hooking up with an uncle to move to the wealthy boonies and open the region's premier

Jamaican restaurant. "I hear that," he says. And then he looks at me.

I look back.

Then he says, "Hey, Dice." He also greets Marsh, but his eyes stay put.

Which prompts a "Hey, Tosh. This is my cousin Pen" out of me.

And Tosh says, "Hey, Ben."

This cracks me up, inappropriate as that may be. "Pen, not Ben," I correct. "As in Penelope."

Blushing, a purplish tint invading his cheeks, he looks at my cousin for the first time. "Sorry about that, Pen-not-Ben." He treats her to a frankly winning smile, straight teeth between lips like a split ripe plum. "Good to meet you."

Pen says, "Yeah," and fixes her gaze somewhere under his left earlobe.

"So, look, man, what's up?" Tosh shifts on the balls of his feet, as though obeying a drum loop only he can hear. Vaguely I wonder if he's like that all the time, perpetual motion in the shower, in bed. "Is this band on or off or what?" He taps Duck's arm in an amiable way. "If it's off, that's cool, only you've had my Beatles anthology forever, dude, and Crane has my didgeridoo." Okay, Tosh Peters is a tad self-involved. It takes him forever to size up the tension among us. "What, is something wrong?" he asks at last.

He looks at me, and my look says *Ding! Ding! Ding!*

"Crane's missing." This from, of all people, Pen. "He's been gone two days. That's why we're all here. Sorry if that interferes with your dream of pop stardom, *Tork*."

Tosh doesn't take the bait. Brow creasing, he passes a palm across his unruly Afro. "Shit. Missing. Two days? And no one's heard from him?"

We start up again, an aimless meander, while filling Tosh in on everything we don't know about Crane's vanishing act. As our path takes us to the edge of the lawn, we pass through a gate into a thriving though unkempt garden. Clearly the Williamses don't retain a groundskeeper, other than someone to cut the grass; Lillian must like her flora au naturel, and Paul must not care. Flowers push up willy-nilly between neglected topiaries and ornamental sculptures. Every few yards, a bench, some made of marble, others with wrought-iron frames.

Marsh sinks onto a seat with a sigh. Pen, back in touch with her nurturing side, sits next to her and holds her around; while Duck, not be outdone in the mother hen role, kneels at her feet and takes one of her hands. Tosh and I prefer to stand, an inch of space between us, and as I again become aware of his steady swerve, I notice myself moving, just barely, in tune with his physical flow.

"Don't worry, Marsh," Duck says. "Wherever Crane is, he *will* come back."

"Do you really think so?" Her hope is a fly in a web.

"Well, yes—of course I do." To me it sounds like he's trying to convince himself as well as Marsh. He releases her hand to sit cross-legged on the ground, pressing fist to lips as though to frap a restless confession. "He wouldn't take off, not now, with his plans to . . . but he couldn't have been serious . . . although he did seem so happy, so sure . . . even though it's utterly bonkers, you both being so young . . ."

Huffing, Pen gives him a swift kick in the haunch. "Out with it, Duck. What the hell are you trying to say?"

"All right, all right!" He lurches onto his knees again. "I know Crane wouldn't have left without you, Marsh, because I know how much he loves you. You see—I saw it!"

We stare at him, stumped.

"Oh, Marsh—he showed me the ring!"

# IV

THE LIGHT IN THE GARDEN IS ALMOST GONE, YET MARSH'S EYES SHINE diamond bright. It takes her a second to locate her tongue, strap it to the syllable: "Ring?"

As in engagement ring? Precursor to wedding ring? No, no, no! Marsh still in high school, Crane barely nudging twenty. Yes, yes, yes! When you're in love, you're in love—what's age got to do with it? I'm too stunned to comment.

Pen, however, has no problem. *"Pfffff!"* she spews. I throw her a scowl—this is so not her business—yet she persists. "What kind of fairy tale are you people stuck in?" She makes bug eyes at all of us. "Clearly I'm the only one here even mildly in touch with reality."

Maybe so—but not for long, since right about then reality goes awry. A heavy, heady scent seizes the atmosphere—the same one I almost OD'd on an hour ago. Now, though, it's not merely the aroma of roses. All around us there's a rustling . . . a bursting. Shrubs that bore only leaves when we entered the garden explode in frantic profusion—think time-lapse photography on crystal meth. On a bower above our heads, buds surge into bloom so fast, the lattice groans with their weight. On every side, we're engulfed.

Marsh, Duck, and even Pen spring to their feet to stand with Tosh and me in a spellbound cluster. This is happening—to all of us. It's not some trick of my mutant mind alone. Together we succumb to impossibility in action. I'm overjoyed, overwhelmed, until all of a sudden the bottom drops out of my bliss. My blue bruise begins to throb, from the surface of my skin to the chambers of my heart, as I fiend for the one I most want to share this moment with.

*Sin!*

Do I shout his name or murmur it or simply feel him so strong, need him so bad, crave him so crazily, that the blunt-force trauma of my desire tweaks this event, spinning it from amazing to menacing. All I know is, adding Sin to the mix makes the roses encroach with belligerence now. And with thorns.

Slender stems encircle, pulling taut like wires, and tines attack. The essence of roses is ether now, and a small, weak part of my brain urges me to breathe it in, gulp it down, and let oblivion take over, anesthetize against the barbs that want my flesh, my blood, my very life. So I do—I breathe, I gulp, I go . . .

When I come to, it's cool, the air no longer sickly sweet but earthy green. The first stars flicker on, and evening calm pervades. I'm out of the garden, flat on my back in the grass.

"Dice? You okay?" Tosh's voice is clear, and close.

Woozily, I pull onto my elbows.

"Hey, Cuz."

Pen's here too, and Marsh and Duck. It's all too reminiscent of that last scene in *The Wizard of Oz*. I'm loath to say, "And you were there! And you—and you!" in case they chuckle indulgently; in case, in fact, they weren't. So I just say, "Things are a little fuzzy . . ."

"You passed out, and then *boom*, it was over," Tosh says. "Then I, uh, Duck and me carried you out."

"Uh-huh," I say, then nip my lip. On one level I want to talk about what happened, but then think, no: the less said, the better. Aside from that black-and-blue mark that thinks it's a tattoo, there hasn't been a whiff of otherworldly weirdness in my life post-Sin. No need to call attention to the perverse rose parade. If I shut up, maybe we can all forget it.

Unfortunately, my cousin feels otherwise. "So, Tosh, guess this was your induction into Dice World."

"Uh . . . huh?" he queries, like he'd rather not know. But Duck rivets on me, like he very much wants to. Willing myself invisible doesn't work, but Marsh steps up.

"Ignore her, Tosh," she says. "Pen's being a bitch."

"Oh?" My cousin flicks a lighter, fires up a doobie. On the exhale she says, "You want to crown Candice Reagan Moskow Miss Average American Teenager?" Squinting, she gestures with the joint. "You're saying where she goes, spooky-dooky doesn't follow?" Hits again, blows smoke. "Don't you think these boys have a right to know what dimensions their bandmate is capable of traveling into?"

"Do you intend to pass that, Pen?" Duck says. "And while you're at it, stop insinuating and start illuminating, hmm?"

"No," says Tosh with terse authority. He gets to his feet and offers his hand, helping me to mine. "We just did battle with berserk rosebushes; I think we should survey the damage, get with some disinfectant." He directs himself to Duck. "You got any hydrogen peroxide in that big house of yours?"

Marsh rises as well and dusts the seat of her pants. "Now there's an idea. We ought to eat something too. That's why Dice passed out, if you ask me. I used my supernatural powers to turn chicken into ashes earlier, and neither Dice or I has had a bite since fourth period."

"Of course," Duck agrees. "First aid first, and then we'll forage."

As we make our way back to the house, I'm still a little shaky, feverish, definitely drained. When the doobie wends my way, I say no to drugs—I don't want to mess with my electrolytes any further. When Duck puts a meaty arm through mine, I eagerly use his bulk for support.

A mistake.

"You know, Dice," he says, slowing us to lag behind. "I've seen some incredible things." Assuming this to be one of his long-winded travelogues, I lean in and even let my lids half close. "The pyramids, the temples of Angkor Wat. Bolivia's Salar de Uyuni—these salt lakes that change color from turquoise to flamingo when the wind blows." His ramble takes on a lulling quality. "Not just natural phenomena, either. Umbanda rituals in Santa Catarina, all right? A voodoo ceremony outside Port-au-Prince."

"Uh-huh," I say, dragging my feet.

"I want you to know, I'm a very open-minded person. I believe, Dice, I believe."

"Yeah? Cool . . ."

"And I know you believe too. Not just because of what Pen was hinting at. I can tell; I can sense it."

*Sure, sure—everyone's a psychic.* I don't say this aloud.

"That's why I feel I can tell you . . ." He lowers the volume a notch. "What we just experienced in the garden confirms certain suspicions of mine."

"That's great, Duck." I am *so* tired. How many miles of lawn to go?

"I didn't want to say it in front of Marsh, but I don't think

Crane is off finding himself, and I don't think he's run away, either." His voice is low as he brings us to a full stop and faces me. "Dice, I believe he's in there . . . someplace." He chucks his head toward the structure before us, a brooding stone beast against the moonlit sky.

I don't get it. "In the house, you mean? Like . . . hiding?"

"Not hiding," he says, gripping my arm now. "Hidden. Stolen."

# V

INVESTIGATING A SUPERNATURAL ABDUCTION DOESN'T EXACTLY JIBE with my goal to be Miss Average American Teenager, so I keep mum as our group troops inside. Duck drops it for the moment and flips the switch in the great hall so we can inspect one another. There are few scratches on anyone, which helps put the freaky flowering in perspective.

"There's got to be some meteorological explanation," Marsh reasons. "It's been so warm for May, and we had all that rain the other day."

"Uh-huh." Tosh is quick to agree. "And the way we were tripping about it, we just must've bumbled around in the bushes."

At a gilt-framed mirror above the mantelpiece, I address a faint red line on my cheek, another across my clavicle. Sure— heat wave, monsoon, klutziness. We merely imagined the ninja thorns, a mass hallucination brought on by purely natural phenomena.

Pen simply snorts. "You said you'd feed us," she reminds Duck.

Ever the solicitous host, he leads us to the larder, where we snack on gourmet packaged goods from the mother country (Lillian Williams retains a nostalgic taste for the shortbreads, lemon curds, and biscuits of her native land). Munching out helps drive the rose garden incident deeper into the recesses of our psyches.

That's when Lillian sweeps in to inform us she couldn't stop Paul from contacting the sheriff to report Crane's disappearance. The cops are on their way.

"We're out of here." Pen grabs her purse, grumbling animosity toward "the pigs" in a way that makes me wonder if this is simply a required aspect of her current phase, or if she's got over an ounce of weed stashed in a zippered compartment. I don't pester her about it, though—I'm good to go too.

For the next few days, I dodge Duck. Not too tough, since here in Swoon, ordinances protect the hills and dales from all but a few unsightly cellular towers, so he can't hound me with calls and texts. And since he's homeschooled, he's not stalking me around Swonowa. Poor guy—his only recourse is the landline at 12 Daisy Lane.

"Duck called," Marsh tells me Thursday afternoon. I'm coming in from chorale—we're doing a precommencement concert—and she's on her way out.

"Cool, thanks." I proceed to litter the downstairs with my gear, eliciting a frown from my housemate—she's kind of a neatnik and I'm sort of not.

"He said it was important."

I scoop up RubyCat and plop to the couch with my furball. "Come on, you know Duck," I say. "He gets a hangnail, he alerts the media. You off to the stables?"

Marsh nods. Of course she is—the Crane situation has only heightened her need for peaceful equine company; she rides each morning and whenever else she can. While everything her father owned had to be sold to pay his debts, Marsh's attorneys finagled a way for her to keep two of the horses, boarding them at a local stable in exchange for cleaning stalls. The mare, Brandy, is hers in every respect—more Marsh's bestie than I am. And then there's Black Jack, who she might've given up if anyone was nuts enough to buy him. Always a bit headstrong and moody— bullish for a horse—once Sin put a saddle on him, that was it, game over: The stallion could be mounted by none other.

"Mac and cheese tonight?" I tempt.

"Oh . . . sure." Marsh shrugs. "Fine."

Such lack of enthusiasm worries me—my mac and cheese rules. The girl is wound tighter than a banjo string, and I can't blame her; in fact, I relate, having also lost the boy of my dreams to who knows where. Sighing, I opt to tend my vegetable patch—how nice and normal is that? I change into grungy shorts and a threadbare tee that has too much sentimental value to join the rag bin, then shove my curls into a haphazard topknot. Once in the shed, I stop short, leery of the Miracle-Gro. *Cut it out!* I tell myself. There'll be no attack of the killer tomatoes; they're just plants—at this point, two inches high. And I really want to be harvesting peppers, cukes, and basil too.

It might be my last chance. The house at 12 Daisy is up for sale. With me set to start college in the city come fall, it just makes sense for me to move home. Yeah, sure, I've had my sights set on Columbia practically since birth, only with everything that went down over the last year . . . let's just say it won't be easy to bid good-bye to Swoon. So I'm out here digging, visions of home-made gazpacho dancing in my head. That's when I hear my name.

Duck, no doubt; the dude is relentless.

"Yo! Dice! You around?"

That Brooklyn brogue—a little tough, a little lazy—definitely not Duck. Getting vertical, I push an escaped tendril out of my face with a dirty glove, and there's Tosh. "Oh . . . hey."

He's pointing at my chest?! No, no, no; he's pointing at the logo on my T-shirt. "Ramones, all right." His hydra of hair bobs approval. "Seminal."

"My mom interviewed Joey once," I say. "She does a celebrity tabloid now—you know, Julia Roberts and Jennifer Aniston and whose husband is screwing the Nazi stripper of the moment— but she used to be cool." Oh, how I blather.

Tosh nods again, rocks to his inner beat. Then, silence. Not really awkward. Just sort of fraught.

Then, "So what's up? What are you doing?"

Thinking of what I'm doing reminds me of how I must be looking. Ratty clothes, no bra, and have I shaved my legs in recent memory? Not that Tosh is dressed to impress, in those checked pants cooks wear. "I don't really know, to tell you the truth," I say. "Before last year, the closest I got to a backyard was Central Park."

"Yeah, we are in the wilderness." He's being funny, and I like funny. I also like how his eyes change color—green-no-gray- no-gold.

"The hinterlands," I banter.

"The outback."

"The provinces."

Are we . . . flirting? It feels that way, with a surge of heat and a twitchy smirk. I pick up the watering can, a convenient prop.

"Yeah, well, good thing the local yokels like curried goat," he says. "Or I'd be at Columbia or some shit."

"Columbia? You're kidding! That's where I'm going." Geek! Geek! Geek! "I mean, I've been accepted, but the future—who knows?"

"Yeah, exactly. Oh, hey, kitty."

R.C. has poked through the cat flap to remind me that kibble doesn't pour itself. Which means I need to stop dicking around, start the people food too. The thought of asking Tosh to dinner occurs, then unsettles. Am I daunted by the prospect of cooking for a pro? Or is it something more, inviting him in akin to a betrayal . . .

"So I guess you're wondering what I'm doing here." He gets to it at last.

I cock my chin in the international posture of *explain, please.*

"Band business."

Oh. Yeah. Band business. Of course.

"It sucks, Crane missing and all—unless he's where he wants to be, and then it's all good—but I don't think we have to stop. Duck ought to play, get his mind off his troubles. Only if I can be selfish a minute, here's the thing: Since you came into the picture, I think this band could actually go somewhere. We're not just three guys wanking anymore."

I remember catching them as Not From Connecticut at a party the Williamses had last summer. What a fateful night that turned out to be. "Whoo . . . ," I say quietly. "NFC!"

Tosh smiles. "Stupid. But then you bust in, and straight up, you give us a real name. Bruise Blue."

Hey, anything would be an improvement. It does have a certain resonance, though.

"That's deep, Dice," he goes on. "That's meaningful."

If he only knew how much—to me.

"And you've got a set of pipes on you. Really."

I've got to appreciate his taste.

"If we worked on it, maybe we could line up a gig, play out. Even without Crane's songs. People love cover bands; they like to hear tunes they know as long as they're done well." He waits a beat, letting his sales pitch sink in. "So what do you say?"

Good question. I can sing; I know I can sing. A solo in chorale? No problem. But front a band, seriously? That first time was just random. The boys jamming, Marsh and me hanging in the studio, and Crane recalling that auspicious hayride last fall. A weather-beaten wagon. A harvest moon. A bunch of kids, a little high. Sin had been making mischief as usual, then settled down and pulled a harmonica out of his pocket, huffing and puffing while Crane strummed his Martin. Next thing I knew, the moonlight was my spotlight for this forceful freestyle, on-the-spot blues song to my boy—a song of woe, a song of warning, a song of what love gone wrong can do.

So last week in the studio, they all got to daring, then begging, then threatening that I better sing right now. Tosh grinned at me, intrigued, and Crane played the intro to that uber-mega-gonzo hit on everybody's iPod right now, so WTF, I obliged. And it was weird: There I was, fooling around with the kind of catchy pop that makes my Cocoa Puffs habit seem healthy, goofing with three other guys, when—*bam!*—a sense of Sin came on strong. So strong, it was like he stood there, nodding to the beat, eyeing me with his signature half smirk, waiting for the bridge so he could chime in on mouth harp.

Yeah. Well. What did he used to call me? Right. "My drowsy thrush."

I loved the feeling. Singing, yeah. The musical bond band members share, sure. But the Sin-ness, the undeniable communion with the boy who wasn't there, that's what seduced me, ensnared me, made me go, *More . . . more . . . more!* So when Duck clapped his hands and cried, "Dice, sing another!" I did. Damn skippy, I did.

"Dice?"

Huh? Oh, Tosh! Here and now, beside my struggling plants, a hungry cat winding between my shins.

"You in?"

Committing to Bruise Blue—and continuing to channel Sin—can't possibly help me in my quest for normalcy. Unless it can. Cushy distractions like a veggie garden and comfort food may muffle the situation but won't abolish it. If I'm ever to heal from this blue bruise, maybe I need to vent, vociferate, howl my head off. Maybe. Maybe not. But "maybe" isn't one of the two answers I can give Tosh.

So I pick one. An answer, that is. "Yes." I say it. What the hell, it's just for the summer—possibly my final summer in Swoon. "I'm in. Sure."

"No shit? For real? Killer! Then we should practice ASAP. Like tomorrow. I already talked to Duck, and he's down. Although I have to work, so it'd be late, like around midnight. I could pick you up. If you want."

Again, the *Y* word. I want. I want very much.

"Hey, you know what I'm thinking? We should do some real blues. Muddy Waters, Robert Johnson, or—what am I saying?—Big Mama Thornton, Bessie Smith . . . you being a female and all . . ."

The dude is getting way ahead of himself, but the truth is, I was raised on the blues—Daddy's revered vinyl, the sleeves in plastic sheeting. I grin at him, shrug in acquiescence, and he takes off, elated.

Later, at the stove, idly stirring cheese into mac, I think of that golden glint in Tosh's eyes. There because he's stoked about the band, how we might "go somewhere." Unless, of course, I put it there.

# VI

THE KUSTARD KUP—SWOON'S KWAINT ALTERNATIVE TO DAIRY Queen—opens for the season Friday. Marsh has been a fixture since age fourteen, and once again she dons the hairnet. What with school, the stables, her overall emotional state, and her first night on the job, you'd assume she'd be exhausted when she's done around eleven. Instead, she's a lightning bolt of jittery blond energy. And she's not alone. Her tumbledown Toyota pulls up the driveway, followed by a far fancier SUV I know full well.

"Hi-yee!" Pen strolls in behind Marsh, spooning from a sundae bigger than her head. "Want some?"

I take her up on two creamy, gooey bites.

"What are you all dressed up for?" my cousin wants to know.

"What are you talking about?" I counter. "I'm not dressed up."

Pen squints, scrutinizes. "Well, you're dressed." As opposed to being in PJs—what every self-respecting homebody wears on Friday nights. Ever the label whore, Pen's anarchist ensemble is nonetheless high-end, making me a tad self-conscious of my thrift-shop special: a man's patterned polyester button-down, circa 1976, cinched at the waist over leggings.

"Pen, come on," says Marsh, who hasn't even sat down yet.

Pen hands over her purse. "Help yourself."

Removing a Baggie of excellent herb, Marsh repairs to the kitchen table to roll a fatty. Pen, meanwhile, flops onto the couch and continues her appraisal. "And is that mascara?"

I make a face. "I'm going to Duck's; we're going to play."

"And how are you getting there? Astral projection?"

It's a fact: A year in Swoon and I still can't operate a motor vehicle—some sort of NYC mental block. "If this is your way of offering me a lift," I say, "no thank you. Tosh is picking me up."

Pen burps. "He is so in love with himself, that one." Ice cream radar in full effect, RubyCat pounces my cousin, sniffing. "Marsh, don't you think?"

"Huh?" Marsh looks up, ponytail swinging. "What?" Damn, she needs to mellow out.

"That guy Tosh," Pen says.

"Hey, don't let her have hot fudge!" I snap. "Chocolate can kill a cat. And so what if he has an ego? It's justified." Tosh is one of those irritatingly gifted people who can wing it on any instrument.

"I'm so sure."

I'm so flippant. "Come, then. Hear for yourself. Marsh, you too." Having her there will be a buffer against Duck; he won't bug me with his *mwa-ha-ha* haunted house obsession if his brother's beloved is around. Plus, Marsh and Duck seem to find comfort in each other—them being practically in-laws already.

So Tosh arrives, and he's all "the more the merrier" (read: he'd love an audience). We pile into Pen's car (I'm carbon footprint fussy—it'd be unconscionable to caravan) and head for the handsome house off the green. Which is in considerable disarray—newspapers, empty bottles, items of Lillian's eccentric wardrobe strewn about the great hall. And here's Duck, splayed on a sofa, his hair in tufts and his eyes puffy.

"Don't mind the mess," he says, heaving himself erect. "Or mind it, I don't care!" Then, "Oh, I'm sorry, don't mind *me*."

He and Marsh cling in greeting, and I begin to doubt this was such a great idea.

Tosh puts a hand on the big guy's shoulder. "You hanging in there, man?"

Duck shakes his head, a woebegone teddy bear, and my heart goes out to him. "It's hard," he admits. "It's been nearly a week. Mum's a wreck, subsisting entirely on white wine and toffee; Father's furious; and the sheriff's department is truly worthless." His shoulders rise and fall like twin anvils. "The worst part is, I've taken Crane for granted all my life. Our family wafts about like vagabonds, wherever the wind and Mummy's whims might take us, but Crane was the constant. Crane was always there."

His gaze is on me during this last part, which makes me squirmy. Duck wants something from me—he's not sure what, and neither am I—yet I just can't bring myself to merge into the paranormal lane. We hold each other's eyes, and then he forces brightness. "Let's rock out, shall we?"

The studio is spacious, wood-paneled, and comfy, hosting a slew of instruments, sheet music, and tablature, plus a computer and various racks of recording gear. The girls sink into plush suede seats side by side while we Bruise Bluers proceed to ignore them. Tosh adjusts the stool at the drum kit, and Duck, who usually plays bass, hovers over his brother's Les Paul, then picks up the SG instead.

"I just want you to know, I'm a crap guitarist," he warns.

"No worries, dude—you're a crap bassist too," Tosh joshes, with a *ba-dum-bum-tish* on tom-tom and cymbal.

I approach the microphone like a curious animal. "Is this on?" Yikes—feedback! "Oops—guess so."

There's a bit of tuning up as we decide not to work on Crane's songs—too weird without him. We toss tune titles around awhile, and then Tosh, a little impatiently, says, "Come on, come on, singer's choice."

"All right, boss man!" Riffling through a stack of lyric sheets, I

pull one out at random—the Ramones' "Teenage Lobotomy"—
and we're off. We do this, we do that, mostly upbeat three-chord
punk and pop, me purposely avoiding the blues and its typically
lovesick verses. I can't tell if we're any good, but Marsh and Pen
seem into it—they applaud, anyway. Then Pen pulls Marsh out
of her chair and they mosh with abandon. Is that a bona fide
smile getting whipped by Marsh's ponytail? It is. For the first
time in a long time, I could kiss my cousin.

After a while Tosh quits the kit, flexing his chops with
one thing after another: guitar, sax, even that whacky pipe of
didgeridoo. I'll cop to it—I'm a little jealous. Much as I love
music, I've always been all thumbs when it comes to any instrument other than my voice. I get over this the second Tosh
attends the piano and rehearsal devolves into a cornball sing-
along.

"Oh, I love this stuff!" he says, thumbing through a thick
tome of Elton John ballads. We harmonize (horribly) on
"Candle in the Wind," then Duck takes a hilarious turn on
lead vocals for "Don't Let the Sun Go Down on Me" (changing the lyrics to "Do let your son . . ."). By the time we get to
"Goodbye Yellow Brick Road," Marsh and Pen have crowded
around, all of us yowling more or less in unison.

"Stop! Stop!" Duck demands at the coda, his face pink and
his smile a beacon. "Stop or I'll pee!"

Tosh throws up his hands. "Please, man! Pee elsewhere!"

So Duck dashes off to the loo and Pen decides to find one too.

"That was so fun, Tosh, really," Marsh says, blowing at her limp bangs. She looks tired, spent—in a good way, for a change.

"Yeah, who knew schmaltz was your forte." I give him a gentle shoulder shove. "I'm impressed."

"You ain't heard nothing till I've butchered Barry Manilow."

Marsh hits up the bar, the mini-fridge tucked beneath, and while I hear her ask, "Water, anyone?" for some reason I don't answer. Neither does Tosh. We just share the bench for a few endless seconds. Then, out of nowhere, a sharp, acute shock of the pain that's more pleasure. For the first time ever in public, in that very private place, my blue bruise starts to throb. Damn right, I flinch!

Does Tosh notice? He must, since he pops up with a "Water! Yes! Water!" and shakes his limbs in their sockets.

In an instant it's gone, no throb, no echo, no trace. Just me wondering what the hell *that* was. I steal a glance at Tosh, who guzzles as he strides around the room, cutting me a way-wide berth. Great. Only now, alone with the baby grand, I can appreciate how cool it is, all curvy construction and satiny polish. Almost like a mythical creature—sturdy legs, a single wing, eighty-eight teeth in its stunning smile. I run my fingers across the keys, warmer than I thought they'd be. Inviting, in fact. And so, out of nowhere—the proverbial clear blue—I begin to play.

Eerily lovely, the melody must draw Tosh and Marsh close

again. Only I'm not aware they're standing there. Nor do I know when Pen and Duck come back into the room. What I do know is A-minor—not the saddest key, more bittersweet, melancholy but not without hope—and three-quarter time. A waltz. Elegant and enduring, the sort of piece a couple might have danced to, out there in the grand hall, back when the house was new. It sweeps and swirls, builds and then ebbs, pouring out of me. And when it's done, my fingers lift from the ivories to my lips.

I look up into the faces of my friends.

Marsh and Tosh radiate clueless glee—pleasantly surprised. Pen's expression is confusion mixed with annoyance—she knows full well I'm as proficient at piano as I am behind the wheel. But Duck, poor Duck, wears a grimace of unadulterated dread.

"Whoa, Dice, where'd that come from?" Tosh asks.

"I have no idea," I softly, slowly admit.

"I do," asserts the stricken Duck. "I recognized it immediately. Crane hummed the damn thing compulsively—every time he came from the east wing!"

 VII

IT'S DIFFICULT IF NOT IMPOSSIBLE TO WRITE DUCK OFF AS A DRAMA queen. Especially as I notice the stink—that's right, stink, stench, malodorous aura—of roses in the room.

"Wow," I concede, purposefully closing the cover on the piano keys. "That's weird."

"Yes, Dice," Duck says. "It is. Perhaps now you'll take me seriously."

Pen leans a knee on the bench. "What's he talking about?"

My eyes are all over the place—on Pen, Marsh, the third eye of the wall. "Duck has this theory . . ."

"What?" Marsh demands, features converging, voice tightening. "About Crane?"

"Yes, Marsh, it is about Crane," Duck says. "And, really, it ought squash any fears you might have that he's been struck by a car or something awful like that."

Right, Duck's got a whole other kind of awful in mind.

"I believe," he says, "that he's still in the house. I believe the house . . . *has* him."

A reflexive puff of disbelief and Tosh breaks the tension; too bad the pieces are so sharp. "Dude, sorry, I know you're upset," he says, palm up. "But come on."

"No, *you* come on." Pen wags a digit. "You don't know anything. You live in Norris." The next town over, it might as well be Pluto. "This is Swoon."

Not one to step off a confrontation, Tosh spews syllables: "Huh? So? What?"

I get up, come between them. "What she's trying to say is . . ." My fingers stray toward Tosh's sleeve, then fall to my side. Is it my priority to make him understand that Swoon is special, and so am I? Or is it time to bring Marsh up to speed on Duck's suspicions—suspicions I can no longer deny? I turn to her. "Look, Marsh, Duck thinks something haunty is happening. And he thinks I can help."

Marsh grips my arm, but Tosh can't get with this—at all.

"Help, then," he says, his eyes gone the gray of everyday reality. "Tell him—no offense—that he's nuts."

"I can't, Tosh. Look, I tried to go along with you guys when you blew off the rose garden episode the other night, but I've had . . . similar experiences—"

"That's right, all her life." Pen offers commentary I so don't need.

"And just now, with the piano?" I go on. "I mean, yeah, it would be remarkable but not necessarily magical if I spontaneously composed a piece of music. And maybe you could argue I've heard it before, caught Crane humming it and then forgot. Only, Tosh, the thing is, I can't play piano. Not 'Frère Jacques,' not 'Twinkle, Twinkle, Little Star,' not even 'Chopsticks,' okay?"

His lips flatten and I hope I'm just imagining that flinch. Turning again to Marsh and Duck, I say, "So now I'm like, fine, freaky is afoot. And, okay, I'm . . . sensitive. But I still don't get what you expect me to do about it."

Stumped, the lot of us. Me, well, I'm distracted—thinking about what Tosh is thinking about, and thinking it can't be good, and mad at myself for thinking about that when I have far more important things to think about.

Then Pen says, "I know: You can do the cards."

The cards. My cards. A present from my oldest, bestest, deadest friend when I hit sixteen. The deck I used to turn to for a clue on what fate was stirring up for me and mine. You know, can't decide how to spend your weekend? Consult the cards. Develop a crush and wonder if it's mildly mutual? Consult the cards. Get the insane notion that your cousin is possessed by the ghost of a boy whose execution you witnessed back in 1769? Consult the cards! Except the cards, my cards, have been put away. Shrouded in a silk scarf, laid to rest in a cigar box, entombed in a suitcase under the bed with other stuff I don't want or need but can't bring myself to toss.

"The cards?" Marsh is mystified. She was babysitting the night last fall when I brought my deck to Caroline Chadwick's slumber party in the hope of outfoxing Sin.

"Tarot," Pen expounds.

Thanks, Pen. But Tosh doesn't make a mad streak for the exit, which I find encouraging.

"Brilliant!" Duck says, then, "Please, Dice, won't you?"

Marsh implores only with her eyes, those big, wet foal eyes that have seen too much tragedy. Suckered!

A shrug, a sigh—the best I can manage to express acquiescence. Except Duck's looking at me like he's ready for a reading on the spot. "What do you think, I tote tarot cards around in my purse, just in case? They're not tampons, you know," I say. "Look, you guys, it's late, I'm fried; I need to be on top of my game to connect with the cosmos." The weekend won't work either—Marsh will be shuttling between the Kustard Kup and visiting her sisters in Torrington, plus my mother's driving up.

"Well, then, Sunday evening?" Duck says. "Sevenish?"

"I can do that," I say.

"Me too," Marsh agrees.

"I'm good." When Pen signs on, I get a twinge of this-has-nothing-to-do-with-you, but I let it slide. This was, after all, her idea.

"Fine," says Tosh. "I work Sunday brunch."

I flick his way. This has even less to do with him, plus skeptical vibes I don't need. But I can't deny that on a certain level I'm glad that, whatever he's thinking, it's not that my gift is just shy of leprosy.

And so, on Sunday, it's under the bed and into the box and over to the Williams place. Lillian and Paul pause their ongoing argument to wave us girls toward the conservatory. That's where we find Duck—on a cushion, legs crossed, fingers kissing.

"Umm . . . Duck?" Marsh calls to him. "We're here."

"Ah!" Lashes fluttering open, he extends his arms to exhibit the position of his fingers, tips of thumbs meeting tips of his rings and pinkies. "The *prana mudra*," he explains. "Pumps the life force."

"That's good," I say. "Pumping the life force is good."

He rises with fluid agility, and I have to bite the inside of my cheek to check my giggle. Clearly the boy raided his mother's jewelry box—there must be thirty pounds of beads, crystals, charms, and amulets around his neck. Tosh arrives in a minute, his usual upbeat vibe subdued for the occasion, and Duck requests that we transit to the east wing without a sound; he'd prefer if his parents didn't know what we're up to.

While previous owners had modernized much of the house over the generations, this portion had gone untouched except for maintenance, necessary repairs. Once we've stolen up the staircase and are free to explore, Duck tells us it had been shut down until the renovation began. "Which, personally, I think was just Father's expensive way to punish Crane."

He grants access to the room where his brother had been learning the not-so-finer points of construction grunt work. A small chamber, with rounded contours, set as it is in a narrow, cylindrical tower. Aside from ladders and toolboxes, a drop cloth across the floor, it's empty. And I mean empty. I feel no "presence" of any kind, but then again, I never actively sought a spirit before—the mofos always came looking for me. Instead I notice only the obvious and earthly. A fine layer of dust everywhere. The air musty, chalky, vaguely chemical and, buried under all that, something else, more unpleasant, and though familiar, I can't place it.

The ornate moldings and decorative ceiling medallions are in the process of being restored, but the most striking aspect is the mantelpiece. That's where the crew must have quit for the weekend—the fireplace is a demo zone—but the mantel is intact and truly a work of art: pure white marble, intricately carved.

Marsh traces the craftsmanship with her fingers, but no one remarks on what the carvings depict: roses.

I soon become conscious of all eyes on me.

"Well," I say. Might as well get this over with. "Let's just sit on the floor and try to get as comfortable as possible."

Only Pen makes a small pout of protest. Of course she's in all black, and of course she'll be covered in chalky, dusty stuff when we're done.

Box, open. Scarf, untied and spread before me. "I'm not going to do a Celtic cross," I say, like they know what a Celtic cross is. "We have some pretty specific questions, so I think if we all focus"—my eyes flick on Tosh—"and keep it open, respectful"—back to the cards—"we might get some answers."

They are quiet around me, heads bowed, concentrating. Cool. I get this party started.

"Where is Crane Williams?" I beseech the tarot. I cut. I reveal. Result: the Tower.

Considering the very room we sit in, Duck's theory is looking pretty good right now.

Three more times I shuffle. "Why did Crane leave?" I beseech, cut, reveal. Result: the Lovers.

A sharp little gasp from Marsh over the courting couple on the card.

Shuffle, shuffle, shuffle for a final query. "Who's responsible for Crane's departure?" Beseech. Cut.

Reveal . . .

This time it's me who gasps. My mouth a horrified O. My hand snatching back as if singed. My eyes springing stinging tears. The card on the silk before me, taunting and tripping and toying with me, is the Hanged Man.

# VIII

ONLY PEN COMPREHENDS MY FREAK-OUT. ONLY PEN KNOWS WHO the Hanged Man is, *our* Hanged Man. So I can't really blame her when she mutters, "Oh, crap." Yet I do shoot her a look that spells out, in no uncertain terms, that if she makes another peep on the subject, I'll cause her bodily harm. Marsh knows Sin as my ex, no more. Duck knows Sin only as that fabulously charismatic devil who hung around last fall. Tosh doesn't know Sin from a stick in the ground. Their ignorance is my, well, not bliss but preference.

"I . . . I don't get it," says Marsh.

I don't either. If I could breathe, maybe it would come to me. I shut my eyes, rub my temples. "Just give me . . ." What's Sin got to do with it? Nothing, nothing, a thousand times nothing. "A minute . . ." Compelling myself to calm down, to finish my sentence. "To interpret this . . ."

The Tower. The Lovers. The Hanged Man.

Mustn't take the images literally, or sweat the orthodox significance of the cards either. Always a tarot dilettante, I've relied on my gut, my gift, to make sense of the messages. That's what I ought to do now—it's not so much what I see as what I feel. So I sandwich the Tower between my hands, and, "Something sudden, a shock, like an explosion, a conflagration. Destruction . . . upheaval . . . rubble."

On to the Lovers. Picking up the card, I say, "This one's a no-brainer: love, sex, passion, happiness—a bond." Feeling it panini-style, I add, "Trust . . . but also temptation . . . communication . . . and mixed signals . . . a bond betrayed."

The last card. The Hanged Man. I let myself look at him. Let myself love him—because I do. "See how he's upside down, more like an animal in a snare than a criminal at the gallows? And the innocence on his face." This is a revelation to me—I'd never noticed it before. "Whatever happened was a mistake." Then I press him to my heart. "He got caught in something he doesn't understand. He stepped into this mess, and he submits, suspended, since what else can he do?"

On the floor, three pictures that mean everything and nothing. "That's it," I say.

"Well, that's bloody bewildering!" Duck spouts. "Really, Dice, you muddled the situation more than illuminated it."

"I am a little rusty," I admit, pulling my legs to my chest

and hugging my shins, my bones heavy with their burden, my psyche drained. Duck, Marsh, all of them—were they expecting divination on demand? Guess I let them down. I won't even look at them now. All I want is to be out of this ruined, acrid room, away from these people, their problems. All I crave is that surreal semiconsciousness that brings my love to me, a state I cannot conjure or control. I lift my head, shake it again. "Sorry, Duck," I say, "but in tarot, as in life, questions often beget questions."

"And that's a good thing!" This, coming from Tosh, rattles our assembly. "No, really," he insists. "Look, I never thought I'd put any credence in trumped-up playing cards, but the reading is a start. Something sparks questions, you follow the questions, keep following until you get the truth." Tosh looks at each of us, then settles on me, his eyes in a green phase, inquisitive, excited. "But I think you can put your deck away, Dice. It said what it had to say."

"So what do you suggest we do next?" Pen shifts from hip to hip. "Hit up the Magic Eight Ball?"

Tosh grins at her indulgently. "How about books. Newspapers." He points to the Tower. "You really believe that one means this house? Well, you might want to find out all you can about the place. Calamity? Upheaval? If it happened, I bet there's a record of it." Tosh gets to his feet, lacing his fingers in a satisfied stretch. His work here is done. "There's a historical society in Norris; I drive by it every day. I'm just saying you might want to check it out."

Follow the questions, huh? Yeah, well, what if I don't feel like it? What if I'd rather curl up in a nice, warm ball of denial? Since first of all I don't believe that Sin has anything to do with the Crane thing—the card popped up in the reading, sure, but anyone could be the Hanged Man in this case. Maybe Crane is the Dangled Dude. And second of all, following the questions won't do much to get Miss Average American Teenager printed under my yearbook photo. I love Marsh, and I'll be there for her emotionally, but I don't see why she can't follow the questions without me. Frankly, our whole crew trying to solve this mystery—all we need is a Great Dane with marbles in his mouth and we could be the next Scooby-Doo!

"Which would make you who, Candida? Velma, right?"

Oh, terrific. Simply swell. Splendid. Ruby Ramirez hasn't come to visit in the longest—ever since I exposed her, in fact, telling her story, our story, to Sin. Flatly, I announce her name. Not that it isn't great to see her, just that she has a way of showing up when I need her—and I'd rather not need her. "You ever hear of privacy?" I am, after all, in the tub, seeking bubbly solace, post-tarot, on Sunday night.

"Between us, baby girl? Since when?"

True that. Ruby and I have no secrets, and we've certainly

seen each other in various compromising positions and states of undress. Joining me here, she's in her birthday suit as she perches on the rim of the tub. The body that was such boy bait as a living, breathing human being hasn't changed a bit, and bountiful waves of brown hair spill across her spine. I have no reply, so she goes on.

"Because, *lo siento*, sweetie, Marsh gets to be Daphne." Leisurely, her flawless manicure wanders through my bathwater. "Duck is . . . what's the preppy one's name?"

"Freddie."

"Right. Freddie. And Shaggy is your new boy."

I grab the soap. Maybe if I hurry up and finish, she'll go away. "Tosh is not my new boy."

Arching an eyebrow, Ruby doesn't push it. To her, males and females can never be just friends.

"So who's Scooby?" I ask, and at the same time we both spout, "Pen!"

"Might as well change her species; she's changed everything else," Ruby observes.

"Funny . . . but I think she's still Pen. She's just going through some shit."

"Generous to a fault, as usual, Candy." Ruby holds one finger high: recognize. "If my cousin messed around with my man? Uh-uh-uh, I don't know I could be so forgiving."

"I think she feels bad enough about that already," I say.

"Among other things. I mean, why gain twenty pounds and chop all your hair off unless you don't want guys to look at you 'that way' ever again?"

Ruby's hair, suddenly, is piled in an elaborate updo the size and general shape of a wedding cake. "I guess," she allows. "Hey, you want me to do your back?"

There she is, equipped with a frothy sea sponge. Without a word, I tilt slightly, lean over, and let her wash the expanse from nape to coccyx, shoulder blade to shoulder blade. Water gushing, sponge scrubbing, her diligent ministrations all so good. Every muscle turns to mush and pleads for more—more strength, more tenderness, more love. Because Ruby does love me, and miss me. A lot. Enough to finish what she instigated the night we concocted our caustic witch's brew? I had only sipped before the goblet slipped from my fingers; Ruby guzzled like it was Gatorade. I woke the next morning with a hangover; Ruby . . . did not. My hand reaches around, finds hers, firmly stills it.

"That was nice." I sit up straight. "Thanks."

*"De nada."* As Ruby flips air, I notice her sporting a diamond the size of a kumquat.

I rinse the sponge and spy, on Ruby's thigh, a single garter trimmed in satin and frilly white lace. "So, Rubes . . ." If she's here, it's no doubt to kibitz on the paranormal soap opera I find myself guest starring in. "Duck thinks his brother was jacked by someone of the poltergeist persuasion. What's your take?"

"*Pffff!*" she spews. "What, you think we all know each other or something? Because let me tell you, we don't have Facebook, all right? There's no Twitter on the other side."

"All right, okay, I'm sorry." I pop the plug. "It's just, Marsh and them expect me to step up, and frankly, I'd rather not. I mean, maybe Crane just got a bad case of commitment-phobia, and instead of giving Marsh a ring, he's off having himself a big old bimbo binge!" Giving voice to my ruminations feels good, and I stand up with a wet *sploosh*. "But then why do I get attacked by rosebushes? And hit the piano like an instant virtuoso?" Water recedes around my calves, around my ankles, to the sound of slurping. "Why do I get myself roped into a tarot reading that implies the only boy I ever loved is behind the whole thing? Why?" I wonder madly as fists form at my sides. "Why?" I wonder madder still as Ruby begins whirling like a cartoon tornado. "Why, goddamn it? It's just . . . not . . . fair."

"Because life isn't fair, Candida," Ruby tells me just before she's sucked down the drain. "And neither is death."

# IX

COME MONDAY, MARSH AND I DITCH SCHOOL TO NOSE AROUND THE local outpost of the Litchfield Historical Society. Now that it's just us (reducing the Scooby-Doo factor), I can let myself enjoy the intrigue a little. Plus, it's a gorgeous day: sunny, breezy, summer jumping the gun. Too bad Marsh is in a mood, our conversation bumpy as the roads are smooth.

"I talked to Duck this morning," she says. "His parents hired a private investigator. Someone fitting Crane's description was seen in Waterbury." She bites her lip. "I mean, if it *was* him, he's alive—but . . . but Waterbury!"

People consider Connecticut the Snooty State, and they're right, but it has its share of rough spots, and most of them, apparently, are in Waterbury. Marsh can't imagine what a sweet, innocent guy like hers would be doing there. "His description?" I say. "I wouldn't worry too much, Marsh—I bet Waterbury is crawling with lanky, sandy-haired guys." This allays her concerns not one iota. "Besides, it's good to cover all the bases. And I bet the private investigator is the best in the business."

We ride in silence awhile, and then Marsh blurts out, "What did you mean by a bond betrayed?"

"What? Oh . . . the reading." I shrug. "I don't know, Marsh. I just . . . pick things up. Intangible transmissions, metaphysical signals. I say what I say because that's what I sense. I wish I could explain what it means."

She turns from the wheel like she's got another question, then opts against it. Scanning the radio dial, I search for something that won't wig her out, even though that means WDNC, the dance station, nothing but soulless, mechanized club bangers. As I tune the radio out of my mind, Tosh jumps into it, and I can't help but smile at having met someone who listens to a different drummer, literally. What a trip it would be if we *did* start doing blues. People our age would probably hate us, but I bet we could land gigs; we'd be like a novelty act, young kids channeling this brutal badass stuff from a bygone era. But of course, we'd have to be good, we'd have to be on it, we'd have to be—

Here.

Marsh has parked in the lot and turned off the engine and is sitting there watching me like I'm in some kind of trance instead of indulging goofy fantasies about appearing on *America's Got Talent*.

I give her a sheepish smile and we go in. The little old lady presiding at the desk is happy to point us in the right direction, and we pull out massive leather-bound tomes. I've always been decent at research, a no-BS 180 to the psychic thing, and I'm soon immersed in an architectural record of the eighteenth century.

"Marsh, come here. I think I found it."

Over my shoulder she reads the description of Forsythe Manor, commissioned by the magistrate Archibald Forsythe, in the town of Swoon, and completed in the year of our Lord 1765. "Sure seems like the place," she concurs.

"And compared to the rest of the town, it was way over-the-top—practically Versailles. I mean, there were some nice houses in Swoon back then, the limestone Congregationalist church, but nothing like Forsythe Manor."

Marsh actually gives a little laugh. "Whoa, Dice, that book must be better than it looks—you sound like you've been there."

I clap my trap, since of course I have been there—a little time tripping with Sin last fall. Closing the book, I tell Marsh we should start on newspapers. "Let's see what we can dig up on Archibald Forsythe," I say. "A magistrate, that's a lawyer, right? Or a judge? Which I guess was a prominent position back in the day, but unless he was collecting graft up the yin-yang, he wouldn't have been able to afford a spread like Forsythe Manor."

Back to the stacks then, and Marsh digs up the next vital bit of info. It even makes her go, "Ooh!"

"What?"

"A wedding announcement," she says, and reads. "'Archibald Randolph Forsythe of Swoon, Connecticut, wedded to Lady Anne Marcella Radcliffe, Devonshire, England, on March the twenty-second, year of our lord 1752.'"

Now I'm reading with her. "'The groom, recently appointed' blah-blah-blah, 'is the son of' yadda-yadda-yadda. 'The bride,' here we go." Luckily I have the manners not to remark on how Archie married into mega-money, and royalty to boot, lest Marsh take it as a slam.

"Is that weird, Dice?" she wonders. "I think Crane and Duck's dad was a regular guy before he met Lady Lillian."

"Weird how? Regular weird, or connected weird?" We've got to ensure, while perusing the vast past, that we focus on clues that relate to the matter at hand.

"Connected weird."

I lay my palm on the notice to see if I get a vibe. Zilch. "We could poke around to see if Lady Anne and Lady Lillian share an ancestor—all those blue bloods were tight," I say. "But I doubt it's important. Let's call it a coincidence and see if we can dig up anything even mildly calamitous or upheaval-y going on in that house."

We read on. We read until we break to pee. We read until

we break for lunch. We read from a place of fascination to a place of absolute boredom. We read about Forsythe's cases, but magistrates basically do misdemeanors, so that's a big snore, and by the time we read about his promotion to a higher court, we're so sick of him we couldn't care less. Lady Anne, on the other hand, seems to have had a life, but suffice it to say the pious *Swoon-Norris Sentinel-Courier* was no *In Star* magazine. It reported on her comings and goings in about as much juicy detail as the departures and arrivals at Kennedy Airport.

"Well," I say at one point. "Looks like Lady Anne stayed in one place long enough to get pregnant. Blah-blah . . . oh, a daughter, 1753 . . ."

"I wouldn't call that calamitous unless she was born with a tail," Marsh says. "Really, Dice, I don't think we're getting anywhere."

I yawn, sip surreptitiously from the water bottle we smuggled in. The clock on the wall reads one forty-five. "I hear you," I say. "Fifteen more minutes."

We agree. Then I find it. The date: 1 January 1769. "Oh, how sad!"

"What?"

"'Fire in Forsythe Manor,' that's the headline. 'The home of magistrate Archibald Forsythe fell prey to fire in the early morning hours yesterday,'" I read. "'The blaze—the cause of which is under investigation—partially destroyed the topmost floor of the east wing. Mr. Forsythe and his wife, Lady Anne Forsythe, heralding the arrival of the New Year with a grand ball on the premises, escaped unharmed, along with their illustrious guests. Yet the fire claimed the life of their daughter, Antonia Radcliffe Forsythe, aged sixteen years . . .'"

Marsh does not take the tragic news well. "Did . . . did you say . . . Antonia?" she asks.

I nod, keeping her in my sights as she takes two shallow breaths in and out.

Then, woodenly, Marsh fills me in about the Saturday night before Crane disappeared. The place: The Spot at Swoon Lake. The purpose: a little makeout session. Yet as the night went on and neither one wanted to go home, they drifted off in each other's arms, on their blanket by the shore. And Crane started talking in his sleep. Mumbling, more like. Groaning. Until all at once he shot up, waking Marsh with a start and the strangled cry of "Antonia!"

A BOND BETRAYED . . . WITH A DEAD GIRL? OH, TO WAVE MY HAND with a cavalier "pshaw!" Trouble is, I know for a fact that phantoms can be seriously persuasive, and a lot firmer than Casper the Friendly would have you believe. If Crane was cheating with Antonia Forsythe, isn't it conceivable he willingly went AWOL? Maybe the rock Duck spied wasn't intended for Marsh at all, which actually makes sense—in the 1700s, it was common to put a ring on it at an early age.

It's almost as if my thoughts ticker across my forehead. Marsh pushes out of her chair and bolts. I tear out after, to find her losing her lunch behind a hedge. Lunch lost, she assures me in a quiet voice that she's fine, she'd just like to go home—she needs to clean up before her shift at the Double K. On the way, she keeps mum; I can only imagine what's raging behind the big round sunglasses that swallow her face.

Finally, as we turn onto Daisy Lane, Marsh says, "I'd appreciate it if you didn't discuss what we dug up today with Duck or Pen . . . or anybody." Too upset even to look at me, she stares straight ahead. "Not yet . . . I just want . . . I don't want . . . I need to process . . ."

"Marsh, of course." The promise springs automatically, yet soon as it does, I wonder how I'll manage to keep it. Following the questions has momentum, like rolling down a hill. Still, a few days shouldn't matter much—in fact, it ought to be beneficial. Marsh is in disaster mode; she needs to chill, see things rationally, remember that Crane's been crazy about her from the get. So I stuff the idea of some eighteenth-century hussy turning his head. "Whatever you say," I vow, though I, too, talk to the windshield.

Once Marsh goes to work, I push the day's research away. Knock out some easy homework, check the progress of my garden, pop in a yoga DVD. But a girl can only putter so much, and the prospect of Antonia Forsythe lurks around the nooks and crannies of my gray matter. Maybe I should eat something . . . or, no, I know: I plug iPod into laptop and start a blues playlist, stuff I could see Bruise Blue doing. Tosh had mentioned Big Mama Thornton; she's kind of an idol. Made "Hound Dog" famous. Everyone thinks Elvis, but no. Plus, she recorded with Muddy Waters and—the phone jangles, and I scowl at an unfamiliar number.

"So what are you up to?" Tosh asks, like he's interested, not as a figure of speech. How quick the scowl reverses.

"Making a mix, actually." Pacing as I speak—not nervous, just . . . energized. "Blues we could do."

"Great minds think like mine!" He laughs when he says it, to show it's a joke, not a gesture of ego. "And it is funny because—well, you heard the latest? About Duck?"

"That they hired a private eye? That a Crane-like individual was spotted in the Waterbury vicinity?"

"That's so this morning," he informs me. "No. The father got the rent-a-cop, but the mother was against it. She figures New York is where a young man goes to 'find himself,' so she's off to the city to snout him. Took Duck with her. He just called me from the Trump SoHo. Him and Mummy booked a suite."

"Yeah. Huh." Flopping onto the couch, I feign disinterest. Get him off the topic so I won't be tempted to bring up the fact-finding mission that occupied most of my day.

"Which is why I'm calling."

Uh-oh . . .

"This might sound cold, but I can't let the trials and tribs of the Williamses dictate my life. So what I'm saying is, I've got a cheap Strat and a Thursday off, and you've got that rocks-into-butter vocal prowess, so what do you say we hang out and see what we can accomplish together? As a duo. Even if just for the interim, till those dudes get back."

Snuggling into the cushions, calf atop kneecap, foot bouncing. A "rocks-into-butter" voice, huh—is that what I have? I say, "Thursday . . ." Three days from now, acceptable advance notice. "Sure, I can do Thursday."

"Cool."

I can *hear* his grin. It keeps me plastered to the sofa awhile, happily contemplating the ceiling. Then I leap up, back to computer, cranking tunes as soon as I can download them, scoping lyric sites, running to the kitchen for a wire whisk microphone. RubyCat demands kibble, and I oblige, but I'm not hungry myself at all. I'm busy. I'm buzzing. I'm bluesing . . .

 XI

"You didn't eat, did you?" Tosh, on the front porch of 12 Daisy Lane. In his hands, this enormous stew pot. At his feet, a bulging shopping bag. Both exude a mingling of spices and tang.

"You brought dinner." I hold the screen door, nose-nodding toward the kitchen, then follow with the paper sack. I haven't eaten, haven't even thought about it, but all at once my appetite is turbocharged.

"No big thang," Tosh says. "It's what I do."

I'm already pawing the packages, arranging containers on the counter. "Oh my God, I haven't had a beef patty in the longest." Am I visibly drooling? "Ooh, and roti. What you do, Tosh, is rock."

He puts his pot on the stove, looking a little disappointed somehow. "I suppose you're into oxtail too, then?" he complains with a half pout. "Here I was, thinking I'd introduce you to a whole new culinary experience."

Bowls, forks, spoons, napkins, lots of napkins. "Sucks, huh?" I say, grinning. "Come on, Tosh, don't tell me you took me for a native Swoonie?" I fill tall glasses with brewed ice tea. "There's not a blond hair on my body, not a polo shirt in my wardrobe— and any plaid is meant to be ironic."

He laughs. "Yeah, dummy me."

Then we're at the table, me moaning my compliments to the chef and him eating them up with as much gusto as we're going at the food. We're chatting about this and that, filling in details of our NYC selves (me: Upper West Side forever; him: Fort Greene via Toronto), clowning, gesticulating with silverware. It's hard to stop shoveling it in—the dude can cook, okay—but I'd rather not be too stuffed to sing, so I cut myself off after seconds. We clear, and load the dishwasher—an inherent rhythm to that as well. Then we look at each other.

And he says, "Uh . . . bathroom?"

I point him in the right direction, then wash up quickly at the kitchen sink.

"I'm in the living room!" I call when I hear him emerge. He unzips his gig bag; I fiddle with lyric sheets, both of us all business. (Wouldn't Ruby snicker, though: "Business. Mm-hmm.")

"'Spoonful'?" I propose.

"Cool," he says. Then, "What, you didn't memorize it?"

The paper in my hand would indicate a no.

"Come on, Dice, you don't need a crutch."

I know what he wants—he wants me to feel it, move with and be moved by the blues. And I can't very well clutch a lyric sheet if we ever get the chance to perform.

"If you forget, make something up."

He's urging, not bullying, like he knows I can do it but it's up to me. So I let the page go. Tosh delivers the riff of intro and then I let loose. Only I don't wag it and brag it à la Howlin' Wolf; I smolder on up to it, like a woman would: *Just a little spoon of your precious love satisfies my soul . . ."*

Enslaved to the song yet owning it too—this yin-yang, push-pull thing going on. Right about then, the we're-not-alone feeling sneaks in like a vapor. Close as a whisper, and that hushed. Until it's not so near, not so quiet. *Thunk!* on the front porch. *Thunk!*

"What the?" Tosh pockets his pick.

The thudding continues, and with it other noises—a screech, a scrambling, a susurrant hiss. Something is out there. No, uh-uh, some *things*. Yet whatever's in here—an amorphous pressure, a tantalizing nontouch—has me rooted to the spot.

Peeling off his Strat, Tosh hurries to the window, then the screen door. He finds the light switch, plunging us into darkness to better see what's happening by moonbeams. "Dice!" Back to the window—for a better view? a safer one?—he beckons.

I want to join him. Too bad I can't move. Until ultimately the ethereal emulsion floats me not to Tosh's side but toward the door, and there they are. Owls and nighthawks perching on the porch rail. Bats like furry black pears hanging from the eaves. Brazen badgers and raccoons snag the best spots, front and center on their haunches, while shyer creatures—deer, skunks, possums—position in the cheap seats across the front lawn. The nocturnal audience stares in at us, beautiful, unblinking.

"Are you seeing this?" Tosh needs confirmation. "It's a casting call for Noah's Ark out there!"

"Yeah," I say, or try to—I'm not sure sound comes out. Then I'm aware of a sweet, insistent throbbing, not just you-know-where but everywhere, the endless cavern gated by my sternum, the delicate nuances of my ears, those ticklish spots on either side of my knees. It makes me acknowledge that what's going on isn't simply animal but spectral. I shut my eyes to the birds and the beasts and open my heart to their sovereign, he who sent them, the one who wants to be here, with me, but cannot.

A breath, a breath, and then the hold breaks into countless intangible crystal splinters. "Tosh, come on . . ." When he doesn't respond, I step deliberately to the window and tug his elbow—the shock that greets my fingers not shocking at all. "Let's just play."

So we do. We play great. Inspired by the confluence of our new fans—some fierce, some mild, all consummately wild—Tosh taps into this articulate yet aching place. As to my singing, well, he doesn't know who I'm singing to; all he hears is the fathomless bruised blue yearning of a girl who lost her love.

 XII

DO ANIMALS COME AND GO OVER THE NEXT HOUR OR SO? I PAY NO attention. Only when car doors slam do I hear the roaring flutter of takeoff, the mad patter of hooves and paws. Then human voices, trilling, cursing, out-and-out bugging.

"Goddamn owl took a crap on me!"

I know that voice—and I don't like it. Teeth clench, dander rises as Marsh, Duck, Pen, and Kurt Libo spill through the front door. *Ucch.* While not opposed to partaking of his product now and then, I do not want Kurt Libo in my house. Of course, none of these people knows that. And judging by the look of them, they're beyond the curve of explanation.

"Hi, Dicey! Hi, Toshy!" Duck rushes up to embrace us both. Profusely.

"Hey, Duck." I wriggle free of his sweaty armpit. "Good to see you."

"Oh, you too!" he effuses. "I missed you! Both of you! So much! Oh, but look: You're together! Lovely!"

Tosh and I trade a glance, then survey our friends. A blissed-out Marsh drops her purse in the middle of the floor and swings our way to kiss me hello like we haven't seen each other in eons. Pen, remarkably, isn't eating, but sips, sloth-eyed, from a large water bottle and leans on Kurt, who looks at me obliquely under his Cro-Mag unibrow.

"Heyyyyy, Dice." Monkey Boy has the temerity to greet me.

"Kurt," I creak, as opposed to, say, launching myself at him, ninja-style.

"Heyyyyy, guess what?" he asks with a leer.

"You've got X."

"Whoa!" from Kurt. In fact, a chorus of whoas. Like I had to be precog to pick that up.

I turn to Tosh. "You know this guy?" I refuse to make a proper introduction. "Swoon's most celebrated dope dealer?"

Tosh flattens his mouth with distaste—mirroring me—but one corner, and then the other, perks up.

Meanwhile, Kurt bounds over, pumps Tosh's hand, slaps him on the biceps. "Hey, whoa, nice axe! Yours, man?"

Marsh, having picked up the Strat, attempts to either tango with it or strangle it. Then Pen approaches and they both tangle up in the strap. Tosh notices but seems more amused than alarmed—he'd called it cheap, but still.

Kurt slings an arm around Tosh and leans toward me. "So, Missy Madame Smarty-pants . . . want a hit? Come on, on me."

"Perhaps you don't realize this is a school night." "Perhaps you don't realize that phenylethylamine turns the brain into Swiss cheese." "Perhaps you don't realize how much I hate, loathe, and abhor you." I could say any of those things. Instead, I say, "Okay."

Having readily succumbed to peer pressure, Tosh and I catch up to our friends' ecstatic mind frame about twenty minutes later—but thanks to mass quantities of Jamaican food still in our digestive tracts, our experience is mellower. Still, we join in for the requisite dancing, and then everybody wants to cuddle R.C., marveling over the softness of her fur. And by now we've paired off. Duck and Marsh, on the living room floor, spinal columns to the couch and heads bent together like wilting flowers, console each other with Crane stories. Pen and Kurt cavort at the old tire that dangles from a backyard elm. Time was, those two might have gotten physical, but no amount of "love drug" can resuscitate that, not with the twenty-pound walls Pen's put up.

The least odd couple sits on the front-porch swing. We're quiet, and for a moment I forget Tosh is here. A pervasive nostalgia sweeps over me—for the swing, the porch, the house, and yes, for Swoon. My mother's recent visit had her meeting with a realtor; the place is on the market now, which makes sense, what with my imminent return to the city for college. Much as I want that, something binds me to this balmy night in the country, with beasts of the field and the essential soul-spark of my true love so close.

"So can I ask you something?"

Hmm? What? Oh, Tosh. "Sure."

"You don't . . . do you have a boyfriend or anything?"

Boy, when he asks a question, he doesn't dick around. "No," I say. I could leave it at that, but if Tosh is going there, don't I owe him, oh, I don't know, a big sign with flashing lights reading: DANGER! So I add, "Not really. I mean, I did, but . . ."

"One of those on-and-off things, huh. Me and Tasha—my ex, yeah, we were Tosh and Tasha, if you can believe—anyway, we were like that for a minute. Then she went away to school and I moved here, and we never officially broke up but . . . we both know it's over." He can be so open about it. Nice for him. "She has an agenda, you know. A checklist. I can't get with that, and besides, I'm more than a few requirements shy."

Musing, I say, "She's lucky. She knows what she wants."

"You don't?"

Have I mentioned how adorable Tosh is? "Ha. Not a clue."

"Yeah."

We hydrate. We stare at nothing. We glide the glider.

"So can I tell you something?"

This is Tosh being coy. It's dark; I wonder what color his eyes are.

"No," I say. "Just kidding. You can tell me anything."

"Good, because I want you to know, it doesn't bother me."

Maybe I missed something. "Excuse me?"

"Your . . . you know, the rosebush ambush and the piano prodigy thing, and let's not forget the beastie bunch tonight. Some people would be freaked by it. Someone else might be into it. But to me, Dice, that woo-woo bugaboo stuff is a facet of who you are. I don't like you in spite of it, and I don't like you because of it. I just like you."

Good to know. And clearly this is where I'm supposed to say, "I like you, too." And I do. But I don't. I mean, I do like him, but I don't tell him. Since what if it's the X talking? We both believe we're sincere in our sentiments, spoken or un-, but we do have some mighty chemicals coursing through our bloodstreams and pitchforking our brain pans, so right now we're both suspect.

The window of opportunity for me to speak must shut with a bang, since Tosh gets off the swing and walks to the rail. I feel like an ass. He likes me, I like him—ergo, kissing should ensue. I stand to go to him, then whirl around—a verbal commotion from the house.

"Marsh, how could you!" Duck wails.

Tosh and I head in.

"I'm sorry, I'm sorry—don't be mad!" Marsh wrings her wrists. "But this is crucial information! And you've been holding out on me for days!" Pacing, pink in the face, Duck rants on. "Why didn't you call? You could have called!"

"I know, I don't know," Marsh says desperately. "I was, I'm confused. I mean, if Crane were cheating with some girl from school, I could compete. But if he left me for Antonia Forsythe— I didn't know what to do. I still don't."

"Who's Antonia Forsythe?" Pen is on the scene, and she must be coming down, since she asks this while poking around the fridge.

"And you!" Duck turns his ire on me. "You knew too. This is my brother's life at stake."

"Who's Antonia Forsythe?" Pen asks again, sniffing a cold patty. "Antonia who?"

Latecomer Kurt, T-shirt grass stained and eyes bleary, means we're all present and accounted for. So I might as well bring everyone into the loop. "The historical society. Marsh and I went, checking for destruction and upheaval. We found out that Duck's house was originally called Forsythe Manor, and Antonia Forsythe was, as they say, to the manor born. And also to the manor died. A fire in the east wing. In 1769."

Pen chews a large bite of seasoned beef, swallows, and pats her lips. "Seventeen sixty-nine?" she says. "Isn't that the year—"

"Yeah, Pen, ding-ding-ding!" I look right at Tosh when I reveal the latest tidbit I figured out: "Antonia Forsythe died in a suspicious fire six months before her father ordered the execution of my ex."

# XIII

THE SUN RISES OVER SWOON, BUT TOSH AND I DON'T WITNESS THIS everyday miracle a deux. He pretty much clears out upon learning that the former flame I don't like to talk about had been dead a few centuries before I met him. Duck also takes his leave, though not till I agree to further explore the spectral situation in the east wing—news of Sin's previous existence further fueling his fixation. Pen? Kurt? I don't know; I don't see them. It's just me and Marsh, sitting atop the backyard picnic table, basking in the colors of a new dawn.

"There always was something special about Sin." So astute, my Marsh. "But I never would've pegged him for a ghost. He seemed so . . . solid."

I really haven't got the energy for this. "When you knew him, he wasn't a ghost. He was something else. And at the end, even I don't know what he was." I crick my neck, right to left,

left to right. "But the craziness that went down around here last fall? His doing. This swath of revenge against the families of Swoon that condemned him—unjustly—for the murder of his beloved."

Marsh swallows. Several times. Since what I just served up is a lot to swallow. Finally she says, "Craziness?" and ponders it some more. "Oh. Right. Only it wasn't all crazy. Con Emerson came out; that was positive. And Crane and I fell in love."

True that. Certainly not intentional, but true.

"So do you think he knew Antonia?"

I snap an automatic no, then allow, "He could have." Antonia = wealthy, with royal British blood; Sin = the bastard half-breed blacksmith. "They wouldn't have traveled in the same circles, but . . . he got around."

This stokes Marsh. "Well, if I thought Duck went nuts when I told him we found evidence of destruction and upheaval, he's even more frantic now," she says. "Sin *is* the Hanged Man from your reading, isn't he?"

I sigh. "You don't want to be too literal, too linear, with these things. All I'll say is, Sin being Sin, he might have known Antonia." I know what's coming next, and Marsh is right on cue.

"Oh, Dice, if he knew her, and they had a"—she tempers her enthusiasm to spare my feelings—"relationship, maybe he could talk to her, help us get Crane back. I mean, that is, if there's any way you could ask him?"

Hope lights her face in the rapidly gaining rays. How can I disappoint her? Yet how can I satisfy her? It's not like I can call Sin up, text him: *Favor?* Although I will admit he's felt much more manifest lately, invading my consciousness outside my dreams, at all hours, in all places. Only no—it's not that random. Sin's been stealing up on me when I'm busy with Bruise Blue . . . busy with Tosh.

Tilted forward on her hip bones, braced on one slender arm, Marsh seems to plead with every ounce of her essence. So I squash my inner turbulence into one compact package. "I don't know," I tell her. "I have no way to contact him, but there may be a way to draw him out."

If it weren't for the music, Tosh might've bailed completely, but he's committed to Bruise Blue. And now that Duck's home from the city (a washout—shocker) and we can be a proper band again, he reaches out about rehearsal. Right now I'm fried—Marsh and I barely managed to somnambulate from class to class today—but hearing him on the phone does perk me up a bit.

"So Sunday afternoon?" he asks above the din of clattering dishware and harried waiters. "I already talked to Duck—he's in."

"Okay," I say, though I'm not exactly thrilled about returning to Forsythe Manor (I can't think of the place as anything else now).

"Good. Cool. Okay. Bye."

*Click.*

Just like that, click. No "What are you up to this weekend?" or even "Have a nice day." Huh. Much as I'd like to avoid analyzing the terse conversation—he's on the clock, he could only grab a minute—I veer there anyway. Could be Tosh quit his crush on me; he'd rather not pursue a girl with a demonic dating history. Could be he never fiended for me at all—his interest begins and ends with Bruise Blue, any flirtation a figment of my imagination. And while I'm obsessing, why put the onus on Tosh? Maybe I'm the one desperate for mooring; I see the band as something to steady me as Swoon starts spinning on its otherworldly axis again. Or maybe I'm fabricating this whole attraction to Tosh in order to get Sin off my brain and conduct myself by the most basic tenets of keeping it real. Of course, if that's the case, it's not exactly working out—whenever Tosh and I start vibing, Sin has a way of making it a bizarre love triangle.

Which gives me an idea. A potentially combustible, probably terrible idea. But since no other occurs to me, I convince myself it's worth the risk.

When Sunday comes, my plan is in place. I also consider it a plus that Marsh won't be present in the studio; it'll be a true practice, and if Duck mentions the east wing, I'll put the kibosh on it, maintain that Marsh ought to be in on any Crane-related endeavor. So just before four, I get on my bike and pedal toward Forsythe Manor.

Tosh is bringing Duck up to speed when I walk in. ". . . I'm talking real old-school."

"Hey," I say.

Both guys return my hey, and Tosh's smile, if small, seems bona fide when he says, "So Duck is down with the blues."

"Yes, well, what are the Stones and Zeppelin if not blues?" he reasons. "And I think it's all very well and good, but I do hope we can work on Crane's songs, too."

"I'm good with that." I fluff out my helmet hair. "We can tweak a blues number, give it a slight punk edge, and try doing a Crane song with a blues feel."

"Right," Tosh agrees. "Once we establish our signature, our style, we can make any song a Bruise Blue song."

So we get to it, and we keep at it, heads down and diligent, for quite a while. When we break, I make my move. Wandering toward the piano, I pick up the volume of Elton John's greatest hits. "Tosh?" I arch an eyebrow. "Will you treat us to some cheese, please?"

Appealing to his ego proves spot-on. Tosh takes a big swig of water and saunters over to the baby grand. "Sure," he says, and sits, making a show of cracking his knuckles and throwing back his 'fro. "What'll it be?"

I leaf through the anthology as if I haven't anything specific in mind. "Ha, 'Crocodile Rock' . . . 'Rocket Man,' that's a good one . . . ooh, I know." Hugging the book to my chest, I take my best shot at coquette: "How about a duet?"

Tosh gives me a bemused look as I place "Don't Go Breaking My Heart" on the music stand. Then he busts out laughing. "A duet," he says. "With you."

I plunk down beside him. "That's right."

"The corniest duet ever written." He shakes his head, incredulous.

"Uh, no, I believe that would be 'Islands in the Stream,'" I counter. "Look, I'm not suggesting we add it to the set list. I just want to sing a song with you." Then I add, with emphasis, "*This* song."

Duck has ambled over to see what we're debating. "Ooh! Dice, will you be channeling your inner Kiki Dee—or your inner RuPaul?"

Tosh rolls his eyes. "Arrgh! You guys are killing me."

"Stop being such a stiff," I cajole, swatting his shoulder. "We worked hard; we deserve a little comic relief." I poke my lip out.

"Do indulge her, Tosh." Duck picks up the SG to play the guitar part. "It could be worse—*I* could be the one to channel Kiki Dee!"

"All right! Okay! All right!" Tosh gives in, briefly studies the sheet in front of him, and cracks his knucks again. Then we do it, we duet. And you know what? It's killer. I'd never heard Tosh sing

before, but he's got a robust tenor that goes well with my contralto, and when we "ooooh-hoooo" in tandem, we soar. Trouble
is, I don't *feel* anything—at least not the feeling I thought this
experiment might provoke. Maybe I should've proposed something heavier, like "Love Hurts," but I knew Duck owned this
anthology and that Elton is a Tosh guilty pleasure. Anyway, now
we're done, and as Duck applauds, I scope Tosh under my lashes.
The boy is beaming. So I place my hand lightly over his and suggest, "How's about giving it the Bruise Blue treatment?"

He holds my gaze and nods, and as we take it from allegretto
to adagio, a lot more than the tempo changes. Our voices come
from a place that's been broken before, and beg that those same
old love crimes won't be committed again. So intimate, so passionate, so scared and yet so willing. Then, upon reaching that
mutual "ooooh-hoooo," joyful in our peppy first rendition but
now with the poignancy of prayer, we—

With the force of a blow from a wrecking ball, Tosh is thrown
from the piano bench. The mic, knocked down by his rocket-
fueled trajectory, hits the floor squealing. Duck leaps back, out
of the way, and I stand, watching in horror the arc of Tosh's
flight, as he tucks into a self-protective ball, only to roll airborne
somersaults. Finally he lands with a thud on the other side of the
room, smashing against the drum kit. Cymbals clang furiously
and then shiver to a stop.

And it comes out of me. I scream, *"SIN!"*

XIV

TOSH LIES CURLED ON HIS SIDE LIKE AN ABUSED CROISSANT. I RUSH OVER and hunker down. Duck does the same. We check for signs of life, get a pulse, call his name. Hazel icons in a corneal slot machine, Tosh's pupils roll back into place. He blinks.

"Tosh, I am so sorry!" Here and there I touch him, gingerly, guiltily. Then I notice the plush nap of the Persian rug; at least he had a cushioned crash. "Are you all right?"

"I don't know. I guess." Pressing his palms, he hoists up to seated. "Didn't know that piano bench had a secret ejector button."

How dare he be goofy! How dare he be sweet! I don't think I can bear it. "Oh, Tosh, I'm sorry," I repeat, and bite my lip so I won't say it again.

He draws up his knees, soles of his One Stars planted, and rubs the back of his head—I bet he'll get a bump. "What up with the apologies? You didn't press the ejector button."

I glance away, and then look back. "Actually, I did. Kind of. Sort of. But I didn't think he would . . . I thought *I* would . . ."

"What . . . who are you talking about?"

Poor, sweet, goofy Tosh, still smiling, though smaller now.

"It was Sin," Duck says soberly.

"Yo, I'm innocent." Tosh hasn't figured out it's a proper noun. He puts up his hands in jest, but his smile shrinks further. "No, really, what'd I do?"

"Sin," I expound. "As in Sinclair Youngblood Powers. Born 1751. Died 1769. Reborn . . . in a way . . . last summer."

The smile is gone. Tosh gets to his feet, with difficulty—he's still shaky. "Your ex," he says slowly. "You called him Sin."

I stand too and shrug ineffectually. Everyone in Swoon goes by a monosyl moniker—Sin's simply suits more than anyone else's.

"And he's a ghost."

"Yes. No. Not anymore," I say. "He was a ghost, and he was possessing Pen. So I tried to exorcise him and, well, oops, made him flesh."

I have to give Tosh credit; he's really trying to work with me here, wrap his brain around it all. "So then what? He was some kind of zombie?"

No, no, no! Not at all! Zombie? Please! A zombie is an animated cadaver. Cold. Stupid. Eats brains. Lurches around like he's wearing overly starched long johns. Sin was hot. Brilliant. Enjoyed mac and cheese, black coffee, had a jones for Gatorade. And he was smooth, so very, very smooth in all his moves. "If you want to get technical, he was a golem," I say defensively, my voice small.

"You keep speaking in past tense," Duck points out. "Yet you believe Sin is responsible for Tosh being catapulted across the room. Explain that."

"I can't," I admit, and turn my arms out. "Look, I haven't seen Sin in six months, but lately, every time we get together to play . . ." I gaze at Tosh now, but somewhere in the vicinity of his left earlobe. "Every time you and me get close, I . . . feel him. And, well, I just wanted (a) to make sure that I wasn't imagining it and (b) find out if there was some way for me to get in touch—"

"Whoa, whoa, whoa!" Tosh springs back as if slapped. "You wanted to duet with me so you could summon him?"

"Tosh, no!" My objection ascends to an octave only dogs can hear. "Not summon, not summon at all," I sorta-kinda lie. "Not really. Anyway, I didn't think he'd use you as a shot put."

Tosh stands there, rubbing the back of his head, a parade of expressions across his face. Meanwhile, Duck scolds, "Whatever you did, Dice, it was most unwise. I didn't know Sin well, but I do recall he was rather . . . unpredictable."

*Thanks, Duck,* I think. "Excuse me, but you're the one who

believes a spirit in this house has made off with your brother. Sin and Antonia were contemporaries. I was hoping to reach him to see if he could shed any light on her."

Duck says, "Oh," then shuts up.

So I turn to look at Tosh again, full-on this time, ready for whatever he has to say to me.

And he says this: "You're right, it has been one big cirque du freak since we started Bruise Blue, but I'm not convinced what's causing it. Maybe it's all Antonia—after all, this is Forsythe freakin' Manor and she's the queen bee-yotch. Maybe it's some other spook—a house this old, could be lots of people died up in here who want to stir shit up. Or maybe it is your jealous ex having a hissy fit. I don't know, only I'll tell you this: I never picked a fight in my life, but I never walked away from one either. I told you the other night, Dice, I like you; I care about you. That hasn't changed. So if Sinclair Youngblood Powers, whatever he is, wherever he is, has a problem with that, too bad. As far as I'm concerned, he can just bring it."

## XV

Fire and brimstone? Thunderbolts and lightning? Fauna gone wild? I anticipated Sin doing *something* once Tosh threw down the gauntlet. Wrong again. Tosh made his speech and no plague was visited upon us. In fact, inertia has set in. Duck's chilled on the whole east wing thing—maybe Sin's hissy fit, as Tosh called it, scared him off. As to Marsh, she's like anyone who suspects her significant other of cheating: Part of her wants to know the truth—every awful dirty detail—but on the flip wishes she could pretend nothing's amiss, and Crane will materialize any second, velvet jewelry box and all. If only the sheriff's department or private dick would report encouraging leads, but both investigations, deemed "ongoing," seem brain-dead.

The last few weeks of high school roll by in a blank blur of term papers and finals. Then Pen flounces into the house and gets in my face with hers.

"Nice labret." Piercing as rebellion is so late twentieth century, but the preppy province of Swoon has always been behind the curve. Then again, if anyone has the pouty mouth for such adornment, it's my cousin.

"You should have heard my mom," Pen says with a satisfied smirk. "A yowl of pain like she was the one taking the needle."

And to think that relationship was once the stuff of Hallmark cards. Learning of her mother's indiscretion with the family dermatologist really sucker punched Pen. It's one thing for you to go off the high diving board into sexual high jinks yourself, something else, very else, for your mom to.

Taking a box of Cocoa Puffs from the kitchen cupboard, Pen circles back and sits across from me at the table, where I'd been finishing off a paper. "But you know my mother, she's soldiering on. Totally gung ho about the party."

Right. The party. Pen couldn't care less, but her mom is tossing a graduation gala—and knowing my aunt Lainie, she'll be crushed if it's not *the* affair of the summer. It's set for the official start of the season, June 21—anything that follows will be by definition an also-ran.

"That's why I'm here," Pen says.

I assumed the purpose of her pop-in was to eat my cereal. Not that I'd begrudge her—Lainie won't allow crap in her home; the woman rolls her own oats for granola.

"To ask if you wanted to play."

Play . . . at the party? "You mean Bruise Blue?"

Pen swallows another palmful. Vaguely I wonder how it feels to eat with a steel rod rammed through your lower lip. "Mm-hmm. There'll be a DJ, but you guys can set up on the patio," she says. "Those Williams boys own enough amplifiers and junk to blow the roof off the Madison Square Garden."

*The* MSG; Pen tends to slaughter her New York references. I narrow my eyes at her. "Are you sure?" What I really want to ask is if our performance is meant solely to annoy Lainie. My aunt likes things just so, and Bruise Blue is so not just so. Is Pen using us as the sonic equivalent of a lip stud?

"Of course I'm sure," she says. "Everyone likes live music. And everyone will be there."

What I need to do is forget Pen's motives, ulterior or not, and consider what's best for me: Do I wish to strut my musical stuff for the discriminating cochleas of Swoon, Norris, and Washington? It's not like I bonded with tons of Swonowa students. When I first got here, I made a few friends by association—they deigned to let me share their air because of Pen—but they don't know what to do with me since my cousin's mutinous makeover. So am I really inclined to make a fool of myself in front of those girls and their ilk?

But why self-deprecate, assume that I'd—we'd—be bad? Bruise Blue are still pretty green, we're raw as sushi, but we do rock. Courtesy of Tosh, for the most part, but Duck doesn't suck and neither do I. Anyway, we're a group; I can't be making this decision for them.

"Golly gee, Dice." Pen gets petulant, slams the cereal box with a rattle. "Don't get too excited."

"No, Pen, sorry, it's a great opportunity," I assure her. "Let me talk to the guys. I'll let you know soonest."

Of course I could predict Tosh's reaction. "Hell, yeah!" To him, playing the party is like a showcase and an investment in future gigs—might not some of the affluent attendees book us to rock their casbahs this summer?

Duck is all for it too. Having a gig gives him a focus. So we agree to practice our asses off for the two weeks before the party. That means Tosh finagling a few more afternoons off and me staying conscious for some post-midnight rehearsals.

The first thing Tosh does when we meet up in the studio is grab my hands and swing my arms like I'm a rag doll. All the while he's smiling a suspension bridge from western Connecticut to Beijing. "You got us a gig!" he singsongs. "Uh, any money in it? No, no, no—kidding! We're playing out. Bruise Blue is playing out."

That enthusiasm's infectious. A lot of "whooing" and "hooing" from the three of us, and only once do I see Duck's eyes turn wetly wistful over his brother's absence.

"Okay, let's get serious." Tosh calls our band meeting to

order. "I think we should keep it short and sweet. Pick a handful of tunes, get them tight as a finger trap."

I laugh, pointing out, "Easy enough—it's not like we've got this enormous repertoire."

"What about that Stones song?" Duck says. "We do that pretty well."

Agreed.

"And Crane's stuff?" Tosh throws out. "The fast one?"

All in favor. I know we're all hoping against hope that he'll be back by then, back and able to join us.

"Let's keep in mind our audience," I remind.

Right, so that uber-mega-gonzo hit on everybody's iPod is in.

"One more ought to do it . . . ," Tosh muses.

I suggest one of the blues classics we'd been kicking around.

"'Spoonful,'" Tosh says, his eyes tipping toward golden. "Genius." Then he hugs me very hard and completely incomprehensibly for about half a second.

Looks like we've got our set list.

XVI

COMMENCEMENT WEEK DOES BRING A CERTAIN LEVEL OF FRENZY. THIS I blame on my parents, typically overstressed, self-obsessed, neurotic New Yorkers that they are. Marsh and I bunk up in the smaller bedroom, ceding them the bigger one. Sure, they could roost at the Leonard place, sprawling on the other side of Daisy Lane in all its posh spaciousness, but Momster and Daddy must believe they can cram months of neglect into a week of high-impact doting. Daddy videotapes every moment—ostensibly for my Nana Lena, who'd be with us except she hasn't ventured beyond the six-block radius surrounding her apartment since they put a Loehmann's on the Upper West Side.

The saving grace? Presents! An antique bracelet with tiny pearls that is completely my taste. A journal too pretty to write in. Clothes, of course. Momster's privy to NYC's finest sample sales, and she went wild. There's stuff for Marsh as well, which is so sweet and was no sweat, since unlike me, heir to the Moskow tush, Marsh has a model's body, and often the best stuff at those fashionista affairs is size negative zero.

"So where would you girls like to go for dinner?" Daddy hopes we'll clamor for the Kendall Wynn Inn. When in Connecticut, he revels in preppy parody—seersucker, badminton, highballs, and stuck-up, old-school restaurants.

"Actually, there's a new place in Norris called Pinch Me Round that's supposed to be fabulous," I say. "It got a five-star review in the *Sentinel-Courier*."

"Ooh. The *Sentinel-Courier*." Momster gets her journalistic snob on like *In Star* is going to win her the Pulitzer, but "fabulous" and "new" snag her nonetheless. It's not till we're in the car that she opines Pinch Me Round is a funny name for a restaurant.

"Not a Jamaican restaurant," I say, explaining that a pinch-me-round is some kind of Caribbean cookie.

Daddy chuckles, saying I'll endanger his quota of white bread and mayonnaise.

I hinted to Tosh that we might come, and the second we're seated, a platter of assorted appetizers appears. My puzzled parents have no clue why, but after we dig into entrées, Tosh comes out of the kitchen in his toque to say hello. Momster and Daddy are all over him, raving about the food, fully impressed that I know the chef. Daddy makes his white bread and mayo joke again, as I cringe, mortified.

"Don't mind my father," I tell Tosh. "He's basically allergic to anything green, so when he comes to the country, we dope him up on so many antihistamines he doesn't know what he's saying."

"No worries, Mr. Moskow, I understand," Tosh says. "Ever since moving here, I get cravings for mayo and butter on the same sandwich."

Momster, all impish grin, must sense the vibe between Tosh and me; she quit the "not nosy, just curious" inquiries about Sin a while ago. On the way home, I preempt any prying by saying Tosh and I are in a band together, which naturally gets Daddy reminiscing about his high school power-pop quartet, the Schmooze.

Yawn indeed. Very much the Nyquil effect. Yet rather than fall into stony slumber, I'm restless in bed next to Marsh, deep in muse mode when she rolls over with a murmured good night. Soon enough I hear her breathing go long and even.

Except the very next second, she's giggling like mad.

"What's so funny?" I ask.

She shoves me in the dark. "Boy, Dice, that must've been some dream!"

Dream? I haven't even been asleep. Oh, but . . . oh, my . . . and then it rushes back to me in a wanton wave. His remarks, his commands, his mouth, his hands. Me begging, laughing, moaning, seriously losing it . . .

"I thought that only happened to guys," Marsh says, still hiccuping hilarity, "when they're like twelve years old."

I hop out of bed, trip over the heap that my mysteriously stripped-off T-shirt and underpants make on the floor, and stumble out.

"Cold shower?" my bestie teases, her giggles following me down the hall.

I don't even turn on the bathroom light. I know what I would see. Skin glowing, nether regions sodden, hair a shambles of snarls, and blue bruise pulsing, raised, alive, and completely unrepentant.

The chorale recital goes well, and afterward there's a tea-and-cookies thingie on the Swonowa quad. Pen attends, which surprises me, until I realize she's there for the shock value—and Mrs. Welch's decadent lemon bars. My parents haven't seen Pen since my birthday in January, when her transformation was just beginning.

"Penny!" bleats my mother. Surely Lainie had bemoaned a report, but only seeing is believing. "How are you, honey?" She goes in for a hug.

"I live, I breathe." Pen, hands to hips, parries the hug.

"Well," Daddy says. "Well, well."

By the time both families convene at the Leonards' for dinner, my parents have adapted to their niece's appearance, though Momster and Lainie do huddle now and then, while Daddy and Pen's father try to find a topic of conversation they can agree to disagree on. Pen and I sit beside each other at the massive oval dining table, she sullenly packing away her mother's gourmet comfort food.

"Everything's delicious, Lainie, as usual," Daddy says.

"Mmm," Momster agrees, but can't resist adding, "I'll have to go on a juice fast after this week. Oh, did I tell you we ate at Pinch Me Round, that new place in Norris, last night? What a feast! Candy's friend is the chef there. A baby like that, a chef!"

"Right, Josh is a real prodigy," Daddy concurs. "Although it was embarrassing having a kid comp us."

"It's Tosh, Daddy," I remind.. "And he's almost twenty-one. And he prefers 'cook' to 'chef,' the way a painter prefers 'painter' to 'artist.' And besides, his aspirations ultimately lie elsewhere—I told you he's a musician."

"A real Renaissance man," Pen grumbles to her meat loaf, though the accusatorial tone is meant for me. "What other Tosh talents will you regale us with next?"

I'm tempted to go on—but I resist. If Pen already suspects that Tosh is into me, I don't want to give her any ammunition—she'll only trash him, and I'm confused enough when it comes to that boy. "Most creative people are multifaceted," I say quietly, keeping it general. "They tend to express themselves in various ways."

"Like you?" Her volume matches mine—our parents can tell we're talking, but not what we're saying. "You sing, you're acing honors English, and you can make dead boys come to life . . ."

Whoa, where'd that come from? And the pinched sneer? The vicious way she's spelunking the cliff of scalloped potatoes à la Lainie on her plate? I shake my head at her, very slowly, only once. "Let's not get into Sin right now."

"Why not?" is her low-level retort. "Isn't that the plan, yours and Marsh's? You think Sin can bring Crane back, so you're going to bring *him* back. Then you and him and Crane and Marsh can enjoy games of doubles tennis and lazy days by the lake." With one finger she taps her cheek. "Oh, but what's Tosh, then? Your side dish?"

So that's it. After pushing me and the world away, orchestrating her own alienation, she's afraid of having a crappy summer. Pen, who'd bounce along so blithely in her bikinis, boys slavering in her wake, has erased the girl she used to be—only that's not enough; she wants to bring me along for the miserable ride. I'd be more pissed if she weren't so blatantly pitiful.

Equally pitiful, the fact that Pen thinks I have such power. Maybe she wouldn't be so cruel if she knew how Sin has been manipulating me lately, and how helpless I've been at every slap and tickle. Sin's the one with the hand full of aces, and the more I muse on it, the clearer it becomes that if he wanted to be with me—really be with me—he would've wielded that magic already. Pen of all people should understand that if it were up to me, I would've brought him back, or gone to him, no matter what or where, a long time ago.

Now's the moment Jordan, the littlest Leonard, chooses to get up from his chair and wangle his way between us. Fascinated by big sister's labret, he pulls her chin to inspect it. Lenient, benevolent, Pen allows this, then sticks out her tongue and snags him onto her lap. Seeing her so loving makes me wistful for Pen to be Pen again.

Only that won't happen—at least not in regard to me. So I push away my comfort food; it's no comfort to me. "I wouldn't worry," I say at last to respond to her scenario. "If Sin can help us rescue Crane, he'll be doing it from very far away."

# XVII

GRADUATION IS ON FRIDAY, TWO DAYS FROM NOW, BUT THE SUMMER solstice kicks off at exactly 7:23 p.m. By Lainie logic, the ideal onset for the grand grad gala. After her dermatological transgression and near-fatal plunge off the Davender Bridge, she'd spent some time exploring the meaning of life. There was a meditation seminar, a chakra tune-up, and a tract on the spiritual ramifications of the seasons. The solstice has new significance, but Lainie being Lainie, it all revolves around her, her family, and now, specifically, her only daughter. The invitations read 7:23 as the soiree's start time.

Besides, "Wednesday is the new Saturday!" Momster delivers a spot-on imitation of her sis. "Oh, Candice, you look adorable! Peter, get the camera!"

Hey, I try—aiming, actually, for retro-chic, with these kitten-heeled pumps from Goodwill, a flared skirt from my mother's recent haul, and a plain tight tank. For coiffure, I watched a beehive how-to video online, and modified it to use only half a can of hairspray and a mere seven hundred bobby pins.

"So tell us more about this band of yours," Daddy says as I mug for the lens.

"You'll dig us," I assure him. "We do a Howlin' Wolf song."

"No kidding!" He is so proud. "Hey, come on, Marsh, get in the act!"

In pointy flats, a pencil skirt, and a sleeveless blouse that zips up the back—a shell, per Momster—Marsh is pure sylph. She let me pile on the eye makeup, but drew the line at overstated updo; fortunately her ponytail works. What a trooper. It's hard, pushing into party mode when she can't be feeling it, but it must be done—forward motion is mandatory.

"I feel kind of silly," she says, lashes heightened by copious coats of mascara.

"Yeah, well, you look kind of gorgeous, so shut up," I say. "Besides, you're in Bruise Blue." She is, for real, on tambourine. We had to hash it out, Tosh and me, but I was adamant. The last thing my girl needs is time on her hands. "You've got to look the part."

She smiles shyly as we pose for Daddy, and then, at precisely 7:22, we cross the road to number 9.

For attire, Lainie requested "grad glad rags!" but word must've gotten out that there'd be a vintage vibe, since most of the girls and a few guys take a stab at the late-fifties/early-sixties thing. None pull it off as well as Duck, resplendent in aquamarine sharkskin, and my mind wanders to what Tosh will wear. It's a little sad the way Pen's out of place at her own party, in a soot-colored baby-doll dress and twelve-rivet combat boots. She stomps around for an hour, deigning to speak to classmates, who deign to speak back, but doesn't seem at ease till her boy Kurt shows. They take off—to smoke up, I surmise.

Stage fright hits the instant I see Tosh—unless those butterflies swoop in for some other reason. All I know is he looks awesome. One-button black suit with tapered pants, striped tie, his ubiquitous One Stars, plus the added element of dark glasses in horn-rim frames. Very much in bluesman mode, his usually buoyant step tempered to a stroll. "Dice, Marsh," he says. "Nice. Very nice."

"What about me?" Duck strikes a pose.

Tosh strokes his chin discerningly. "You? You'll do." Then he cracks a smile.

As a unit, we cruise by the performing space—Duck and Tosh had come over earlier to set up—then mingle and mesh. Caroline Chadwick and her whole crew compliment Marsh and me on our ensembles, and I suppose it's genuine. Wick and Marsh used to be tight, but that went south after Marsh did in Daddy Demento. The DJ is decent, and people are dancing—including my parents, who, I must admit, know how to throw down and don't look too ridiculous.

I wish we could play already, but Tosh insisted the ambiance would be all wrong if it wasn't at least partway dark. This being the longest day of the year, that could take a while. I find myself scoping the sky until the aubergine of twilight settles in around us. I give him a nudge and he nods decisively. "Let's do this."

But first, a word from our sponsor.

"Hey, hey, hey!" the DJ calls. "The parents of tonight's honored grad-to-be have something to say!"

Aunt Lainie and Uncle Gordon tipsily toddle up to the booth while flutes of bubbly are pressed on all celebrants. "I hope I won't get in trouble serving one itsy-bitsy toast to minors." Itsy-bitsy, that's pure Lainie parlance. "But I look at you young people, and you're so grown-up and poised and beautiful . . ."

Plenty of heartfelt hoo-ha about life journeys ensues, but I can't really concentrate with Tosh so very right behind me, his breath a caress against my neck.

"That spoon, that spoon, that spoonful . . ."

Him hushing the chorus makes me jumpy, and no way can I chalk it up to preshow jitters.

"Shhh!" I turn to him—my cheek meets his lips—and quickly turn back.

Gordon and Lainie must announce their daughter, since there's a smatter of claps, and then a pause—no Pen in sight. The sound starts up again as eventually my red-eyed, snickering cousin clomps up. Oozing sarcasm, she lifts her flute and with a deadpan "Go, Lancers" downs its contents in a few deep swallows.

Awkward reigns till the DJ regains control. "Everybody, please give a Swonowa welcome to Bruise Blue."

The response seems thunderous—collective relief, no doubt. Following Tosh's measured gait, we assume the area of patio sectioned off with flickering votives. It's not dark-dark, but dark enough. The scent of fancy finger food mates with heady honeysuckle. Then I hear the sticks clack behind me: one-two-three-four.

Our short and sweet set list is strategic. We kick it off with our mega-hit cover, and once the crowd realizes we're doing it— Bruise Blue–style—we have them eating out of our palms. Next up, "Tumbling Dice" (what else?) off the Stones' *Exile on Main Street*, which garners extreme approval, particularly among the parents, who sing along to every line.

"Thank you very much," I say, and giggle out the last of my tension. "Guess everyone knows those two. And let's give it up for Duck, okay; he just learned that guitar lick like yesterday." The boy raises both fists, then flops in a flamboyant bow. "Usually, Duck plays bass in Bruise Blue, but as some of you may know, his brother, Crane Williams, is . . . well, we don't know where. Nobody does. And for the Williamses, and Crane's girlfriend Marsh, these last few weeks have been incredibly difficult.

Because Crane is so great—he's kind and smart and sensitive and beautiful." My voice cracks, and I need a second. I spot Paul and Lillian among the guests, and they're actually holding hands, their eyes wet. "So we all hope that if we put our prayers together, however we define the notion of prayer, Crane will come back to us very soon." Loud encouragement swells, lofting those prayers into the night air. Even though Crane didn't go to school with us, he was known, and liked, and the idea of him being gone without a trace is having its emotional effect on every person here. "Anyway," I say, "now we'd like to play one of Crane's songs. He wrote it for Marsh. It's called 'Swear.'"

*I will do it, I will dare*
*I will show you, I will share*
*I will call you 'cause I care*
*I will love you, ooh, I swear*

A power-chord promise of devotion, it would've been a puff piece under ordinary circumstances; now I don't know how I manage to pull those lyrics off, or how Marsh avoids a full-on faint. The tune clocks in at less than three minutes, then we dive next into "Spoonful," our finale. Duck thumps the bass line on the SG. Marsh shimmies the beat against her slim hip. And Tosh, stepping from the kit and taking up his Strat, can't resist a bit of showboating.

First he channels Hendrix, twiddling about a thousand and one notes, then turns his back on the party to snag my eyes, playing the intro exclusively for me, all tied up sweet and tight like the ribbon on a present. Yeah, well, we never did *this* in rehearsal. I can't tell if he's trying to transmit some meaningful message or just crowd teasing, but I like it. A lot. So much, I smile with my lips sealed, indicating he ought to do it again. Ultimately, when I do start singing, the tune takes on a sultrier swagger, a touch more heat. *"Just a little spoon of your precious love satisfies my soul."*

So now we're good and done. And they, all of them—the top tier of Swonowa High School seniors, several select parents, even the grumpy grad of honor—drench us in raucous applause. They want more, but we can't oblige; even if we had an encore, Bruise Blue is spent, seriously. After a bunch more thanks and thanks again and really, thank you, we walk off.

My stride suddenly quickens; I need some space right now. Kitten heels sink into the lush Leonard lawn as I beeline for the side of the house. Behind me, I can hear the start of the booming dance track the DJ had cued up, and something else . . . my name.

"Dice . . ."

With his tie loosened and his shades pocketed, Tosh reaches for my arm. I light his face with my smile, and notice an expression there I'd never seen before, an *I can do anything* look that's more than cocky confidence. It's exultant, it's righteous, it's *knowing*, and it gives my chin the most curious upward tilt. I'd comment, but as I breathe—inhaling my own name as it issues again from Tosh's mouth—he puts that mouth on mine.

# XVIII

A KISS. THAT'S ALL IT TAKES. HOW SIMPLE! HOW STUPID! IF ONLY I had known! True, it couldn't have been just any kiss. Only a fully conscious, eyes-wide-open kiss. Not a lazy, blasé, why-not-kiss kiss—only a deliberate, purposeful, passionate kiss. In fact, it's possible that only this kiss, Tosh's kiss—his sweet, sure, triumphant kiss—could make what happens happen.

First, the earth moves. Not like an earthquake; it's much more subtle—an undulation. When our kiss breaks and Tosh leans me back against the wall of the house, I see that he felt it too. He straddles his legs around mine and rests his forearms on either side of my shoulders, gaze unwavering, and we prepare for kiss, the sequel. Since after all, cliché or not, the earth moved. Naturally, in our conceit, we think it's *us*.

Damn, are we dumb.

Then the sky moves. Forget cloudburst, forget hailstones,

more like the stars elect to descend a little closer, give us a taste of their heat, their eighty-billion-degree fireball dominance, their ability to demolish on a whim, at will. But what whim? Whose will? I'm beginning to wonder.

Finally, *I* move. Under my skirt, my thighs press together—the way thighs will when you kiss a boy for the first time, half daring him to part them, half hoping he won't try—and the left one, bruised blue, starts to tremble. The right one picks up on this. Then all of me is trembling, and I mean all, inside and out, the eggs in my ovaries, the alveoli in my lungs, the squishy protective fluid my brain floats in, and, of course, the concentrated mass of membranes and sparks that amount to my brain itself. I clench my lids in an effort to still the trembling, yet even as I do, I accept it's in vain.

"You're shaking . . ."

Tosh is about to gather me in his arms again, I know it, and my eyes fly open as I realize that's a very bad idea.

"Tosh, let me go."

"I don't understand . . ."

"I know, I know, but you really need to let me go."

"But, Dice—why?"

My own reply is preempted.

"Because if you do not, you'll leave me no recourse than to do you bodily harm."

Out of the earth, out of the stars, and out of *me*. Him. Here.

Now. So close—an inch away, less, his back to the wall of the Leonard house. The smell of him: horses, dirt, iron, impudence. His voice so calm; I know that calm. As Tosh shifts his gaze, I see his Adam's apple spike. And I wonder how long we'll stay like this, the three of us, within this strange, awful angle of intimacy—an endless moment? a brief eternity?

As I watch, reckoning takes Tosh's face. Of course. In the escalating lunacy his life has been since deciding "Hey, that moon-tan chick with the indigo eyes and barn door butt, I kinda-sorta like her," this is the obvious next step. Yeah. Right. Sure. Uh-huh. Her boyfriend's back. The dead guy.

# PART II

# THE GATE

 XIX

To extricate himself with maximum dignity and minimal damage, Tosh pushes off with his arms, releasing me from their castle keep. One step away, he says, "I guess you two need to talk."

Us two. Hmm. So far I have yet to make the smallest signal to acknowledge Sin, though I sense him modify from supine to sideways along the wall—the better to examine me.

One more step, and Tosh goes on: "I just want you to know, I'm not afraid of you."

His breath on me, as always with its hint of apples, Sin addresses the boy he caught in so compromising a position. "That would make you either very brave or very foolish. I care not which. But do leave us."

To Tosh, I nod accordance. No—I don't nod; I bobble, I'm a bobblehead, a bobblehead with a big, ridiculous beehive.

"All right." Eyes so gray, tone so grave, the boy who just kissed me tells me, "I'll see you."

And as Tosh turns to walk away, a proprietary knuckle sweeps a tendril off my cheek and behind my ear. "You've done something to your hair."

Oh, please—is that how it's going to be? Casual commentary, sparkling repartee. It's a game I'm good at, but right now I don't have the wherewithal to engage. In fact, it seems that I can't move.

"I cannot say I find it becoming."

My head is a grenade, and Sin plumbs for a pin, finds one, pulls it out. No explosion.

"It does display your neck and shoulders nicely."

He mines another, and another; a hank of hair falls free, and still I stare straight ahead.

"But it's all about artifice; in fact, reeks of it—"

He inhales the polymers and solvents of Aqua Net.

"Whatever upholds this construction, it's not you, Dice."

One more pin, and with a silent *crash, bang, boom,* the whole mess dishevels around me. At which point Sin heaves off the wall to take the stance Tosh relinquished, his long legs astride, his arms bracketing.

"Now, this . . . ," he says. "This is you."

Seeing him cures my paralysis. I blink for clarity and drink him in. High bones, thick brows, and heavy lids, the muscled mouth full on the bottom and sculpted on top. Finally I plunge into those bottomless black eyes. I say his name, bracing for the crush of his full weight against me. Except it doesn't come. Instead, he searches me, as though for something he'd left when we were last together, truly together, as opposed to in a dream that's not a dream. His stare marauds, tearing at the fibers of my soul with far less delicacy than he undid my hairdo, and it hurts. So I tell him, "Stop."

"Stop? Stop what? I'm just . . . looking . . ." He defies me. "Or is this a preemptive stop? Do you think me about to ravage you? Kiss you black and blue and deaf and blind?" His eyes gleam, ice on coal. "No, Dice. Not to fear." For a flash one corner of his mouth ascends in the uneven smirk that's the essence of his mien, and then reclaims sobriety. "I will not. I cannot."

With that he leans flat to the wall again. I cast my gaze skyward, then it's my turn to roll onto my side and study him. Dark blue jeans, plain white tee—his basic gear, although last I saw him he was all dressed up in his birthday suit. My hand on his jaw, I guide his face to mine. I read his pain like print. "What's going on, Sin?"

"Your betrayal," he says. "That's what's going on." Stern and deliberate, he removes my hand. "How long did I spend in limbo, this trap of not-quite-oblivion, only to return and find you in the arms of another?"

I want to tell him he's being unfair, but if roles were reversed, can I honestly say my reaction wouldn't be the same? True, I forgave him many offenses—including deflowering my cousin. But I hadn't witnessed them in flagrante delicto, plus she was merely a means to an end, and he was a different person then . . . if "person" isn't exactly the right word.

"Wait, hey, whoa." My voice is soft, but I do object. Maybe I've got some 'splaining to do, but he's up first. As in, where he's been these last six, seven months? We fell asleep together in a tangle of limbs and sighs in front of the fire and I woke up alone. "Sin, come on. You abandon me without a—"

"Abandon? You think—" He shakes his head, consults the stars. "That's not what happened. I simply . . . it was . . . something. I don't know."

Well, that's illuminating. Yet in a way, good to hear. I never wanted to believe he'd meant to leave me.

"But how I suffered—"

Now I'm starting to get mad. "*You* suffered . . ."

"Unable to be with you, unable to let you go."

He does seem distraught. "I . . . I'm sorry, Sin. But it was the same for me."

"It was *not* the same," he insists. "You had your life, your friends. The pleasure of your senses—all six of them. Your appetites. Books, music, food, drink. You had day, you had night."

All of it meaningless without him. "Don't you know I would have gone with you, anywhere?"

He's not listening. He's off the wall now, literally, three paces this way, three paces that. "I had nothing," he fumes. "Just this narcotic haze, this druggy *Dammerschlaf,* and the maddening omnipresent awareness of you."

Could that be true? Then what of his visits? "But, Sin, you would come to me—"

"When you called, yes, I—"

What is he saying? "No! You would just . . . be there. I couldn't—"

"As usual, Dice, you underestimate your power." He stops, smacking fist to palm in frustration, then flings a finger. "It was you who brought me to your bed, and then, to torment me, to throw it in my face when you dallied with that—"

He's so wrong. "That's not . . . I didn't—I wouldn't." My hands flounder, sightless birds trying to find purchase on windblown branches. "Sin, please—I love you."

With the speed of flame, he snatches me by the shoulders—the brunt makes me gasp—and looks at me, in me, that searching, questing, stare. "Love." The word dissolves on his tongue. "If it's me you love, what were you doing with him?"

I start to speak, as if I have an answer—but I realize I have none.

"I saw you, Dice," he goes on, the skin-sheathed steel of his grip tightening. "Saw you with your throat arched and your eyes slit and your lips parted."

Yeah . . . that would be me.

"And do not tell me it was pure desire, just lust, because you, dear lady, don't operate that way." He's maneuvered me against the wall again, as if he might nail me there. "I know about you . . . and I know about love." He lets go, as if his truths burned his hands.

And then I hear "Shut up, Marsh, Dice is fine—she's Dice!" Pen, it's Pen I hear. "I invited you to smoke—not to whine."

It takes a beat, but the pun penetrates Kurt Libo's skull. "Huh-huh," he chuckles. "Yeah, beer's all right—but no *whine*. We don't want any *whine*."

"Just spark it up, Kurt, okay."

He does, and it's a mighty spliff—I can see it in the flare of his Zippo. What's more, they can see us.

Pen's chin threatens to violate her cleavage. Marsh clutches her arm. The two of them freeze on the spot. But Kurt lunges forward, bellowing, "Holy crap! Screw me hard and smack me stupid! Sin!"

Who banishes all emotion from his eyes. "Kurt, you devil!" But it's me he shows his smile, savage thing that it is. Then he slings an arm around his old cohort's shoulder. "Tell me what kind of trouble you've been getting up to—and let's see if I can't dig you deeper."

## XX

"YOUR HAIR IS WRECKED." PEN'S NOT BEING MEAN, JUST STATING FACT.
"Marsh, give her your ponytail thing."

Having flanked and funneled me into the house, my girls
now take stock of my state in the downstairs powder room off
the Leonard kitchen. The great thing is, they ask no questions.
They witnessed Sin with their own eyes—the how and why
details are irrelevant. All that matters, as they can plainly see, is
I'm not happy. So they proceed with damage control.

Marsh whips off her elastic and I take it, but conferring with
the mirror I don't know where to start. Masses of sticky curl
obtrude from the circumference of my head. I look hilarious. I
feel hysterical. The combination makes me giggle.

"Here, let me." Pen tackles the top, making the sides spring
out like Bozo. She grapples with the nape and the crown poufs
up, a huge geyser of hair. "No use."

"You're screwed till you can wash it," Marsh says.

Pen agrees. "Sneak upstairs if you want, use the shampoo and stuff in my shower."

Not a bad idea. But I get a better one. "Or I could just jump in the pool."

Pen's grin is instantaneous. "You could," she says. "We all could."

"You mean . . ." Marsh is not so sure about this.

"Let me grab towels!" Pen zips into the nearby laundry alcove.

I kick off my heels. Peel off my tank top. Giggle some more.

Back in a flash, Pen throws a heap on the sink, and in one fluid motion yanks her dress over her head. I haven't seen her Rubenesque proportions in the buff before, and I decide that she's beautiful, still beautiful, still Pen.

"Damn," she says, hoisting a leg onto the toilet to unlace her clodhoppers. "Tight in here with the three of us."

Marsh lingers by the door, hands clasped, considering. Then she recognizes that it all makes perfect sense: Sinclair Young-blood Powers is back in town. Time to get naked! Off comes her nice new outfit.

We wrap ourselves in Egyptian-cotton terry.

"Ready?" I query.

"Set," Marsh accedes.

"Go!" Pen shrieks.

It is on, a whooping and hollering circuitous route to the

pool that cleaves a path through the guests. I catch sight of my parents, whose faces register a bemused respect. Oh, there's Wick and her flabbergasted gaggle. And Duck. And Tosh. All in a blur. We reach the edge, lose our vestige of modesty, leap high, hug knees to boobs, and hit the surface in a three-part cannonball salute. Water ballet it is not. But, Houston, we have splashdown.

Oooh, ahhh, how I need this! This cold, this wet, this hard slap on the ass, this total submission to submersion. Instantly it brings my fever down, the sting of chlorine even having an astringent effect on my mental facilities. True, the delirious dip is only making my hair situation worse, but that's okay—a bottle of conditioner, a wide-tooth comb, I'll deal with it later.

Once I hit bottom, I further recall that swimming is so not my forte. Panic ought to set in any second, so I tune my internal GPS for shallower environs and begin to dog-paddle. Soon as I get footing, I'm laughing. It seems we set off a chain reaction. All around, by the glow of tiki torches and in-ground lights, Swonowa seniors are losing their minds and their party clothes, going native and jumping in. With a few clean strokes, Marsh is at my side, and then Pen. High fives all around as we congratulate each other on a job well done.

Duck may have been the first to launch. Looking more walrus than Winnie the Pooh, he swings our way. "You girls are brilliant!" he lauds. "Brava!"

"Check out my mother," Pen says with a chuck of her chin. Mincing poolside, Lainie attempts to instill order, but that's not going to happen.

"Yeah, well, I just hope no adults consent to join the fun," I say. "The sight of my parents in the nude would require therapy they can ill afford."

Pen scrambles onto Duck's slick shoulders, challenging, "Chicken fight! Who wants to chicken fight?"

Marsh gives an "Eek" of surprise as a boy from our Spanish class swims between her legs and lifts her up, but I guess she figures *when in Rome . . .* since she kicks her vehicle (whose name is Dennis Purvis; of course, we call him Purv) and with a yowl goes for Pen with ferocious glee.

I move toward the edge, wrap my arms around the ledge, and kick in front of me as I watch the match. That's where I am when Tosh finds me.

"You go next?" he asks.

"Oh. Hey. No," I say. "Not much of a swimmer. More of a not-drowner."

"Really? Me, man, summer in New York, I was all about Coney, Riis Park, Jones Beach—you couldn't keep me out of the water, and talk about reckless, none of that 'wait half an hour after eating' either."

Tosh is so cute. I smile at him. Here we are, naked, me and the boy whose mouth recently seized mine, surrounded by all these other naked people, and it should be weird, very weird, yet it's only mildly weird. Which is weird. Then I see Tosh is not entirely naked. Around his neck, a silver chain with a small circular pendant, a medal of some kind. I never noticed it before, and I wonder if he always wears it, tucked under his T-shirt.

"So . . . how are you otherwise?"

I'm honest with him. I tell him, "I don't know."

"Yeah," he says. "I hear that. But I can still call you, right? I mean, I'll call you. About practice and stuff. After graduation. Hey, by the way, congratulations and all that."

See what I mean? Just mildly weird. "Thanks."

"I'm going to get in line for the diving board."

I tell him okay and see you, and I watch him lumber off in that clumsy way you have when you walk in the water. As he lifts onto the ladder, I dunk myself—I just can't look.

# XXI

"Candice Reagan Moskow . . ."

I'm out of my seat, down the aisle, up the stairs of the proscenium to accept my diploma. Moving the tassel from right to left, I walk off, down, back, done. It's cool, but in the aftermath of solstice night, graduation is anticlimactic. Tonight, tomorrow, are other parties, a few that I was invited to prior to fronting both Bruise Blue's debut and the skinny-dipping bacchanal, several I'm "reminded" about (those invites apparently lost in cyberspace). But I think not. Too much on my mind.

"Are you sure you won't come?" Marsh isn't doing the party circuit either; she switched shifts with another custard slinger to get time off to spend with her fam. New Pop has a timeshare in Newport, and I'm welcome to join them for seafood and sailing.

"No offense," I tell her from my lolling collapse on the

couch, "but I need some post-parental decompression."

Head cocked, lip nipped, she studies me at length. Much as I ached to spill about my kiss with Tosh and how it did or didn't spark Sin's subsequent comeback, bitching about an embarrassment of testosterone riches with her boy still mysteriously AWOL just feels wrong. So off she goes, and here I lie, the battlefield for a civil war between thought and feeling. The largest of issues: Sin, of course. Who. I. Still. Love. That is *not* at issue—I have loved him from the get, and miserably ever after. The very idea that he is near yet not here is the definition of unfair. And insane. And just plain stupid.

Now that it's established that my love is not in question, I can sideline Sin to take up Tosh. Have I been leading him on? Using him, a captured flag in my attempt to negotiate a normal life? No, even Sin pegged it as real. Of course I care for Tosh; just how much and in what way I was moving toward discovering when Sin barged in.

So, Sin, front and center again—the what, why, and how of him. All along I'd thought he was in charge from some unidentified beyond, my blue bruise—his dark mark—evidence of that. Only to hear him rant that this is my fault. I'm the reason he couldn't find peace; I'm the one who ordered him to my bed and then, as my attraction to another grew, brought him closer and closer to this, his latest infernal, unnatural existence. Which does make a certain psychotic sense: The turmoil of my emotions—intact for Sin, incipient for Tosh—igniting à la nuclear fission or the celestial big bang.

If so, what sort of monster have I blunderingly conjured this time? Where's the mortal soul he so gladly embraced that November night by the fire? Left behind, clearly, or fatally wounded or on hold or . . . I don't know, but Sin sans soul is bad news for this town, and for me, and I just cannot imagine what I ever did to deserve this.

"Wah, wah, wah!"

I hike up on my elbows, direct a glare toward the fireplace. We don't own a bearskin rug—the Reagan-Moskows do not do fur—but Ruby Ramirez has brought her own, and she poses on it, languorous, a fledgling centerfold.

"Don't freak," she says, plucking the material. "It's faux."

I tuck my legs, composing myself for what she has to impart (like I have a choice). "What, I'm not allowed to complain even within the confines of my own brain?"

"Go ahead, Candida, wail all you want." She too sits up, slipping on a sheer peignoir. "But that and a MetroCard will get you to Times Square."

True. "So do you have a solution, oh wise one? Or did you just get lost on your way to a *Playboy* shoot?"

"No solutions, only suggestions," she says. "And I suggest you get over yourself. In other words, why are you so ready to take responsibility for this, and by 'this' I mean the resurrection of a very naughty boy? It may not be about you at all."

Not about me? Then who? I stare at her. She stares back with "duh" dripping all over her face like Carrie's prom queen makeup.

"Oh . . . crap . . ." I really have been in me-me-me mode. "Antonia!"

Soon as I mention her name, Duck pleads into the phone that I come over post haste. I take my bike, but before entering Forsythe Manor, venture onto the lawn for the garden. Pausing at the gate, I glance up, not surprised to find the east-wing tower window rising directly above. Up there, that small, round room, *her* room; this spot where I stand, her view.

I lay my hand on the latch, mustering the courage to go in. That's when I notice the gate itself is a tribute to the roses it guards. Buds and leaves of iron wind around the bars and nestle in the curlicues, leading to the grille's centerpiece: a large, fully open bloom, each petal finely wrought and perfectly placed. The detail is exquisite; the craftsmanship a counterpart to the carved marble mantel in the tower room. That Antonia must've been into roses big-time—and her parents spared no expense placating her passion.

Beyond the gate, rose perfume beckons. Curiosity trumps apprehension and I lift the latch, wandering into this untended eden until I reach the bower. There's still plenty of light, and I can see the colors—soft pastels, as opposed to riotous brights. The bushes are laden and all abuzz, countless bees listing and weaving as if drunk on the pollen.

Sitting on the bench, I no longer feel threatened. In fact, it's incredibly peaceful here, and the fragrance is sublime—how could I have found it off-putting? A smile spreads, and I stretch drowsily. Contact high from that potent stuff the bees are swilling? The last few days catching up to me? Mm, wouldn't a nap be nice. I'm here for a reason, though, aren't I? Yeah, well, whatever it is can wait. I won't even sleep; just rest my eyes. If only the bench weren't so hard. Nudging the ground with my rubber-capped toe, I find it far softer, so I settle there among the clover and fallen petals . . . curl onto my side . . . cradle my head with my arm . . .

And then somebody's shaking me by the shoulders. Who even knows I'm here? Right, Duck—he must've grown impatient. I'd tell him to let me be but can't seem to make the effort, so I burrow into the cushion of one arm and swat with the other.

Only damn, he's persistent. I flip onto my back, unglue my lids—and encounter small, close-set, red-rimmed eyes set in a face white as powder. Duck being wide-eyed and ruddy, this is so not Duck grappling with me on the pliant earth. My mouth is open, which would be good if a loud, urgent "get off me!" would spew. Or forget articulate command—at this point I'd take a bark, a bellow, a nice resounding scream. Nada. Greasy strands of hair brush my cheeks. Breath that would make an onion cry. Desperately I swipe at the ghoulish visage above me.

*Knee! Elbow! Heel!* Luckily, my mind can still holler like a drill sergeant, alerting me to body parts proven effective in encounters such as these. I hook with my right arm and connect with what might be a nose, then scramble to my feet and tear out. Find the gate, fumble with the latch, slam free. Only once I'm out on the lawn does my scream, loud and urgent, return to me.

# XXII

MULTITASKING — AS IN SCREAMING AND RUNNING AT THE SAME time—I ram smack into Duck. This serves to renew my scream and make him scream too. Unless his scream is triggered by the garden ghoul coming straight for us, arm extended, in a limping gallop.

"Girlie! Boychik! Please! Enough with yelling! Please!"

Possibly, he's not a ghoul. Possibly, he's . . . just a guy. A little old guy in grimy clothes. As to his pallor . . . some kind of dust?

"Please, thank you, for stopping yelling." He holds a small hand to his heart, catches his breath. "I am sorry, very sorry. Young lady, please forgive . . ." Skeptically, he squints at Duck. "You are Mr. Williams?"

"Mr. Williams is my father," says Duck, as we both struggle to regain composure. "I'm Duck. Who are you?"

The man raises his chin. "I am Stanislaw. You are Duck? This is name?"

Duck huffs. "It's a nickname, all right." He looks at me, a sweaty wash across his brow. "Dice, are you all right? What the hell happened?"

"Uh . . . not exactly sure?" Although I get the strong conviction I'm about to become embarrassed.

"Mr. Duck, nice girlie, please. I explain." Stanislaw slaps at his thinning hair. "I am not bad man." He thumps his chest. "I am craftsman, how to say, plaster master. All the way from New Jersey I come."

To me it sounds like he's come a lot farther than that.

"Are you trying to say you work in the house?" Duck demands.

"*Da.*" Stanislaw points to the tower. "I am for fix ceiling. Make . . ." He kisses the tips of dirty but delicate fingers.

"Yes, I understand. That doesn't explain what you were doing in the garden . . . with her." Duck sets a comforting paw between my scapulae.

Stanislaw looks askance, mildly abashed. "For weeks, I am there, and see from the window this garden. Today I am done; I think to see this garden from closer." With a tsk-tsk-tsk, he shakes his head. "All of respect, Mr. Duck, but that garden . . ." Small, careful hands flail in the international gesture of disarray. "Still, very beautiful, and so many flowers." Now he pulls a utility knife from the pocket of his overalls, brandishing the blade.

"So I am, 'Stanislaw, you cut some roses for your wife!'" He shrugs. "That is bad, maybe? But that is all my bad, just that, to take some roses for the woman I love." He closes the blade, returns it to his pocket. "Then I see young lady, like so." In the air, a flat line. "Is she hurt? Make faint? I go help! It is truthful!" He turns to me. "I make fright on you, nice girlie. I am sorry."

Yeah, uh-huh—embarrassed all right. "Uh, no, Mr. Stanislaw—I'm the one who's sorry." I turn to Duck. "When I got here, I don't know, I wanted to check out the garden." Up and down, sheepish, with my shoulders. "Then . . . guess I crashed."

Duck still seems dubious, but he says, "Well . . . as long as you're sure you're not hurt, Dice."

I nod. "And you, Mr. Stanislaw? I think I kind of got you in the nose."

Touching his nose, he winces slightly. Still, "It is fine nose," he says.

"Then I suppose it's all right," Duck decides magnanimously. "No harm done. Please, cut as many roses as you like."

"Mr. Duck, you are nice young man. I had some, but then dropped. So: I will go?"

"Yes, do . . . go right ahead."

Only then I think New Jersey's got to be a good four hours away. I could run to the house, dampen some paper towels, grab a sheet of tinfoil. It's a Lainie trick; you double wrap the stems to preserve them for the ride.

"Hey . . . Mr. Stanislaw?" He swivels with a quizzical half grin, hands in his overalls pockets. "Aren't you worried the flowers won't survive the trip?" I ask, then offer, "I know a way to keep them alive, if you like. You wouldn't want to bring dead roses home to your wife."

The half grin spreads to full, and I see that Mr. Stanislaw hasn't got very good teeth. "My wife? Oh, nice girlie, is okay— she will not mind," he says, stroking the blade in his pocket. "My wife, she is also dead. Dead roses will be very perfect for her."

Taking off toward the garden gate, he la-la-la's a little tune. Somewhat off-key, but I know it, of course—that same bitter-sweet waltz I ad-libbed on the baby grand.

# XXIII

DEAD FLOWERS FOR A DEAD LOVE. CREEPY, YET MOTIVATING—ONWARD!

"So," I say to Duck as we head up the lawn. "You talk to Tosh?"

"Briefly." He plucks errant petals from my hair. "I wanted to bask in our glory, but you know how it is in that madhouse he calls a restaurant."

"Mm." Not one to kiss and tell, our Tosh. "I thought he might have mentioned that he . . . we . . . anyway, Sin's back in town."

"No! Really?"

"Yeah, really. He crashed Pen's party, then disappeared with Kurt. And I have every intention of grilling him about Antonia but . . ." Best to keep it simple. "We kinda-sorta had a fight, and I'm not sure where to find him."

"Well, once a party crasher always a party crasher," Duck points out astutely. "There are parties galore tonight. But of course, you'd know that better than I."

Astute and on target—if a bit pouty (ah, the social inequities of the homeschooled). "You're right. I do. Want to be my date?"

"*Bien sûr!* Only, Dice . . . are you . . . prepared to go out?"

I read his face: My cutoffs/sneakers/T-shirt represent a whopping fashion don't. "Duck, you know what? I have a mother," I inform him. "And never once did I hear her say, 'Is *that* what you're *wearing*?'"

He flaps his arms. "Suit yourself. But I need preen time."

It's not quite dusk. "You got fifteen minutes."

He takes twenty. Then we head for the garage. The Williams automobile collection includes a Rolls-Royce I once had the pleasure of riding in (after I had the displeasure of stealing it). Duck's everyday ride is a humble hybrid, which normally would be fine by me. Except . . .

"Hey." I put my hand on his arm. "Can we take the Cutlass?" Since Crane's disappearance, someone tucked it under a dun-colored cover.

"I cannot understand you, Dice," Duck says. "You'll party hop dressed like that, but you care about the car you roll up in?"

I smile small. Before Crane bought the Cutlass—lovingly restored by Libo, who despite numerous faults is a primo mechanic—Sin had it on permanent loan. He'll know the engine's distinctive roar from half a mile away; the better to psych him out.

"Indulge me," I say, and together we remove the polypropylene shroud. The keys are in the ignition. I take shotgun, and Duck starts her up.

"Where to, madame?"

Good question. There are the upper-echelon affairs, thrown by kids whose families have held sway in Swoon for generations. Those would've been the places to scope Sin last fall, when he focused on the progeny of those he deemed responsible for his untimely death. Things are different now, with my boy on the loose without such an agenda. No doubt he'll be after fresh meat, though—innocent meat. "Take Bantam Road," I say.

Mary-Kate Kale remains a proud member of abstinence alliance Pure Love Covenant, the ranks of which, locally, dwindled after Sin's tear through town. I know her from chorale (she the owner of an appropriately angelic soprano) and personally never had a problem with her; she doesn't proselytize or spout rhetoric, and she's smart (number three in our class). Ergo, I trust her party to crawl with not just Swoon's remaining virgins but also the sort of brainiacs who can tell you exactly what marijuana does upon entering the bloodstream, only not from experience. Fertile territory for Sin and Kurt's enterprise.

It's a relatively small group. Swoon doesn't produce a lot of "nerds" or "geeks." Most kids who show such inclinations get it burned out of them at an early age. Surely there's some ritual to which I, an outsider, am not privy, during which the *Preppy*

*Handbook* is quoted and names are scalped. Sort of like a bris . . . except not. Those who slipped through the cracks congregate at Mary-Kate's tonight: Eliza Lee Warren and Melissa Jane Pratt (PLC girls), S. Roland Furman (our valedictorian), and every Asian in our graduating class (all four of them). A few other people I may not have noticed at Swonowa, due to their wise decision to keep a low profile, now, among their own, seem interesting, animated. And hobnobbing quite contentedly, Sinclair Youngblood Powers.

If he's rattled by the roar of the Cutlass pulling up, it doesn't show; he simply lofts a cup of punch in salute as Duck and I make our entrance into the Kale backyard. Like me, he's dressed down. Yet something about the way jeans and a plain white tee fit his lean, precise frame elevates the prosaic pieces to what all men's fashion aspires to. Not curly, not wavy, more like whorly, his dark hair drapes casually to just past his collar; his sideburns stop right where they should, as if by their own intention and not a razor's. There's a slight lift to the left side of his upper lip, but then it drops evenly into place. Duck pours me a cup of punch and I take a sip. (Unspiked. Shocker.) Then we wend our way over.

A gentleman never disregards a lady's approach, so Sin greets me with a brusque "Dice." My companion he treats to a smile. "Is that Duck Williams? Dude!" Then a half-hug-with-pec-bump-and-back-slap.

Duck blushes happily. "Sin . . . you remember me?"

"I'll never forget that hayride," he says, and the deliberate way he won't look at me feels like the slow insertion of a knife. "Then we partied at Con Emerson's, right?"

The reference brings Duck from crimson to an almost fuchsia. That's the night he and Con—the Swonowa Lancers' macho linebacker—began their scandalous fling. See Duck rack his brain for a bon mot to trivialize the whole thing. See the need for it broken by Kurt Libo, who bounds into our circle.

"You guys want to see something scientific?"

Startled whiz kids barely have a chance to scoff before Kurt smushes his palms together, then smears his cheekbones and the bridge of his nose with glowing acid-green war paint. The exhibit makes me cringe, and I can feel Sin seethe—once you've been dead a few times, you gain a greater respect for life, even that of insects.

Finally, a cough. "*Photinus pyralis*, one of the few phosphorescent land species," says Jeremy Patel, who will imminently cure AIDS. "Though of course it's prevalent among aquatic organisms—phytoplankton, jellyfish, and the like."

Of course, as nods around us concur. Kurt lunges, as if to spread the rest of the radiant guts on Jeremy's forehead, but Sin cuts off the move with a glance. Kurt drops his hand, surreptitiously wiping organic goo on his cargos, while Sin gently captures a bug out of the air to cradle between heart line and lifeline.

"How quintessentially summery they are," he says. "And how sad."

A girl I don't know reaches timidly for Sin's hand, then tilts it to look inside. "It's beautiful," she says, beaming up at him. "Like an art deco design, the clean lines, the symmetry."

Our hostess and her PLC pals move in for a peek, something they'd taken for granted all their lives suddenly as compelling and unique as E.T. Sin flattens his hand to set his quarry free, but it seems content right where it is.

"Why sad, Sin?" Mary-Kate inquires sweetly.

He sighs, then says, "Their time is so brief; two weeks at the most, isn't it?" Jeremy nods affirmation. "While they're here, they're rife with imperative—to live, to mate—but with none of the frenzied scuttle you see in other creatures." I swear that bit is directed at me. "They glide, they float. Even the way they light—so largo yet so blithe. They don't know they're bound to die."

Can the boy ooze or what? Everyone rapt by his eloquence, his aura, his Sin-ness, as if he emits some potent substance. One by one the girls, even a few guys, reach for Sin's hand to admire his antennaed mascot.

"Funny you should mention the blinking," Jeremy says. "Since it is believed to be intrinsic to the breeding ritual."

Mildly Sin says, "Is that so?" and smiles at his own hand, where a second firefly has joined the first.

"You see, it's the males who do the flying," Jeremy continues, "while the females will choose a branch or a leaf to land on."

Fireflies form epaulettes on Sin's shoulders; clusters attach like medals to the front of his PWT.

Jeremy makes a high-pitched sort of snort. "They should call the girls fire*lies*." Others, incredibly, enjoy this joke. "They just *lie* there and blink messages. Love messages."

Bending his elbows, Sin turns his palms down so *Photinus pyralis* can land on his knuckles like rings, align across his wrists like beads in a bracelet.

"That's how the males find them and, you know, *woo* them." Excited by his own lecture, Jeremy shines, but he's overpowered by Sin, who now has a halo of boy lightning bugs circling his head.

"Sin!" Mary-Kate, all in awe. "You're like a Christmas tree!"

"It's amazing!" Eliza Lee Warren and Melissa Jane Pratt tout in tandem, hands folding spontaneously in prayer.

"*You're* amazing . . . ," the girl I don't know tells Sin.

Kurt can no longer restrain himself. He goes, "Huh . . . huh-huh . . ."

"They do seem to like me, don't they?" Sin employs the full extent of his half-up, half-down, skewed smile. And then he extends his arms to his sides and drops his chin, mimicking the pose of the most renowned wrongly hanged man in the history of humankind. Any second, M-K and Co. will drop to their knees in worship. I'll cop to being a bit agape myself.

Sin knows exactly how long to play it, and when he lifts his head, he briefly levels his gaze on me. Then he gives a whoop and a rock star jeté. All the lady lightning bugs lift from him at once and waft away, suitors in slow but steady pursuit.

# XXIV

WITH MINDS AROUND HIM NEWLY OPEN, SIN SPIES KURT, ABOUT TO fire one up. He separates jerk from joint, presenting the latter to our hostess. "Would it be all right?"

"Oh . . ." Shallow-set eyes, snip of nose, and smudge of mouth all attempt to meet in the middle of Mary-Kate's face. Dare she? Oh, but she'd never! They don't call it demon weed for nothing! Except . . . oh . . . Deliberation presents an excuse to step closer to Sin. She's still pinching herself—*the* Sin Powers at *her* party—and he's so sensitive and intelligent, poetic, even, the way he speaks, nothing like the gossip that went around about him last fall. You'd need to be as clairvoyant as a can of soup to divine this girl. "Can I make a confession?" She flutters a signal no doubt adapted from the female firefly. "I've never tried it before."

"It's interesting," Sin opines. "The way it alters perception.

And this"—a swipe beneath nostrils for verification—"is the best there is." That's all. He'll make no other pitch or chiding comment or insinuation that this is her last chance. There she stands at the precipice while he simply waits, holding her eyes as if he's got a century. Now, propelled by mischief, nothing more, he taps the white paper tip to her bottom lip and then withdraws it.

Mary-Kate giggles. Like she just invented giggles. And in that moment understands how malleable absolutes like "never" can be.

I, for one, haven't got a century. Still, I watch and wait and (the decision has been made) smoke and chat and munch the "smart" snacks and stand around and walk around, basically what you do at a party. Really I'm biding time, angling for my perfect opportunity, until I remember that "perfect" is a lot like "never." With Duck giving me prodding stares, I steel myself and go up to Sin by a fig tree. With him, the girl I don't know. "Excuse me," I say, which she reads correctly as "Back off, bitch."

Then we're face-to-face. "Look. Hey. Please." I cast syllables. He can take his pick or collect all three. "Cute routine with the fireflies—taking the flea circus concept to the next level."

"You know I have an affinity to the animal kingdom; why not the insect world as well," he says. "I suppose that's why . . . uh"—he gestures toward the retreating girl—"she suggested I volunteer at Walden Haven."

I've heard of the place, an animal refuge off Stag Flank Road. They take in injured wildlife, nurse them back to health, and release them to their natural habitats. What a noble way for Sin to spend his summer days.

"It's humans," he continues bitterly, "that confound me."

I lower my eyes, raise them with effort. "Sin, I know you're mad at me—"

"'Mad' does not begin to do justice to what I am at you." His brows knit, his tone subterranean.

"Still, I need to talk to you about something, and it has nothing to do with us."

He doesn't say, "There *is* no us." Part of him wants to, I'm sure. Instead he says nothing, so I forge on.

"Okay, so, last month, Duck's brother Crane went AWOL. Some people believe he just took off for, oh, whatever reason a guy would have to leave the girl he loves . . ." I feel my lip wobble and I bite it. "The family he loves, the band he started that's coming together." I inhale. Exhale. "Only from day one Duck's been trying to convince me something strange and sinister and not just guy-going-guy is going on." Am I making sense? Must be, since Sin still seems to be listening. "But I didn't want to hear him, because I'm done with strange and sinister, okay; I want nice, I want normal . . ." Again, reign it in, stick to the subject. "Only after a while I can't deny that things are happening and evidence is piling up. Like getting attacked by rosebushes. And me playing the piano when I can't even play the kazoo. And you, Sin, okay—you happening. Yeah, I think it's *you* making you happen; and clearly you think it's me . . ."

This is coming out badly. I thread my fingers through the curls at my temples and pull, aiming to straighten out my thoughts. One last shot: "Sin, look, here's the thing: It wasn't me kissing Tosh that brought you back. It was Antonia Forsythe."

The reaction is delayed, and not at all what I expect. Sin busts out laughing. Not his derisive wolf bark but that genuine response to something truly ludicrous. His dimple creases and a bona fide twinkle ignites his eyes and I know he wants to share with me just how silly-nutty-whacky it is. For a second, until he doesn't. Dimple: shut down. Twinkle: still bright but the antithesis of merry. "Antonia Forsythe," he says, "would make Mary-Kate Kale resemble a cross between Lady Gaga and Countess Báthory."

Lady Gaga I'm familiar with—and apparently Sin has caught up on his pop culture gaps in the last few days. As to this Báthory person, I make a mental note to Google her later.

"So you know her?"

"Antonia Forsythe? I knew her, past tense, as an innocent dimwit." Sin rakes his forelock, gazes skyward, and returns his eyes to me, twinkle now tarnished to a dull *how dare you*. "I know that she died horribly—consumed by flames while her oblivious parents entertained glamorously in the great hall. And I know that her father's gavel condemned me." He's trying to contain himself, show no emotion; he lowers his voice even further, his mouth barely moves. "If you mean to propose any impropriety between me and that poor unfortunate, I warn you, my lady, you insult me. And you've reached your limit for that already."

Innocent dimwit. Poor unfortunate. Descriptions that don't exactly jibe with the image I'd concocted. My portrait's of the pampered only child of adoring parents, her every utterance marveled at, her every wish fulfilled. Considering her mother's regal background and frequent comings and goings, I assumed she enjoyed a London education, a Parisian wardrobe, a Viennese pastry chef, and a Pekingese lapdog. Surely Antonia was the envy of her peers, things being pretty straitlaced in eighteenth-century Swoon. Now, in the burning ire of Sin's eyes, I'm abashed at my shallow assessment, based on a few lines from a long-ago newspaper, some fancy decorative touches to her living space, and my own prejudices.

Yet, well, since I'm already here, I might as well shove the other foot and both elbows into my mouth. Besides, he's so righteous about Antonia Forsythe, yet he had no qualms about corrupting M-K Kale (not that a few tokes of the skunky-sticky ever corrupted anyone, but I need fuel).

"I don't mean to insult you," I say, "but I'm obliged to Marsh, and to Duck, to find out all I can about Crane—me being the designated occultist around here. So if you'll hear me out and shed what light you can, I'll let you be and you won't have to talk to me ever again."

The loyalty I show my friends must suit his strong, albeit skewed, sense of honor. He folds his arms across his chest in a posture that bids me continue.

"Okay, first, this little ditty ring any bells?" Note for note, I la-la-la what I've come to think of as Antonia's tune.

I'd forgotten the effect my singing has on Sin; in the space of an instant his face melts, then hardens. "It is hers," he confirms.

"Do you know the lyrics?" I figure they could contain a clue.

He shakes his head. "She would hum it incessantly. But were there words, I never heard them."

"All right, Sin, look. I know you view her a certain way, but according to Marsh, the Saturday night before Crane vanished, he called out Antonia's name in his sleep. So is it possible she isn't so immaculate?" He does me the courtesy of pondering it, then murmurs something I don't catch. "What did you say?"

"Women. I said, 'Women.'" The way his arms are folded, I now see, keeps his heavy heart from dropping out of him. "With their fans and veils. With their smiles and insistence on politesse. Whatever really goes on in there, I certainly cannot tell."

I allow his trope against my gender. "Okay, Sin, here's something less arcane than the average female." I tell him of our sojourn to the east wing of Forsythe Manor; I tell him of the tarot reading. "Three questions, three cards: the Tower, the Lovers, and the Hanged Man. If you can unequivocally assure me that the Hanged Man isn't you—that in no way is your latest incarnation here in Swoon tied to Crane and Antonia, then fine, I'll give it up."

His arms fall to his sides and his chin points to his pain. "The cards would not read false; your interpretation must have some grain of sense," he admits, resigned, as he lifts his head. "I can assure you of nothing, my lady. I can only tell you what I know."

# XXV

I'll take it — without interruption from the giddy guests at Mary-Kate's. Duck included.

"Are you getting anywhere?" he asks under his breath as Sin and I locate him on the sidelines of lawn chess.

"Like pulling teeth," I answer quietly. "From Jaws." Then I turn it up. "You about good to go?"

"I'm sure I can drag myself away."

Apparently Sin sees no reason to tell Kurt we're out, so the three of us quit for the Cutlass. I ask Duck if we can drop him off and borrow the car, implying that Sin won't speak in front of anyone else. I don't know if that's true, but the boy's mood improves when he slides into the driver's seat. First stop, Forsythe Manor, to deposit Duck. Idling in front of that imposing structure sparks a fever in me. Sin stares at the house too, as if to strip it to the beams for its secrets. Yet right now my sense is that neither one of us is a match for the place. Welcome taunts from every window, challenges from every stone, and once a familiar fragrance assails, I urge him, "Let's get out of here."

The top down, the night delicious, the country roads a set of French curves—the part of me able to "be here now" is digging this. The rest of me tenses and tugs, impatient, unsure. "Do you want to just go to my house?"

"No." Clearly indecision isn't among his faults—and on second thought, I must concur. I have no desire to revisit the scene of our love under current circumstances.

"The green is right here," he points out, though we're headed in the opposite direction. "Shall I turn around?"

"Please, no!" The village green, with its mighty ash tree—site of his long-ago execution, Pen's near-fatal tumble, and the ceremony I performed that loosed Sin on Swoon . . . . "Just drive." I lift my profile to the stars and steal what snatches of "be here now" that I can.

Which is how we wind up at the lake. The spot on the lake, known as the Spot, is where Swoon's idle youth come to swim, smoke, lay out, make out—all away from prying eyes. At least that's what it's like by day. I've never been to the Spot after hours. Not that I know what time it is; the Cutlass's dashboard clock is stuck at an eternal 7:40—one aspect of loving restoration Libo didn't bother to address. There are few cars in the area where we park; pop music fizzes from one.

The wooded trail to the lakefront is narrow, and we have no flashlight, but whatever sort of being Sin is, this is no deterrent. "Take my hand," he says, reaching for me with scarcely a backward glance, simply ensuring I don't sprain an ankle, crack a tooth. Chivalrous as ever.

But I do as he says; I take his hand. It's hard. It's warm. It's roughly callused. And safe and strong and capable of countless things, great and awful. Everything I remember his hand to be. How much simple hand-to-hand contact meant to us once, when he was a ghost in occupation of my cousin, and touch was the means to our encounters. How far beyond touch we traveled, all our senses locked and loaded, minds and bodies to their limits, hopscotching time. Yet at its core, it all comes down to this, the unconditional trust, the completeness, of our two hands joined. Is he thinking that now, as he leads and I follow?

Toward the bottom, the path dips more steeply, our steps come faster, and Sin whirls me onto the lakefront with force enough to sunder us. But he holds on. Until, deliberately, he lets go.

Not quite sandy, not quite pebbled, the shore isn't as hospitable here as in more populated, and therefore pedicured, stretches of Swoon Lake. Such is the price of privacy. I'm too nervous to sit still, anyway, and Sin also seems to favor motion. The moon is low, and sloppily halved, a custard pie torn in two. Lapping ripples provide soft percussion. I want to lose my shoes and wade ankle deep in water I know is freezing; I want to remark on how freezing it is, how crazy I am to wade; and I want more than anything to hold Sin's hand again. But that's not going to be. He'll tell his tale more to the lake than to me. Any wonder that after all this I'm now in no hurry for him to begin.

"To me," he begins anyway, "Antonia Forsythe was a shy, odd, awkward girl."

And beautiful? I won't ask, but I want to know.

"Though her gowns were surely made by renowned couturiers, they never seemed to fit, abrading at the wrist, buckling in the bodice. Still, she was lovely in her way. Fragile, with porcelain skin and gray eyes, a somewhat pointed chin. Her two most striking features, though, were opposites. First, her mouth—tiny, perpetually pursed, a rosebud afraid to bloom. In counterpoint, her hands—long and bony, and highly unusual for a girl of her stature, she used them. Not for embroidery or tatting lace, but in her garden. Antonia was always there."

Among the roses. Snipping, pruning, watering, mulching. How would Sin react if he knew I had a garden, prosaic as my veggies may be. Laugh, probably.

"Or so it appeared to me, since that's where I'd see her. Archibald Forsythe, the 'spare no expense' type with his wife's money, commissioned me to build a gate for her stone garden wall, and he wanted something special—"

"Yes . . ." I'm scarcely aware that I speak, and I break Sin's flow, but I'm floored—I had no idea the gate was his creation. "I know," I stammer. "It's still there. A work of art."

A brusque thank-you and he picks up again. "What a joy to design something, create something. Horseshoes were my stock in trade; this was a rare opportunity, yet I hoped it might lead to more. I'd met Hannah by then, and I knew we were destined. I wanted to provide the best for her."

Hannah Miles. Sin's first love. Redheaded spitfire who gambled with her life. And lost.

"Since the work was so painstaking, I set up a temporary forge on the premises. I'd get my routine farrier affairs out of the way and then repair to Forsythe Manor. Antonia would linger, half-hidden among her roses, whenever I toiled nearby. I did find it strange she'd be permitted to, considering my . . . reputation."

Reputation, ha! Deserved reputation, as in *fact*. Sinclair Youngblood Powers never met an urge he didn't indulge, and before he fell for Hannah, visited many a bed and hayloft and forest clearing and scullery floor and maybe even this very lakeshore with any number of women and girls drawn to his dark charms.

"But Lady Anne seemed to have little interest in her daughter, and Archibald was busy climbing the pole of judiciary ambition, so Antonia roamed. Of course, there was nothing untoward about it—there was only Hannah in my eyes, and Antonia spoke not a word to me. She'd skitter about when I was near, humming squeakily, her lips screwed up in seriousness. In truth it confounded me to be in the presence of a lady who did not seek my attention."

Ah, Sin. Still Sin. I cannot help but smile.

"The damnedest thing, till it struck me: Antonia was an imbecile."

Right, uh-huh. Only a mo-mo would be immune to his allure.

"A numbskull waif with neglectful parents—naturally, she gained my sympathy. I'd smile, remark on her lovely roses—but never get a glimmer of response. So imagine my astonishment when she kissed me!"

Aha! Innocent idiot, my ass!

"It was the day I installed the gate. Late summer, and a blazing afternoon; I was having a devil of a time lining up the hinges, cursing myself for having wrought so massive and unwieldy an object. The last thing on my mind was Antonia Forsythe. Oh, how I struggled and swore, stripped to the waist in the heat. When I finally got it, I stood back to admire my success, and then—in part to test it but also just to let loose, I launched myself with a howl and swung. An embarrassing position to be caught in by the young mistress of the house."

I'll bet.

"Yes, I noticed Antonia then, still as an alabaster statue in her ill-fitting frills. Yet feeling my oats as I was, I hopped off and called to her. 'Come see, my lady! See if it's not the grandest gate in this great colony of Connecticut! See if it's not a worthy trustee of your flowery treasures!'"

Flowery treasures? Yeesh . . .

"Advance she did, her eyes wide, her mouth strict, and with those nimble, spidery fingers reached for the flower at the center of the gate. She hesitated, then began caressing each petal and the crevices between. At last she turned to me, hand at her throat, eyes brimming tears, and then she was upon me, quick as a cat, with an ardent—albeit clumsy—kiss. The things that shot through my mind in that moment, beyond shock, of course: amusement, repulsion, pity.

"So much depended upon what I did next. Hence, while I turned my cheek to escape her lips and avoid her gaze, I held her to me. Held her firmly, held her close, till the excited writhe of thrill was spent and she was still. Then I loosed her hands and placed them at her sides. She gazed at me, glowing; but her mouth, that tortured little orifice, was locked in a grimace, a travesty of a true smile. It pained me to look at her. There on the grass, my sweated-through shirt. I flung it on, mumbling something—maybe just her name and a one-word apology— and left."

At a gallop, no doubt.

"Forthwith the next day I dismantled my station and received from Archibald Forsythe accolades for my artistry and payment in full. I never returned to the manor, and in assessing the incident over the next week, I came to believe that Antonia, lonely, doltish creature that she was, had simply been overcome with gratitude."

Pausing, Sin looks out at the lake and up at the half-pie moon, and then he looks at me. "And I still do. Please convey my sympathies to Marsh and Duck, but since you insisted I reflect upon Antonia Forsythe, I can now maintain with clarity of conscience that she has nothing to do with Crane Williams's departure, Dice. And neither do I."

With that he turns away and begins trudging back to the woods.

## XXVI

HE WAS THERE; I WAS NOT. IF SIN SAYS THERE WAS NOTHING MORE to Antonia's kiss than a klutzy thank-you from a "special" person, he ought to know. Their relationship was just as he said—brief, benign, innocent . . . and over. What's more, in his estimation, the Easter bunny has a greater capacity for evil. Yet those rapacious roses, the waltz that won't get out of my head, the insinuated omen of the tarot cards—and let's not forget Ruby's recent visit—I'm having difficulty accepting that the young mistress of Forsythe Manor is as simple as Sin insists. I can't shrug off the feeling that some unfinished business from the summer of 1768 has got to come to full flower.

My reasonable, commonsense side remains dedicated to the proposition that Crane Williams is enjoying a vision quest or final fling. My woo-woo psychic flip side? It's pretty damn sure someone or something in that grand house near the green purposefully plucked my best friend's boyfriend out of the atmosphere. Both sides are united, committed to following the questions till the truth comes out. Trouble is, having heard Sin's "end of story" story, I've got no clue what the next question might be.

Any wonder I tossed and turned all night? Lucky me, Sin did actually pull over instead of just booting me out onto Daisy Lane, but he left the motor running and his sights on the windshield. I mumbled good night and got out, dragging my heart with me. Now, contemplating the ceiling, purring furball for a bedmate, I recall telling him that if he shared his tale, he'd never need speak to me again. The idea that he'll take me up on it weighs me down like there's a hippo on my belly instead of a cat. Yeah, well, I've got to get up anyway. The real estate lady will be showing the house today and it's a wreck. Plus, I've got to deal with Duck.

"The good news is you've got a Sin Powers original on the premises," I tell him, phone cinched to my ear as I gather laundry. "He built your garden gate." Then the bad news, Sin's rationale for absolving Antonia Forsythe, and himself, in regard to Crane. "Basically, we're back to square one."

Duck absorbs this with a sigh. "Well, that utterly sucks," he says. "Father fired the detective and hired a new one. Mum's got a slew of new pharmaceuticals. And I'm so bored and blue and simply . . ."

"Don't worry, Duck." That creaky, cranky old joint he lives in had plenty of other inhabitants between Antonia's time and now; maybe one of them is spooking up the place, and if not the evildoer behind Crane's abduction, then able to offer a few clues. "We'll stay positive, okay, and we'll keep each other sane. We'll hang; we'll play music . . ."

Oops, that slips out. How can I salvage my relationship with Sin if I keep seeing Tosh? Assuming I want to salvage it. Since, say I do win him back, how long will he stick around this time? Tosh, at least, lives in Norris and has no ties to the netherworld. Maybe I've had enough of Sin's drama; maybe I've moved on . . .

"True, there is the band." Duck snaps me out of my musings. "Tomorrow's Sunday, so Tosh ought to be free by evening. Will Marsh be back from Newport?"

"Oh, uh, I don't know. Why don't you check with Tosh and I'll hit Marsh and we'll confirm tomorrow. But-right-now-got-to-go-see-you-later-bye." I rush off, then scurry around in rudimentary cleanup mode. The agent arrives with a couple of NYC retirees who've convinced themselves that their golden years will be shinier in a pastoral setting. I try making myself scarce, but at one point I catch the woman giving me that *do you live out here all alone, dear?* look.

I set off on a bike ride before the next prospective buyers can bug, and when I return, Pen's at my kitchen table, on my laptop, a bowl of my Cocoa Puffs and (remarkably, something that doesn't belong to me) a gallon of latte frostee at her elbow.

"Yo," she says.

*Yo*, I think. Please.

"Hope you don't mind, but your place has got to be my home away from home now that school's over," she says. "Remember how my mother used to hound me about the hazardous effects of tanning? Well, now she's all like, 'Why don't you go outside? Get some sunshine!'"

"*Mi, su*," I tell her. Then *mi* takes a few long sips of *su*'s high-octane beverage.

"Ooh, now this is cool . . ."

What, some tribal pattern from a tattoo site? I peer over her shoulder:

---

CHEST-AH-FEST!
Local Bands . . . Local Beats . . .
Local Arts . . . Local Eats . . .
July 10th & 11th
Noon to Midnight

---

"For this," Pen says, "I'd get some sun. But hopefully it'll be cloudy."

A grassroots music festival does sound fun. And fun, we could all use some of that. By then for sure—okay, maybe—Crane will be back. We ought to make a plan. "Where's it at?" I ask.

"Southeast of here." Pen's mapping it already. "Not too far. We should definitely go." She gives me bright eyes and a slanted smile. "You know what . . . ," she says. "Bruise Blue should play."

Tosh would wet his pants. "Oh . . . but how?"

"I'll find out," she says, then adds, almost to herself, "Of course, by now they may have the lineup all set . . ." Clicking around the site, she asks, "Dice, do you guys have a demo?"

A demo? "Of course not—we've just been dicking around."

"How am I supposed to get you this gig without letting them hear any music?"

I look at her. "Who are you, our manager?"

She looks back. "Why not? You need one."

She'd rock. Except there's one variable she hasn't taken into account. "You want the job? Talk to Tosh," I tell her. "Bruise Blue is more his band than anyone's; he's our arranger and really the driving force behind the whole thing. And it's no secret how much you love Tosh."

Eyes glued to the screen, Pen says, "I'll have to deal. You're right about his talent. And you've got to have at least one hot straight guy in the band."

A quick, ripe flush rises at the comment. My cousin is among the multitudes that know nothing of the kiss I enjoyed against the wall of her house with said hot straight guy. I bite my lip. Discussing him with Pen could help me decipher my tangled desires. "You think Tosh is hot?"

"Me? No, *I* don't. Technically, he is, though. It's just an observation. About the band." She closes the laptop. "All I know is you better start working on new material. Like how about some more original songs? And the covers you do had better be commercial." Girl sure sounds like a manager. "You need to record something, make an MP3 at the next practice. Which is when? Or you know what, I'll just talk to Tosh. Since apparently I have to get his *approval*."

I start to say something, then stop. Practice, shmactice. I'd put Bruise Blue on a way back burner, but rehearsal = the studio = Forsythe Manor. I'm tugged to that place like a fish on a line. So I locate Tosh's info, slap it on a pad, hand it to Pen. "Here you go, boss."

Sucking at her latte, she seems to commit it to memory.


Fresh from Newport, Marsh meets us in the studio that Sunday at six, her kid sisters in tow. Their mother and New Pop will steal an extra day and night of vacation, Marsh happily agreeing to watch the girls—focusing on them will keep her mind off her woes and her mood relatively buoyant. We notch it up more when we tell her about Chest-ah-Fest. Everybody's juiced about it: A bona fide gig could mean tons of opportunities.

"I can play the tambourine," says Willa, who's baby blond and sparkling.

"No you can't," counters Charlotte, who shares big sister's large foal eyes.

They'd been quiet, almost awed, for the first half hour, but take after take of "Swear"—digitally documenting it for our demo—has made them antsy.

Pen steps in—she's killer with kids. "You guys know what? Mrs. Williams has got the most yummiest snacks in the kitchen. They're English! Doesn't that sound good?" Will and Char bob agreeably and Pen leads them out. "Back in a flash, and then enough of 'Swear' already. I want to hear that other Stones song." Over her shoulder, she says, "I'm not so sure Dice can pull off 'Sympathy for the Devil.'"

Oh, come on—if anyone has sympathy for the devil, I do. Want proof? The Williams place being so close to the Swoon town center, everybody's cell phone actually works. Mine vibrates my butt, and I pull it out, saying hullo to an unidentified caller.

"Dice."

Pulse quickening, temperature rising—it's ridiculous, embarrassing, the effect Sin's voice has on me. I curl into myself, hoping to deflect attention from my bandmates. "Uh . . . hey," I say. "What's up?"

He tells me. My reaction puts all eyes on me. I can't help it. The word spews out in horror and disbelief: *"Jail!?"*

# XXVII

Sin on Swoon lockdown—again! Unjustly—again! Or so I leap to assume.

"I've been taken in for driving a vehicle registered to Crane Williams."

His voice is composed, but how he must hate this. Forget Sin's centuries-long feud with local law enforcement; it's got to be killing him, calling me for rescue. Who knew he even had my number; I can't remember him ever reaching for me this way. I guess I'm flattered to be his one phone call—a toss-up, no doubt, between me and Kurt.

"Though I've yet to be charged with any crime," he goes on, "so far they are not partial to my assurances that the car had been loaned to me. Apparently they're unaware that Crane has a brother called Duck; indeed, one of the officers is of the opinion that I'm a smart-ass."

"Simon, his real name's Simon," I say. "Don't worry, Sin; I'm with Duck now. We'll be right there."

The Swoon PD is in the center of town, maybe even on the same site as Sin's initial incarceration, prior to his capital punishment. I can't help but wonder what's keeping him there this time around. The Sin I knew last fall had a highly hypnotic patter; he could talk his way into and out of virtually anything. If that failed, with his brute golem brawn, he could simply pull apart the bars of any Podunk prison cell. Is he merely mortal in his current incarnation? The thought of him sitting there, head in hands, helpless on a bench, mystifies me.

Swoon hardly being a hotbed of nefarious activity, the police station is far from bustling, and since we're with Duck's parents, we get prompt attention. Paul Williams does ample fist shaking and foot stamping, and we manage to spring Sin, and the impounded vehicle, in under an hour. Charm no worse for wear, Sin apologizes to the Williamses for the unconscionable inconvenience, thanks them for their efforts on his behalf, and insists that they rely on him for anything, anything at all, so that he might repay his debt. Then they drive home in their car (not the Rolls, just the Jag), while Duck, Sin, and I take the Cutlass.

"Where would you like us to drop you?" Duck asks.

Sin doesn't answer at first. Then, from a demoralized slouch across the backseat, he says, "I simply don't know." He really is at a loss, like he has no reason for being now. Since, clearly, his reason for being isn't me.

Duck and I trade a queasy look. "You're welcome to join us at the house," he offers.

Ooh, bad idea. Duck still must not know how Sin discovered me and Tosh midclinch. And now Sin sits up, leaning between the bucket seats, vaguely heartened.

"We're rehearsing, of course," Duck adds. "But as I remember, you're quite musical too. Perhaps you'd like to sit in?"

Sin sinks again, fuming, futile.

Holding the headrest, I swivel to study him, and our eyes engage for about an eon. Then we're up the drive of Forsythe Manor, and he says, at length, "Very well. Why not."

Why not? A thousand scenarios flit through my head as we enter the house.

"That was fast," Pen says. "Good, now we can—" She stops, snapping her trap with an audible clack of perfect teeth. Clearly she didn't expect us to go completely insane within sixty minutes. Except for the flash glance at her party, she's had no confrontation with Sin. It's been a long time coming. Chipped ebony manicure sinking into the arm of her deep suede chair, she holds herself back, though from what—leaping up to hug him, or slug him? Instead she simply stares, probably recounting internally the litany of things the boy did to her, how monstrous they were, and how she loved every minute.

If he's thrown by her ravaged hair, studded lip, and extra pounds, it doesn't register, yet he can't fully meet her eye, either. "Pen," he says hoarsely. "I hope you're well."

Narrowing her eyes, she can't look away. "Oh, I'm well," she tells him. "Well as hell."

Meanwhile, Tosh would no doubt like to grow wings. Maybe he's kicking himself for not telling Duck details of his previous encounter with Sinclair Youngblood Powers. Maybe he thinks throwing the two of them together again was my idea—and I wish he'd look at me so I could give him a *don't look at me* look.

The only one who can be relatively normal about it all is Marsh. Of course, I haven't had a chance to tell her yet how not helpful he's been on the Antonia tip. She ambles over, puts a light hand on his shoulder, and kisses his cheek. "Sin," she says, her smile a Kustard Kup confection. "It's good to see you."

"Thank you, Marsh. You too." He takes her into a quick but true embrace, then says, "I've learned about Crane. I wish there was something I could do."

"There isn't?" Blanching, her eyes fly from Sin to me and back again. "But we . . . you . . . Antonia . . ."

At the mention of the name, he seems to struggle—his posture tightening, his expression wavering. He'd told me, absolutely adamant, that the girl with whom he'd had a passing acquaintance centuries ago is dead, gone, buried, and beyond the scope of our current situation. Yet somehow Marsh's anxiety strikes him in a way my inquiry of the other night did not—as though her slim frame might collapse, her fraught eyes burst with tears. Maybe he's actually getting it now, how it felt for her to hear her true love break from a dream with "Antonia!" cracking his larynx.

Only Marsh does not buckle, does not bawl; she's stronger than she looks and sniffs, hard, to thwart the threat of sobs that's with her constantly now. "It's okay, Sin—I understand." She says that, though of course she understands nothing but heartache and loss. "It's just really hard . . . to be without . . ."

"I know," Sin says, turning from her to me, and I think, *I know too.*

The painful moment passes and Duck, no doubt verging on weeping himself, mans up and turns deferentially to Tosh. "I hope it's all right that I asked Sin to jam."

Tosh responds like cement. Small blessing, though—he knows it wasn't my brilliant idea.

"Crane had always meant to learn harmonica," Duck continues, roving the room, panning the clutter. "Give me a second . . . or several; I'll find one."

Tosh to Sin: "You play harp?"

Sin to Tosh: "Some."

Tosh mulls. "We could use another melodic line. Could work."

"Here we are!" Duck wags a vinyl pouch. "Ooh, look, there's a bunch. Lovely!"

He tosses it to Sin, who lifts an arm to snatch it from the air without altering the ram-tough posture he and Tosh maintain. Removing a C harp, he blows through a riff, lickety-split, and then another, chug-chug-chuggier. Tosh's foot can't stop itself—it taps—and his lush lips turn up. I begin to think this might actually, somehow, impossibly, turn out okay.

So we go, Sin adding fills to the still uber-mega-gonzo hit we've claimed for our own, lending even more of a Bruise Blue stamp. Making music dissipates weirdness, not entirely, but enough to make me think maybe Sin could join as a full-fledged member. It would certainly address Pen's point about male sex appeal. I'm musing on the notion when little Willa rushes into the room.

"Hey!" she calls out breathlessly. "Hey! You guys! Did you see Char?" She skips up to her sister, and Marsh bends to her, magnetized. "I know I'm not supposed to interrupt, but we were playing hide-and-seek and I looked everywhere. So if Char's here, she interrupted first!"

"Nope, she's not in here," Marsh says. "You probably didn't look very hard."

"But I did. I looked really hard. I looked everywhere."

Marsh crouches to get eye to eye. "What do you mean everywhere? You were supposed to stay in the great hall with Mrs. Williams."

Willa swings her arms; Willa stomps her feet. "Mrs. Williams got tired. Mrs. Williams said she took a pill and had to lie down." Willa wiggles; Willa squirms.

This is . . . not right. This is . . . very wrong. I know by the cold, hard squeeze on my heart. I know by the hot stars behind my eyes. I know because of a certain scent and a certain tune, the nasty familiarity of both.

"So I was it, and I looked and I called and I even did 'olly olly oxen free,' but she still wouldn't come out." Willa rubs her nose; Willa scratches her butt. And when she does that, three crushed, wilted scraps fall from her grasp.

By now Marsh has sunk all the way to the floor, clutching her littlest sister in a sort of stranglehold. I hunker down and pick up . . . rose petals. "Hey, Will—what are you doing with these?" I ask her quietly.

With one finger she touches the fragment of flower and looks at me, like: *What's that got to do with the price of tea in Tibet?* "I don't know," she says. "I found them looking for Char." Her skinny shoulders rise and fall. "They're all over the place."

It's not that I don't believe her when I stand and head for the door. I wish I didn't believe her, but I do, so I'm not surprised when I pull it back and a flood of petals falls across the threshold.

# XXVIII

AND SO A SÉANCE ENSUES. NOT IMMEDIATELY, NO. FIRST, MARSH AND Pen whisk Willa off for a sleepover at 9 Daisy Lane, while the boys and I split up for a top-to-bottom, inside-and-out search, in case I'm delusional and Charlotte's snug as a bug in an armoire or gazebo.

It occurs to me that two of our scouting posse (namely, Tosh and Sin) might be inclined to exit through a rear door and keep on going. Neither one has much invested in this, their only connection to the whole quagmire being me. Poor Tosh didn't sign up for any of it—he just wanted to do music. As to Sin, he's shown no sign that he forgives me (nor have I asked him to), and bottom line, he owes me nothing. All I know is, boy drama can't be my priority right now. The rose garden is, and I tear through it, calling for Char. I'm on my way back—empty-handed—when Pen pulls up the drive.

Part Bambi, part zombie, Marsh runs toward me. She doesn't ask. I don't tell. I simply put an arm around her. We walk a few steps, and then she stops. "I'm not going in there," she says.

"All right, it's cool," I tell her. "How about the porch? We'll sit on the porch and wait for the guys . . ." A mourning dove coos an unconvincing lullaby. Weeds make treacherous advances across the front lawn. Evening arrives like a friend who's not your friend anymore—she's just someone you know. One by one, Duck and Tosh and Sin find us, nobody making a sound till somebody does.

"That bitch." It's Marsh, wounded yet willful. "I'll kill her." No one mentions that her enemy's already dead. "My boy-friend, my sister . . . I don't get it—what does Antonia Forsythe have against me?"

It sure seems like a vendetta. I think back to the Marshalls I'd met in Swoon in the summer of 1769. Marsh's malevolent ancestor was a horse trader—a horse thief, according to Sin. What if he had some drama with the Forsythes, and it's taken their daughter this long to try and settle the score? A question worth following, I suppose, but if Antonia was as timid and sheltered as Sin describes, I doubt she'd have had much per-sonal interaction with the likes of Patrick Marshall.

"If only I could talk to her." Marsh begins to pace, holding herself at the elbows, holding herself together. "Reason with her, beg her . . ." Her voice breaks like a balsa model airplane.

"Come on, Marsh." Pen steps up and stills our girl, sits her down again. Then she looks at me and utters the *S* word. Like I was the star pupil in some spiritualism elective at Swonowa. Really, to me, medium is a burger order. Above all, let's remember the last time I played ritual roulette—what a major fiasco that was.

"I . . . I don't—I never." I flatten my lips. "What if I screw up?"

Silence. Clearly my capacity for error is legend. Then someone points out, "Things couldn't get much worse."

How's that for a vote of confidence?

We've all seen the same movies. Which means we don't know jack. So a pit stop in Duck's room so I can log on for research. This takes all of three minutes.

"You got a dish or a jar or something?" I ask. "Preferably not plastic."

Duck dumps a cache of butterscotch from a crystal bowl onto his dresser and hands it to me. "Might this do?"

I heft it. "Better not be a priceless antique." If we do make contact and Antonia's in a mood, I wouldn't want her smashing it into a million pieces . . . against anyone's skull. I indicate the pillar candles arranged along his headboard. "Grab a couple of those, too."

Once ensconced in the tower room, we settle onto the floor.

Boy-girl-boy-girl—funny, it just works out that way, me between Tosh and Sin. Never have I felt so intensely sandwiched, but I readjust my focus. I gaze about in the splish-splash light. Newly finished ceiling above, shapeless humps under drop cloths, torn-apart hearth. Antonia's carved mantel is nowhere in sight; it must have been removed for safety while the workers fix the fireplace.

"Apparently it's smart to start with a prayer of protection," I say, positioning the crystal dish in the center of our circle. "Guess we can skip that." After all, we're courting a potentially evil spirit. "So, basically, I'm going to ask for access, and whatever I say, just *think* on it, with me. No stray thoughts." I look to Marsh. "No jumping ahead to, 'Where's Charlotte?' 'Where's Crane?' We need to be . . . present with the presence."

Squelch the gadgets, huddle in a little closer, everybody's fingertips on the rim of the bowl. Here we go, WTF, I wing it.

"We in this circle respectfully ask permission to make contact with the dead." I pause a beat. "We mean no harm to anyone, alive or deceased." Another beat. "We're reaching out to a spirit we believe is in this house." Beat . . . beat . . . beat . . . "If you can communicate with us, please move this planchette, or—"

*Whoooooooooooo!*

Whoa, that was fast. The moan is low, but loud enough, coming from everywhere at once. "Are you the spirit of this house?" I ask. "Are you—"

182

*Whoooooooooooo!* Louder now. Across from me, Marsh's features tense with a rigid mix of terror and determination. On either side, Sin and Tosh lean forward and in, their shoulders cinching mine. The whole circle tightens, like a noose.

*Whoooooooooooo-hoooooooooo!*

Huh? I don't see Antonia Forsythe as the whoo-hoo type. And why is the mocking moan vaguely familiar?

*Booooooo-yaaaaah!* And then a cackle—a cackle I know exceedingly well . . .

"Yo, what you playing? Duck, duck, goose or some shit?"

Black muslin, white apron—the modest garb of a pre-Revolutionary housemaid sure doesn't suit the ghost who strikes a pose above our heads.

"Hey, Rubes," I say. "Nice dress. So what brings you all the way to the east wing?"

She answers my question with a question—quintessential Ruby. "Aren't you going to introduce me to your friends?"

Glancing around, I can't tell if they're scared or stoked or what. Mostly, they seem bewildered by our haunted hook-up—as in, how do I know this girl? And what should I tell them: Meet my bestie from the city, who's awesome except for the fact she tried to kill me once? I keep it simple. "This is Ruby. We go back." Then I latch her eyes. "The way you eavesdrop on my life, you ought to know everyone. And no offense, but I can see you anytime."

"None taken, *chica,* but you need me now," she informs. "Why you think I have this stupid getup on?"

Actually, I'm stymied.

She wiggles her neck. "Damn, Dida, you're not going anywhere without a spirit guide, and clearly that's me." She lifts her muslin skirt and curtsies. "I'm here to serve, m'lady. So come on, let me in."

Does she mean to sit among us, join the circle? I didn't see anything online tipping me off to that. Wide-eyed with wonder, my friends trust me to do what's best. Only Sin, who knows the whole sad Ruby story, regards her with narrowed, skeptical appraisal.

Focusing on me, she flips in the air to hover upside down. "Look, first, you can lose the crystal ball, I mean bowl." She picks it up, examines the label. "Waterford, huh? Nice. But unnecessary." She returns it to the floor. "It's more effective if you hold hands. So come on, scooch over . . ."

Sin addresses her warily with just one word: "Why?"

Somersaulting into a crouch she lets her gaze linger on his, irises of lucid amber holding steady against his onyx ore. "You know why."

Sin must debate internally, then he shrugs. "I believe we must allow her," he says. "Physical contact produces energy. Energy is the essence, the substance of the human soul. Whether in living body or spectral figment or sequestered in an object, a place.

A tree, for instance." His case, for centuries. "Or a house." The matter of the moment. "Of all our senses, touch is beyond intellect, beyond emotion, pure spirit."

Ruby gleams at me. "Touch, Candida!" That winsome wheedling. "I want to get corporeal for real. Touch! Even if just for a minute. Touch. It's what we miss most, all of us—the dead and the restless. Touch. That's what we crave here in the trenches of eternity. Touch! I know he did." Again she tilts her chin at Sin. "I know I do." Her smile glows with truth. "And so does she. Ooh, yeah—her especially. She craves it like crazy."

# XXIX

HAVE YOU HUGGED YOUR BEST FRIEND TODAY? DO IT. SHE FEELS GOOD, doesn't she? Solid, maybe a little moist—flesh, bones, muscle, pulse. She feels like what she had for lunch and the patronizing speech she got from some authority figure and the zoom in her mood when she tried on those cute shoes she doesn't need. She feels real. That's how Ruby feels to me when I reach up and pull her from the air to the floor. That's how I feel to her. The two of us on our knees, in our arms, among other people who, despite varying degrees of desperation, at this very second, don't even exist. It's just us. The only difference between how we feel right now and the way you feel with your girl is we know how fleeting it is. You think you'll be there for her and her for you forever. Yeah. Well. We used to feel that way too. Now the tighter we hug, the less we can hold on.

"I really want to help," Ruby says, into my eyes, into my heart.

Of course she does. She wants to help find Char and Crane, which is crucial, and she also wants to set right what's wrong with us.

"Come on then," I tell her. "We got business."

So now she's settled between Sin and me, everybody holding hands, and she intones, "I am open . . ."

And I feel her open, become conductive, agar in a petri dish, inviting whatever disturbance or impulse I might beckon from beyond.

"I am given," Ruby says to the unseen spirits of Forsythe Manor. "I am able. I belong to the souls of the circle and the souls surrounding the circle; I am the circle. I am yours. Use me."

So I do. "Is there someone in this house that will communicate with us?" I ask. We wait. I rephrase, putting the imperative into the situation, adding a "please." I start again: "Please, if there is—"

"Relax, relax, won't you? I'm coming." The voice rises from Ruby's throat—arched, bright, and clipped—and with a slight electrical tingle, she transforms. "Yes. Well. Here I am. Hello. How do you do?"

The hand now in mine is a lily—soft, delicate, and white. This can't be the hand of Antonia Forsythe, devout horticulturalist. "Who are you?"

"Why, I'm Earline Hampford, of course. Call me Early. Everybody does, because I am *so* ahead of my time. But if you don't know me, hmm—you don't look like friends of Reg's, but surely anything's possible. Do you know my husband, Reginald Hampford? Dreadful bore that he is."

Ghost Girl sure can gab. Well, it's not like she has to breathe. And who wouldn't be an ego storm after years of dead quiet? Sin was a tour de force of self-involvement, yakking till dawn to deliver his story when I first summoned him. Across the circle I sense Marsh's frustration—it's Antonia she wants, not this chatterbox; I try to send calming vibes. Right now it's Earline Hampford or nobody, and maybe she'll prove a fruitful lead.

"Would you like the nickel tour? Drafty old house, I hope not," Early prattles on. "Can't imagine why Reg bought it except that it was cheap, the old piker—you should hear him brag. I detest, simply detest, when he speaks about money. Terribly boring, money. I don't know a thing about it, except how to spend it. Fortunately, Reg doesn't require me to know anything. All I have to do is look pretty."

She does. A soigné sylph, twenty, tops, with a cap of corrugated platinum hair worn close to her scalp. Pausing for praise, she poses with her knees swung one way and her torso the other, lips painted crimson. And here's a dress Ruby would approve of: slim cut, sleeveless, adorned by beaded fringe that reflects the candlelight. A matching purse dangles by a chain from one shoulder. I'm about to give Early the flattery she's fishing for, but let's just say her attention's been diverted.

"Well, well, aren't you the big six," she says to the boy on her right, splitting her lips into a gap-toothed smile, adorable in its imperfection. "What do they call you?"

"They call me Sin."

A trilling arpeggio of laughter. "I bet they do!" Early performs a feline head butt to his shoulder, yet as she leans into Sin, her hungry eyes travel the circle. When they alight on Tosh, I think they might fall out of her head. "Eat my applesauce," she murmurs. "I bet you're a musician. Hmm? Do you play jazz?"

"Uh, jazz?" Tosh seems embarrassed. "Not so much . . ."

"No? Oh, that's all right. You're still the berries in my book."

"Hey!" This is from Pen, but Early's occupied. "I said, 'hey!'" My cousin is unaccustomed to being ignored. "You're a flapper, right?"

Early cocks her head. "Bearcat, sister," she corrects. "No one *says* she's a flapper. They call us that but, *pfff*, what do they know!" She lets go of my hand—the break in the chain having no ill effect on her density—and pulls several slim items from her purse. "Ciggy, anybody?" she says, offering a case around. Getting no takers, she sticks a smoke into a jeweled holder and lights it. "Say, how come we're all sitting on the floor?" She squints through her ascending plume. "Some kind of game, hmm? Games are very big around here. Is it—oh!" She gasps delightedly. "I know! It's a séance, isn't it? I'm getting the heebie-jeebies already. Just leave it to Early Hampford to hostess a séance! I'll certainly make the pages tomorrow—and I do mean the Hartford pages, if not all the way to Boston."

An allusion to the society section of the newspaper, no doubt. Makes sense, too. In my quick scan online earlier, I noted that spiritualism was a huge fad in the 1920s. As to Early's continued presence without physical contact, I chalk it up to the magnetic energy of our rapt attention—as long as we find her fascinating, she's got her hooks in.

"Well, we reach anybody?" She seems to have ID'd me as running this spook show. "Hmm? Have we got us a ghost?"

"In fact," I say, "we have."

Early's round eyes gape wider. "Really? Who?"

I'm right in her face when I say, "You!" Then I lean back and let it sink in.

"Me? Wh-what do you . . ." She chews it, swallows it, pats her sleek pelt of hair. "Hmm. Yes. Well. In all the excitement, I'd forgotten about that. I am dead, aren't I?"

I nod. "Sorry. And you must've died in this house—since you're still here."

"And gruesomely, too." Duck pipes up. "Since otherwise you'd be at rest." Clearly he's been reading up.

"Was it gruesome?" Pen, a recent convert to gorno, naturally wants to know.

"Oh, yes! Terribly gruesome!" Early hikes her knees up to her chest and dips her head to drain all the drama she can.

191

"It was the hooch! An awful batch, but we were swilling it anyway—that was the game. The more of the nasty stuff you could handle, the more points you racked up, and I was doing splendidly, until I wasn't, and old Reg had them put me on the chaise . . ."

"Oh, I know about that," Pen says. "With alcohol poisoning, you're supposed to sleep it off on your side, not your back, so you won't asphyxiate on your own vomit. Is that what happened?" The absence of dismemberment disappoints, apparently.

Early's shoulders hike and dip. "I turned the most ghastly shade of periwinkle, which clashed with my dress."

Nobody groans out loud or rolls their eyes, but the temper of our collective impatience must message Early somehow. "Say," she says, crushing her ciggy in the Waterford bowl. "You people haven't come to see me at all, have you?"

I try a sympathetic expression. "Actually . . ."

"Figures! Never could get any real swells to come out here to the boondocks after Reg locked me up and threw away the key." She casts a theatrical glance toward the ceiling. "Now here I am, dead as a doornail, and I still can't attract any good eggs." She sighs and begins to fade. "Well, guess I ought to be getting back, then."

"No! Wait!" Marsh cries.

Narrowing her eyes, Early appraises Marsh. Maybe she detects a resemblance, since she says, "It's about the kid, isn't it?"

"Yes," Marsh says quickly. "A little girl, my sister?"

Early lights another cigarette. "Really, if I knew what people saw in them—kids, that is—I would've had one myself."

I put a hand on her arm. "Early, please," I say. "Can you tell us anything about her, anything at all?"

"Well, she's just arrived. And not that I've been paying attention, since I couldn't care less, but she's not dead, if that helps."

With a choked sob of relief, Marsh sags heavily onto Duck.

"That is helpful, so helpful," I say encouragingly. "She disappeared from our world a few hours ago, but we don't know why, or how."

"Why, I couldn't tell you," Early says. "But how? That's easy. See here." She stands—at five foot zip a tiny girl for such a whopping personality—and strolls to the fireplace, flicking ashes at the hearth. "This was sealed up as long as I lived here, and as long as I've been dead here, too. Now that it's all busted up, you can tell there was a reason."

Could the recent demolition of Antonia's fireplace have opened a sort of passage? I join her there, stare into the blank space. At first, I see nothing. Then I blink, shift my focus slightly . . . and I see *everything*.

XXX

ONE AFTERNOON A FEW MONTHS AGO, I'M FOLDING LAUNDRY, ZONING out, when I notice through the window a small flock of birds going round and round in the cloudless sky. The slant of sun, combined with the speed and unison of their choreography, creates this flickering, high-velocity vortex, a cycle of splashes in space that's entirely organic yet appears mechanical, like an alien invention designed to stupefy earthlings like me. That's as close as I can get to describing what confronts me in the tower-room fireplace.

Initially, anyway. Peer between the gaps in the "birds" and there's the entire past, the pedestrian present, and the unfolding future, all in a simultaneous, spiraling stream. Unfortunately, it hurts to watch—hurts like a brain giving birth to a helix of subway trains during eternal rush hour—so I need to frame my focus on only a small slice. This also hurts to watch, but in a different way, since what I see is lives, and deaths, the lives and deaths of people who met their ends in this house.

I say something. Probably "Oh my God." Behind me I'm vaguely aware of my friends, only no way can I acknowledge them. The people before me captivate in IMAX 3-D. There's Antonia Forsythe—I recognize her from Sin's description—lacing into her ill-fitting gown, sipping tea alone in a corner, seated at an escritoire in this very room . . . and writhing in flames. Here's Earline Hampford, kicking up her heels in a manic Charleston, guzzling bathtub gin like there's no tomorrow . . . and there isn't. All of them, a patchwork quilt of fine intentions, broken dreams, clandestine trysts, bitter betrayals, mundane day-to-days, and occasional strikes of brilliance, valor, sacrifice, madness.

The lives are engaging in a reality-TV sort of way, but the deaths are truly five-star entertainment—if you're a five-star sicko. Each one dripping comic-book colors. Each one bellowing hell-bound screams. Each one awful: suicide, murder, tragic accident, disfiguring disease, butchered childbirth. No one passed easy here at Forsythe Manor, and they're all still here, none at peace. Now that I know the architecture of agony this house represents, how can I be certain it was Antonia who trapped first Crane and then Charlotte into its wretched confines? Maybe Sin's been right about her all along; maybe her roses and her waltz weren't seductions but warnings.

"It's a passage," I murmur, mostly to myself, and back away. From this perspective the hearth is perfectly ordinary again, but it dawns on me that this is where it all began—the sparks of Antonia's demise starting right here. Following her death, the Forsythes must have bricked it up, then quit using the wing altogether, and ultimately sold the place, defeated. In all the years since, this prime square footage lay fallow. Until . . .

"All she had to do . . . ," I propose, "was reach through here . . ." Needing to form the words, articulate the horror. "And snatch them."

Now my gaze wheels dizzily around. Ruby's done an *hasta la vista* (bubbly, vapid Early gone as well). The rest of my friends take turns peering at the firebox, up the flue, into the chimney. Finally they gawp at me as if trying to pick a flattering motif for my straitjacket.

All but one. Spine curved, palms on thighs, Sin continues to examine the seemingly benign space. He's sensitive, intuitive, just like me. Always has been, even as a kid, just like me. Marsh and Pen, Duck and Tosh, they wouldn't see it, couldn't. But Sin . . . ? He straightens and faces us, smacking his hands as if they're tainted by centuries of soot and lurid death.

"Well?" I demand.

"Like a small flock of birds in a certain slant of sun."

Exactly. Precisely. Absolutely. Yes.

"A fissure torn between the mortal and spectral planes."

Okay, sure, that sounds good—official.

"And? Sin, what are you saying?" Marsh is in no shape for this, and it shows.

"Dice called it a passage; I see it more as a gate—a gate that swings both ways." He looks at me as if this might be the very reason he returned to Swoon, then over to Marsh in answer. "I do believe that Crane and Charlotte were taken via that gate. And I consider it my duty to go after them."

 XXXI

"Not without me," I tell him. Naturally, I expect an argument. Naturally, I get one.

"I won't permit it," Sin says with irritating finality.

Rather than splatter our spat all over the others, I tug his arm, and we retreat to the rounded alcove that rises above Antonia's garden. "Your duty?" I say. "Mighty noble and all, but I'm the one who's obliged to Marsh. Plus, two can cover more ground than one, and we don't have time to screw around. Crane and Charlotte are human beings—remember those? They like food, water?"

"You needn't lecture me on mortal frailty—these last few days, I've seen my share. What I don't know and cannot predict are the perils beyond the gate." He looks out the window and back at me. "This isn't a matter of receding in time, as we did last fall, but stepping into time itself. Anything that ever has or will transpire in this house might lie behind any door. You've glimpsed some of the atrocity from the safety of this side. Dice—" Sensing I'm about to interrupt, he takes my elbow firmly, pins me with his stare. "I won't let you expose yourself to such danger."

*Why not?* I wonder. Is it simply that, should something befall me there, he wouldn't want it on his conscience? Has he got one of those these days? Or is it more? The depths of his eyes remain oblique, but I've got the audacity of stupidity to let myself believe it's love. Of its own volition my head bows in reverence to that love, and I feel the warm storm build behind my eyes. With intent I lift my chin, raise my gaze, and his is still upon me. Like it never left. Like it never will.

"Oh . . . ," he says with a softness he rarely allows. "Dice. Please. Don't. Cry."

"I'm not crying." I sniff; I brave a smile. "Look, Sin, unless you're prepared to physically restrain me, I'll only follow you through the gate anyway. I'm not afraid—no, hear me out: As long as we encounter events that already happened, we're safe. I mean, nothing bad ever happened to me here, or to you, right? It'll be just like an amusement park spook house—scary but harmless."

A slow nod of concurrence. Not that he knows what an amusement park is.

"As long as we're careful not to disrupt anything," I pound the point, "no matter how heinous; as long as we stay in our lane, scope Crane and Char and yank them back through the fissure, we should be okay."

"And if we encounter things yet to happen?" he asks. "Potential futures that involve you and I?"

There is that risk. How could we not attempt to fiddle with the future? "We make a pact, here and now," I tell him. "No matter what, we slam the door; we walk away."

Rubbing the muscles at his neck, Sin knows when he's licked. "Agreed."

We both look toward the hearth, our friends assembled there. Marsh and Duck like two trees struck by lightning that fell on each other and found support. Next to them, Pen and Tosh, heads bent, seeming so . . . civilized. That's a first.

Pen says, "So you're going?" as Sin and I approach.

"Because we were thinking," Tosh jumps in, "maybe you should each tie a rope to your ankle, and we'd hold the other end—sort of the surf-leash concept?"

Logical, in a *Poltergeist* kind of way, but this isn't the movies. I smile at him, then her—realizing they came up with it together. "That's an idea," I say, "but I don't think so. Don't worry." I glance at Sin. "We'll check for each other." How we'll do that when we split up, I'm not sure, but I keep my game face on.

"We'd best get started," he says.

I steel myself for the ride to anywhere.

"Wait a second." It's Tosh. Reaching into his shirt, he removes the necklace I noticed the night of the mass skinny-dip. "Dice, do me a favor—wear this."

A small silver medal—an angel with a sword and shield; a slain devil, belly-up, at his feet. With deft digits Tosh fastens the clasp at my nape. "Saint Michael," he whispers deliberately, and I sense him looking past my cheek. "Protection from demons." Demons beyond the gate? Or the one I'm traveling with? What do I know from saints? For that matter, despite my experience, what do I really know from demons? I pat the pendant, warm from his skin, against my absence of cleavage. It's not so much the Saint Michael but the mojo of Tosh I'm taking with me.

Turning to him, my palm cupped on his shoulder, I say, "Thank you." Then I plant a kiss—it's a print, not a peck, but I put it on his cheek, where I know it belongs. Then I step away from him. The step that takes me to Sin's side.

Navigating the fissure proves tricky. Since as soon as we walk toward it—that flock of birds in a certain slant of sun—it vanishes from view. I put out a hand and touch only air, then stone. We try different angles, looking up, looking down—our friends eyeing us with polite discomfit—and then stand back.

"Any ideas?" I ask Sin.

He mulls. "We're being pedantic. Here, give me your hand."

I don't know where he's going with this, but I give it a shot.

"Look for the fissure; tell me when you see it."

I find it; I tell him.

"Good. Close your eyes and forget it. Instead, see the gate."

The gate I see is the gate Sin built, the gate to Antonia's garden.

"Now we climb it . . ."

With my free hand I grasp the iron bar. Right foot onto the rung, then left. Sin, beside me, does the same. Together, we swing.

Passing through feels like swallowing a melon seed. A mistake. A mistake we make on purpose. Even though it's the fissure that does the swallowing, Sin and I the seed, once I reach the other side, I wonder about the wisdom of this journey—what mutant fruit might result if our seed were to take root.

# XXXII

HERE WE ARE, AGAIN AND STILL, IN ANTONIA'S ROOM. IT *IS* HER ROOM. Furnished with her stuff. Canopy bed with downy coverlet, tall bureau, dressing table. There's a washbasin and pitcher with pastilles of soap in the shape of roses; I pick one up, inhale the scent. In the alcove overlooking her garden sits the small writing desk, elegant stationery set upon it. The mantelpiece bears but a single vase with a single bud, no other curios, dolls, or mementos a girl might collect.

Sin stands rigid in the middle of the room, heels together, hands clasped at the base of his spine. Sinclair Youngblood Powers, ill at ease in a lady's boudoir? Unlikely, unless previous insinuation of immodesty still has him smarting. Or maybe he just wants to get on with it.

Yeah, well, me too. "So how do you want to do this? We each take a floor?"

"I suppose," he says. "Time *is* of the essence. Let's do the wing first, since we're here. I'll go downstairs."

"Fine," I say. "We'll split the second floor, and move on to the main house if we have to." At the door I pause, survey his face. "I want to thank you for doing this, Sin."

"No need," he says curtly, and descends.

Alone now, I let my fingers trail the wall. The manor seems grand enough without this superfluous addition. Archibald Forsythe compensating for a small penis? Lady Anne nostalgic for some palace from her youth? I creak open a door—dark emptiness inside. Then I remember: The east wing was Antonia's domain. Had it been built exclusively for her? Were the Forsythes ashamed of their dimwit daughter, locking her away where fancy guests and their own sensibilities wouldn't be offended? Soon as the thought occurs, I hear her waltz. Distant, beyond this hall, beyond this floor. Quickly I check the remaining rooms—all blank voids—and hit the stairs. Though Sin and I planned to reconnoiter on the second floor, I blow past the landing, sure that the wing is a washout. I need to pursue the music.

It beckons, louder now. Also different, the way it plays. Before, I'd heard my own voice in my own head; now it calls from outside with an eerie, hollow quality . . . an organ? I scope around at the foot of the steps, rush toward the great hall. Only once here, Antonia's tune is displaced by a tuxedoed figure at a piano—a turbulent composition, Tchaikovsky or some fellow mad Russian. A small assembly leans forward in upholstered chairs, enthralled, and I'm taken in too, ducking for cover behind the potted palms that decorate the hall. From here, I note the high collars and puffed sleeves of the ladies' attire—very Victorian.

The pianist finishes with a flourish, and one woman leaps from her seat, applauding with passion. Scornful faces disapprove— such a display inappropriate in this prim and proper age. Naturally, I'm thinking along "you go, girl" lines when a sickening wave seizes me. I'd seen this woman earlier, peering through the fissure, and now the room shifts and I'm spying on that same scene again, up close and personal, for real. They're alone in the room, maestro and devotee. He—mustachioed, nose like a pump handle, eyes ice blue. She—honey-haired, bosomy, screaming. With one hand he holds her torn chemise, with the other he beats her viciously, and though she screams, screams for her life, her eyes maintain that same rapture as when her abusive beloved pummeled the keys.

I stumble out, and as I reel into the foyer, in front of the main stairs, Antonia's teasing melody comes again. I chase along a familiar hallway, but barge into a room I'd not been inside before. Mucho macho—massive leather chairs, a desk the size of Texas, mounted game staring glassily from the walls. Behind the desk a military man, shoulders like cinder blocks, looks straight at me.

"Close the door, Private."

It's an order, so I obey. The soldier motions for my approach. He's got the neck and nostrils of a bull, but the saddest eyes I've ever seen.

"You know, Private, I never wanted to join this man's army."

Where are we, time-wise? I can't tell. A uniform is a uniform.

"I wanted to be an actor. Do you find that strange?"

I need to reply. I go with "No, sir."

He grins. "It seems as though I'll finally get to play my scene."

I note the decorations across his chest, the pistol on the blotter before him, the brisk, professional manner in which he inserts the gun barrel and pulls the trigger, adding an abstract pattern to the drapes behind him. It elicits a scream. From me. The soldier has nothing to scream with anymore.

Out of there, out of there, out of there. Toward wherever, wherever, wherever. The studio, as it happens. Although now it appears to be a salon, an intimate alternative to the great hall, where a patron of the arts could entertain in style. Fine furniture, gilt-framed paintings, sculpture on pedestals, an elegant harp, and, against one wall, some kind of small keyboard.

Except forget the decor, I'm far more interested in the room's animate objects: Antonia Forsythe and Sinclair Young-blood Powers. She in pleats, ruffles, the ubiquitous fichu of mid-eighteenth-century fashion; he in breeches and frock coat. Weird, since Sin told me his acquaintance with the adolescent mistress had been confined to the garden. If he wasn't outright lying (which I've never known Sin to do), the scene I've burst in on is currently unfolding or lies ahead. Either way, a singeing dry-ice sensation courses through me—the cold of exclusion, the burn of betrayal—but I can't do a damn thing about it, only sidestep to observe from the shelter of a panel screen.

There is no music now. Nonetheless, they dance. And how happy Antonia seems. Not that she'll be landing any Aquafresh commercials, but she's overcome her reluctance to smile, and her porcelain skin glows. Maybe she hums to him; he certainly holds her close enough to hear as he sweeps her expertly around the room. *Totally innocuous*, I tell myself, trying to shed my eavesdropper's anger. On their next swing around, Antonia molds herself to Sin, nesting in the curve of his neck. Hers is a posture of utter surrender, his of entitled command, as his steps become broader, deeper. Now encompassing more of the floor, he pilots her deftly around tables and chairs, statues in silent testimony to this increasingly giddy waltz. With a panther's grace and a lion's pride, he takes her for a ride, twirling and dipping, her head and shoulders ultimately arching as her pelvis implants to his center of, among other things, gravity.

Around again, ruling the room, Sin practically brushes the panel screen that I now stand beside, rather than behind. That's right, in plain sight, hands on hips and, quite possibly, blowing steam out of both ears. Close enough to smell them, close enough to smack them, for that split second until they glide off.

"Never was any good at 'look but don't touch' myself," comes a haughty voice behind me. And then a haughty giggle, if there is such a thing. "Especially when 'touch' is a euphemism for scratch her eyes out."

# XXXIII

PEELING MY ATTENTION FROM THE *SYTYCD* WANNABES, I FIND Earline Hampford at my elbow.

"Really, sister, come away," she urges, and she's right. Whether waltzing in the past, present, or future, Sin and Antonia can't be disturbed. As I force myself from the room, Early links an arm through mine, and I fall in with her saucy saunter. "What would you say to a bottle of champagne?" she wants to know.

"I'd say, 'Hello, bottle of champagne.'" Bubbly being a weakness of mine.

"Goody. Because ever since you living started hopping the fence, things have really been picking up on this side of eternity. The quality of the hooch, for instance. I'd had to settle for the same swill that killed me for eons, but now the floodgates are open!"

We amble by the dining room, Early's prattle helping me

get a handle on this skewed plane of existence. "What else is new?"

"Hmm, well, we're all here at once now, anyone who ever died in this crummy joint," she says. "It's not like we're all making whoopee, but we are aware of one another." Early clicks a flame to the tip of a cigarette. "It's like being at a railway station: Arrivals, departures, various trains on various tracks, and while you see your fellow travelers, you stick to your own schedule." She taps her temple. "Savvy sister that I am, though, I've figured out how to boost their juice."

The way this girl smokes and drinks, it's probably best she died young and left a beautiful corpse. They didn't have Botox or rehab in her day; she wouldn't have aged well.

"The post-Prohibition stuff is the bee's knees. Have a look-see at my cold closet!"

We've entered the kitchen: linoleum tile, cumbersome appliances, and a breakfast nook with wooden benches. Early opens a built-in cabinet with a huge block of ice on one shelf and champagne bottles fitted sardine-style on the other.

"Thoroughly modern, hmm?" Early says. "I insisted. Told Reg, 'Reg, you may have slapped the cuffs on me, but I will not play the humble country wife at that stodgy old house. You rig it up right and maybe, *maybe*, I'll deign to live there." She rips the foil and unscrews the hood, then pops the cork with a blast, allowing minimal overflow. Clearly, she's done this before. "Cheers!" Early lofts the bottle, taking a sip before handing it to me.

I slake, ignoring the pesky inner voice that counsels sobriety in this unstable kaleidoscope of time. Early watches admiringly as I guzzle with gusto. Then, giggling, I hand back the bottle and wipe my mouth on my wrist.

"So . . ." Early motions toward the nook with the base of the bottle. "What brings you to our little corner of damnation, hmm?"

From my sense of her attention span, no way she'd sit through the director's cut, so I whisk her through an edit. "Basically," I say, "we're on the hunt for Crane and Charlotte, but we've got to be careful not to tamper with anything on this side. Which isn't easy, with all these events streaming simultaneously. Already it feels like doing ballet in combat boots."

Early pats her platinum crimp in contemplation. "Well," she says, "Antonia I've noticed, of course, moping about in too much gown." She shifts in the booth, hiking her own skirt higher and crossing her legs at the thigh. "And naturally, I sensed that Crane of yours the instant he arrived; getting a corporeal type is headline news here in the dead zone—only she must have him locked up like a crown jewel because I haven't caught a glimpse." Now she leans forward and plucks my arm conspiratorially. "But the kid? She's pretty much got free rein. When I spied her, she was right there at the counter, the self-sufficient little thing, standing on a foot stool and making sandwiches. If she doesn't come skipping along any minute, there's a nursery on the second floor, all kinds of dolls and toys—you might check there."

A nursery? Makes sense. "Thanks, Early—good idea." I should get up there, post haste. Maybe just a few more swigs, and a few more digs for insight. "The thing is, I was convinced Antonia was—*is*—behind all this. Only Sin thinks she's innocent, incapable . . . feeble-minded, in fact. And once I got a load of all the evil lurking in this place, I started tilting his way. Now though . . . the look on her face while they danced, delirious, maybe, but not stupid . . ." Clueless as ever, I shake my head. "I guess I'm looking for motive. *Why* would she want to kidnap Crane, or Char?"

Early drains the bottle. Daintily, she hiccups. "Why, why, dragonfly!" She recrosses her legs a bit impatiently. "Reasons! Really! Why does anyone do anything?"

To her, a rhetorical question. In Early Hampford's wasted life, death, and afterlife, everything's always been random. But it's not that way for most people. Most people do have a point, a purpose—or feel we need one. Why does anyone do anything? Musing on that, I hit on one major reason: We do what we do for love.

"There's one thing you should know about us ghosts, even wet blankets like your Antonia," Early goes on. "We ab-so-lute-ly adore games. You know, all the rules we've had to follow in life . . ."

Rules? Doesn't seem to me Early abided by many . . .

"Now we just want to play . . ."

That rings true. Ruby's even more mischievous in death; in life, she had so much to prove—how hot she was, how cool, how desirable, how untouchable. And Sin! In a way I miss his roguish ghost gags—the telekinesis of the Leonard Labor Day barbecue, the way he inspired Pen's feats of gymnastics sans underwear at the Lancers/Trailblazers showdown. As a representative of the living, I'll admit there's a certain appeal to a place like this—party central 24/7, playmates like bad girl Early, all the bubbles you can imbibe—

"Dice!?"

My name, on Sin's mouth, interrupts my reverie.

"In here, big boy!" Early answers for me.

He barrels into the kitchen, then stops with a wide-legged stance in front of the nook. The jeans and PWT Sin; no sign of the old-fashioned garb he sported in the salon. I wag a few fingers; then I burp. Early ogles him candidly.

"Dice . . . you've—you've been drinking!"

Early snickers. "Ooh, a real swifty!"

"I've been gathering intelligence," I say defensively, except it comes out "tin-ell-o-gence." Which is funny. So I giggle.

So does Early. "You are just too darb, Dice," she says, which

I figure is a compliment. "Shall I pop another bottie?"

Sin leans his fists on the table. "I think you've both had enough."

"Never!" Early cackles. "I don't know the meaning of the word."

But now Sin's eyes are on me, and adroit as he is at hiding emotion in their facets, I see the amusement there. I smile at him, my smile chock-full of the main reason anyone does anything.

# XXXIV

"EAST WING? SECOND FLOOR?" GENTLE YET FIRM AND FRANKLY flabbergasted, Sin hoists me from the table and steers me away from the influence of Earline Hampford. "We were to meet, if you recall?"

"Yeah, yeah, yeah. But I heard 'Miss Forsythe's Minuet' or whatever. I went to investigate." Uh-huh: "vin-est-o-gate."

"*Vin*, indeed," he says. "Dice, this is most unlike you. First to flit off like that, then swill to the point of—"

"Look, I'm fine," I tell him. And I am. For the most part. Cognizant enough to milk my condition and cling to his arm for balance. "A little tipsy is all."

He's dubious. "Nonetheless, I was concerned. Some of the things I've seen here."

I lay my head on his shoulder, wincing as we walk past the great hall and I get an unbidden instant replay of the beating I watched in there. "I've seen stuff too," I say. We've reached the main staircase, and I grab for the newel, aiming to straighten up, sober up, lose the ditzy drunk-girl routine, which is cute for only maybe half a minute. Instead, I lose my grip on the post, spin around, and windmilling woozily, plop to the bottom step. Looking up at Sin, I say, "Whoops . . ."

"You could do with some fresh air." On one knee in front of me, he makes a vain attempt to sweep my hair back.

"Wait, wait. I've got a thingie . . ." I dig in my pocket for the wriggle of elastic, gather my mess into a low tail that probably looks like it belongs on a beaver. "You're right," I agree, our faces close. "It is hot in herrrre. But can we go out? I mean, what happens to the whole mortal/spectral plane deal when we leave the premises? I'm thinking it might be an all-exits-final situation." Itch-you-station. Great.

He lends an arm, helps me up. "Possible," he concedes. "Perhaps the porch."

We risk it. Sin pours me into a chair before seating himself catty-corner. There's a breeze. It ripples the trees and shrubs that frame the property and cools my skin. A splash of lightning turns the sky to lilac; thunder mumbles more than rumbles, very far off.

"Early *was* helpful, by the way," I say, filling him in on her view of this warped dimension. "Plus, she saw Charlotte making sandwiches, so no matter what, our people won't starve here. It's possible for the living to ingest—" Another burp, the last vestiges of champagne. "Excuse me." Blushing in the dark, I press my fingers to my lips.

Sin no longer bothers to suppress his smirk; I see the gleam of teeth as the left side of his mouth spikes. "You're excused."

We're quiet a minute, then I ask him, "So, Sin, you know my number?"

It's been on my mind, but it takes him aback. "Now I must beg your pardon."

"My number, my cell number. Before—" Was it really mere hours ago? "When you were in lockdown, you called me. I can't remember you ever calling me, so—"

"Ah," he says. "That. In truth, Dice, I have no idea what your number might be." He leans forward, wrists on his spread knees, and beseeches the floor. Then he swivels his head toward me. "They told me I could make a call, so I picked up the phone and thought of you . . . and there you were. Your voice. Your 'hullo?'"

Glad I asked. I square my shoulders and smile inside all the way to Uruguay. Then I say, "Oh, I forgot to tell you the most important thing. Early says there's a nursery, a kid's paradise, apparently."

"We should go, then, if you're up to it." He slaps his thighs.

"Yep, I'm good." This is actually true.

"And this time, let's stay together, shall we?"

I'm all for that. As we ascend, I steel myself for what ugliness might greet us on the second floor. I also debate telling him how I watched him and Antonia waltz in the salon—and decide against it. If Sin was, is, or will be compelled to take the girl in his arms, I'll just have to trust it's in the best interest of all. We enter the corridor on tenterhooks, neither of us eager to throw wide a door. Toward the end, we hear the preoccupied murmurs of a child. Charlotte.

Seated serenely, shins against floor, she's surrounded herself with a select group of stuffed animals and dolls. There's a miniature tea set in front of her, and she's so intent on serving her guests, she doesn't notice us come in. Softly I call her name.

"Oh. Hi, Dice." She says it as if expecting me, then absorbs Sin with an enigmatic stare—I'm not sure if she remembers him—before lowering her gaze to her party. "Thank you all so much for coming," she says. "I hope we can do it again very soon." With that, she stands and walks over to us. "Okay, I'm ready."

I edge my eyes to Sin, then grin at the girl. "Ready?"

"To go back," she says. "I bet Willa cried when she couldn't find me. She does that—she gets frustrated and then she cries. Because she's still so little."

"I see," I say. "So . . . do you know how to get back, Char?"

She tilts her head quizzically. "Not exactly. Don't you?"

I take her hand and give it a squeeze. "Not exactly. But we'll figure it out. I think we have to go to the round room first."

"Oh, yes," Charlotte agrees. "Down the big stairs and then up the skinny stairs. It's a lot of walking. It's okay. I'm not tired."

How much like Marsh she is—the wide eyes, the trooper attitude. "You're not?" It must be after midnight in the real world. "Well, that's good. What about hungry? Are you hungry, Char?"

"Nope," she says. "We ate."

Again my glance consults Sin. "Who's we?" I ask mildly.

"Me and Crane. I made sandwiches, all by myself. Then I put them on a tray and—" She stops, as if maybe she's said too much.

Rather than push, I change tactics. "Oh, Crane. How's he doing?"

"He's fine." Her tone is cagey, noncommittal, and then she says, "You know what? I am tired." She pokes Sin. "You could carry me. Piggyback."

"Of course, dear lady." Sin assumes the position, and she clambers up, resting her cheek against his broad left lat, end of discussion. We're all quiet now, climbing to the tower. Mostly I muse on how to proceed. Do we put Char to sleep in the fluffy canopy bed and continue searching for Crane? Or swing back on the gate, delivering our bird-in-the-hand to safety, and then come back for the errant boy?

Notions that get shoved aside the second we enter Antonia's

room. Softly lit by several silver candelabra, it has been prepared in our absence. Before, a lone bud stood on the mantel; now the entire space is filled, flooded, flush. A riot of roses, plus grasses and sprigs of baby's breath to set them off, arranged in vases and strewn about in heaps.

"Wow!" Charlotte capers from Sin's shoulders. He and I exchange incredulity and watch the child dart around, blissing big-time in this bumblebee fantasy. Every color, from almost black purple to the fairest pales to the near-neon of tropical fish, even some with double-hued petals—yellow tinged with tangerine, pink that bleeds red. The bed is a collage of whites— milk, ivory, birch, bone—and all blooms; the stems, leaves and thorns removed, a sublime, satiny blanket. Most extraordinary, on the escritoire, a ribbon-sashed bouquet of blue roses. Drawn to them—I've never seen such beauty—I notice they rest atop a creamy envelope. It's addressed, in careful calligraphy, with just one word. A name:

*Sinclair* . . .

# XXXV

My Darling—

Be steady my hand! Be smooth my quill!
Oh the thrill, after all these years, of writing
to you. Yet even as the fire claimed my life,
I knew our love was not to end. When first
I found my spirit released, I was plagued by
an indescribable loneliness, a yearning for
you. Then I felt your essence enter my house,
calling to me powerfully—and so enabling me
to contrive the clever plan that shall at long
last unite us. Anon comes the moment you will
be in my arms, and I in yours! It is gladly
and with good faith that I return this child,

*the final piece in the trail that leads you to me.
Likewise shall I cede to the land of the living
the young man I have sequestered, <u>after</u> you
join me upon yonder bridal bed to fulfill the
vow you swore to me, now and for eternity. Till
then—so sweet! so soon!—I remain . . .*

*Yours—*
*Antonia*

Me, a gloating "told you so"? Nope. I won't remark that
for a feeb, Antonia Forsythe has quite a rich vocabulary—if,
irony intended, a tad flowery. As Sin lets the letter flutter to the
desk, I pick it up and read for myself, then wait for him to say
something.

He does. "She's deranged . . ." His seething is a measured
hiss. After all, Charlotte's here in the room with us, and who
knows if the she-demon herself isn't eavesdropping. "I swore no
vow to that wretch!"

I want to believe him, so I do, offering the faith in my eyes.
"Yeah, well, clearly she thinks you have," I whisper. "And she's
gone to a lot of trouble to get you to make good on it." I scan
the monogrammed sheet once more. Deranged? Damn skippy,
bartering Crane for Sin as though human beings were tokens
in a game. Yet under the insanity lies doubt, and it's doubt that

fuels Antonia: If she were so sure Sin had made a pledge to her, she wouldn't need a hostage. It's terrorism of the heart—crazy, yet crafty.

"Trouble for nothing." Sin indicates Charlotte with a slash of chin. "Collect the child. We're out of here."

"Without Crane?" Of course we're not.

Stumped, stricken, he lets a hand fly up, then fall to his side. I focus on Charlotte. She knows where our boy's been stashed. They shared sandwiches together, picnicking in one of the manor's many rooms. Yet she's Little Miss Mum, thanks to some coercion—a promise, maybe, or a threat. Looks like I'll need to trick her. Motioning Sin away, I crouch where she plays among the roses, making selections from a pink stack while humming, distractedly, that familiar tune.

"Wow, you're picking really pretty ones, Char," I say. "Are they for a bouquet?"

She nods. "Uh-huh. Two. One for Will and one for Marsh."

"That's so thoughtful. But will it be all right . . . with Antonia?"

Hesitating, Charlotte considers the stem between her fingers. "I . . . I think so. I mean, she has so many flowers. Wouldn't she want to share?"

"Gee, I don't know." I choose a bloom myself and regard it uncertainly. "I never met Antonia. What's she like?"

She has to think about it. "Nice, I guess. We were playing with all the toys and stuff, but then for no reason she got mad and pinched me, hard. Only right after that we went to the kitchen, and she let me have whatever I wanted. Although she didn't have any mayo." Charlotte smirks, remembering. "She didn't even know what mayo was!"

"That's funny!" I tap her nose with the rose. "What kind of sandwiches did you have?"

"Definitely not mutton!" she says, and laughs. "It smelled gross, and besides, Crane wouldn't eat it because mutton is a meat and he's a vegetarian. Are you a vegetarian, Dice?"

"Me? Uh-uh. But of course I know Crane is—we're good friends. He's in our band and everything." Charlotte's face turns wary, like she'd rather not talk about him. Major manipulation is due. I glance at Sin, lounging impatiently along the wall. "Yeah, he's like the leader of the band, actually. But he hasn't been around, so we all really miss him." Cue the heavy sigh. "No one misses him as much as Marsh, though." I place a hand on Charlotte's arm, but she evades my gaze. "Marsh misses Crane like crazy. She's so sad, she even cries sometimes . . . a lot." Really edging the kid's emo-meter. "I don't think even the biggest bouquet could cheer her up. But you know what will?" She looks up hopefully. "If we could find Crane, get him—"

One push too far—but it's not Charlotte who reacts. Instead it's like a monster amplifier hid amid the roses was suddenly cranked to eleven, blasting Antonia's blasted waltz. Ugly with distortion, the tsunami of sound shakes Forsythe Manor to its foundation. Charlotte gives a shriek that I can't hear, and I grab her, cushioning her head against my chest. Sin leaps from his post and stoops, her skinny limbs circling his neck and torso, while I get vertical. Ushering us out, Sin lays his free hand between my shoulder blades, but I sidestep to snatch Antonia's letter and in that instant see every single petal drop from its sepal, leaving litter atremble on the floor and a ravaged forest of barren stems.

The bilious bellow seems to assault from everywhere at once, spreading through the corridor and narrow stairwell like choking sonic smoke. The steps and banister quake so violently I'm sure they'll splinter as we hurry down, but we reach the bottom and charge into the main house unscathed. Just in time for the remix: Books, knickknacks, china, picture frames, anything not bolted down, adds smashing, crashing contributions to the din. Furniture stamps on wooden legs like an insatiable audience demanding an encore. The very floorboards, which are bolted down, rattle in the racket and threaten mutiny.

The impulse, of course, is to get the hell out of here. The danger—what annihilating void might await beyond these dimension-flouting environs—doesn't even occur to me. Yet just as my fingers touch the heavy brass doorknob, the noise is no more. The house is still. Almost silent, but not quite. Antonia's waltz continues to play, with that eerie, almost wheezy, hollow tone. It no longer violates every square inch of mass in the manor, but now has an identifiable source. So we—Sin, Charlotte whimpering in his arms, and me at his side—follow it to the salon.

There, at the small keyboard I'd noticed earlier, sits the girl who would steal Sin.

# XXXVI

A GIFTED MUSICIAN ANTONIA FORSYTHE IS NOT. FEATURES PINCHED and shoulders hunched, she plinks and plunks and plods her way through the piece, in its own way as painful as the cacophony we just endured. A few feet inside the room, we wait for her to finish, but I get the feeling that if Sin were carrying an ax instead of an innocent child, he'd storm to the instrument and go lumberjack on its ass. Even as he lowers Charlotte to the floor, I sense his muscles twitch, anxious to throw off this practice of restraint, this facade of courtesy.

Antonia knows we're there, since like any poor player the awareness affects her performance. First she loses the rhythm and then (small blessing) speeds up, but in her favor, I'll admit she doesn't fumble the notes. Which speaks volumes about her: She is precise, she is determined, she will let nothing dissuade her. Great. My nemesis is a sociopath with bloodhound tendencies who, as an added bonus, is already dead and ergo indestructible.

We'd come upon her in profile, and when she's finally done making Strauss or Chopin or whatever lesser composer turn over in his tomb, Antonia slides her outsized hands from the keys and swivels to face us fully. Her malnourished mouth widens slightly in her poor excuse for a smile, those gray eyes emitting a dull pewter gleam. Then she rises from the bench to execute an inelegant curtsy, and bows her head.

Dutifully, Char begins to applaud, and without much enthusiasm, Sin and I take her lead. This springs Antonia straight for Sin, ignoring me entirely and lavishing him with a worshipful gaze before dropping her eyes again.

This girl, this girl—we all know a girl like this, since most of us at some point have been a girl like this. Sure, fine, some are born freak-of-nature flirts, genetically programmed for playful allure, the hair flip and come-hither glance as basic as the taste for chocolate. Valentine's Day in kindergarten? They've got the fat stack of cards. Pen was like that, though you might not believe it, seeing her now. Most of us, though, need a minute to find our way with guys, and what's good about that is, once we get it, it's unique—it's ours. A subtle, quiet charm for some, or a rough-and-tumble tomboy appeal. For me, it's all about banter—I may not be the hottest chick in the room, but I've got the teasing, testing, verbal tug-of-war thing down. As to

230

this girl, this Antonia, she still hasn't figured it out yet, and I almost feel sorry for her.

Except right now I'm too uncomfortable for empathy. Somebody has to say something. With a nudge of my elbow, I nominate Sin. Maybe he'd prefer to wring her neck, but ultimately he pronounces her name. Antonia looks up eagerly.

With all the control he can muster, Sin says, "I believe you have some explaining to do."

At that, the girl's mouth puckers and her cheeks puff with triumph, even mirth, as she holds that spade of a chin high in defiance. Antonia's game—a game without rules or logic, played in an arena of death and nonsense—is clearly going her way. Then, bitch has the nerve to shrug. Shrug! She jacked Crane Williams, causing his family and as-yet-still-unofficial fiancée untold worry and grief, and God knows what kind of trauma she's inflicted on poor Charlotte, and all she can do is shrug!

Sin clenches his fists at his sides. "See here, Antonia, you've committed some egregious offenses, and seem to have done so maliciously. What's more, if I read your letter correctly, you've acted upon the notion that I . . . made you some sort of promise—"

The word she's been waiting to hear. Antonia launches herself at Sin, no doubt the way she did that inauspicious afternoon in her garden. This time, though, he's not so sensitive;

this time, he refuses the solace of his body. Ripping at her tentacles, hurling her away with a grunt. Antonia stumbles, then regains her footing only to throw herself onto a settee and proceed to sob convulsively.

I shake my head at Sin. "Nice job."

"Dice, please, do not berate me. She must be a numbskull, as I've said all along!" His low growl is as harsh as any shout. "What makes her think I—when I did not, I never—"

"All right, all right," I say. My turn to take a stab at it, girl to girl. I sit on the floor beside the distraught figure. Dubious, the wisdom of this move—she could haul off and smack me with one of those bony mitts—but I place a hand on her upper back. I rub gently. I coo soothingly. Then I take her by the shoulder and prompt her to face me.

"Hey, Antonia? You know me, don't you?" A safe assumption, since she's been mucking around with me and my friends for the past month, yet her stare is blank through her tears. "I'm Dice. Candice, but everyone calls me Dice. And, look . . . I know I'm an outsider on this whole situation between you and Sinclair, but sometimes an objective opinion can be helpful. You know? I'm not here to make trouble for you. I just want to understand what's going on. So you think you could please stop crying and sort of fill me in . . . ?"

Am I getting anywhere? I can't tell. At any rate, Antonia doesn't seem to be gearing up for a physical smackdown. Still, that infuriating orifice in her face seems screwed tighter than ever, not a rose afraid to bloom but one that withered before it got the chance. As of yet, not a single, solitary word has squeaked out of it.

That's when I feel a tugging on my T-shirt. Charlotte has elected to join us.

"Hey, Char," I say, and put an arm around her, drawing her into the chummy circle of chick-bonding I'm trying to manufacture here.

Only Antonia looks at the little girl in the oddest way—the way you look at a jacket you thought was so cute in the store but then got home and wondered why you wasted your money on such a thing, a jacket that's not in the least bit cute and doesn't even fit. You're mad at yourself, but you project the feeling onto the offending piece of outerwear. Stupid jacket. Ugly jacket. You could rip it to shreds.

Char evades Antonia's look and instead gives me one of intent. Then she cups her hand to her mouth and leans into my ear. Her whisper, heated by excitement, imparts crucial information: "Excuse me, Dice, but don't you know Antonia doesn't talk?"

# XXXVII

Guess that explains why certain eighteenth-century Swoonies never had an actual conversation. Still, expressions can speak louder than words—the malevolent glare Antonia just leveled on Charlotte, for instance. Creeped out, I return my attention to the still sniveling woman scorned. "Pardon me, won't you?" I say, my manner decorous. "The child is tired; I'll just attend to her."

Taking Charlotte's hand with an authoritative squeeze, I march her to one of the salon's small sofas. No doubt she *is* exhausted; at least, she's eager enough to docilely toe off her shoes and settle onto the cushions. A pillow for her head, a shawl as a blanket, I rig up an impromptu bed and, as I do, glance at Sin, standing in the spot of his recent pouncing as if soldered there.

He's had a rough night too. For one thing, he hates to be

wrong—and, damn, was he ever wrong about Antonia. Plus, that ruckus she pulled earlier was straight out of *Haunting for Dummies*, yet he fell for it just the same. Cool in the crisis but nonetheless affected, rattled, dare I say afraid, if not for himself, then for Char and me. Him, Sin Powers, wickedest mofo this town has ever known, thrown by the caprice of a novice. He runs a palm over his thick hair and looks this way; our eyes latch—the confusion and concern I see there, the wondering: *What have I done to bring this upon us?*

We really need to huddle, strategize, only any intimacy between us is sure to ratchet the mistress of Madhouse Manor up to new heights of whacko. I perch on the corner of Charlotte's settee and wish her good night, then lightly stroke her hair as I try to collect the pieces of this puzzle. The effort to organize my thoughts makes me want to curl up next to her and pull the plug on my brain. Too bad this isn't about what I want. Wired, weary, I walk to where I'm equidistant between a rock and a mental case. I clear my throat. I get their attention.

"I want you both to know that Charlotte and I will be leaving shortly." Sin scowls, narrow-eyed, but Antonia's expression couldn't be more delighted—she perks up in her seat and sucks back snot, her silent lips upturned as much as they'll allow. "I recognize that you two have personal matters that our presence—my presence—infringes upon. I also know that the sooner you"—I have to gulp to get this out—"reach an understanding, the sooner our friend Crane will be returned to his loved ones"—I lean my gaze on Antonia now—"gladly and in good faith." Since, hey, just because she's twisted doesn't mean she won't honor her word.

If objections rise to Sin's gorge, he swallows them as now I approach Antonia. She rises to meet my eyes. "I do so wish you and I could have had a conversation." Smile: small, a flawless facsimile of genuine. Tone: moderately dulcet. Inside I'm spitting—I hate to lie—but I'm not an actor's daughter for nothing. "We have much in common: Music, but of course you know that. Oh, and horticulture—I've started my first garden this summer, merely vegetables, nothing grand like yours, but I do enjoy it." Palm to palm at my sternum, with all the sincerity of *namaste,* I continue: "Anyway, I must thank you for your hospitality." Then I let my glance waft to Charlotte. "We'd be on our way right now, only look at her, so peaceful—these last few hours have been such a hubbub, I'm hoping you might consent to let her sleep till dawn?"

Antonia agrees with a tilt of her head, yet I sense confliction there. Victory is so close she can taste it—soon, she and Sin will be on their way to yonder bridal *blech.* Yet I don't believe anyone ever spoke to her as I just have—with not only kindness but interest. To me, it's clear: Antonia Forsythe has never had a real friend.

"As for me, I simply . . ." Closing the space between us,

searching for the term—oh, right. "I have to use the chamber pot." She puckers her mouth and tops it with three fingers, faintly a-blush over my confession. "I'm sure I'll find my way unaccompanied," I say, and with a quick, deferential curtsy, I am out of there.

In truth, I do need to pee, but this is—for the moment, anyway—my last-ditch attempt to locate Crane. I hurry along, peeking behind every door. Inured by now to sordid criminal scenes, I say, "Don't mind me," to the valet I spy slipping arsenic into his employer's whiskey and turn a blind eye to a murderous adulteress. Just before the great hall, where in the Williams residence a rather lavish powder room lies, there is in fact a WC. Clearly I've entered a more modern era since rather than an oversized pitcher under a bench, the facilities resemble what I'm used to. I drop my jeans and drawers and sit, and then I get company.

"Hey there, sister."

You know someone's your friend when you have no problem peeing in her presence. "Hey yourself," I tell Early. Finishing up, I wash at the pedestal sink and lower face to faucet for a few quenching slurps.

"How goes the sleuthing?"

I *shhh!* her automatically. Then, catching the two of us in the mirror—she a head shorter—I feel a sudden pang. Cute, bright, doomed—a victim of her appetites. Maybe, if things were different—no loveless marriage, no rambling house in the middle of nowhere—Early might've found a calling, led a full and fulfilling life. The 1920s were revolutionary for women—Josephine Baker, Coco Chanel, Amelia Earhart, Edna St. Vincent Millay. Why not this saucy charmer with the challenging, gap-toothed grin? Poor baby bearcat. If only I could take her with us, but of course I know I can't. I let the water run to conceal our voices and turn from the glass.

"Look, Early, we found Charlotte in the nursery." I stroke her arm from shoulder to wrist. "Thank you again for the tip."

"So what's next, hmm?" She hops up onto the sink, slinging one gam over the other. "How do you and your sinfully delicious fella intend to deal with that moony Antonia?"

"Not sure," I admit. "First thing I've got to do is get Charlotte back."

Early widens her eyes, fastidious lashes reaching toward thinly plucked brows. "You . . . you're leaving?"

"Just till I can get the kid home safe. Unless . . . you haven't run into Crane, have you?"

Sliding off the sink, Early's face gets wistful and stubborn at once, like a little kid when bedtime is announced. I think I know why: I'm just the sort of good egg she could get used to, and I guess the lonely dead like having a live one around. "No . . . ," she says, petulant, and fishes around in her etui for lipstick. With meticulous precision, she refreshes her pout in the mirror, then turns back to me. "Righty-o!" she says, and shrugs, and then grabs me for an emphatic hug. *Touch!* I hear Ruby in my head and squeeze the small girl tight. "Don't take any wooden nickels."

"I won't," I say, only Early's already bounced, leaving nothing but a smirch of crimson cosmetic on my shoulder.

# XXXVIII

"Are you sure you want to do this?" Sin asks somberly as we mount the east wing steps. We being all four of us.

"Yes, of course." I am such a liar. "You and Antonia need to be alone."

The tower room has been restored to floral extravagance—decadent heaps and neat arrangements, blue roses on the desk, mounds of white on the bed.

"Antonia, may I pick a bouquet for my sisters?"

Pleased by the entreaty, our petal princess gives Charlotte a magnanimous nod.

"Will you help me choose? I want it to be just right."

Really, I could kiss the kid! Now Sin and I can steal a tête-à-tête. Apples on his breath, the otherwise earthy-animal essence of him—I get the strong weakness that defines me when he's this near.

"I cannot believe you're leaving me alone with her!"

That makes two of us. "I've got to get Char back—Marsh will be out of her mind," I murmur. "Besides, it might be smart to divide and conquer. Once I'm gone, Lady Loony's guard will go down and you and she—"

He grips my arm reflexively. "You're not suggesting I—we—consummate—"

The very idea makes me gag. "Of course not. Just . . . placate her. Distract her. Romance her." What, I'm giving him a refresher course in how to be Sin? "And while you're at it, scope Crane. I'll meet you—"

The rustle of silk over taffeta tells me to can it. Antonia has led Charlotte to the mantel, the girl's arms laden. My eyes on Sin's—if only I could dive their depths, drown there. Then I think, WTF: Antonia must realize what he means to me; she won't buy a casual farewell. So I'll make it a good-bye for the record books. I go to him. Fit my peaks and hollows to the topography of his frame. Press my full length against him—the muscles beneath the denim and cotton, my cheek to the triangular treasure of skin exposed at his V-neck. Take in the mingling of glandular excretions, the heart and brain and sex and soul and Sin of him. Demanding and devoted, under and around, my arms hold him like he's mine. And with crush and comfort and purpose and promise, his body and everything that vessel contains owns me in kind. Completely. For a breath, a beat. Then we part.

"Come, Char, let me have some of those," I say, striving to keep the quaver from my voice. "You'll need to grab onto the gate." We stand at the hearth. I look to Sin. "Help me . . . help us find it."

"Let it find you," he says.

Since that's how it's done: surrender control, forget focus.

"The pinwheel!" cries Char; that's how the fissure appears to her.

"Now close your eyes . . ."

And here is the gate, our iron ferry home. *Don't!* warns a scared and selfish part of me. *Don't leave him!* I acknowledge it, I validate it, and then I ignore it.

"Oh. Hey. Sorry."

Two startled dudes in overalls leap from the fireplace as if scorched, one of them losing his hammer with a clunk. Having allowed Charlotte to sleep through sunrise, we now enter the living world with the workday already in progress.

"Excuse us," I mumble. "Come on, Char, let's go wake Duck."

"Mm-kay. But Dice? I don't want these anymore."

"Yeah," I say, collecting the bedeviled bouquets. "I don't blame you." Bloom over stem, out the open window with the lot.

En route to Duck's room, we manage to avoid smacking into his parents. I rap on what I hope I remember to be his door and slip in, rather than loiter in the hall. Sun slants through the shaft in the shutters, but the boy is out, on his stomach, the edge of the sheet throttled in one fist. I say his name a few times, then go for a shoulder poke.

*"Hnghwuph?!"* He jolts like a jack-in-the-box, gingery hair in clumps. "Oh! Dice! And Char—oh, thank goodness!"

He tumbles from bed, belly of rising dough atop the waistband of SpongeBob boxers, his a.m. chubby thrusting one yellow rectangle front and center. It's the most normal sight in the world, and I love him so much right now. I wish I could tell him his brother came with us and is just down the hall getting fussed over by Lillian and Paul. Instead, I tell him some fast truth. Then I notice Charlotte riveted. "Char, don't stare."

"But Dice, he's got a big bump in his underpants."

It feels so good to giggle. "That happens to boys in the morning sometimes."

Hastily Duck pulls on shorts he picks off the rug. He adds a fresh T-shirt and the moccasins he scuffs around in. "Let me run you girls home. Or I suppose you'd prefer Pen's house? That's where Marsh went, after you and Sin . . ."

Of course. Marsh couldn't bear to head home with Charlotte kidnapped; she couldn't camp out on the drop cloth in the east wing, either. Being near Willa was as close to comfort as she'd get last night. Nodding, I say, "Right, let's crash their slumber party. I bet Pen's mom will make us all waffles or something."

Waffles *and* something (namely, blueberry pancakes) before

Lainie toddles off to tennis. We get the little ones set up in the breakfast nook before taking it to the Leonard dining room. I pull Antonia's missive from my jeans pocket. "Read it and creep," I say as they pass it around.

"So Sin's still there? With her?"

"Is he staying? For good?"

"What kind of vow? What does she mean?"

I feel like a target in a shooting gallery. "I don't know, and she's not talking—literally," I say. "Antonia's mute, which explains the lack of communication between her and Sin. Who absolutely denies pledging her so much as a stick of gum. But yeah, I left him to stall her and scope Crane—Charlotte saw him, by the way, and he's okay—"

"Couldn't she lead you to him?" Logical, Duck. "Oh, but she must!"

"That's . . . complicated," I say. "I don't know what the kid knows, but she's scared of Antonia, for good reason." I recap the earsplitting play of ghost girl's extreme sport.

"Oh God—poor Char," Marsh groans. "Duck, you know I want Crane back as much as you do, but my sister's traumatized enough."

I jump in before those two can get further at odds. "The way things are on the other side, I doubt it would do any good to give Char the third degree. Even if she identifies what room Crane's in, Antonia may have him stashed in a different century. Who knows—she may even be able to shuffle him around at will."

Like in a game. Ghosts ab-so-lute-ly adore games. I'm starting to feel pretty pawnish myself, and realize that's what we all are—human tokens on Antonia's high-stakes chessboard. My head reels. Slamming caffeine doesn't help. The four of us push gluey pancake residue across our plates, slumped and silent.

Then Pen, for whom subtle segues don't exist, says, "Tell me this: Does Bruise Blue still intend to do Chest-ah-Fest? Because I got the email—we're in."

The girl's priorities are way out of whack. Our expressions convey this succinctly.

"What?" she blunders on like a blond Sherman tank. "My reputation is on the line. If we're going to bail, I need to let them know."

I could spike her head like a volleyball. Then again, Bruise Blue is crucial to all of us, on both sides of the gate. Music is a mighty force, and the band is our bond—we can't let Antonia Forsythe continue to pluck us apart. "Uh . . . when is it again?"

"The tenth and eleventh. They have us down for the second day."

"Of July?" Damn, I am time-trashed. "And what's today?"

"The twenty-sixth. Of June," Pen says. "Do you need the year?"

I make a face and do the math. Almost two weeks to practice, assuming Sin and I wrap things up fast beyond the fissure.

Can we? How? What's our next move? Damn, I've got to swing the gate again. "We should play," I say, "but I just . . . I've got to . . ." Break down? Yeah, that's it. I shove aside my plate and clunk my head to the table.

A disgruntled noise from Pen, but Marsh hustles to kneel beside my seat. Her cool hand against my neck supports me, sustains me, helps me tap a new strain of strength. I straighten up and smile at her.

"How's this?" she proposes. "Dice, you get some sleep—the spectral jet lag must be awful. Tonight, when you're rested . . ." She trails off, then gets tough. "You and Sin can take care of business, bring Crane home, and we'll be a sextet at Chest-ah-Fest."

The hope in her voice. The faith in her eyes. Her trust in the power of love and music and, well, Sin and me. Maybe Marsh is crossing a bridge made of toothpicks, but hope and faith and trust are all we've got.

An abyss of sleep, deep and luxuriously dreamless, until I hear Marsh in the hallway. Sluggish, I weave to the bedroom door and steady myself on the jamb.

"Oh, Dice, I woke you." She lopes up.

"No, no, it's cool—I've got to get up anyway." Still, I fumble toward the bed, and Marsh follows, perching on the edge, sort of talking to the air.

"I wish I knew how to thank you, Dice. To go over there in

the first place, and then leave Sin so you could bring Char back. It's just—" She looks at me, away again. "I've always been the big sister. Even with my mom, her being kind of flighty, me always having to get between her and my dad. But with you, I feel—no, I know—I've really got someone, no matter what. It's like that with Crane, I guess—or it was—but when he first disappeared, my reaction was that he was over me. With you, whatever happens, wherever you are . . . you're there, for me . . ."

It's nice she feels that way; even nicer she's expressing it. In the house Marsh grew up in, showing emotion was like wetting the bed. Only right now, with everything so close to the surface, I want to avoid an emotional eruption of my own. One quick hug while I tell her, "Shut up or I'll have to start calling you Mush." Then I check the clock. Eleven hours unconscious and I'm still in a fog. "I better shower."

When the hot spray hits, my brain kicks in, calling roll on my obsessions. Sin? Indeed. Antonia? Yeah, lucky me. Crane? Yep. Tosh? Mm-hmm, him too. At least Marsh's sister is safely squared away. I reach for my pouf and lather up, then . . . ! My mark, my bruise, that indelible blue badge of desire and testament to true love. It's gone. What? How? When? A slow fade that began on the solstice with Sin's return to this realm? Or did it vanish in a heartbeat—now that I'm here and he's there, beyond the gate . . . with her? More urgent, *why*? Because I said "gone," but it's not quite gone: It's some other kind of emblem now. White, whiter than my surrounding moon tan, and raised, thickened—a scar.

Yet while my fingertips detect the change, the area itself is devoid of sensation. I scrub there. Nothing. Scratch there. More nothing. Pinch, hard. Just numb, as though a few inches of flesh had been surgically supplanted with an analgesic. Bittersweet as the pain had been, this nothing, this non-pain, really bites. Some signal from Antonia, a malicious display of victory? Or from Sin, my white scar his white flag of surrender? Could it be that despite prior protestation, he's come to accept that she and he—

No, no, no! That's nuts. Can't be, won't be. If anything the scar is an SOS, a sign that Sin's in peril. Hop out, dry off, fling on clothes, and dash downstairs.

Marsh is there, car keys in hand.

Too much to say, so we say nothing till we get to Forsythe Manor.

Then she tells me, "Duck said he'd be in the studio."

He's not alone. Facing each other, Pen and Tosh straddle the piano bench. Tosh gets up when he sees me. We come toward each other until we stop. Then, with a little lunge, his arms come around me. For a second it's awkward, and then it's awesome, since Pen joins in, and Duck and Marsh. The group hug almost hurts. After all, I was never that girl—the girl in the middle of a tight-knit clique, the girl who was part of something. Basically it had always been Ruby and me—we had other friends who were cool and all, but we were all we needed, all we believed in. This is different. This is Bruise Blue. I belong to these people. What I'm about to do I'll do for us.

Except I don't get a chance.

The studio door flings wide—no knock, no nothing—and in strides Sin.

True, his stride is hampered by a steamer trunk that must weigh as much as a baby elephant, the way he's lugging it. He throws it down with a *thunk*. And if the old-fashioned leather-bound chest looks anachronistic in the modern studio setting, so does Antonia Forsythe in her finest faille and brocade gown.

# PART III

# THE GAME

# XXXIX

TWIGGY FINGERS SNAG HIS SLEEVE AS SIN LEADS THE INCONGRUOUSLY costumed monstress into our midst.

"Allow me to present Miss Antonia Forsythe," he says formally, steering her toward Pen. "Miss Penelope Leonard . . ." Pen gives her paw like an obedient puppy.

"Mr. Simon Williams . . . Miss Kristin Marshall . . . Mr. Tosh Peters . . ."

Shock value must keep Marsh and Duck from tackling Antonia, demanding Crane's return. After all, it's not every day they meet the dead, and this girl-ghost-your-guess-as-good-as-mine exudes palpable clout—a chill dampness coupled with that sickly sweet rose perfume that steals in on an inhale and creeps from the lungs to the blood. I didn't sense it on the other side, but I get a whiff now, as does everyone else. Each in turn extends a hand, manipulated like marionettes. For every intro,

Antonia curtsies minimally, a courtesy she chooses but isn't required to bestow.

"And of course you know Dice."

The penurious smile. And then she says, "Indubitably."

That's right, a thin, timid, wispy sound, but it's a sound and she makes it. In response, my own vocal chords seem initially paralyzed; then I choke out, "You—can—talk."

The look Antonia gives me, the eighteenth-century equivalent of *Duh!* "It has been ages since I've wished to speak. Yet now there is so very much to say." Her rain-cloud glance reviews me. "One day, dear Dice, perhaps we shall have our overdue chat about music and horticulture. Although at present more pressing matters ought be addressed. Such as the gentleman who's been my companion of late."

A cracked cry from Marsh, and Duck almost shouts his brother's name.

"Crane, indeed." Recognizing Duck as a current inhabitant of her ancestral home, Antonia fastens onto his arm and proceeds to drop the subject. "At first I thought it impertinent to arrive without invitation, but Sinclair's urging was so . . . adamant." Inclining her head his way, she flaps pale, scant lashes before returning her attention to us. "Then it occurred, there'd be no breach of etiquette—since this is, after all, my house." The heiress to Forsythe Manor allows her gaze to roam. "Everything's so different now," she says, and as her eyes rest on mine, adds, "But then again, so am I."

Still attached to Duck, she begins to tour the studio. "Is it not interesting, though, that the more things change, the more they remain? Since this was for the most part a music room when last I dwelt here." As Antonia muses, her voice gains vigor. "Whenever my mother, the Lady Anne Forsythe, was in town, she preferred to entertain here. Such artistic friends she had—the most amusing people, though few as artistic and amusing as she." Antonia pauses and strokes the air. "Her instrument prevailed here—she was quite an accomplished harpist." Then wanders on, Duck in a trance at her side. "And here, by this wall, was my virginals."

Her what? I can't have heard correctly—right now I don't trust any of my senses. It's incredible that we'd allow her to lead us along, literally or figuratively, considering the crimes she perpetrated against us. Then again, that was as a silent ghost on the far side of the spectral divide. We've got even greater cause for caution now, since who knows what she's capable of, this immortal and possibly amoral being. And whom do we have to thank for that? I pry my crazy-glued soles off the floor and sidle his way. "Sin?" I say innocuously. "A word, if I may?"

Antonia's apparently enjoying herself, raising no alarms as Sin and I convene in a corner. "Dice," he begins, "before you lay blame, remember you're the one who left me alone with her. I implored you not to—"

255

"For a *day*!" I hiss. "You were alone with her for a day—"

"The longest day of my existence. She followed me every-where, a scrap on my boot heel. I'd sit in a chair and she'd be behind me, stroking my hair, massaging my shoulders—or she'd fall at my feet and put her head in my lap . . ."

Okay, *eww*. But I'd better hear him out. To avoid arousing Antonia's suspicion, I nudge Sin toward the bar as his litany continues. "She brought out this get-up—"

Yeah, that: full pre-Revolutionary regalia. The height of fash-ion and finery, too—not his humble farrier's garb. A skirted, collarless coat and ruffled cravat, with leather spatterdashes below his breeches. It's the outfit he wore when I glimpsed him and Antonia waltzing, and he carries it with the same poise and aplomb as his typical gear.

"So I thought, to appease her, I'd put it on—quickly, so that, once dressed, I might search for Crane. Only she allowed me no privacy! Stood there while I disrobed, hiding her eyes behind her hands, but Dice, I assure you she was peeking!"

*Bitch!* I smolder inside, bending to the mini-fridge. "Bev-erage?" I invite aloud, rummaging through the stock.

"At one point, I began to stride through the house, throw-ing back doors and calling Crane's name," Sin says. "She trailed all the way—tittering in this . . . this . . . titter! I took her by the shoulders as if to shake his location out of her, but she just tightened her lips and lofted her chin."

I fill an ice bucket. Clearly, Antonia was in mime mode the whole time on the other side. Speech must be a phenomenon of crossing over. What other new attributes might she have acquired?

"So I changed tactics, complaining of boredom, which is when she urged me into this room," Sin goes on. "She poured me a brandy and then sat at her virginals—"

Her *whatsit*? "Excuse me?"

"The damned harpsichord she pounds upon. It's called a virginals—yes, with an *s*, despite the singular."

I remember it from the salon. The wooden keyboard overly embellished with a relief of roses in mother-of-pearl, as if adornment could compensate for the player's lack of talent.

"She only seems to know the one damned song."

How easy to envision Antonia, daughter of this regal hostess, dutifully practicing her little piece. I can even see a younger version—age twelve, when the Forsythes first took up residence in the grand manor—being trotted out to play for guests, only to screw it up and be . . . not punished, not chastised, just shunted aside, ignored. Maybe that's when she lapsed into silence, the early stirrings of insanity.

"I asked her to dance—if only to stop the awful plinking." Naturally Sin can boogie down without music, just part of his something-something. "And that's when I began to speculate . . . what would happen to Antonia were she to attempt the voyage?"

I find a kitschy set of tiki-god cups and have to stop myself from knocking Sin upside the head with one.

"After all, as a ghost, I couldn't walk among men. I was entirely dependent on you, Dice, if you recall."

Uh-huh. I recall.

"Were it not for your touch, I'd have had no substance at all. And were it not for the rite that golemized me, I'd probably still be rambling around inside your cousin."

Okay, if I were Sin, I might think along the same lines. But isn't he forgetting one tall, thin, and kidnapped thing?

"Hence, as a plan began to formulate, I filled her ear with the marvels of the modern world. Teased her with motor vehicles and television and smartphones. Tempted her with the freedom women now enjoy—no burden of corsets, panniers, or petticoats. Specifically, I spoke of you and your friends, the camaraderie you share, the band—"

Oh, no he didn't! He did *not* tell Antonia she could be in Bruise Blue!

"Dice, it was ideal. I'd swing her through—and see her no more. Be free of her! And in vanquishing her, release Crane, of course."

Of course? Well, you never could accuse Sin of pessimism. I'm flipping tabs on soda cans, filling tiki cups.

"I knew she'd agreed when our waltz was done," he says. "Her gaze assured me she'd follow me anywhere."

258

Yeah—I know the look.

"And then she did the damnedest thing. Perhaps she recalled the failure of her first attempt to kiss me, since rather than launch herself at my lips, she knelt and, squeezing my hand, planted one there. Dismally, as you'd expect—more protracted nip than kiss." He scopes the room quickly. "Left a mark, too." Hiking up his left shirt cuff, he exposes the spot.

Which is when I spill soda all over the tray. A tiny wound—a hickey, okay—bright pink and shaped exactly like a rosebud. And all at once I know. The moment Antonia put her brand on my man, my blue bruise turned to insensate scar. Sin may not realize it yet, but with horror I do: The rosebud love bite won't be gone by tomorrow; that nasty little nibble on his wrist will keep him under her thumb! If only I'd warned him when I saw the two of them dancing, but I had no idea it would lead to this.

"*Dice!*" He hisses for my attention.

I right the soda can, grab a bar towel to sop up the mess. "Who's thirsty?" I somehow creak.

As Bruise Blue gathers around, glad to have something to do, Antonia dips her nose into the effervescence. "Oh!" she softly squeals.

Coca-Cola: just another marvel of the modern age.

"Sinclair . . . ?" she begins deferentially. "Shall we toast?"

Sin looks like he might projectile vomit, yet he must agree. "If you wish."

"Indeed, but before we do"—Antonia sends her gray gaze around—"I'm sure you are all concerned about your dear Crane."

"Yes!" It spasms out of Duck as Marsh snags his elbow. Manning up, he says, "We are quite concerned."

"Then permit me to assure you that he's perfectly all right. And while I gather you are anxious for reunion, there are still some arrangements to be made. However, you have my word"—an adoring glance at Sin—"*our* word, that Crane, like all of you, will most certainly dance at the wedding."

# XL

Uh-huh, that's right, wedding. With her small smile and reserved tones, Antonia tells us that while she's after no elaborate social affair, certain practical priorities must be dealt with, chief among them the purchase of a home. The trunk she had Sin tote from her era contains her dowry. In solid gold. Which she's ever so pleased to learn retained its value. The house they acquire needn't be grand—truly, the most modest quarters would suffice—but until it's found, the bride-to-be will require accommodations. Naturally, she wouldn't dream of imposing on the family currently residing at Forsythe Manor and, furthermore, has had her fill of the place, centuries' worth. Sighing, Antonia finishes her refreshment and wonders if she might enjoy another—like many a mortal, she's found the sugar-caffeine combo an instantaneous addiction.

Can I blame the same substances for what comes out of my

mouth next? "It might be best if you stayed with Marsh and me." Few invitations are extended more reluctantly, but it does seem best. My girl and I can bunk up—she's not fussy—and that way we can track Antonia while figuring out how exactly to destroy her.

"Dice, how kind of you," she says. "And where is it that you reside?"

"Where? Oh, we're on Daisy."

"Daisy Lane!" The titter. "How could *I*—"

"Daisy Lane is quite fashionable now," Sin interrupts before she can trash my hood. Sternly he adds, "And I'm sure you'll be made comfortable."

"Yes, I too am sure," Antonia defers. "Thank you, Dice. I'd be most happy to accept."

Next morning I stew while coffee brews. We'd trooped in just before 3:00 a.m. Tosh had insisted Bruise Blue get some practice in—hello? Chest-ah-Fest?—but everyone was too distracted to accomplish much. Despite the fact that the cause of our distraction was off on a stroll with her beau—how terribly she'd missed her garden and oh! wouldn't it be lovely to be wed beneath the bower!

In a word, *blech* . . .

Now, gazing out at my own backyard, I take in the low, overcast sky, the densely humid air, the way the grass seems burdened by the dew, and perceive a change has come. Yeah, and whoever said "Change is good" didn't know what he was talking about. A pall has fallen over the town, and once again I feel the call to set things right in Swoon; only difference is, I haven't got an inkling what I'm up against.

Except that it's embodied in the fragile girl now mincing into the kitchen. The cami and capris Marsh generously left out for her hang on her frame. With limp, undone hair reaching below her shoulders, her chin and nose look longer, her mousy mouth more grim. Only Antonia's alloy eyes—flat, unfeeling— hint at her power, and I quell the shiver they give me.

In fact, I aim to psych her out as I lean against the counter in the tank top and boy shorts I slept in. Bitch is on my turf now. Comfortable in my ample body and loose, leonine curls, I watch her levelly, then pull up from my slouch into a strong mountain pose. "Coffee?"

She murmurs a demurral, much preferring tea.

"You sure?" I pour myself a mug. "I'd get used to it if I were you. Sin loves his coffee, especially when he gets out of bed in the morning." The insinuation being that I've been with Sin when he gets out of bed in the morning, the insinuation being a lie. Antonia gets the insinuation—balefully, she blinks—but bottom line this tough-chick act is so not me. Does the spider try to bully the fly? No—the spider's just the spider. I sigh. "How about some Cocoa Puffs then?"

"Cocoa Puffs?"

"Like mush, only not mushy—at least not right away." We take it to the table. One bite and Antonia's in heaven. Unfortunately, that's a metaphor. In fact, she goes at her bowl with such gusto, I can't help but wonder if crossing the threshold into this time, this life, may have been her plan all along—why settle for yonder bridal bed in a world that's dead when she could have Sin amid the vibrant energy and tasty, convenient breakfast foods of the here and now?

"Where is Miss Marsh this morning?" she inquires, spoon and eyebrow aloft. "Is she the sort to while away the day abed?"

"Are you kidding? Marsh is the most industrious person I know. She's up at dawn and over to the stables—she cleans stalls in exchange for keeping her horses—"

"Horses?" Antonia had her first motorized vehicular experience last night.

"People have them for fun, for sport—not for transportation," I explain. "Anyway, now that school's over, Marsh is likely to pull a double shift at the Kustard Kup after her ride."

"Yes, Sinclair mentioned that today's woman often engages in labor. Have you a . . . shift?"

Do I need to go into how my parents work their butts off so I can enjoy my teenage years, especially since the nasty death of my best friend, which almost took me with her? I don't. I shake my head. "I don't have a job. I volunteer at the library, though."

"Ah, charity. How admirable." She clasps her hands and beams. "Of course, it cannot compare to the work Sinclair intends to take up with those unfortunate creatures at Walden Haven."

Guess he told her about that. A flicker of jealousy that Sin would share any detail of his life, even an impersonal tidbit about administering care to ailing squirrels. "Well, Marsh has to work," I say with a shrug. "She needs to earn money. She's had a hard life, hasn't had the advantages you and I have had."

Antonia pats her mouth with a napkin. "Advantages do not necessarily translate to an easy life."

Which is true, but I gloss over it. "The sucky part is, Marsh is such an awesome person. She didn't deserve any of the crap she's had to deal with. That's why, when she and Crane fell in love, everyone was like, yes, yay, finally." Am I getting through to her at all? "And they really are in love," I go on. "It's not a crush or a game or . . ." What's the word? "A dalliance. It's real. It's true. They're committed."

She deigns to look at me. "Yes," she says. "Like Sinclair and I."

*What makes you think he loves you? What makes you think he can even stand the sight of you?!* The need to know careens around my brain like reverb. Tact, however, is key. I muster some semblance of sisterly interest to say, "So you and Sin had quite a romance, huh?"

Chick chat being both foreign and enticing, Antonia takes

the bait. "It is true," she reveals, blushing slightly. "Our court-ship did not unfold along conventional lines, but that's one of the aspects that made it so very special."

Nodding, I urge her gently. "But somehow it got messed with, right? Your parents, I'll bet. Or some other girl—some hussy. Must have been awful." I wait a beat, watch her. "What happened?"

Like a cell door slamming, she shuts down. "What hap-pened?" Antonia repeats icily. "I died. That is what happened."

Robotically, she resumes crunching Cocoa Puffs. I pour a bowl for myself, add milk, and then circle back to where this conversation started. "Anyway, Antonia, I was telling you about Marsh because she's such a good friend to me. And she could be your friend too."

"Indeed, I expect to have many friends. Educated, talented friends that we might have to supper and—"

"Right," I cut her off. "But friendship is a two-way street." Whee, that soars over her head, for obvious reasons. "It's about mutual respect and empathy and understanding. Being there for her, helping her get what she wants, what she needs. Even if that means putting your friend before yourself." I catch her gaze drifting to the fascinating reading on the side panel of the cereal box. "Antonia, do you follow me at all?"

"Yes, Dice." She blinks in my direction. "I believe so."

"Good." I eke out a smile. "So if you want to be Marsh's

friend and have her be your friend, why not let Crane come home . . ." I cannot manage to form the words "before the wedding" so I go with "Sooner rather than later? Like today? Marsh would be so happy. We all would."

Antonia considers this. She really, truly seems to. Unless she's just screwing with me. Ultimately, she says, "If I comprehend correctly, friends do things for each other. At times subjugating their own desires for the benefit of a friend."

Could it be? "That's right, Antonia. You got it."

"Well then," she says. "If Marsh wishes to be my friend, she wouldn't want me to do anything that might interfere with my wedding." She smoothes the napkin, the motion implying she'd much prefer linen to paper. "So no, I'm afraid I won't be able release Crane till Sinclair and I have taken our vows."

# XLI

How long are we to continue this charade? At least till I get back from the library. Story time is on my slate this morning, and I can't imagine anything more depressing than fairy tales. Valiant knights, beautiful princesses, happily ever afters—I'd rather read aloud the stock listings from *The Wall Street Journal*. Still, I manage to pull my head out of my butt for two separate sessions, and then shelve a rack of books. By the time I'm back on my bike, the oppressive weather has lifted and the boosted mood I get from the kids sticks with me.

So much so, the thought of Antonia Forsythe's stimulating company has me pedaling in the opposite direction. Where am I going? Not a clue. I'm just going, and it feels good as hill segues into dale and the byways bend and blend. Fifteen minutes later, I find myself on a familiar stretch, Stag Flank Road, where Marsh used to live. Sort of the outskirts of Swoon. Kind of the wrong side of the tracks. As ghetto as it gets in northwestern C-T, ramshackle ranch houses giving way to double-wides giving way to nothing but scrappy posted land on either side and bumpy gravel under my wheels. I speed by the former Marshall place with a passing wince for the nastiness that went down there, and keep on whizzing, so the small sign, half-obscured by sumac, nearly escapes my peripheral vision. I slow down, pull a U-ie, and hop off in front. Walden Haven.

Pine needles and other forest detritus crunch louder than I like—I definitely get the sense that sneaking in is my best move. An old truck parked in front, and by old I mean crappy, not the fancily refurbished vintage rides popular among certain Swoonies. Ah, like this one. The sleek, cared-for Cutlass is practically a museum piece next to the rusty, dented Ford. I leave my bike and, avoiding the trailer I assume serves as Walden Haven's office, make my way into the refuge.

There's a series of wooden pens, like small barns, I guess, or big sheds. From inside, some intermittent screeching and snuffling, nature on the mend and no doubt getting restless. Beyond these, a large enclosure fenced by chain link and—oh! oh! ohhhhh! I spy Sin from the side, sitting on his heels, attending to the most amazing creature on the planet. All ears and eyes and legs like those on a spinning wheel. Soft brown coat sprinkled with dollops of cream. The fawn's entire body, from flap of tail to wet black snout, wiggles with the efforts of his hunger as he nurses from the bottle my boy holds aloft. I am spellbound.

Yet I have to go nearer; I *have* to! Quiet, quiet . . . closer, closer. Afraid I'll unsettle or upset, but the busy little beast is oblivious, intensely occupied. So—softly, softly, so, so softly—I whisper, "Ohhhh, Sin!"

He tilts his head toward me, smile in full, like he knew I was there all along. "Incredible, is he not?"

"Yes! He is!" I mirror Sin's pose, shins against the ground. "He's a boy?"

"Indeed." Making short work of his lunch, too—good thing Sin's got a second course at the ready. "A buck." He says it like a proud papa.

"Wow, really? So he'll have antlers and everything?" City kid raised in a pet-free condo, sidewalk pigeons and subway rats represent the bulk of my exposure to wildlife. This past year in Swoon was a crash course in critters—one of the pangs to my solar plexus whenever I think about leaving.

Stoically, Sin says, "If he lives." The thought of him not living makes me want to die. "His mother was hit by a car; some local road-crew fellow found the carcass, and this little one nearby." The fawn chugalugs, his trusting eyes on Sin's face. "I suppose he got lucky."

An orphan himself, he must relate. There's even an element of abandonment to him, here on the litter of leaves, framed all around by pine and beech. Thing is, it looks good on him. Black hair unruly, rough hint of stubble along his jaw, the brooding knit of his brow. He's lost some weight—his musculature lean beneath the thin white tee, the planes of his face more prominent. The state of him stirs me in a whole new way. Last fall, gleefully in charge of his own havoc, Sin was every ounce the reckless knave. Now, grappling to do what's right, he confronts an enemy he feels impossibly responsible—somehow! but *how*?!—for arming against us.

Seeing him this way, my resolve against Antonia turns molten and then casts hard as armor. "Oh, Sin . . ." It seeps out of me.

The fawn, whom I thought would never stop sucking, abruptly does. Sin chucks him gently on the chest. "All right, Luther—had enough, have you?" He proffers the nipple a few more times, just in case. Baby buck totters away, stands perfectly still, and then all four legs fold simultaneously—*boom!* We look at him with idiotic exultation, then at each other. Eventually, our smiles wane.

Sin says, "So here we are."

"Yeah," I say. "Any ideas?"

"I wish I had, Dice, but we don't even know what the blasted bitch *is*." Frustration in his mien, mixed with a bit of begrudged respect for the mystery of it all.

"Then let's tackle *why* she is," I say. "To me, the root of her power is some subversion on love—her love for you, and her conviction that it's returned. Your vow."

"My *vow*." The word is a fetid sore.

Which reminds me. "Let me see your hand," I say, getting vertical with urgency. "The left one."

Eyeing me curiously, Sin stands to place his palm against the fence. There it is, spitefully bright as when I first noticed it, the tiny, terrible rose tattoo. My spirit takes a plunge; my eyes follow suit.

"Dice, what troubles you?"

"There, that." I poke the spot. "Antonia's logo."

"What the . . . ?" He rubs it with a confounded finger.

"Sin, it's not lipstick; it's not coming off." I never spoke to him of my blue bruise, but he must sense the certainty in my voice. "It indicates her hold on you, her influence," I say. "It ensures that you won't walk away from this, that you'll do her bidding and . . ." We both know Antonia's ultimate goal—there's no need for me to finish.

"Damn and defy her!" he seethes. "I won't walk away from this because it would be reprehensible to do so. I'm putting up with it for Crane's sake—for Marsh and Duck. Not for Antonia or any sully on my skin."

I believe Sin's nobility; I believe his valor. Too bad I also believe Antonia's capacity for the opposite. Plus, right now I detect distinct bemusement in his face. "What?"

"Nothing, nothing at all," he dismisses. Then, "Blast it—I *am* compelled to fetch her for a promenade along the village green."

I say, "Great."

We get quiet, and once again Sin smushes the spot.

"Does it hurt?" I ask.

He shakes his head. I consider that a plus—pain would suggest potency—and all at once my spirit surfaces. "Look, Antonia's all about tricks and traps and sneaky maneuvers. She has to be, because her love is impure. Crazy, yes. Powerful, yes. But tainted. Deep inside her love there is a seed of doubt."

Sin studies me, and then he gets me. While the chain link between us is too much metaphor for our imprisoned situation, his fingers twine mine, flouting the steel. "Perhaps her doubt will do her in."

My smile isn't wide, but it's steady. "If we can figure it out, cultivate it—exploit it." Yet how to manage that?

He feels my thoughts. "It appears the time is ripe for another turn at the tarot."

It's an idea. The only one we've got. "All right, I'll do it. Only it'd be great to have your vibe, your energy. You'll have to come over when she's not around, except she's always around—or maybe I can meet you some—?"

"What do you think this is, Powers? A petting zoo?"

I spin to the nasal bark behind me. It belongs to a bleached blonde in too-tight jeans, Walden Haven T-shirt knotted at her midriff. A haggard face, etched by a perpetual scowl. A face that's been laughed in and lied to and left standing, waiting, alone. It's pretty clear, without the slightest precog sweep, that whoever this woman is, she prefers animals to people, and has her reasons.

"Alice," Sin says, which is all I'll get as an intro, and all I really want. "Dice is a friend of mine. She just happened by."

"You do amazing things here," I say, not to make amends for kinda-sorta trespassing, but because it's true. This place is populated by so much roadkill as far as the world is concerned, and if some burned-out, hard-luck shrew steps up to save them, she deserves a lot more than my lame-o praise.

Alice affords me nothing but a sniff. "Well, tell her to happen bye-bye. You've got shit to shovel."

Clearly I don't snap to her orders as quickly as she'd like, since she starts lumbering toward me. I give my boy an optimistic parting glance. While we haven't set a time or place, we do kinda-sorta have a plan. So I say, "Okay, see you . . ."

He says, "Yes." And, "Soon."

On my way out I shove a hand in my jeans pocket to pull out everything—the folded ten, the crumpled ones, the coins, the lint. I open the door to the trailer and toss the lot inside. Call it a donation.

"Soon," Sin said. I believe him. Faith, hope, trust—intangibles I use like spider silk. One way or the other, he'll find me, as he always does, as I always find him. And together we'll find a way out of this.

# XLII

SEEING TOSH'S CAR IN MY DRIVEWAY, I BEELINE FOR THE BACKYARD. OUR unresolved issues have been hovering patiently; maybe now we can settle a few—a concept that for all its emotional potential seems appealing compared to everything else we're dealing with. But are we to get some alone time? Apparently not, judging by the female laughter that wafts my way. Pen, of course—though I scarcely recognize my cousin minus the enormous milkshake that masquerades as coffee. And is that a splash of the breezy citrus cologne that had long been her hallmark?

"Hey," I say, wheeling my bike. Then I stop short. My lowly veggie garden has been . . . not merely transplanted but completely transformed. The tomatoes have been moved to a sunnier spot and staked with sticks and twine—which they need, since they've grown a foot in my absence and sprouted dozens of tiny yellow flowers. Meanwhile, a piece of broken lattice that was collecting dust in the shed has been arched for the cucumbers, whose vines now recline along it with curlicue tendrils, large, healthy leaves, and citrine blossoms of their own. Here, basil plants are now basil bushes, with white and purple flowers streaming from their tops. There, parsley and oregano are, well, parsley and oregano—a miraculous improvement on a mound of dirt. Finally, the catnip I'd put in is now up to my shins and bound to make R.C. the most popular kitty in the neighborhood. The whole patch is a free-for-all Disneyland for butterflies, ladybugs, and bees. "What the hell happened . . . ?"

Pen laughs. "Antonia happened. She was knee deep when I got here."

"Yeah," says Tosh. "We were just saying how you'd freak."

"And, uh, where is Antonia now?"

"Bathing." Pen purses her lips and pipes down her tone in mimicry. "She was perspiring most profusely."

I traipse my fingers through the rampant greenery. Was Antonia being . . . nice? Or just flaunting her mojo? Could anyone capable of bringing forth so much life be 100 percent bad?

Pen shifts gears. "Uh, anyway, don't be mad, but I'm taking her to Torrington. There's this place on Old Hickory Road . . ." Sounds quaint but Old Hickory Road is practically a superhighway, lined with strip malls and shopping plazas—J.Crew and Talbots as far as the eye can see. And something else. "That place, uh, Bentley's or Bucky's?"

278

I bug my eyes. "Buckley's Bridal, Connecticut's wedding warehouse." Anyone who ever wrestled with insomnia has seen the ads on late-night cable. "You're taking Antonia to buy a wedding dress." I say it flatly, since it's not a question.

My cousin nips a guilty cuticle. "It looks that way."

Refreshed from her bath, Antonia glides into the backyard, dressed in another loaner from Marsh, who must be in the shower herself now, cleaning up from stable duty. "I'm ready, Pen," she declares. "Oh, Dice, good afternoon."

I stare at her. "Antonia," I begin. "My . . ." Can I even employ a possessive pronoun anymore? "The garden. It's amazing." And then I cough up, "Thank you."

Dismissively she says, "Pish-posh, is it not what friends are for? Although I would recommend some flower beds—there." She aims a knobby knuckle. "There, as well. Perhaps Pen and I can find some on our return from the bridal shop. Oh, Dice, do you wish to come, help me choose my gown? Pen says this shop has so very, very many, I don't know how I'll possibly decide."

"Uh, no, thanks." I creak out the syllables. Then I suggest they sprint through Torrington Commons for a few sartorial staples, too, so Antonia needn't keep ransacking Marsh's wardrobe. When they're off, I look at Tosh, who's no doubt gone brain-dead from the girl talk. "I'm going to make lunch," I say. "You want a sandwich?"

"No, thanks—got to get to work," he says. "I just came by to find out what everyone was doing on the Fourth."

The Fourth? Oh, of July. Fireworks, watermelon, right, whoo-hoo.

"I guess your mind's been on other things. But the way we've been whipping ourselves over this gig, I figured we deserve a reprieve, maybe go up to Meriden Falls."

Meriden Falls? "Never heard of it."

"Me neither, but Pen says they're spectacular. It's in a state park. We could pack a picnic, hike to the falls, hang out. Really make a day of it." He's giving me the hard sell. "Plus, Pen says there'll be a ton of people, so we should print up flyers for our Chest-ah-Fest appearance and just paper the whole field, hype Bruise Blue like bandits."

Now it makes sense. "Sounds great. It's just . . . it's hard to make plans right now."

He nods. "I'll bet. You must be . . . I can't even imagine."

But he'd *try* to imagine. For all his hubris and ambition, he can get over himself when it matters. "Oh, Tosh," I say helplessly, "you don't know the half of what went down here last year, with Sin and everything."

"Actually," he says, "Pen and I were talking last night, and she filled me in. Not that I understand any of it. But I do know that you and Sin, well, Pen says you guys belong together and . . ." He trails off.

Belong together. Whatever that means. We're certainly not together now. Even if it weren't for the Antonia drama, would we have reconciled? Maybe me and Tosh? "I need to give this back." My fingers reach abruptly for the clasp at my neck.

"No." He's here, very close, and he means it. "Dice, my grandmother gave me that medal when I was a little kid. She's from Guadalupe, one of the small islands; all kinds of superstitions down there—but I never messed with any of it. Saint Michael lived in my underwear drawer for years till I moved here and thought . . . well, I don't know what I thought, but I don't think it was about ghosts and golems and whatnot. Funny how things work out."

Funny. Right.

"But at this point, they're not worked out. So if Saint Michael is worth a damn, I want him right here." He touches the chain where it lies against my skin. "When everything settles down, if you want to give him back, okay—maybe. Till then, Dice, please. Wear it. Close to your heart. For me, all right?"

His eyes are golden, his aim true. "All right."

"Promise? Swear?"

I smile for him. "Promise," I say. "Swear."

As if the words make a lick of sense to me.

# XLIII

THE VEGGIE PATCH IS A WONDER. I'M STILL MARVELING AT IT WHEN Marsh finds me.

"Hey . . ." She stands at the perimeter.

"Crazy, huh?" She can only nod, ambivalent in her awe, and all at once I flash on Charlotte. Her admission up in the tower room that Antonia had pinched her. Hard. But for no reason? Not if the kid now bears a bright pink blemish. Just one more way for our demon in residence to hedge her bet. If Antonia's imprint can induce Sin to escort her bony butt around town, there's no telling what it might persuade a little girl to do. Crap, I can't let Marsh know what I'm thinking—one more worry and she'll implode. "Turkey sandwich?"

"Totally," she says, eager to step away from the garden. "I'm starved."

Avocado, provolone, I slap lunch together fast, and Marsh

and I carry our plates to the wicker table on the porch.

"You know where Pen took Antonia?" I ask her.

"To miles of styles for bridal aisles, and prices you'll say 'I do!' to," she quotes the corny commercial. "Unbelievable."

*Really,* I think, and get angry. We ought to be counseling *Marsh* at Buckley's Bridal and planning her shower and whatever else it is you do for your be-ringed bestie. Changing the subject, I tell her about the fawn.

"You went to Walden Haven—and lived?" Her brows get lost in her bangs. "That Alice Boyle is a piece of work. She and my dad had a few run-ins over the years."

"Well, she did throw me out," I say. "But Sin seems to know how to handle her."

Marsh pokes a slice of escaping avocado. "How is Sin?"

"Hanging in there. It's just . . . he's so different now. You remember him last year, so cocky, so confident. He thought he knew everything. Now, with all this, he admits he knows nothing. And with his hands tied . . ." More like his testicles in a straitjacket.

"Oh, Dice, it's awful," she agrees, beset by guilt. "If it weren't for Crane, and me and Duck, he'd tell Antonia to go screw herself."

How true. We'd shove that undead automaton into her steamer trunk with all her doubloons to weight it and toss the sucker off the Davender Bridge. I treat myself to a half smile, then shake off the fantasy. "The thing is, I'm into him more now than ever," I say. "Sin used to be a bad boy. Now he's a good man, or he's trying to be. Except it's not easy . . ." In other words, he's still Sinclair Youngblood Powers. He of the battleship libido. The cutthroat charisma. That instinctive comprehension of mortal carnality. "He's . . . he's . . ."

He's here is what he is. The Cutlass cruises up the drive, and he gets out. Hastily cleaning up the dishes, Marsh says, "Hey, Sin . . . uh, Dice, I've got to . . . uh . . ." She flits inside and I don't stop her.

"Perfect timing," I tell him. "Antonia Forsythe has left the building."

"It's no accident; I saw Pen's car. They stopped, told me of their devil's errand."

He looks hungry. And I so want to feed him. "Sandwich?"

"I'd love a bite . . . perhaps after."

Well, he's got his priorities straight. Only I need a cool, calm dim to read by. The glaring sun of a summer afternoon won't cut it for tarot cards. He'll have to come inside, for the first time since the last time. Can he handle that? Can I? I gaze beyond the porch rail, through the light of the lovely day, then turn to Sin. He's already at the screen door, holding it open for me.

It would've been called the parlor back in the day. Simple stone hearth. Pine plank floor. The furnishings—a cozy rag rug, a bentwood rocker—cast-offs from our NYC apartment, Nana Lena, and the Leonards, plus a few flea-market finds. It was here that Sin and I began and ended our one and only night (though in between hit every room, not to mention backyard antics on the tire swing). I'm seeing us, slo-mo, across my cranial widescreen; closing my eyes only fine-tunes the focus.

"I'll get my deck," I say.

Once upstairs I tell Marsh what's what and ask her to add her energy.

Oddly, she refuses. "I'll add it from up here."

"Marsh, you're dusting. This is no time to multitask."

"I'll stop." She puts down her rag. "I'll sit very still and concentrate."

Finally, I get it—she truly is the best. She knows I long to be close to Sin, alone with him, here, where we belong. "Marsh," I say, "first things first, okay. We need you; Crane needs you." I go to my dresser, the cards no longer entombed beneath the bed.

Convinced or coerced, Marsh comes down with me, and the three of us sit cross-legged on the rug. "There are many different ways to read," I preamble. "After a while, you just figure out your own spreads." For this, six cards, three under three. I untie the scarf; encase the deck between my palms; inhale and exhale to cleanse the vibe. "Think with me now, feel with me . . ." As I shuffle, shuffle, shuffle.

"This is our aspect: what we're dealing with." I lay down the Moon. Madness, hysteria, deception, delusion. Antonia in a nutshell—emphasis on "nuts."

"This is our effect: why things are the way they are." I produce the Five of Cups. Absolute emptiness, sudden disappointment, heartache born of treachery from those you trust. So Antonia was robbed, violated, betrayed. By Sin . . . or someone else?

"This is our secret: the essential factor that eludes us." I uncover the Five of Swords. Spite, malice, interference. It'll bleed you out, rather than kill you quick. Ouch.

Not a pretty patchwork so far. "Well, this is where we're at," I say. "Now what can we do about it?"

I start a second line of cards. "Here's one possibility." A naked woman astride a lion, spine arched in fearless abandon, her tangle of hair streaming. The proverbial wild card? Yes and no. The one called Lust goes beyond blind desire; it means having the strength to let yourself go and believe that you'll prevail.

"Here's another way to go." The Two of Wands. A force of nature. Energy in action. Making things happen. Getting things done.

"And finally, our outcome, our answer, a peek at our fate." I flip it. The Universe. "Well, duh." I actually say that aloud.

"What does is it mean, Dice?" Marsh asks.

"The last card is the last card, the final card in the major arcana," I try to explain. "The Universe basically stands for completion. Good or bad, deliverance or disaster, whatever happens, happens. It's over. Over and done. Over and out. The end."

# XLIV

SIN UNFOLDS HIS LEGS AND LIES ON THE RUG. MARSH RETURNS TO HER unfinished dusting. I simply stare down the spread. Glaringly obvious. An utter mystery. If I could view it objectively, I'd be intrigued, but since I can't, I wend my eyes onto something far easier on them—Sinclair Youngblood Powers in full supine splendor, hands clasped to cradle his skull, the ankle-over-ankle length of him so innocently inviting. That's right, innocent. While Sin can be fully in charge of his charms, in moments like this he defines ingenuous. A natural man. I can almost forget the six vital, vexing images arranged on the floor between us and believe that right now he's planning our evening—eat out, order in, or cook.

I indulge the reverie till Sin turns onto his side. Regards the cards, then me, then the spread again. "So the Moon is our lunatic mistress, yes?" he muses at the top line, and then wags a finger at the follow-up. "Someone hurt her, someone she thought she could trust . . ." He lifts his gaze again. "Someone *I* presume *you* presume to be *me*." The thought did occur, but I don't reply. "Yet there's still a missing piece to our puzzle . . ."

"Not bad for a newbie." I point to the last card. "So how do you suggest we get here?"

"Apparently, whatever we do will get us there—win, lose, or draw, the end is the end. But you and I are both too willful to be carried by the wind." He studies our alternatives. "Employ these magic wands? That's your bailiwick, my clever witch."

A teasing endearment, but I bristle at the term, shifting my weight from hip to hip. "Fairies use wands," I remind him tartly. "Not witches."

"Point taken," he murmurs, moving on to run a pensive finger alongside Lust. "Yet I'm more inclined to a fundamental approach."

At that, he rolls over to contemplate the ceiling again. Gears engage behind his eyes. Where they take him, he's not telling. Sin's more the type to show than tell. And that concerns me. Since the last time Sin carried out one of his schemes, he loosed Antonia into our world.

Not to mention under my roof. As the days go on, I feel like I'm running a B&B in the fifth circle of hell. My unholy guest fusses about the smallest details, like the proper spoon for one's

Cocoa Puffs and the optimum temperature for its milk. And, granted, there's a reason she's technologically impaired, but the girl has barely got the swing of the light switch. She won't lift a single knobby finger around here (Forsythe Manor must've had servants up the wazoo), yet whenever there's housework afoot—Marsh maneuvering the vacuum, me throwing together a meal—she watches intently, like we're some fascinating reality show.

Of course, I do get to keep tabs on her and monitor her interactions with Sin. Fortunately, her demands on him are few. Governed by her bitten rosebud, he'll drop by for a compulsory visit or escort her to the Kustard Kup. Maybe that's how woo got pitched in the 1700s, but to me, Antonia's wrapped up in this childish concept of courting without an inkling as to what makes a real relationship. The notion of them kissing or otherwise getting busy on "yonder bridal bed" doesn't creep me out in the least—I simply can't imagine it.

As to how Sin spends the rest of his time, that I can imagine. I imagine there's been a trip to Hartford to convert portions of Antonia's fourteen-carat dowry into cash and investments (he wouldn't let piddling Swoon Savings and Loan handle his finances). I imagine he and Kurt Libo are nurturing some hydroponic product somewhere (though for that he really ought to involve his betrothed—I'm getting tomatoes as big as grapefruits out here). One thing I don't have to imagine is what he does for creative fulfillment—that I know for fact.

Sin has officially joined Bruise Blue—and our rigorous Chest-ah-Fest rehearsal schedule means I get to see him nightly. I'm really digging how we work together: I'll sing a line, and he'll echo on harp, tweaking the melody slightly. There's an intimacy to it, like we're speaking our own language, and it's as close to a private exchange as we get. Since of course Antonia attends every session. She can't enjoy our music much—the Bruise Blue sound is a far cry from classical waltz—but she's always there. I count my blessings that she doesn't try to get in on the act, or offer any opinions. Simply sinks into one of the plush suede chairs, cold Coke in her cold hand, to fixate on Sin's every lick and line, more like his slaver than his lover. If she could fit him with a collar and leash, she would, and that does creep me out. Really, like I don't have enough reasons to sing the blues.

 XLV

---

# BRUISE BLUE

**Dice** = vox & magix

**Duck** = bass & guitar

**Marsh** = hits & kisses

**Sin** = huffs & puffs

**Tosh** = this, that & the other thing

Empowering punk. Redefining rock. With the
backbone and bloodline of music born in
secrets, slavery, and sex.

**BRUISE BLUE.** We're gonna hurt you.
You're gonna love it . . .

Pen presents a printout at the studio tonight. We pass it around and weigh in.

Sin: I approve. Makes me sound like the big, bad wolf.

Marsh (ever wary): Hits & kisses? I'm not sure I get it . . .

Tosh: That's the idea, a bit of mystery.

Duck: Oh, it's cute, Marsh. But mine's so straight—and I'm so not. Can I be . . . how about rhythm & grooves?

Pen: Absolutely. Done!

Me (finally): I like it. I think it's . . . us. You came up with this, Pen?

She and Tosh check each other. Then she takes the paper back, reading it like she forgot what was on it. "Me and Tosh," she says. "We batted ideas around. Over email."

"Uh-huh," I say. "So what's it for?"

"Everything, ultimately," Tosh enthuses. "The Bruise Blue website, our Facebook page, iTunes . . ."

iTunes? Damn, that boy dreams big. I feel like the slacker in the act. All I do is show up and sing, mostly for therapeutic purposes.

"But right now," Pen picks up his thread, "it's for the Chest-ah-Fest flyer. So if you guys don't mind . . ." She breaks out her camera. "Photo session."

"Pen, no!" Marsh objects. "You could've warned us. I didn't even wash my hair today." It's not that she's vain—just shy.

"Exactly why I didn't warn you. I knew you'd bitch," my cousin counters. "Besides, shut up. You get out of bed looking like you sleep on the cover of *Vogue*."

Marsh implores me with a grimace, but I only shrug. I couldn't care less.

"Please, Marsh? Oh, pretty please, nuts and cherries and cream, just like your very best sundae?" Duck cajoles. He's such a ham, and anything to do with the band helps him forget his troubles.

Pen poses us against the stacks of studio equipment, then decides that's "too busy" and piles us onto the sofa instead. "Okay, you guys, let's see some attitude."

We mug.

"You call that attitude? Come on, give me badass!"

We scowl.

"Damn it, people, don't look so miserable. I want sizzle! I want smolder!"

Sounds to me like she wants Sin.

Who's all too willing to oblige. By rising off the couch, cuing up some music, and proceeding to get us in the mood. By "us" I mean everyone. In the room, across the nation, and around the globe. Boy, girl, gay, straight. A sigh in your ear. A tickle up your spine. A tremor in your underpants. Sin Powers is moving, and you are not immune.

Not that he's moving much. Not at first. Just a tad. Very,

very slowly. A boot heel. An eyebrow. Every muscle involved in a deep, from-the-diaphragm moan . . . except his comes out silently, a private dispatch for you and only you, addressing that most sensitive sex organ: your brain. What does he transmit? It's for you and he alone to share. But you get the message, all right. Sin Powers knows how to reach you. Reach . . . you . . . right . . . there . . .

So you start to throb where you throb, and melt where you melt, and get hot, hot, hot—all over. He's well aware. He feels it, too. And with his next move—that upper left quadrant of lip elevating the littlest bit—he demonstrates approval. He's pleased with you. And pleasing Sin Powers is the greatest pleasure you've ever known. So far . . .

Then a hint of his hips—an orbit of adventure, a theme park ride with no safety belts. A tilt of his head that let's you know there's more in store. He rubs his thigh as though the constraint of his jeans and society in general is too much to bear. And when he plucks the front of his plain white tee, that special concavity between navel and sternum, he sends another message—you're making him as hot as he's making you. Uh-huh. Mm-hmm. Look what you do to him; look at him now. He's grown a foot taller and a foot longer. It's all your doing. Proud of yourself?

Now the music picks up, a tempting tempo, tribal and ribald and ancient as earth. He's ready to move for real. Are you? Since it's everyone-out-on-the-floor time. Done teasing, done taunting, Sin Powers is bursting at the seams and set to burst all over you. Spin you and split you, flip you forward, bend you backward, throw you down. Listen up: Hear the quickening pulse as his thick, bright blood pumps, pumps, pumps. Come close, closer than atoms. Give what you've got, all of it, everything, to this rhapsodic sirocco of parry and thrust, build and break, rise and fall. Succumb. Surrender. Submit. If you're a living, breathing, heaving human being, you have no choice.

Oh, but you're not? You're an accidentally-on-purpose freak of demented damnation. Soulfully stunted, never nurtured, ignorant to primal bliss. Driven by perversity and obstinate ironclad fallacy. Well, then, when Sinclair Youngblood Powers snaps and slides and leans like a cholo, pops and locks and cranks that yank, you fly from your seat, chewing your fingers, and run from the room as fast as you can.

# XLVI

LET'S JUST SAY SIN IS TAKING THE LUST CARD LITERALLY — AND FINDING major inspiration. Judging by the band photos that result, it's contagious. The Bruise Blue flyer shows a messy mélange of waving limbs, wild hair, and wicked grins. Out of focus, yet very much on target. How Pen managed to snap away while taking part in Sin's spontaneous dance party is definitely to her credit. She wanted sizzle, she wanted smolder? Well, she captured it. If I didn't know us, and someone handed me a piece of paper boasting about Bruise Blue, I'd want to check us out. We look like a hurricane—the kind you can't wait to get swept up in.

Unless you're Antonia Forsythe.

From the edge of my eye I watched her flee, freaked out and shaken up. So the orgiastic goings-on offended her? Good! Finally, a few points for our side. No one followed her out, but I guess she made it to 12 Daisy Lane well enough on foot. The next day she spends in bed, recovering, refusing even to see Sin when he pays his obligatory call. I wonder if she's planning to attend today's jaunt to Meriden Falls.

I'm up early, and Marsh skips the stables so we can prep, packing coolers with sandwiches, drinks, and treats. We work in tandem, in harmony, giggling and gabbing happily, making things happen, getting things done. Yet as I spin to the spice rack—curried chicken salad is on the menu—I see her. Antonia. How long has she been standing there, grasping the collar of her long chenille robe, glaring at us?

"Good morning and excuse me," I say sprightly, elbowing her out of my way.

Antonia skitters, fetching her preferred breakfast spoon. Marsh and I try to impress upon her the meaning of Independence Day, but her bland response shows little interest. Surely the great soon-to-be-state of Connecticut was already buzzing over taxation without representation back in her day, but I sense Antonia didn't concern herself with anything beyond her roses and her illusory romance.

We take two cars: Me and Marsh in the Duck-mobile, Pen with Tosh riding shotgun and Sin and Antonia in back. Seating arrangements that thrill me to no end. Luckily, Meriden Falls is only about an hour away, and with cool tunes and good friends, the time flies. It's still morning when we arrive, but this is clearly a popular destination, the parking lot already half full. As we pile out, I notice Sin is in rare form. Only no, not rare—not rare at all.

The robust timbre of his voice, that rakish swagger in his stride, the way clover-sweet air and sparkling sunshine seem like his attendants—or his accomplices. I'm struck with a slo-mo replay of the first day Sin set foot on the Swonowa quad, every head turning with the need to know: Who *is* that guy? Now as then, his magnetism beguiles like the bell of an ice cream truck. That rock-god routine at the photo session was merely a prelude—Sin Powers is back, in full effect.

Once we start hauling out our stuff, he starts showing off—juggling Marsh's backpack, Tosh's soccer ball, and a small watermelon. I'm nervous for the melon, what a big, splashy mess it would make if Sin were too mishandle a pass, but he soon tires of his own clowning. Stacking three coolers, he leads the way out of the lot.

As to Antonia? She's left to fend for herself. I can't imagine he was outright rude to her en route, but he certainly seems to have forgotten her now, strutting ahead carefree as Huck Finn with a week full of Sundays. How awful she must feel, tagging along on the fringes of our group, but what am I supposed to do, loop my arm through hers and inquire chummily about her china pattern? Antonia is unwanted, and I unwant her more than anyone. Except maybe Sin. The tarot threw down a gauntlet and he's picked it up. And I get the sense he's just begun.

Doubling my pace, I reach his side. "You act like you know where you're going."

He slants his glance my way, smile the slightest bit vulpine. "You call it Meriden, we called it Scatacook," he says. "I'm sure I told you my adopted mother often had me stay among my tribe. We'd come out this way to fish." He hoists the coolers to readjust the weight. "Damn, woman, what are we picnicking on, boulders?"

By now we've reached an optimal tree—lavish low boughs offering maximum shade over lush, spongy lawn. Our gear goes down and we're next, lolling in the grass. Sin lasts maybe two minutes horizontal; aggressive energy has him up and kicking the soccer ball around.

"Might I ask what you brought this for if you're going to sit on your ass all day?" he chides Tosh, to my shock and amusement. "Come on, get up."

To my further shock and amusement, Tosh does get up, and soon Marsh and Duck join the frolic.

"Don't you want to play?" I ask Pen, who was always such a jock.

The scrunch of her features, the level of her lashes—what she'd like to do is talk, I can tell, really talk, like we used to. Then she flicks at Antonia—the usurper, the outsider—and fakes a non-committal shrug. My resentment builds like lit coals. Could be Antonia senses it; she pulls a magazine from her tote and begins to leaf through it.

"Go for a walk?" I prod my cousin.

The moment has passed, though. Pen plucks at a tuft of grass in front of her. "Maybe later . . ."

Something's up with her. I'm curious but I don't push. "Okay, well, whenever." I flop, lulled by drifting clouds into a doze, only next thing I know, I snap to, a poke from my subconscious: *Dice, you don't want to miss this!* Lifting to my elbows, at first I think Sin has found himself a pet—a round, bouncy pet. Then I see it's the soccer ball—the way he manipulates it with the sides and soles of his feet make it chase his heels like a frisky puppy. For seconds at a time he lifts off the ground, glissades over and hovers atop the ball, defying gravity.

Pen's caught on too, and Antonia puts aside *Modern Bride*. We stand for a better view, since now a crowd is gathering. Grinding old-school industrial music cranks from a boom box nearby, egging Sin on. The freestyle moves become ballet-meets-capoeira-meets-hip-hop as he handstands and backflips, popping his rubber buddy off parts of his body—not to mention Tosh's Afro, Duck's belly, and Marsh's butt as she shrieks with laughter. People are clapping and stomping, whooing and hooing. Pen seizes the moment to press Bruise Blue flyers on the burgeoning mob. Feeding off the frenzy, Sin tops himself with increasingly impossible gyrations until, for a grand finale, he head-bangs the ball into the air. It falls to earth I know not where. Unless of course it actually goes into orbit.

# XLVII

With a single piece of extreme-sports performance art, Sin has established a following. Care to guess how many of this eager coterie are female? Naturally, some have boyfriends, and they instruct these boyfriends to drag their blankets and baskets over *there*—i.e., where we are. Said boyfriends actually oblige. Since who wouldn't want to hang out with that mad, rad, bad . . . what's his name? Sin?! No way! Holy crap . . .

So our small crew swells, and Sin, in the center, holds court, looking less than lordly in frayed shorts and not much else. Shoved and shunted by the gaggle, Antonia winds up yet again on the rim. For how could she possibly compete with specimens like these, she with her hunched posture, frail speech, and cement-colored eyes, they with their spray-on tans, dazzling teeth, and twenty-first-century boobs? Tupperware offerings of fried chicken and banana bread, plus assorted other temptations not necessarily edible are made as newcomers jockey for position.

"Sin, let me put lotion on your shoulders—you don't want to burn!"

"Sin, try my potato salad—it's a blue-ribbon winner at the county fair!"

"Sin, have you heard this song? Here, use my earbuds . . ."

Am I jealous? Damn skippy! But I've figured out Sin's scheme: He's giving his bride-to-be a preview of coming attractions. The future Mrs. Powers will have to put up with mucho female attention. Is this the life—nay, the eternity—she wants, forever facing a revolving bevy of cuter, cooler, more lascivious competition? He'll show her exactly how desirable he is, which ought to cure her crush and prove without doubt that he never made her any vow. How could he swear to love anyone? He's Sinclair Youngblood Powers, and he loves everyone. So, ladies, ladies, please—form an orderly line!

Catching a glimpse of Antonia huddling by herself, big hands clinging to bony elbows, I think Sin's ploy might be doing the trick. So as the congregation of girls grasps and weaves, I'm feeling very much the more the merrier, and sure, I'd love a piece of fried chicken, why not. One tasty drumstick later, I don't even know where Antonia is, but I do need a napkin, badly. I make my way toward the stash I packed, and that's when I spy her. What draws my eye is the flash of sun on her very large knife, and I feel my blood flow backward. What is she doing? What should I do? Holler an alarm, choke-slam her evil ass? Wait . . . now what? Sin extends toward the blade-wielding whack job. Obedient eyes lowered, she hands off her deadly weapon. He grabs the hilt, then calls to his minions: "Hey! Who wants watermelon?"

"Me!!!" comes the chorus.

Right, *phew,* silly me! We do have a watermelon, and wouldn't its sugary juice be great after all that savory stuff?

"Bring . . . me . . . the melon!" Sin commands.

"The melon! The melon!" comes the exuberant if vaguely aberrant chant.

I'm cracking up as Duck presents the fruit, round as the soccer ball, almost twice the size. He places it before Sin like a sacrifice and trots up to where Marsh and Pen and Tosh and I have gravitated toward one another. Sin, seated, lifts to his knees, the knife poised. Antonia has stood back, out of the picture, perhaps for a better view of her beloved as he readies for this bizarre and hilarious rite. Everyone quiets down as he sonorously intones: "On this most auspicious day of our nation's history, I hereby slaughter this proud and noble gourd in honor of the great state of Connecticut!"

There are cheers as Sin brings the point to pierce the rind. Except the thing before him is no longer a gourd. It's a bomb, a grenade, a cannonball—and it explodes. Our cheers become one confused, united scream. Chunks of wet pink meat and hard green shrapnel go flying, a rain of seeds like bullets. The picnic erupts into panic, our new best friends running for cover, tripping over coolers, slipping on Frisbees. Ultimately, as the fallout settles, it's clear that no one's really been injured. Only it's just us again, Sin's sycophants scattered.

Talk about buzzkill. Nothing like nuclear fruit to get this party finished. Sin especially seems at a loss, having found the soccer ball and stalking off to kick it around solo. Either he's being a big baby or strategizing his next maneuver. Marsh and I pick up the carnage, while Antonia fastidiously attends to herself with a sanitizing wipe, a cruel twist to her contracted smile. Chalk one up in her column. Yeah, sure, she had nothing to do with the patch that produced the melon, but given her prowess with plants, I unequivocally hold her responsible for its detonation.

So what are we going to do now—pack it in and head for Swoon? That would suck.

"Hey . . ." Tosh, a voice of reason. "Are we hiking to the falls or what?"

That's right, the falls. Somewhere to go, something to see.

"We really should," pipes Pen, who's been there. "So gorgeous. And the trail's not too tough."

It seems unanimous, except no one moves toward Sin. Well,

I've seen him in worse moods, so it's up to me. "The consensus is we should take a hike."

He checks me from under his forelock and says, "All right."

That was easy.

There's a picturesque covered bridge that I bet has graced many a postcard, and then the trail begins. "Tough," I find, is a relative term. The way down is certainly steep. By and large we're dressed for it; only Antonia, who eschewed sneakers during her spree through Torrington Commons, wears pink lace-up espadrilles. She's clearly having difficulty on the path, and Sin suffers the grip of her fingers as she baby steps. Despite this hampered progress, we're soon feeling mist on our skin as we come upon the dramatic cascade pounding some seventy-five feet toward the Housatonic River.

Wows abound all around. Then we stand quietly, admiring the magnificence. It's hard to be with Sin in the presence of wonder yet unable to share it in any direct way. The light touch of his hand at my sacrum, a hushed adjective in my ear, that's all I want right now. He's here, though, scant inches away. We exist on the same plane, in the same place, at the same time. I try to be grateful for that.

Pen pulls out her camera and snaps away.

"Please, Pen," Antonia says, posing stiffly. "Please do take one of Sinclair and I."

I assume she'll want a print and, in her skewed view, see a

happy couple. Even though, once the shutter clicks, Sin can't wait to extricate himself from her possessive proximity. He leaps to the guardrail, the slim margin of safety between tourists and the coursing water, the jagged limestone drop. As he makes it his tightrope, my breath catches in my throat. Last fall, such a feat wouldn't have given me cause to blink—a golem feels no pain, a golem can't be killed. Only there's no way of telling which, if any, immortal attributes Sin retains in his current incarnation—and I don't want to find out.

The question is, as his loose-limbed strut and mock-drunk reels grow increasingly reckless: Does *he*?

# XLVIII

THINK ABOUT IT. I AM. SIN COMES CRASHING BACK INTO THIS world to find the girl he loves in someone else's arms. Days later he discovers himself doomed by a pledge he can't recall making. Every minute since his return has been dredged in disappointment and pinioned by madness. Do acrobatics without a net really seem such a strange choice for him now? Could he be so unhappy that flouting fate above jagged rocks and roaring water appears to be a viable option?

I flash on our friends. All they see is Sin being Sin—and they're digging it. Sin the daredevil, adding to his repertoire of risk. But what do they really know—nothing. What do they really care—nothing. The only true empathy I get right now feels like a bug in my ear as I catch Antonia watching, veiled terror in her storm-horizon eyes. Of course, she *would* be afraid. On her side of the fissure, she had Sin on lock through infinity.

But here, might he be fallible, might he be able to escape her—through death? Icky, that she and I should share a fear—but then again, we share a love. Initially, then, Antonia's anxiety heightens mine; only now, all at once, with a ragged, unbidden laugh—my breath shaking free of my throat—I lose it.

Sinclair Youngblood Powers loves life. Not eternal life, immortal life, reasonable facsimile of life—but real life. If life is what he's got right now, he'll live it to the limit, yes. But trifle with it, abuse it, take it for granted? Never. If Sin is alive, he is blessed, and no one knows it more than he. So I laugh with relief and I laugh with assurance as my boy cartwheels the length of the rail to dismount right in front of me.

"There's a series of lesser falls yonder," he announces to all, not the least bit winded by his extra-extra exertions. "If anyone should care to forge on."

I care to. You bet I do. "Sounds cool," I say. Murmurs of assent ensue, though some a bit hesitant. Duck in particular looks like he's had enough activity for one day. And Antonia, well, if she had her way, she and Sin would be sitting on a blanket in the field, alone. But we all go along—pausing only when Sin slips under the rail to divert from the main trail.

"A shortcut," he says.

There's minimal debate about whether or not to continue, but I'm right behind Sin, and ultimately they are too. The path we take is rugged and even steeper—plus I'm sure elements of overgrowth are poison ivy, poison oak, or poison something. Concentration keeps us quiet as we make our way, each to our own thoughts, though when mine wander to the one absent from this expedition, I realize Marsh must be musing the same sad way, and Duck, too. Crane. The collective mood lightens when we hear a lilting gurgle in three-part harmony. Before us, our reward: a trio of smaller cascades that strike my fancy as the sirens myth, singing while brushing their hair.

Across from these falls, a wide, flat expanse of rock—shaded and sheltered from view. We gather there and marvel, still not saying much; some splendor defies language. Anything I could tell Sin—how amazing this all is, how much I appreciate his bringing us here—isn't necessary. He knows. Glancing toward him, I find his eyes already on me.

"There's more," he says after a while.

"I believe I'll stay," Duck says dreamily, prone on the stone, cheek pillowed on beefy biceps. "I'm explored out."

"That might be wise." Sin's gaze sweeps off and down. "This next bit is somewhat tricky."

"I'll stay too." Marsh is stretched out next to Duck, still hypnotized by the sparkling spill. "But you'll come around this way to get us, right?"

"Of course," Sin assures her.

Which is when a weird thing happens. Here's Pen and Tosh, all set to join us, and then they don't. Do I see Pen tug Tosh's belt loop? Do I watch them exchange a flurry of silent communiqués? Maybe, or maybe I imagine it—but they're not coming.

As to the persistent gray mouse in the pink espadrilles? I don't know. I don't pay attention. The trek begins with a slight upward grade, and then, suddenly, there's a sheer drop. For Sin it's like stepping off a box. For me, stepping off a skyscraper. He leaps down and looks up at me. My look says *no way*. So he takes a moment to survey the rock wall, patting and plumbing it.

"Aha, yes, this will work," I hear him say with confidence. "Dice, come here. I've found a couple of chinks."

Skeptically I near the rim. "A couple of what?"

"A ladder. Of sorts. Listen to me, this is what I want you to do . . ."

The instructions are so simple. Support myself with my upper-body strength while dangling my entire lower body off the edge of the earth. Then fit my toe into this tiny indentation he's spied. After which he'll direct my other leg toward the next notch, and so on, until he can reach up and guide me the rest of the way. There is of course no way this will ever happen. Unless I trust him completely. Which I do. Lo and behold, I'm down.

I turn around and we are close. We are alone. We are breath on breath. And he knows why I've come with him—that it has nothing to do with yet another collection of hidden waterfalls. He knows I would come with him anywhere. Even places he wouldn't want me to enter, to wit the mysterious void that kept us apart for six months. He also knows what will transpire next—and so do I. He is going to look at me, and then he is going to say my name, and then he is going to take me . . . take me . . . take me back.

Except . . . "It's not much further," he says, his voice so hoarse, so low. "There is a place . . . I want you to see . . ."

When he takes my hand, I feel like we're already there. Then we actually come upon it. Eden. Has to be. We've gone deep to the bottom of a canyon, falls on either side, each one with a slightly different cadence, a slightly different song. Ferns and mosses feed on the stone, while vines and ivy tangle and sway like euphoric folk dancers. At our feet a brook flows merrily and yet travels nowhere—since this, after all, is paradise. There's nowhere else to go.

For a moment we stand, existing for each other. Only this, only us. Sin lets go of my hand to cup my face, and then he is kissing me. We are lost and found, and nothing—time, space, imperative, eternity—can keep us apart.

## XLIX

ONE OF THESE DAYS, I'M GOING TO GET DRESSED. I MEAN *DRESSED*: Starting with stockings, two of them—forget tights, I'm talking the kind that clip onto garters. Over the undies, some sort of snug, silken slip. Followed by a dress, or possibly a suit and blouse—either way there will be buttons involved, a plethora. Certainly a zipper, at least one. And a belt. Maybe even a bow, at the throat or at the back. The shoes will also require a closing mechanism, laced up or ankle strapped—no pump, no loafer, no mule. The rationale for all this fastidious layering and fastening? An interview or audition? Dinner at the poshest place to commemorate some milestone or achievement? No. The sole purpose in getting dressed is to be undressed, by him, slowly, for however long it takes.

Of course I intend to return the favor. For he will also be dressed. As in *dressed*. Each item fitting superbly, the sum of the parts giving me a small gasp at the sight of him. Then, passion balanced by patience, I'll attend to necktie knot and cuff link cross, buttons, buckle, shirtfront, fly. Employ deft digits, one article at a time, kneeling when necessary, circling him as is my pleasure, relishing the task, leisurely but not lazily, all the way to completion.

Will I go first, keeping everything on till he's entirely undone? Or vice versa, submit to my own delicious undoing and then take to him wearing only a smile and some earrings? Or maybe we'll take turns, call-and-response disrobing, piece by piece by tossed-aside piece.

Or maybe not. Maybe neither of us will ever deign to put clothes on again. We'll live in the haven of the canyon, and if by chance I ever come upon the soft bit of fabric he now guides gently over my belly, my breasts, my face, and away, I'll view the faded artifact and wonder what one did with such a thing. In fact, as he observes me briefly against the sumptuous natural backdrop, my entire past wavers, recedes—here and now is all there is.

Closing on me for another kiss, Sin finds between my breasts another man's talisman. His fingers curl around the warm silver circle. The clasp imprints the skin where the base of my neck meets my uppermost vertebra. There's pressure as he looks from his fist to my soul, and for a second I think he'll break the chain, send Saint Michael into the churning current.

Then he releases the amulet—conceding, I guess, that there's evil he cannot protect me from. Mustn't let his ego interfere with anything that might keep me from harm.

So now he returns to tender, finding places to kiss as uncharted as our idyll. The off-center peak of my hairline, the contours of my suprasternal notch. I'm exploring, too, across terrain that shivers and hardens and swells. As to language—explanations, propositions, defenses—it's as obsolete as my discarded T-shirt. The only sounds that matter are the rushing water, the rustling of creatures in league with our love, our own breath and sighs.

Except what's that? A terrible sound that begins from above and comes toward us at speed. So we separate, look up. Crashing through the brush, bouncing off the crags, plummeting, unstoppable, down the steep canyon wall, too fast to see beyond a blur. Until it hits the bottom. Then we do see, all too well.

Antonia has landed facedown in the rocky brook bed. Clearly, she is broken. Utterly still. Shattered limbs at impossible angles. The brisk current is the only thing that moves, Sin and I staring frozen at the contorted body.

"I should . . . collect her," he says finally, and we both draw to the bank. He steps into the stream and lifts her with the effort of picking up a dish rag. She is limp in his arms, her neck in his elbow crook, her arms and legs cold cooked noodles. As he carries her past me, I see sightless, gelid whites in her head, irises sunken far into her skull. Antonia is dead.

But we already knew that. And those darned dead, they don't die twice. So it should come as no surprise when the jerks and jolts begin, rebooting whatever diabolical impulses keep Antonia animate on this side of existence. Her arms lock around Sin with a spasm, eyeballs falling into place. "Oh, Sinclair . . ." Her voice like tin, her will like iron. "I do love you so."

I find my T-shirt and pull it back on as Sin sets Antonia back to her feet. The look the dead girl gives me turns my blood to gasoline.

It's a killer climb up the canyon. There are moments I want to stop, and I do stop. Then I keep on going. Concentration is key—if I lose my grip on an outcropping or trip on a root, I'll take a tumble, and unlike Antonia, I won't get up. Which is exactly what she wants.

I don't know how much Antonia saw of Sin and me on the bank, but it changed her, penetrating the glassine surface of her insanity, reaching its squishy, vulnerable core and smacking it, hard. I'm not some bimbo on the picnic grounds she can scare away with a stunt. For the first time, Antonia actually perceives me as a viable rival. The look she gave me by the river's edge— the dull, dead, impenetrable stare, lead-based paint on a weapon of mass destruction—cannot be misconstrued.

So I'm careful, very careful, as I pick my way out of paradise.

I pause to catch my breath and regain my game face. Because the truth is, I'm afraid. And I can't let Antonia see that.

It's not till we hook back up with the others and head toward the field that I notice she's changed physically, too. Always sort of clumsy, now thanks to the fall, she lumbers with a stiff lurch, her pelvis out of whack, the left shoulder slightly higher than the right, her spinal column askew so it looks like she's craning to hear something. I flash on her staggering along to "Here Comes the Bride" and it sparks a giggle. Antonia sends her awful eyes my way, but I keep my composure, fear masked by mirth. My own step, lighter and unencumbered, allows me to sail past her.

Soon as we're in the car, heading back to Swoon, Marsh and Duck pounce.

"Start talking," Marsh says. "What happened? Between you and Sin . . . and her."

Duck doesn't even bother turning on the radio. "And don't leave anything out," he says. "We're just dying to know!"

Dying. Unfortunate word choice, but I get the point. Only how to tell them? What happened? Nothing but everything. The most wonderful thing that could possibly happen—and the most terrifying. I'm crazy in love; I'm scared out of my wits. I lean between the two front seats and look from one friend to the other—can they read the messed-up message in my eyes?

"The good news is," I start, "Sin and I . . . we sort of . . . kissed and made up."

Marsh gives a little yelp. "You kissed! Does that mean you're back together?"

Does it? I don't know. "Well, we were interrupted—that's the bad news. Our eighteenth-century interloper got a peek, and it didn't sit very well with her." I lean back in my seat. "I don't want to be alarmist, but I need to figure a way out of all this, fast. Because there's no doubt in my mind: Antonia intends to kill me."

 L

A FIREWORKS DISPLAY IS SET FOR NINE ON THE SWOON VILLAGE GREEN. Macy's has nothing to worry about—I went last year; it's no big deal. In fact, I think I'll pass. I like to go, "Ooh!" as much as the next person, but noise and crowds are just what my nerves don't need right now. Better devote time alone to the latest tweak in the freak show of my life: How to thwart Antonia Forsythe's plans to do me in.

Which means stop thinking like myself and start thinking like a psycho. Obvious methods—your shooting, your stabbing, your strangulation—are out; surely it would irk Sin if she came at me with those. It's got to look like an accident. Pinch of undetectable poison in my Cocoa Puffs, perhaps? This notion occurs just as I'm pecking at picnic leftovers. Had Antonia been alone with this stuff? Watch me lose my appetite, then wander out to the porch. Daisy Lane is dead, the falling night serene.

Sitting on the glider, I gaze toward the Leonard house. My cousin seemed psyched about the fireworks, and that makes me glad. Pen's gained new enthusiasm in general lately, which I chalk up to her anarchist phase actually paying off. At times it seems put on, but I think it's helping her deal with her issues—including her behavior during Sin's seductive tenure last fall. No way could she regain her perky naïveté, but she's moving forward to discover herself, develop herself, grow up.

As if musing can summon, guess whose headlamps cast their beacon on my driveway. For a moment the car goes dark, then Pen and Tosh debark. Talk about an unlikely twosome. Must be some band business that cannot wait.

"No pyrotechnics for you kids?"

"Seen one crossette, seen 'em all," Pen says, throwing Tosh a glance. "We wanted to talk to you, if you've got a sec."

Uh-oh. Am I mangling lyrics again? Does my stage presence need an extreme makeover? "Sure," I say. "What about?"

Tentatively they check each other. Then, not tentatively, Pen says, "This," hooking Tosh at the neck and planting a big, fat, juicy one right on his ripe-plum lips. Sliding his arms around her waist, he pulls her in for emphasis. Fireworks? They're igniting their own.

Then they quit and turn to me.

Some psychic, huh—I never saw it coming. "Uh . . . whoa."

And they say, "Yeah." Together.

The corners of my mouth shoot up. "Interesting," I say.

Once she would have been coy; Pen is now candid. "You're cool with this?"

"Completely," I say. Because I am. Shocked, sure, what with how Pen trashed the guy from the get. As to Tosh and me, that couldn't have gone far before fizzling; we're too much alike to click beyond friends. What I see in them is beautiful. Hope, faith, trust—the trinity in action. They are clearly so into each other; how could I have missed it?

"Good, because we were . . . I was a little worried," Pen says. "Tosh told me you two almost . . . more than almost . . . and if you thought . . . because I've done some shitty things . . ."

"Pen, please." I get up and hug her. Then I hug Tosh. Then I hug them both. Hand to heart, I say, "I am utterly ecstatic for you guys." Yeah, except for the tiny twinge that envies how easy it is for them. All they have to do to be in love is to fall in love. I sit back heavily on the swing. "Just keep the sickening PDA to a minimum."

"Definitely." Pen posts next to Tosh on the porch rail. "Although, back at you," she says, leering. "According to Duck, you and Sin are making some PG-13 progress."

"Oh, that's true. Sin and me, we're good. Except for the fact that his bride-to-be wants to murder me."

"What?" She plops down at my side. "Spill!"

Guess Duck didn't want to bear bad news. Best as I can, I

give her the gist. "So I have to be vigilant," I sum up. "Let's call it added incentive to figure out how to beat her." Frustration seeps from me with a sigh. "Sin's running a ploy of his own. He thinks if she gets a taste of what being with him is really like, she'll get over him. That's what all his showing off was about today."

Pen *pffff*s. "Right, like that'll work. Antonia will nuke the nearest organic object, and buh-bye bimbos." She gets it—that's a comfort.

"You probably shouldn't be alone with her, Dice," Tosh says.

My cousin concurs. "I can come around in the morning when Marsh is at the stables."

Nice, but never. "Pen, please. Marsh leaves at dawn; you'd sleep till the crack of noon every day if you could." I pull Saint Michael from my shirt and give him a pat. "No worries. I got my boy here."

A faint whisper of *boom* from town. The sky in that direction turns a hazy pale. A celebration of freedom is under way. It rallies me. "Look, you guys, you have my official blessing, so why don't you toddle off. Really, it's cool. I'm safe for the moment, with Antonia at the fireworks with Sin, and after the day I've had, I wouldn't mind being alone awhile."

They scope me skeptically. Neither one moves.

"Tell you what. Go to the green and plaster patriotic Swoonies with Bruise Blue flyers, then swing by and pick me up for practice."

That gets them. With a squeeze of my knee, Pen says, "Okay. See you in an hour."

I watch them go. Pen and Tosh. Tosh and Pen. Go figure. They make me smile. Sitting by myself, expecting to seek my own counsel, I find myself singing aloud instead. Absently at first, then with greater conviction and volume. A special sort of song. A spiritual. Learned it at the neighborhood kids' choir Momster enrolled me in—I must've been what, seven?

*"Gonna lay down my sword and shield . . ."*

It lifts me up, in that light-at-the-end-of-the-tunnel sort of way. Trouble is, I've yet to catch the merest glimmer of light. My sword and shield are around my neck, the only defense I've got. I don't see myself laying them down any time soon.

## LI

THE TIME IS NIGH. ANTONIA HAD LEFT A DEPOSIT ON SOME SEVEN gowns at Buckley's Bridal Warehouse, and now she must make her decision. Pen will serve as chauffeur and fashion consultant, but Pen is running late. As Antonia, dressed and ready, reels into the kitchen with her newly skewed stomp, I tell her so, then add casually, "By the way, after breakfast, you'll need to pack a bag."

An eyebrow wings. "I beg your pardon?"

"Just for a few days. My mother's driving up from the city." This is true. *In Star* affiliates with the Hamptons Film Festival every Fourth; Momster spent the holiday in serious schmooze mode and desperately needs R & R. Or so she insists—I'm betting she wants to check what's stalling the sale of the house. Maybe the agent told her I'm running a home for wayward demons up in here, so not a plus for property value.

"Pen suggested you stay with her." Got to love the girl for stepping up, faking friendship with our monstress. And with my mother and cousin running interference, I expect to breathe a bit easier. "You'll like it at the Leonards'," I say. "It's far more posh than this old place."

Absorbing this, Antonia sits at the table for her Cocoa Puffs fix. "Very well," she says. "But I do wish you wouldn't denigrate this house, Dice. I find the quaint environs ever so charming." She pours a bowl. "The decor is rather shabby, of course, but the structure itself is sound. At least, I do hope so, since Sinclair and I agreed last night that we shall purchase it. Properly appointed"—she sweeps her hand—"it ought make a lovely honeymoon cottage."

My house? The site of and shrine to the most incredible night of my life? That. Cannot. Happen.

"Indubitably, we'll import everything from France." She lets her glance survey the space. "Cabriolet chairs . . . a chandelier . . . oh, if only we could find a virginals like the one I used to play." Then she looks at me, lips pursed and chin high. "And upstairs, certainly, the most sumptuous bed . . ."

Baiting the enemy isn't smart, but sometimes a girl can't help it. "Certainly," I say. "And considering these brutal Connecticut winters, don't forget the Louis XV bed warmer. You'll need it."

Antonia hasn't got a retort—I'm not even sure she got the implication. Instead she says, "Such details are inconsequential.

330

What's important is, once our offer on this house is accepted—and surely it will be—we can pick a day and engage the justice of the peace." Pout in place, she upends the milk container over her bowl. Too bad it's empty.

An insignificant victory, but I mug smug nonetheless. "Please do forgive me," I say. "I must have taken the last drop."

Antonia regards her still-dry cereal, then looks at me and sighs. "Dice—dear, *dear* Dice—I do so wish you and I might reach a truce."

This ought to be interesting. I lean back and let her bring it.

She extracts a single ball of puffed corn from her bowl, pops it in her mouth, and chews pensively. Then she begins. "I was raised in a pious era and led a sheltered life, but I am not a fool."

That's one thing I never took her for.

"These last several days, I've become immersed in the ways of modernity. The morals of your age—or should I say the lack thereof . . ."

Another chocolate morsel as she carefully composes her phrases.

"Ergo, much as I disdain the thought, I accept that you have had some sort of . . . liaison with Sinclair."

I grit my teeth. If she calls me a slattern—that's eighteenth-century for "slut"—she'll be picking Cocoa Puff crumbs out of her hair for days.

"Yet in many ways you seem so decent . . . a lady."

331

*Gee, thanks!* I think.

"So you must agree that a crude, brief encounter—the sort a man of many appetites might easily fall prey to—cannot compare or compete with true, abiding love. A love that transcends time. A love to endure for eternity."

Oh, cue the strings!

"A love that has been sworn to me."

Again with the sworn! Antonia pops another CP, shakes her head. "Can you imagine, that in the weeks that followed upon my death, there had been speculation that I deliberately caused the conflagration in the east wing? Captive wraith that I was, I heard my parents bemoan this tawdry rumor." Pale lashes reach for the ceiling as reflectively she goes on. "An errant cinder caught my quilt, and it is true, I failed to immediately douse it—seeking, I suppose, to draw attention to myself, alone in my room while a ball was under way in the great hall." She pauses, for effect or regret. "A fatal error, for soon the roaring red display engulfed me."

I gulp down a lump hearing the specifics of her mortal end.

Yet Antonia can shrug, blasé about it now. "Alas, it was my fate to meet the flames," she says. "But take my own life? Perish the notion! No girl with so great a love and rich a future would do such a thing."

With her next contemplative Cocoa Puff, Antonia glances off. "Of course, my parents had no knowledge of Sinclair and I. He being common, they would never have approved. Indeed, from the day he pledged his troth, I began to amass my dowry, pilfering it gold piece by gold piece from my mother's coffer."

Her eyes get a nasty glimmer, ice on slate, as she offers this illicit info—and then they grow misty with remembered misery. "I knew not what kept Sinclair from claiming me, as days went to weeks and weeks to months. My garden fell to seed, the rosebush branches barren, yet I'd pull on my cloak and wander therein, waiting for him. It did baffle me; it did pain me greatly—but I knew he would come."

What's prompting this confession, I can't be sure. Maybe Antonia just wants me to understand her before she does me in. Her revelations have got me mesmerized. Groundless as it is, her love was—*is*—solid, hammered in the forge of her heart. Yet all those months of waiting surely planted that flaw of doubt in her otherwise steadfast conviction.

Now she lofts her chin to declare, "And I was right, for here we are, centuries later, set to wed."

Summoning sympathy, I gaze at her across the table. "I appreciate your sharing all this, Antonia," I say. "But actually, Sin told me he can't recall pledging—"

She throws me a glare. "Surely whatever he told you was to quell your prying. Sinclair respects that what exists between us is none of your affair."

Okay, I expected a rationale along those lines. And now Antonia regards me as though weighing whether to go on.

Which she decides to do. "I will allow, however, that you played a pivotal role in bringing Sinclair and I together again. And it is my hope that if I convey to you what that was, you'll quit your salacious attempts to . . . to distract him."

I breathe. I blink. Antonia assumes this to mean I bid her continue.

"You see, Dice—dear, *dear* Dice—were it not for you, I mightn't have conceived it possible that he and I could be reunited . . ."

I still breathe. I still blink. Only what Antonia delivers in that needle-on-a-chalkboard scratch is starting to mess with my motor functions.

"For centuries I wandered Forsythe Manor bereft, a lost soul in my own home, one among many tortured, aimless spirits . . ."

Where had I heard that before? Right, in the letter to Sin we found on her escritoire. She'd described her loneliness, her yearning . . .

"Then one evening *you* came, and you sang, and with your voice you channeled my beloved."

The letter went on—how she then felt his essence calling out to her . . .

"Such a silly trifle of a song, so loud and brash. Yet you evoked him."

Did I? I did. Damn right, I did. When I sing, Sin is there. Sin is always there. That first time in the studio, Tosh checking me with those gold to green to honey eyes, Sin was no doubt extra there. I felt him. I wasn't the only one.

"I sensed his presence powerfully."

The dull glimmer of Antonia's dead gaze. The strained intensity of her tone. Am I still breathing? Still blinking?

"And then . . . what is the expression? Oh, yes, I took it from there."

Though she's stopped gnashing cereal, Antonia shows her teeth—vicious, tiny, relentless thorns. How can I breathe? How can I blink?

"With the fissure opened, the sorcery proved simple. The scent of my roses, the lilt of my waltz, and Crane Williams belonged to me. After that, the magic gained momentum. My flowers entrancing. My music beckoning. Again you came to the house—in your short skirt, that bruise upon your leg. I could not help but note how it bound you to him."

So that's how she got the idea. Now her bitter pink bitten brand jails my man as effectively as a ball and chain.

"I was imbued!" Antonia carries on as her fingers flex and clench. "I could do anything! And then there he was, my Sinclair, swinging the iron gate, come to me, come *for* me, come to fulfill his vow."

Antonia rises from the table, her fractured frame and contorted face as repulsive a loogie as hell ever spat. And now I cannot breathe; now I cannot blink.

"The love so long denied finally mine! Everything I ever wanted is coming to fruition. A beautiful gown of flowing white, a home of my own, and my Sinclair, more handsome and noble than I even recall, soon—soon!—to be mine, body and soul."

The truth hurts, they say, but that's all they say—they don't say how it hurts. That's because each painful truth has it's own unique recipe for agony. This one—the ugly, undeniable truth that I'm responsible for setting Antonia's game in motion—is an eaten-up-alive sensation. From the inside, from the outside, a rapacious force devours me. Except it doesn't. Because I'm still here. Breathing. Blinking. Knowing.

Knowing that my voice turned traitor in the worst possible way. Knowing that again—again!—some misbegotten kernel of magic rose up in me to lead me astray. Knowing that Antonia Forsythe was my sinister silent partner in summoning Sin. Knowing that the partnership has been terminated, with her still holding the all-important trump card: Crane Williams stashed away in the spectral cyclotron beyond the gate.

What an illuminating morning this is proving to be. My brain bulges with new knowledge, a helium balloon. It lifts me from the table, lofts me from the room, and leads me out the back door. Angry red wrecking balls, tomatoes burden their stalks. Cucumbers threaten like truncheons from their vines.

Herbs conspire in a potpourri of flagrant fragrant mockery. *Et tu, vegetables?* I wonder vaguely as I drift toward the perimeter of the riotous patch.

"Oh, Dice. *Dear* Dice." She has pursued me to the garden. "My confession has disturbed you." She moves toward me, gesturing with a spindly, spidery hand.

"You . . . you violated me . . ." It's all I can manage.

Antonia doesn't exactly smile. "Lambs are for slaughter. Horses are for . . . for sport, yes, nowadays. And people like you, so sensitive, so susceptible to those beyond the grave—surely you accept your purpose."

My purpose. And now, purpose served, I'm supposed to step aside? Apparently.

"So I must urge you to stop imposing yourself between Sinclair and I. I urge you most strongly."

And if I don't? She'll maintain her murderous agenda against me, that's for certain. She might even mess with Charlotte (climb that ladder, little girl; sip the stuff under the sink; play with matches . . .) or renege on her promise to release Crane. A moment passes, and it's as though I can see the garden ripen, drawing off her evil energy.

"I truly am sorry for you, Dice," Antonia says. "I'm well aware that you love him. But he is mine."

A skeletal shackle—frigid, rigid, horrible—her fingers fall on my wrist. I wrench away. Yet I do see sorrow in Antonia's eyes, porous charcoal flecks of it. Then she breathes, and blinks, and all that's there is the hard, gray granite of her determination.

"Goodness, Pen shall be here shortly," she says. "I must run and pack my bag. Indeed, it ought be pleasant, visiting with my neighbors across the lane."

## LII

ANTONIA'S REVELATION HAS ME SHAKEN UP, BUT WITH MOMSTER IN the house, I've got to play it down. Aside from a CliffsNotes version murmured to Marsh in bed last night, I haven't said a word about it but of course can think of nothing else. My voice—that contralto renegade, that melodious turncoat. My magic—much as I try to bury and obliterate it in my quest for Average American Teenhood, those pesky paranormal traits find a way to bite me in the butt. My love—Antonia implied that if I back off Sin, she'll spare my life. Only what is life without the one you love? Before long my mother will notice something's wrong and want to "discuss" why I'm so "evasive" and "sullen," and no way can I get into it with her.

Fortunately, she's awakened this morning by a call from the realtor that fully occupies her mind.

"Really?" she says. "Really? *Really!*"

Apparently, the realtor got really, really real. We have an offer on the house. Quite a healthy offer, for the full asking price. In cash. No mortgage, no muss, no fuss.

"In today's market—incredible!" she marvels. "The deal is going to happen fast; we'd need to be out within a month. We can do that, can't we, sweetie?"

"We" meaning "me," but I nod dumbly. By mid-August, Marsh will have to suck it up and rejoin her sisters in Torrington, and I'll be safely ensconced on the Upper West Side. Ample time to prep for Columbia—do some shopping, scope my schedule, definitely book a hair appointment. Beauty salons in the land of silken blondes are incompetent with natural curls. I'll cop to it: I'm glad my spiral glory makes me stand out here. Only it's gotten so raggedy lately, I've been wearing it up a lot, or in two long braids—the 'do I do for a cookout chez Leonard tonight.

Soon as we arrive, I see that Antonia's been busy. Bouquets abound, and they're all wild. Having left her hosts' carefully tended annuals untouched in their boxes, she must have combed the fields of Swoon for daisies, Queen Anne's lace, thistle—weeds, basically—to weave the ingenious constructions that adorn the patio.

Uncle Gordon presides at the grill, slabs of steak on a platter beside him. My kid cousins and some buddies wage war with water guns while the playmates' parents sip sangria. Lainie urges Momster to regale her guests with insider gossip from the

Hamptons. She does, but seems more fascinated by the revolving teenage contingent.

She picks right up on the body language between Pen and Tosh and throws me some sympathy—she'd been sure I had a thing brewing with him. Her expression turns to flummoxed when Pen introduces the timid, cloddish Antonia. Then she loses it completely when one of her favorite Swoonies rolls up.

"Sinclair!" Okay, the woman is just in from hanging with Brad and Angelina and Quentin and Woody, yet here she is, all a-gush at the sight of my boy.

"Ms. Reagan!" He clasps both her hands, but that won't do—Momster moves in for a kiss on both cheeks, and I mean cheeks, not air. "It's wonderful to see you—lovely as ever."

"Oh, stop." She swats him, then beams at me, assuming that if Pen's with Tosh, I got the better deal. "Candice didn't tell me you were back in town."

Her smile is soon to sour. Spazzy stomp in full effect, Antonia approaches to lynch Sin's elbow. For a second it seems he'll shake her off like a mosquito, but he composes himself, stonily intoning, "May I present my fiancée, Ms. Reagan?"

Good thing the Leonards lit citronella torches, since if there were mosquitoes, an entire swarm could fly into Momster's gaping maw. "Your . . . yes—no," she stammers. "We've met."

Dinner, fortunately, is served, my mother deliberately chewing her steak as if that could engender clarity. In fact, the entire meal proceeds mechanically, the mood wound tight. Though Sin does sit beside his betrothed, he chats mostly with Momster, inquiring about Daddy and how both their careers are faring, before segueing into the New York music scene. Tosh joins for this part of the conversation, my mother relaxing to reminisce about the glory days of CBGB.

"The bathroom? We dubbed it the Toilet Seat of Death," she says, swirling her sangria. "And the backstage graffiti you would not believe. But it did have the city's best sound system, and of course everyone paid their dues there."

Much as I enjoy the oral history of punk rock, I'm taken by the most delicious fantasy: Sin and me emigrating from Swoon, living together in some sixth-floor walk-up, taking the clubs and coffeehouses of NYC by storm, a girl/boy vox/harp blues-based sonic sensation. He sits directly across from me now—looking so fine, speaking so earnestly, laughing so warmly—so close yet so far. Hmm, well, maybe not so far . . .

I do something. I can't resist. Slip off a sandal. Extend a leg. Then tap, tap, tap against the boy's boot. His face ignites, and obscuring his half smirk with a napkin, he glances down like he dropped something. With a quick dip he leans over, scoops up my foot, and tucks it in his lap. This requires scrunching on my part, which naturally I do, tenting my fingers in front of my chin and spacing out dreamily.

First, I'm treated to gentle, diligent massage. Ball, arch, heel, and tendon, then each little piggy gets a sweet, insistent squeeze. I'd be purring right now if I had the equipment. It feels so divine, my other foot promptly gets jealous. Sin being Sin, he moves on to tickle. I bite my tongue—technically the tickle is restricted to my sole, but I feel it surge electrically up my thigh and then some. My head lolls left as I feel myself go damp. This is too good, too good, too good. I can barely bear it, and then I can't bear it at all—I squirm, wriggle, blurt a giggle.

This puts a bump in Momster's nostalgia lane; she glances at me. But Sin abruptly stops, so I smile guilelessly. Then he starts in again, all at once, surprising me—my next thrash more pronounced. Now Antonia gives me the eye—and chills me to the spleen. Once more Sin quits, planting both elbows innocently on the table. "Dice," he asks with faux concern, "are you feeling all right?"

"Mm, perfectly . . ." Fun's over, I assume, only to have Sin seize, then pull. All I can do is scrunch further as he nestles my size seven to indicate precisely how much he's digging this. Which elicits a gasp heard round the table. I've sunk so far in my chair, I'm visible only from the clavicle up. The heat rising to my skin is surely evident in the waning sun. My eyes flash at Sin to cease and desist, but he refuses, and like a curtain falling on some bizarre tragicomedy, Antonia lowers her lashes to gaze in her companion's lap. Sin, still focused on me, adjusts with a thrust to drive home the dimensions of his pleasure once more before finally relinquishing his hold.

I take back my foot, then sit up in my seat. Busily, I reach for water, have several cooling sips. "Well," I say. "Wow. That was so good. Uncle Gordon, that steak, yuh-mee!" I push my plate. "But you know I left room for dessert!"

"Oh!" That reminds my aunt. "Wait till you see the pièce de résistance!" She looks to her daughter. "Penny, won't you help?"

My cousin starts to grumble, but Tosh gets up, and so do I; Pen concedes and we follow Lainie like ducklings. In the kitchen she reveals two miniature braziers; on a tray she has graham crackers, chocolate, and marshmallows set up. "What's a cookout without s'mores!" Aunt Lainie asks rhetorically as we hustle back to the guests.

The children cheer. So do the adults, as if tipsy from more than wine. In fact, the whole vibe on the patio has changed. Nothing like Sin Powers exercising a foot fetish to loosen things up. A sultry dusk is upon us now, and the blue flames rising from the roasters add a mystical tinge. Pen's brother Silas, in his excitement, starts clambering onto the table.

"No, no, let me help you." Laughing as she scolds, Pen moves into supervisory mode. I join her—the sooner we get s'mores into their paws, the sooner we can indulge.

"I want one with lots of mush-mellow!" Jordan squeals.

"Okay, okay," I tell my cousin. "Here you go, this one's major mush-mellowy."

With the single-digit set attended to, Pen prepares an especially gooey goody for Tosh, then taunts him with it. He goes for a grab, but she parries, painting his lips with melted chocolate. He flicks his tongue, then snatches her wrist to eat the treat from her fingers. Their sexy s'mores-play gives me a pang—these same confections happened to be on the menu one special night last fall—but now I'm aware of a gunmetal glare aimed at me with menace. And the air grows ripe with night-blooming jasmine. And the wildflower centerpieces stir in their pots, ready to stretch off their stems. And just as I jerk away from the latest weapons in Antonia's floral arsenal, deadly scamps of blue spring off the grate of the brazier to set my braids on fire.

# LIII

STOP, DROP, AND ROLL. YOU KNOW THAT—YOU LEARNED IT IN grade school. Ever find yourself on fire, kiddies, just stop, drop, and roll. Trouble is, you find yourself on fire, you can't remember a damn thing you learned in grade school, much less your name, your species, your planet. Plus, what's happening fast and right here feels slo-mo and far away—it takes forever to register that someone is on fire and that someone is you.

So I stand there ablaze as Sin comes leaping across the table, tackling me to crash on the paving stones. He lathes me onto the lawn, smothering Antonia's soldiers of flame. At least, that's what I'll state for the record—I can't really keep up in a linear way. Like when, exactly, do I notice the screams, my mother's loudest among them? When do I realize that acrid smell isn't tar being laid down the road? And when does it all go impossibly still, Sin's full weight on me, his face so close, his eyes frantic?

I say his name.

He says mine.

Next thing I know, I'm in the shower, fully clothed, then soaking wet across the ivory damask duvet of my aunt and uncle's bed. Snippets of my mother's ongoing freak-out—ambulance! emergency room! provincial country doctor!—filter in. As it happens, one of the Leonards' dinner guests *is* a provincial country doctor, and he's already deemed my burns minor—no charring, no blistering. He phones in a prescription for ointment (me) and tranquilizers (Momster). It's cool. I'm fine. The main thing bothering me right now is how badly I'm bound to look like a poodle.

"I look like a poodle, don't I?"

It's late afternoon on Sunday in the backyard of 12 Daisy Lane and I'm surrounded by mostly supportive female energy. Mostly, since Antonia Forsythe is here and her energy has already been tried and convicted in the supreme court of my cranium. Not that I've outright accused her of anything. What good would that do? Antonia has her own agenda and she was heeding it. I need to take responsibility for my own actions: I'm the one who chose to play some very dangerous footsie. I'm the one who let my guard down around the girl hell-bent to kill me. Now, having submitted to Pen's scissors, I've got to take responsibility for that, too.

"Oh, sweetie . . ." is the best my mother can muster.

"You don't look like a poodle," Pen insists, admiring her handiwork. "You look like the kick-ass frontwoman of the most righteous neo-blues-rock-pop-soul-punk band in northwestern C-T."

Marsh nips a cuticle and studies me. "It's . . . different," she says. "It'll take some getting used to."

Antonia says nothing, sitting removed at the picnic table, her own locks hanging limply to veil her expression.

"All right." I huff a brave sigh. "Let me see."

Pen offers a hand mirror. Schizo side part. Choppy spill of tendrils across my right eye. Much of the left side got scorched to cinders, so what could be salvaged now reaches only to the bottom of my earlobe. Hmm. Well. The new length shows off my bone structure, while the long, asymmetrical bangs effectively conceal the red zigzag burn on my jaw. Around back, I finger-comb what feels like a picket fence designed by Salvador Dalí on an absinthe binge. "I don't look like a poodle," I say at length. "I look like I could scare poodles . . . pit bulls too." I pass the mirror back to Pen. "Thanks," I tell her. "You did your best."

My mother slings an arm around me, gives it another shot. "I think you look fabulous, Candice." There's a tense, tight catch in her tone; I'm her only child, and I've cheated death more times than she cares to count. "Up here you might be considered a bit outré, but soon you'll be back in the city, where you belong."

Where I belong. Right. Need I mention whose idea it was to move my ass to Swoon in the first place? I do not. Once Pen leaves, Antonia in tow, and Marsh goes to the Double K, Momster and I whip up a simple dinner and pop in a chick flick. She hasn't said word one about Sin's impending marriage to Pen's strange, awkward friend—clearly she's trying to respect my boundaries. Which I appreciate; I haven't got the strength to spin a convincing story for her.

"Don't forget to contact those moving companies," she reminds the next a.m. Then a hug—careful of my healing skin—and she gets in her rental to brave the long commute.

I sit on the porch alone. Few Swoonies make the daily drive to New York for work, but plenty go to Hartford and Stamford, and soon Daisy Lane is a-purr with luxury vehicles. On the heels of the husbands, the real housewives of Swoon, off to Pilates and pedicures and other idle errands. Everybody in a car—windows up, AC on, satellite radios programmed to preferences, carbon footprint be damned. Momster's right: It will be good to get back to the city—sidewalks, pedestrians, subways, straphangers. Even the noise pollution will feel welcome after this, the country lane gone quiet again, the morning reassuming its lazy summer serenity, the only sound breeze through the trees and the intermittent enterprise of insects.

Except what's that clattering madly up the road? Too tall,

too wild, too magnificent for anything made by man. Sleek and so alive, a symphony of muscles under gleaming ebony hide. Black Jack, with Sin astride, spurring him on. Pounding hooves at full gallop. A stuttering, high-pitched announcement as boy reins beast to a rearing halt. His eyes are lit, his breathing a rasp, as his boots hit the drive with a clunk. He's looking more gaunt than ever. "God!" he says. Followed by "Damn!" And then "Carburetor!"

Yeah, well, a vintage ride can be finicky. So Sin found alternative transport. Every morning since the s'mores incident, at the stroke of nine, he's come to check on my condition. At first, I was barely aware. Then I got all insecure, sweating my appearance. Oddly, today, with Sin about to view my new 'do, my vanity vanishes, my ego gone with it.

He lets the stallion graze on the lawn and mounts the porch steps. I stand to face him. Without a word he sweeps aside my tumbledown bangs. He examines the zigzag on my chin, lowers his gaze to the Rorschach on my shoulder. Then his eyes return to mine.

"You were never more beautiful," he says.

"Yeah," I say. "Right." Then I say, "Coffee?"

Heartened by my resilience, he smirks and nods, and while he ties Black Jack to the rail, I go inside to brew a fresh pot. Sin and I sit in the kitchen, splitting one of Aunt Lainie's fresh-baked muffins, a get-well gift. Conversation flows like, well, coffee. We chat about the cranky car. The fawn at Walden Haven. The incongruous coupling of Tosh and Pen. Even the weather. Briefly we discuss tonight's rehearsal—my first in four days, the last before Chest-ah-Fest. We get around to everything and anything, except the one topic we lack coherent language for. It's almost as if the upcoming show is our last hurrah. Antonia in her lunacy must see it as leniency, a concession—she's allowing Sin to sow this one last wild oat. Once it's over, there'll be no more forestalling the long, slow walk to the electric chair—I mean, altar. And then what? A speedy annulment after Antonia delivers Crane? *If* she delivers Crane? I push the thoughts away. All I want is this morning, this muffin, this moment with my man. Lapsing into copacetic silence, we polish off the pot.

Sin thanks me for the fuel, and then dips into the sugar bowl. "Come with me," he says.

Out on the lawn, he clicks in his throat to alert Black Jack. "His turn for a treat," Sin tells me, placing two cubes in my palm.

Nervously I smile as Sin unhitches his ride, then offer up the squares of sweet. Black Jack gives me an equine grin, his yellow teeth the size of matchbooks, and bows his humongous head. Lips like velvet on rubber, with spiky whiskers attached. A tongue like a totally separate animal, squishy and persistent, that resides inside him. It's all kind of icky and sticky and wondrous, and I love it like a big horse loves sugar.

Mouth against my ear, Sin translates. "He says, 'Mmmm.'" Then it's as though he hits a wall. "Damn it, Dice, I'm no good at this!" he thunders. "You *know* me. I was born for pleasure; I was built for bliss. I'm like him!" He slaps the stallion's rump, gets a whinny of agreement. "Yet here I am, serving a demented sovereign who thinks she owns the rights to my very soul. Her digging roots . . . her clinging vines . . . I want to do the right thing, Dice, I do . . ." His fingers curl to strangle an intangible. "But I want *you* . . . I want *us* . . ."

He has what he wants then, wary of my wounds but with no less abandon, his broad-daylight front-lawn kiss incredible.

"I am so in love with you." He says it to me, through and through me. "Yet if the force of my love is not enough to damn Antonia Forsythe to the hell she has earned, I fear nothing will be."

He is so in love with me. He said it, he did. He means it, he does. Long as I'd yearned to hear those words, much as I ache to return his ardor, I press pause. "Sin, come on—it's the caffeine talking." I reach up to train his face on mine. "Look at me, Sin. Listen to me. You haven't said 'I do' yet—so you don't. You *don't*. Just keep your head, okay."

He holds my gaze an instant longer. Then he says, "Quite right," and is up in the saddle and on his way. What else can we do but get on with our day, do the things that suck up our seconds, murder our minutes, devour our hours. Time, something we *can* kill.

Later, at the studio, music is my medicine, rhythm my salve. I pour my heart out. I give my bandmates goose bumps. I give myself goose bumps. I may be powerless in half a million ways, but I am ready for this gig.

Assuming, that is, I live through tomorrow night. Tomorrow night is bound to be the most challenging of my entire existence. I fear tomorrow night with every fiber of my being, but I will face my fear. A fear, in fact, that has nothing to do with Antonia Forsythe; a primordial fear that precedes Antonia Forsythe. Tomorrow night, much to my dread and against my better judgment, I'm going camping.

# PART IV

# THE GIG

# LIV

BRUISE BLUE SNAGGED A MOST EXCELLENT EIGHT O'CLOCK SLOT on the second night of Chest-ah-Fest. Because the promoters were so blown away by our demo? No, because the promoters are socialists who elected the lineup by lottery. Originally, we were all to drive up the day of, dig the scene, do our set, bask in rapturous applause, and head home. Then Pen and Marsh concocted the camping scheme, presenting it to me as an escape from all I've been through. Like peeing in the woods is this huge reward. I must've been delirious, under the influence of prescription-strength Tylenol, when I agreed.

Me, sleep al fresco in the wilderness? Technically there'll be a tent, a thin scrap of polyester that hardly constitutes shelter in my book. In my book, doors don't have zippers; doors have knobs and, more important, locks. The one saving grace? The tent sleeps three, and Antonia—dear, *dear* Antonia—isn't invited to this girls' night way out. If she wants to attend the festival, she'll have to drive up with the guys and the gear tomorrow, the Pinch Me Round catering van pitching in as tour bus.

"It's going to be great," Marsh assures as we load Pen's car.

I do mean load. Marsh might have been some Girl Scout superstar, merit badges on top of merit badges—she really can start a fire by striking flint against steel. Pen, however, believes a happy camper is a pampered camper, and the Leonards own all the latest top-of-the-line equipment. I'm like, *Yay, Pen!*

Soon as Swoon recedes behind us, my apprehension gains a sort of excitement. Not over the show, though—that's still a day away. Definitely not about sleeping on the ground. More a sense that something awaits me, something inevitable, destined. Of course, my improved mood might simply be due to the growing distance between myself and a certain monstress.

"So, Pen, regale us with tales of you and Tosh," I say. It's the first time us three are together to feast on the details.

"Oh, I don't know," she demurs. "There's not much to tell."

I get her: hesitant to flaunt with Marsh and me mired in romantic miasma. I swivel to the backseat for affirmation, then poke my cousin. "Look, we want to know, blow by blow. Your happiness is our happiness. Chicken soup for the love-lorn soul."

A modicum of arm-twisting and, "Well, I guess it began the day we met—how could I not like a boy who called me Ben?"

Pen says. "Only I didn't want to like him. I didn't want to like anyone. I put a lot of energy into not liking him." She fiddles with her dashboard devices. "Then . . . it was the night Sin came through the fissure with you-know-who. Tosh and I got to talking. Stuff started spilling out. About Sin and what went on around here last fall. Things he did, things *I* did, not nice things." She leaps for the HOV lane. "Then I told him about you, Dice, and how you kept it together, never losing yourself, but never giving up on Sin either. Tosh took it all in and was sort of speechless for a while."

Which must've freaked her out. Tosh has a ready opinion on everything. The silent type the dude is not.

"Finally, he goes, 'She *believes* in him.' 'She' meaning you. 'Always did. Still does. Never quit for a heartbeat. That's some true love right there.' Then he looked at me. 'The kind of love that makes you believe in love. Hard, maybe. Scary, yeah. But true.' And . . . you know how Tosh's eyes change color?"

Uh-huh, I do know.

"Well, they were the warmest honey-gold when he said, 'I want to be in love like that.' I looked straight back at him. And then we knew."

Pen gets a whole lot of "awwww" for that, and then proceeds to prattle on about their first touch and their first kiss and their first fight—yeah, it happened already. She talks so much, so ebulliently, we almost whiz right by our exit.

"Chester!" I yelp, oddly panicked that we'll pass it. "Pen, Chester!"

"Oops!" My cousin slices three lanes, nearly causing three accidents, that could've got us killed three times. Still, we take the ramp unscathed. Clearly, I've got a date with fate in Chester.

Excuse me, Chest-ah—the preferred pronunciation of Connecticut Yankees. A pretty little hamlet all done up in gingerbread buildings and deciduous trees. With a libertarian university nearby and a creative, crunchy-granola vibe, it's an ideal locale for an arts and music jamboree. We pass through the main drag before heading out to the festival grounds, several miles west along Route 6.

Woodstock it ain't, but the area's already starting to bustle and buzz. First we arrive at a midway, where food and craft vendors are setting up. Pen pulls in at the registration booth; we take care of business and pay for our campsite (as "talent," we get a reduced rate). While there, we grab a schedule. Band names alone indicate an eclectic affair, everything from chamber music to doom metal.

"Whoo-hoo, check it out!" Pen points with pride. There we are, Bruise Blue, right there in print.

We roll onto a flat field footed by a nice-sized stage, the sight of which frightens me a little, in that healthy, normal, stagefrighty way. Now up a slight grade that levels off to a parking lot and, beyond that, another field, where tents sprout like brightly colored mushrooms. With impressive speed and efficiency, Marsh transforms a rain slicker and a couple of oversized flexi straws into our domed domicile. Then out come the LED lanterns, portable stove, stocked coolers, air mattress, triple-plush sleeping bags, and canvas folding chairs. Okay, maybe my first foray into roughing it won't be too rough. Glancing around, I note the shack-like bathroom facilities, getting only minimal heebie-jeebies. Farther on, ringing the field, are woods. Dense, deep, dark woods. The kind of woods those Brothers Grimm were so fond of setting their more sinister stories in. Still, the tingle that trips along my recently shorn nape isn't completely unpleasant.

"Dice?" Marsh tags my elbow.

Chest-ah-Fest, here we come.

The promoters, socialist or not, have got to be stoked. Early afternoon and the midway is hopping—not bad for a weekday in the hub of nowhere. A lot of people our age, most of the style statements in the tie-dye-and-hemp vein, but really everything from middle-of-the-road mall mode to thrift-shop geek chic represents. There are also parental types strolling around with tots attached. Plus wandering amusements—a juggler on a unicycle, two chicks that look like twins yodeling over ukulele.

Our first stop is for sustenance, which leans heavy to the

vegan side. "Tofu tacos?" I propose, and we get in line. Squirt enough hot sauce and they're not bad at all.

Music isn't set to start till three, so after lunch we cruise the kiosks hawking art, crafts, jewelry, et al. Other services are available too—face painting, Tui-Na massage, henna tattoos . . .

I stop. A hand-lettered banner: MYSTIC CRYSTAL REVELATIONS. A beautiful boy: wheat-blond hair, tawny eyes, more freckles than a constellation has stars, no shirt. He sits on a hassock in the lotus position. Before him, a display of agate, malachite, other geological specimens purported to have spiritual properties. Behind him, a striped tent that seems cobbled together out of clown pants.

Even though he's no more than twelve, thirteen tops—and despite our own romantic entanglements—he's so cute, Marsh, Pen, and I can't help but tell him "Hiiiii!" in three-part harmony.

Hands in prayer position, he greets us with a *"Namaste,"* while drinking us in like we're one big juice box. Then he calls "Fracas?" over his shoulder. "Someone here for an aura audit."

A what? For who? I have no clue till through the flap comes a girl in a thin, gauzy blouse, faded denim skirt, and dollar-store flip-flops. Other than that, she absolutely defies description, since she refuses to look the same from one second to the next. At first she's merely medium: medium height, medium build, plain brown hair, a couple of pimples dotting a fair complexion; the kind of girl who fills high school hallways across

America. Then the tilt of her eyes, the tint of her skin, the texture of her hair all segue to suggest someone of Slavic descent, followed by Asian, then Middle Eastern, then African, then, impossibly, with a heightening and lightening of bone and tone and tress, the full 180 to Nordic. And in a beat she's back where she started.

"Hello." It comes out in a dozen different dialects, through an enigmatic smile.

Peripherally I notice Marsh and Pen getting a lesson in crystals from the topless cutie-pie, so I meet the gaze of every-girl. There's no doubt: She's the reason for the expectant trickle I've been feeling since we started this trip. So how come I step away?

"I'm Fracas," she says. "Please come in."

Another step, though more to the side. "Why . . . what for?"

"You need your aura analyzed. Even Regis could tell"— she tips her head toward the crystal kid—"and Regis can be obtuse—he wouldn't know poison ivy on his own penis." Her accent finally seems to settle, yet I still can't pin it—it's the voice of anywhere. The way she speaks of the boy, he can only be her brother. "You will have to come in, though; it's near impossible to give an accurate reading in daylight."

Yeah, I know all about the proper light to read by.

Shifting, morphing, Fracas continues. "Yet I already get a sense . . ." With an arm full of bangles, she strokes the space between us. "You're blighted . . . blindsided . . . blocked . . ."

This snags my girls' attention.

"What are you doing?" Pen wants to know, a protective edge in her voice.

"I read auras," she explains.

"She's the best," hypes her bro.

"But your friend seems afraid to learn her true colors."

Pen and Marsh are confused. In their estimation, I don't do fear.

"I'm not afraid," I say. "I've just got enough hocus-pocus in my life."

"Hmm . . . so that's it?" Bracing herself on the table, Fracas leans forward and blows on me. A vague hint of spearmint gum, a stronger sense of probing. Despite her ever-changing visage, the caring in it is constant.

I sigh. "Are you affordable?"

Fracas says, "Very," and lifts the corner of the flap.

Enter the clown pants. Alone.

"Sit anywhere," she invites. "Comfort is key."

You couldn't be more comfortable in a bubble bath. The floor an ocean of cushion. A barely there essence of bergamot. Muted illumination glowing from spheres overhead. Most remarkable, the air inside the tent, as if you've woken up next to someone you love, only instead of his breath falling on your face, it circulates around you. My whole body smiles as I sink, limbs growing longer and heavier, muscles and tendons slackening like the strings of a down-tuned guitar.

"It's nice in here," I tell her.

"Vagabonding makes it a challenge—you want to travel light—but we try."

She asks my name and tries it out a few times. "All right now, Dice, I'll probably babble a bit and seem like I'm spazzing." She twirls her hands in front of her chest. "That's how I release my impressions—like a toddler with alphabet blocks. Then, once everything's out, I'll sort it, explain what I see."

"Babble on," I say. "Full spaz ahead."

Fracas looks at me. Then she un-looks at me. I know that unlook; it's the same way I found the spectral fissure in Antonia's tower room. Makes sense that her focus would fracture and split, since she's looking not at me but all around me.

And Fracas says, "Oh . . ." And then, "Ah." She circumnavigates my cross-legged form, barefoot now on the pillows with a sure, steady tread. Once in front of me again she kneels to part my aura like a curtain, then scoops some up and rubs it on like lotion. "Ooh . . . you're a rainbow . . . a rainbow of blue. Every blue hue. The enlightened cool of the morning sky . . . the clear, royal blue of great power. The colors of calm and sensitivity, loyalty, and valiance. And love, of course, radiant and true."

Only now concern enters her spaced-out orbs. "Oh, but there's deep-pain blue, too, and terrible fear: the swell of the sea in a storm, that murky midnight that's almost black." Fracas emits a soft, sympathetic tsk. "That's where you hide . . . or try to . . . only this enemy . . . you cannot hide. This enemy is close, this enemy is canny, and no matter how deep you go into that blue-black, you cannot get away."

I'm hearing this—and it's making me mad. "Enough!" Waving my hand, I break Fracas from her trance, get her off my aura. "Look, I know I have an enemy, all right. And I know I haven't done much to vanquish her. But not for one single second have I tried to run away."

Fracas composes herself, all of herself, every girl in the world coalescing inside her. "Uh-huh, well, you do have your hands full." She regains her level gaze and trains it straight on me. "But that's not the foe I'm referring to. The one I see you running from is you, Dice. You."

# LV

WHAT'S FASTER, THE SPEED OF LIGHT OR THE SPEED OF SOUND? Damned if I know, but the speed of denial has them both beat.

"You don't know what you're talking about," I tell Fracas.

Who doesn't buy it. "I don't claim to know anything—*I'm no precog.*"

Denial rolls its eyes.

"I just call it as I see it. So why don't I hurry up and finish—you might as well get your fifteen dollars' worth."

*Fifteen dollars?!* denial scoffs. *What a scam!*

"First things first: Blue resides in the throat; it rules the voice. You must be a singer."

Denial stares her down. "Good guess, seeing as I *am* at a music festival." Why is denial such a bitch? More gently, I say, "My band plays tomorrow night."

Fracas looks like a billion girls who just aced their SATs.

"There's a lot of sapphire in your aura, same as your eyes, which shows you're intuitive, sensitive. You feel—big-time—but with you it's all about altruism, compassion, an outward rather than selfish sensitivity." She tries not to stare at my crazy hair, my healing flesh. "As to your own emotions and their . . . ramifications, you can take your knocks . . . and you have."

Around now denial wants out, scopes for a split in the clown pants. But Fracas moves on.

"There's also this bold, clear cobalt and azure, blues beyond sensitivity. Blues of clairvoyance. Blues of power." She pauses before positing another impression. "The combo, the deep and the bright in equal measure, that makes you highly . . . susceptible. You draw spirits like velvet picks up lint."

Denial sticks its fingers in its ears, going, "La-la-la-la-la-la!" at the top of its lungs.

"Around the rim, a cool, pale blue—the calm, peaceful color of faith and hope. Also a sign that no matter what, you'll ride it out, you'll deal."

Denial would agree with that, if denial were listening.

"That brings us to the blue-black. These . . . globules of it. Like oil in water. There's this beautiful clear blue sea of power and purity, plagued with blobs of fear." As if she can predict denial's next defensive feint, Fracas shakes her head, adamant. "Fear of your own abilities. Fear of your own authority. That's what you so desperately want to avoid: your own spiritual prowess." She bites her lip, like she just doesn't get it, then shakes her head again. "And the fear is growing, feeding itself—metastasizing."

Guess what denial does next? Uh-huh, holds its breath. Till it turns . . .

"Dice, you spoke of an enemy. I'm going to assume that he or she has some heavy-duty mojo. Well, I can pretty much guarantee: Until you embrace your true blue awesomeness, you'll be useless against this other force."

Want to know why denial's so fast? Because it thinks if it can get there first, it can blot out the truth. Only truth trumps denial. If someone's in your face, filling you with truth, denial doesn't stand a chance.

Still, I insist: "I just want to be normal."

"Go ahead," Fracas says. "Be normal. Normal and dead."

Huffing acceptance, setting my lips in a line, I face facts. Normal's not going to cut it. Not for me. Not this time, anyway. My aura has a serious oil spill, and if I don't do something about it, the damage will be irreversible. I need more than hope and faith and belief in love. I need to get my good up to the level of Antonia's evil.

Breath comes out of me once more, long, blue breath. "So what do I do?"

"Oh . . . ," Fracas says. "I really don't know."

"You don't know?" Weakly, from afar, denial goes: *What'd you expect for fifteen bucks?*

Fracas turns her palms up. "Dice, I read auras. I don't write them; I don't edit them. The best I can offer is a chakra tune-up, but I'm not a therapist for energy fields; I'm no Doctor Aura." She glides her hands along her thighs and sits on her haunches. "How you go about embracing your power is something you'll have to figure out for yourself."

"Hey, Dice?" Denial again? No, Marsh. "You about done in there?"

And Pen. "Come on, the first band is going on."

My girls, apparently, have had their fill of mystic crystal education.

"In a minute," I call toward the fly of the clown pants, then face Fracas. "So I'm screwed."

"No." She smiles, and the world's girls smile with her. "Let me show you something."

Glances around for a particular pillow, one with a hidden seam. Splits it with a fingertip and delves the stuffing. Comes out with a small suede pouch. Before she even shows me what's inside, I hear it. A beautiful "om" softly intoned by an umpteen choir. As she loosens the string, I can smell it—a remarkable, complex aroma I couldn't identify if I studied it for a thousand years. All I know, inhaling, is how it opens me to every possibility on earth and beyond.

Now Fracas empties the contents into the hollow of her hand. This small, rough stone. A stone that sings. A stone that exudes the essence of ever-unfolding wisdom. A stone that also glows from within. When she extends it toward me, all the girls of Fracas cluster closer.

"Whoa," I say. "What is that?"

The glow in her face is the glow of the stone. "I have no idea. I don't know what it is, where it came from. I don't even know how I got it—it's like I've always had it." She dips her hand and the little rock rolls into mine. "All I know is what it does."

I know bupkis about chakras, but I must have a bunch because that's where I feel the stone, glowing and singing and scenting, sensing, smiling, knowing. This "Ahhh!" comes out of me.

"I call it a journey gem," Fracas says.

My hands like a book, my sights on the stone.

"You put it under your pillow, and you have a dream that's not a dream."

I'm familiar with the state.

"Wherever you go, you'll find out what you need to know."

Only in my version, I never left the bed.

"I loan it out occasionally."

That's just crazy. "You'd trust another person with something so precious?"

"I don't have to. It always comes back."

I tear my eyes off it with effort. "You'd . . . loan it to me?"

Fracas smirks. "No, I'm just showing it to you to torture you."

I match her smirk.

"You'll have to give me something for it, though. You know, collateral."

I don't have much money on me, but maybe between Pen and Marsh I could scrape together a decent deposit. "Let me see what kind of cash—"

"No, not money." She stop signs. "Haven't you got something of real value, something of meaning to you?"

Only intangibles—the memory of yesterday morning: Sin charging up the drive on Black Jack, the words "I am so in love with you," his last delicious kiss. "Fracas, I'm camping," I tell her. "I left the family jewels at home." Except . . . No, I can't. I promised. It's not even mine to give. Yet as one hand closes around the stone, the other goes to the chain at my neck. Silver Saint Michael, with his sword and shield. My borrowed guardian in exchange for a borrowed guide. "Will this do?"

Examining the amulet, Fracas says, "This will do fine. In fact it's perfect." She slides the chain over her head, passes me the pouch. "Only one caveat . . ."

"Dice! Come on!" My best friends. The first band.

"Yeah, in a sec!" I look at Fracas: *Spill!*

"What happens on your journey is yours—your experience, your knowledge, your responsibility," she says. "The more you divulge, the more you dilute."

Yeah, yeah: What happens in Chest-ah stays in Chest-ah. "Got it," I say, burying her treasure in my pocket, then pulling out some bills to pay for the reading. Crumpled tender on the cushion, I tell her thanks.

"You're welcome," Fracas says, tucking Saint Michael into her gauzy blouse. "I'll take good care."

"Di-iiice!!!" Whining in unison outside the clown pants.

I look at the reader, all of her, all the girls in the world. "Yeah," I tell her . . . them. "Me too."

## LVI

feel free to counter with a frivolous "What should I wear?" or the far wiser "Do you *really* know how to get there?" Still, the question is rhetorical since the obvious and only answer is sure, yeah, of course. If you're me, anyway. Ruby wants to party, so I'm in.

Even though I am beyond whipped. It was one long day of rocking out (except for the brief indoor detour for my aura audit), with the last band finishing around midnight. Then we gathered round a campfire and sang corny songs—including "Kumbaya" and something called, I kid you not, "On Top of Spaghetti." Now, despite the creepy moniker of "mummy bag," this sleep sack feels mighty snug—I'm in no great rush to unzip. Yet I lift to an elbow and check my girl. A toga party, judging by her outfit. Ought to be fun.

Quiet as a mummy, I crawl out. And what do you know: I'm

also garbed in a flowing gown, gathered at one shoulder and knotted under my boobs with a braided cord. Too bad I didn't bring my gladiator sandals; instead I scope for my sneakers.

"Come on!" Ruby is so impatient.

"Shhh!" I am *not* braving the wilderness barefoot.

Fuzzily, "Dice?"

See, now she's gone and woken Marsh. "I'm just going to pee," I lie.

"Should I come?"

How much do I love her? "No," I say. "I'm not scared." Another lie.

"Mm-kay." She rolls over, mumbling, "Take . . . flashlight."

I would, only I don't need it. Tonight, the only accessory to her elegant attire, Ruby sports a ghostly luminescence. Did I say accessory? Make that necessity. The sky has a cataract of cloud, the night the color of my worst fear. Ruby grabs my hand and leads the way, winding easily among the tents toward the fortress of trees.

Things only get murkier when we enter the forest, and my typically gabby dead friend is being atypically quiet. The better to hear the snaps, crunches, and fluttering of whatever else is up and around, attending to nocturnal doings. Ultimately, I begin to hear other sounds: strains of music, lilting laughter—party palaver, no doubt. Then, right where the trees seem most impenetrable, a figure emerges and hails us.

"May I see your invitation?" The statuesque girl wears an

obelisk of hair rising straight off her head. She needs the extra height like Forsythe Manor needs the east wing.

Take it away, Ruby. Since here's when she'll go, "We're on the list," or "We're friends of Jamal or Thurston or Dorian," or "Invitation? We don't need no stinking invitation!"

Except Ruby nudges me, and then I know—I've got this. There's a pocket in my gown; lo and behold, it contains a card. A tarot card. The Two of Wands. A force of nature. Energy in action. Making things happen, getting things done. I flash it like an all-access pass.

Which apparently it is. "Ah!" The WNBA wannabe seems impressed. "A seeker of dominion! This way, please."

I flick to Ruby, my smile all: *Success!*

Smiling back, but smaller, she says, "Have fun, Dida."

"What do you mean, have fun? You're not going in?"

"Nah," she says. "Not for me."

The big girl looks off, disinterested, her jaw like a pickle jar—but I get the message: No ghosts allowed. That makes me sad, but Ruby doesn't seem offended. In fact, her smile's turned sweeter, and she seems happy—happy for me, happy for her.

"All right," I tell her. "See you." The instant I step through the trees, I get a pang like I might not, ever again.

Okay, this is the most fabulous party ever. Ever! No, really: I have gotten down at some serious scenes. The red carpet kind

Momster's magazine kicks out for celebs. Impromptu jump-offs when parents unexpectedly leave town. Last year's Swonowa homecoming dance—as awesome as it was awful. Snores in comparison. I mean this party is the *shit*!

First of all, it's in a palace. Except "in" is a misnomer, since walls, floors, ceilings are irrelevant. We're swinging from star shine, the sky suddenly clear and heaven this happening new neighborhood. I cavort across the air (guess I didn't need my One Stars, huh), dancing my ass off. How can I not? The band is phenomenal, thumping at the bottom, swirling at the top. Accordion to zither, every instrument has its part in the celestial rhapsody. And somebody's drumming on a hollow tree. Someone else wails on a massive conch shell. And who knew pebbles swirling in an eddy could sound so cool.

Wherever I turn, mass quantities of the delectable and intoxicating. Parfaits and layer cakes, pomegranates and grapes. My champagne glass is a self-fulfilling prophecy. Only let's forget the ambience for a second; let's talk about this crowd. Okay, in a word: gorgeous! Whoo-hoo, to the big and strong! Shout out, to the slender and lithe! Holla back, to the fat and sassy! Every conceivable shape and hue, and strutting proud. Some opt to be naked. Others dress simply. Still others are done up, *waaaaay* up, the fabrics literally alive, the designs defining creation.

Hey! There's Sin! Or damn, he sure looks like my boy. I jump and wave, and he sees me, smirking his smirk, beckoning to me with . . . not his harmonica; this funny row of narrow pipes. We gravitate toward each other, but with so many fellow revelers wanting our attention, this may take a minute. A minute for so many hugs and kisses, so many toasts and salutations. Oh, no matter! Time is an obsolete concept here. So I sip and sup and scintillate, orbiting ever closer to the one I love. I'll reach his side, dance in his arms, let that beard caress my cheek and find out if it tickles.

On the fringe of the sylvan soiree, I notice a most unlikely guest. A wallflower here? Guess it's true: Every party has a pooper; that's why they invited . . . Antonia. Hair gone to gnarled briars. Long fingers strangling one another like swamp grass. Twin traps with guillotine blades staring out of a gray-green face. I'm smart enough not to engage that gaze, since whether that's the Antonia I know or some kind of avatar, tonight she's more potent than ever, clearly a peer of these people.

Whoa, whoa, whoa—wait! Did I say people? Silly me! These aren't people. I get it now: This is the disco of the deities, and I'm throwing down with gods. Only that's got to be a mistake. Once they find out I'm a phony, they'll toss me right out. Unless they have other plans for my insignificant ass. Here, alone, in the thick of their supreme company, I start tripping on terror. No Ruby at my side. No Saint Michael around my neck. A whole new level of Antonia Forsythe looming. I scope the magnificent multitude for the one who resembles Sin—and there he is. Only my Sin hasn't got horns. My Sin doesn't have hooves. The god's eyes find mine, their jet sparkle familiar but the immortal impunity far surpassing that of the Sin I know, or knew, in any incarnation. And me, without bravado, without protection, the thread count of my bedsheet chic meaningless.

Languorous now, these beatific beings encroach from all sides, in no rush as they serenely close in on me. Edge me in toward . . . is that an altar? As in sacrificial? Damn, if it's a virgin they're after, they'll be disappointed. An elevated alabaster slab, with stairs on four sides and arced on top like a basket handle. I start to climb; I see no choice. My blood is sludge, no: oil. The blue-black platelets of fear Fracas saw in my aura now clogging my veins. Why did Ruby drag me here? Why would such majestics bother with the likes of me? Why does anyone do anything? Wait, I know this: love. Maybe I'm not about to be slaughtered . . . but heard. Maybe I haven't been led to an abattoir but a podium, a cool, smooth soapbox on which to make my plea. What had the giantess said when I flipped my Two of Wands?

"I seek dominion!" I gaze out into the glen of gods, beseech the sublimity surrounding me.

Hey, you want bread, you go to a bakery. You want pastrami, you do deli. I'm in the market for power—my own personal power—and it seems I've come to the right place. For the glorious assembly hearkens to me, and I see no scythes or torches, only pure, exalted radiance.

380

It's spiel or no spiel, and I pick spiel. I start with: "Hi." Then remember my manners: "Thank you for the opportunity to speak at this sacred forum." Then go on, hand to heart: "I'm Dice, and I'm a girl, a mortal girl, and I'm good with that, really. I'm not looking to trade on my soul or upgrade to death-defying status. Except the thing is, I do have certain gifts, gifts I've been ducking for as long as I can remember. Now I'm ready to acknowledge those gifts because, I won't lie, I need them. My life and the lives of those I love are in peril. I want to accept these abilities, nurture them, and put them to use." My eyes roam my judges, my potential redeemers, their faces impassive and their postures impossibly, perfectly still. "Only my powers are dormant inside me; they need a serious kick-start." I open my arms in urgency. "Who will waken the goddess within?"

The consortium is quiet, then comes a rustling, a parting—a vision. Her dress is pearl and her crown is jeweled and she strums this large, ornate lute-type thing. "I am Saraswati," she sings, her voice divine. "I am Hathor, I am Benten, I am Cerridwen . . ." With every name, she subtly morphs—her colors, her costume, her implements—reminding me of Fracas, except not the least bit earthly. "Wisdom, music, art, communication—these I rule. And I sense in you reverence for and talent in my purview. I will waken their power in you." So saying, the goddess places a kiss on my lips.

"Thank you, my goddess." I say this humbly as I can, no

easy feat with the wealth that floods me. "I cherish your gift, and will use it well."

With that she glides off, and for a moment, nothing. Then another goddess approaches, riding a golden stag. Adornments writhe on her body—sequined serpents that they are. Nestled between her parted thighs, a lion cub gives me a sphinxlike stare. "I am Arduinna, Diana, Flidais, Vida . . ." Her countenance, too, evolves with every name she utters. Gently she heels her mount up to meet me. "I rule the forest and am revered by all creatures. I sense in you respect and admiration for my subjects, and will grant you a bond with them all." Leaning close, she presses her lips to mine.

"Thank you, my goddess." Again, striving for modesty as my soul ignites. "I cherish your gift, and will use it well."

As the stag takes to the air, there comes a high-pitched screech from the sort of brutish bird I've seen a lot in northwestern C-T. Iridescent blue-black feathers. A beak like the business end of a pair of pliers. Talons deadly as garrotes. Brilliant eyes that know all and spare nothing. Circling the podium, round and round, then flapping in my face. Not sure how to respond to this, I, well, wing it, raising my arm, elbow crooked, in offer as a perch. The avian—crow, raven, whatever—must approve, landing heavily on my wrist, then bopping up to my biceps.

Quite clearly—not to mention casually—she speaks into my ear. "I'm Morrigan-Persephone-Isis-Hel, et al, et cetera, yadda-

yadda-yadda. I've come in this less-than-formidable form since that's what you can handle."

I say, "Uh . . . okay."

"So here's the deal. I rule death. I rule war. The underworld is my domain and it suits me fine. Human will? Mine to manipulate. Yet I'm the immortal's immortal, reigning over phantoms and demons, worshipped by witches." She puffs the plumage at her ruff, rolling her neck like a boxer before a bout. "These other ladies"—she says it like "losers"—"they're warm and cuddly and their blessings will basically buy you a free lunch. But I'm the one you want, Dice-Dice-bay-bee. I'm the one you need. I embody magic. I epitomize magic. I *am* magic." With that kind of fluent braggadocio, she clearly missed her calling—schooling south Bronx rappers and north Jersey mobsters. "Too bad for you I don't take no mess."

Lunging with her bill, she snatches a hank of bangs near my temple, then pulls the strands all the way taut. Emitting something like a half cackle, half chuckle, she lets go, and the curl boings back.

"All this time, you had my power in you," the belligerent bird continues, "and what did you do? Deny me. Reject me. Piss me off, that's what." She hops along my arm, cocks her head to clock me from a new perspective. Petulant, she preens her feathers, then hops back to my ear. "Now all of a sudden that old blue-black magic ain't so bad."

I shrug, giving the raven a ride. "What can I tell you?"

A cynical croak. "Don't *tell* me shit," she says. "*Beg* me, bitch."

We are eyeball to eyeball in a staring contest. Morrigan Et Cetera is absolutely right: I'm in need of major mojo. Only I never begged anyone for a goddess damn thing, and I'm not about to start. So I say, "No way, lady. I already *asked* you nicely. Look, you should be glad I didn't abuse your power, treat it like a toy or an entitlement. I know the difference between firecrackers and WMDs. And you know what? My arm is getting tired. So are you going to bless me or what?"

With a flaunt of wingspan, she flies off, ululating at oblivion. Then she turns around, comes back, and—ready, aim, fire—unloads on top of my head. Through clenched teeth I mutter, "Thank you, my goddess. I cherish your gift, and will use it well," since I take that as a yes.

# LVII

THE SUN IS AN IMPRESSIONIST PAINTER, DAUBING AND STREAKING his canvas of sky. Or it could just be me perceiving morning in a whole new way. I lounge against a hillside and thrill at the world awhile, and when solitude runs its course, I see what's shaking in the tent. Which is not much. Pen and even Marsh still asleep. Digging for toiletries, I don't worry about making noise.

Marsh is a morning person; she's okay with this. "Hey . . ." She zips out. "This is one for the record books."

Me being up before her, she means. If she only knew. "The whole sleeping-on-the-ground-in-a-glorified-body-bag thing. So how about we check out the swimming hole?"

She undoes and redoes her ponytail in two neat sweeps, no comb or brush required. "What swimming hole?"

"Weren't they talking about it at the campfire?"

She nips a lip. "Not that I remember."

Not that I remember either. "Well, there is one."

"Shut up." Pen, immobile except for her grouchy mouth.

"Sorry, can't," I say. "Too excited. We're going to the swimming hole."

"There's a swimming hole?"

Do I look like an unreliable narrator?

My cousin considers, then snuggles deeper in her sack. "Tell me all about it . . . in about four, five hours."

"No." I crawl her way and proceed to noogie. "You said let's go camping, so now I'm camping and I'm pretty sure visiting a swimming hole is an integral part of the process."

Pen smacks my hands, thrashes to vertical, rubs her face. "What's that in your hair, Dice? Is that . . . *ewww*!"

Marsh has a look. "Bird poo! Lucky you!"

That's what I'm counting on, but I steer the convo back to our a.m. activities.

"I didn't even bring a suit," Pen puts in.

Marsh gives her a goggle, like: *Pen, it's a swimming hole. No tops, no bottoms, no problem.*

Eventually, with help from camp-stove coffee, we get motivated. Me leading, like I know the way. Which I don't. There *is* a swimming hole, of that I'm sure—I'm just not sure why I'm sure. Maybe I stumbled on it coming back from the wingding in the woods, a wrong turn gone right. To be honest, everything post–crow encounter is kind of a blur, the way things get at a party where you're the guest of honor. Once I passed muster with the diva of death, there were no more hesitant rustlings and lone approaches from the gods. The kick-ass corvid took off, and then I took on this dazzling receiving line. Sort of like the bat mitzvah I never had, only rather than distant relatives and Upper West Side snobs, I greeted superior beings, and instead of checks, they shed their grace on me.

True, not every deity had blessings to bestow, but that's fine. Like, am I really concerned about my fertility right now? I am not. And what about the green-tinged, snaggle-headed swamp thing? I figure Antonia has that one on lock, along with any other agriculture-type gods. All I know is, I came out of there amply laden, and while I have no clue what to do with my newly awakened abilities, I'm assuming it will be a learn-by-doing thing. Just keep my eyes open (all three of them) and my senses attuned, and opportunity ought to knock.

"I am sweating my boobs off," Pen complains. "Just so you know."

"Well," I tell her, "you'll really appreciate an ice-cold dip, then."

She huffs. "If we ever find it."

"Really, Dice." Marsh pauses to scan the sky. "We've been hiking at least an hour. You do know where you're taking us, don't you?"

"Uh-huh," I say, forging on, to very shortly afterward announce: "Ta-da!"

My girls reward me with wows.

The path leading to this hidden haven, unlike the treacherous route to the lower falls at Scatacook, is a piece of cake. We bound down easily, Marsh and Pen insisting they never doubted me. Gurgling water calls to us, and we come upon a wide expanse of flat black rock, where we spread our towels and shed our clothes. Guess I win the strip-off, because no way am I going to be the rotten egg. I race toward the ledge and dive.

A move that elicits sharp alarms. Since, after all, I don't exactly swim, much less dive. Yet as I plummet, I remember last night's tête-à-tête with Yemaja a.k.a. Latis a.k.a. Chalchihuitlicue, who sent my water willies down the drain and clued me in on this secret spot. I slice the surface, my spirit soaring higher the deeper my body delves. Down I go, down, down, till I graze the bottom with my fingertips, somersault, and surge up, up, up, to fling droplets into halos that glitter in the sun.

My girls, of course, took the plunge a beat behind. They rise up an instant later, babbling astonished admonishments and praise.

"Dice, are you crazy?!"

"You could have cracked your skull!"

"You looked so beautiful!"

"Weren't you scared?"

388

"We were so scared!"

"Since when can you swim?"

"Since when do you dive?"

I haven't any answers beyond gasps and giggles. They'll come to accept the change in me; right now they're still too stunned to keep on me about it. Together we glide to the side and climb out, and as we bask in the hazy bliss, another memory steals up on me:

—*I am Pan and I am Pashupati and I am Cernunnos and*—

—*I know who you are.*

—*The lord of desire,* your *desire.*

—*Yeah, uh-huh . . .*

—*You doubt it? There lies a pasture not far from here where we can be alone, and I will release you, inspire you, introduce you to passions you never imagined. And you, my lamb, have a vast imagination, I can tell.*

—*Tempting. But I don't think so.*

—*You cannot rebuff me! Gaze upon my phallus!*

—*It's . . . very nice. Really. But there is a boy*—

—*A* boy*?! I am a god!*

—*I know, I know. A bit too much god for this girl. Besides, my boy, he's a lot like you—except for the woolly-bully satyr pants. So think of it this way: When me and him are together—and we will be together—it'll be in tribute to you. Well, not completely, but I bet you'll get some vicarious pleasure out of it.*

—*Vicarious pleasure? I? The nerve!*

—*Sorry . . .*

—*So there is nothing I can do for you? Did you not come here . . . wanting?*

—*Yeah, but I got what I wanted. Come on, don't pout. Look, I could use a ride. To my campsite. It's just beyond the woods . . .*

—*A ride. To your campsite. You are too cruel. But very well, my lamb, I'll shepherd you there. Climb on!*

# LVIII

REALITY SNEAKS UP SHORTLY BEFORE NOON. ADEQUATE CELL PHONE
reception at the Chest-ah-Fest grounds puts Pen back in business
mode immediately. There's a bit of verbal bob and weave with her
boy—Tosh informing her they've been at the festival half an hour
and already unloaded the gear; where have *we* been? She calms
him down, arranges coordinates to hook up on the midway for
lunch. Marsh and I hang back at the campsite, noshing on provi-
sions brought from home, then amble over to the festival.

That's when we notice Sin squiring Antonia through the
throng. Marsh snags my belt loop as the ultimate odd couple
investigates a kiosk.

"Oh, Dice," she says haltingly. "They're looking at rings."

"It's all right," I tell her. "Really."

We put it in gear. "You made it," I say, marching up.

Sin has swapped his PWT for a tapered shirt of apropos

lapis lazuli. The other wardrobe addition: a pair of mirrored aviators. I can't see his eyes, but I see his smile. It's bittersweet and strained, but it's his and he's made it mine. "An interminable journey," he says, "but yes."

A silver-haired silversmith bedecked in her own baubles sits behind her wares. She reminds me a little of Duck and Crane's mom. "You make beautiful things," I tell her, admiring a cuff inlaid with abalone.

"Everything here is silver," Antonia complains. "I should think we'd want gold, at the very least. I read on the Internet machine that platinum is most precious. Oh, and I did espy some lovely diamond-encrusted rings on the Tiffany and Company dot com." She suctions the arm of her begrudging groom-to-be. Behind those shades, he could be anywhere. "Still, I have always believed a simple gold band ought suffice. No cause for ostentation—so long as the love shines bright."

Marsh pokes me in sickened amusement—I bug my eyes at her, like: *Stop!*

Sin, meanwhile, gives an equine stomp. "If there's nothing here you want," he says, "shall we move on?"

"No!" Fiercely she tugs his hand. And presses the place above his wrist like it's his control button—or do I just imagine that? Unwittingly my fingers trace the still unfeeling swatch along my thigh. "Let us choose trinkets for the ceremony. We can find more suitable rings later."

392

The ceremony. The actual exchange of vows. It seems . . . imminent. "So you've set the date," I say numbly.

"Indeed," Antonia says. "This Saturday at four, on the grounds of my erstwhile estate."

*This* Saturday. Mere days away. Between now and then, I'd better be a very busy girl.


The Chest-ah-Fest crowd is as eclectic as Connecticut gets: mostly white, yeah; mostly monied, sure; but all ages, kids to crusties, and that works for Bruise Blue. The way we tinge every tune with throwback blues flavor makes our sound old-school and cutting-edge at once. So it's fair to say they're digging us— and we're feeding on the energy. As musical director, Tosh is popping—he'll flex on drums, then leave the kit to handle more intricate guitar parts while Duck picks up the bass to keep the beat. Still, I'd say it's the vibe between Sin and me that has our listeners on lock.

When he first got with Bruise Blue, we were at odds—that lent an interesting tension to the music. But now we're in it together, and everything we've been through pours into our songs—the passion, the peril, the battles, the bliss. Though I'm the aggressor, my vocals demanding his echoes, Sin is there for every taunt and invitation, licking it up and down and side-ways. Except when he solos—then he's on top, chest and belly muscles pumping wails through his harp. All the while, we're conscious that this is a show, fusing with our bandmates for public entertainment, yet it's intrinsically all about us—Sin and I might as well be deep in that canyon again, the only boy and girl in the world.

In the swirling mass in front of us, a few figures I recognize.

Right up front, big and beautiful, Pen bops around, loose and loud and jubilant—our number one fan. Bruise Blue wouldn't be here if not for her, and despite a few lapses while under the influence last fall, she's always been there for me. She's not the flighty, flirty girl of a year ago, but a woman in the cerulean stage of love, and I beam at her, wishing every happiness her way.

Over there, my new friend Fracas dances with herself and all the girls on this blue planet. Her journey gem, its duty done, is safe in my front pocket, soon to be exchanged for Saint Michael. Can Fracas read the results of my trip in my aura, the blots of fear banished, my deep and my bright in full effect?

Finally, a stilted figure in clothes that don't quite fit, Antonia neither blends in nor stands out. It's like she's a forgotten knapsack, something to be swerved around or accidentally trampled. That I'd feel anything for her besides hate or fear should surprise me but doesn't. It sucks to be her, and always has—all she really evokes in me is pity. Can I show mercy and still not falter, expunge her from our lives forever without sending her straight to hell?

That question, posed to the blessings newly activated inside me, sparks my psyche. Inspired, I take a bow and shout major thank-yous, then ask permission to switch things up a bit.

Taking the mic from the stand, I holler, "How's about a little freestyle?"

They holler back affirmative, and I stroll to the kit. Tosh gives me a look like: *What the?* My smile says: *Just trust.*

"Come on now, Tosh, give me a blues shuffle, huh?" I snap my fingers. "A very basic groove."

He delivers—not too fast, not too slow, just enough high hat, just enough strut.

"And Duck, you know I'm partial to A-minor . . ."

If he didn't, he does now, and he gives it to me, gives it to me good.

"Now, Marsh here—she's my girl. She's knows aaaaalll about it, and she's going to make it clear to you." Losing what's left of her inhibitions, Marsh shakes and shimmies, and they love her for it.

Finally, Sin. Stroke him sweet along the jaw. Place a palm against his heart. Dive into his eyes. Say nothing, till the crowd hurls excitement. I wink at them and say to him, "And you, Sin Powers . . ." Beat . . . "*You* . . ." Beat. "Oh my boy, you know exactly what to do . . ."

At center stage, I feel for my cue and rely on all the gifts within me when I spill . . .

*You and she go back a while*
*She won't let you go*
*She don't speak, she don't smile,*
*She won't let you go*
*She don't talk but she done told me,*
*Yeah, she told me so*
*She won't let you, she won't let you,*
*  she won't let you go.*

Marsh, right up close beside me, bangs that curvy cymbal box against her hip. With her throat arched and her eyes slit and her lips parted. Yeah, uh-huh, that way.

*I don't know you very well*
*But boy I know you good*
*I won't ask but I can tell*
*Just what's in your blood*
*I don't make the flowers grow*
*I ain't no sold-out show*
*And she won't let you, she won't let you,*
*  she won't let you go.*

Now Duck, for all his teddy-bear cuddliness, has been around the globe and around the block. He comes up on my other side with a sure and tender touch on the SG. And behind me, the boy who's got my back as well as my beat puts in slurry harmony just where it belongs to spur my lament to the next level, my voice finding an even more plaintive spot.

*Why she think she got a claim?*
*Why she think she got a right?*
*Now we're caught in her cruel game*
*And she can play all night*
*She got hands and she got eyes*
*Yeah, she got them on the prize*
*She won't let you, she won't let you,*
*    she won't let you go.*

I have no shame. I'm in the open-door confessional. This is my purge, my complete indecent exposure. My ache, my anger, my excoriation. Too intimate to admit, too honest to share, I'm doing it anyway. I have no clue how it works, how blues music, born of pain, can make me feel so good, but it does. My weakness is my strength, and when I feel it, I lay it on the man I'd do anything for. Sin solos to strip his own soul for me—breath believing as his mouth makes a miracle. And when he's done, I take it back, take it all the way.

*So she want to fight a duel*
*She sharpening her claws*

*Don't she know that I'm no fool*
*I ain't no just because*
*Doesn't matter what you said*
*What you promised, what you did*
*She gonna let you go, she gonna let you,*
    *she gonna let you go*
*I can take her, I'm gonna make her,*
    *she gonna let you go.*

Good and done, I send my eyes to the sky. It's that infinite blue of dusk, cool yet warm, far yet close, and host to a filling silver moon. *Hey, moon,* I think, *you crazy, random thing, you don't scare me.* Since just above you, small but a billion times more bright, the first star of evening shines. It shines for me.

# LIX

I KNOW, I KNOW—ME AND MY ARCANE OBSERVATIONS ON THE heavens. Yeah, well, here's another: The cosmos has got to be female, beset by fluctuating hormones and major mood swings. Since once minute you're onstage with your band, wowing newfound fans. The next you're alone in your own kitchen—not even the cat for commiseration—wondering how things got so bad. Specifically, the dismal conditions at 12 Daisy Lane.

I'm pretty adept at ignoring a mess, but this is no mere mess—this is a shambles. Tower of dishes in the sink, clothes and magazines willy-nilly, every surface splattered and splotched. The bathroom is its own special science project, the kind that demands a hazmat suit. Now, I realize Momster was visiting, and the woman definitely has tumbleweed tendencies. Plus, Marsh may have slacked on the tidy tip, having pulled extra shifts at work to snag time off for Chest-ah-Fest. As for me, recuperating from the s'mores incident, maybe I wasn't all that concerned about leaving a trail of crumbs in my wake. Yet all those factors combined couldn't possibly wreak this kind of wreckage. I stand in the middle, mystified, when Marsh walks in from her morning ride.

"I was thinking you might never come back," I tell her. "You saw the place and decided you'd rather live in a barn."

"I did run out of here screaming, 'Oh, the horror,'" she admits, puzzling over a lone sock lying on the sideboard.

"It's like we've been marauded . . ."

That's when Antonia descends with her saccharine "good morning"—and I know. The destruction has got to be her doing. After all, she'd spent some twenty-four hours home alone, left to her own devices. I have every intention of calling her on it, but instead can only gawp. The girl has gone green. All that fun in the sun at Chest-ah-Fest must have tweaked her undead melanin to give her skin a freakish cast (who knew to recommend an SPF of 15 or higher?). So I simply stare as she opens a cupboard, closes it, peers in the basin, and ultimately inquires of Marsh and me, "How am I to enjoy my Cocoa Puffs with no clean dishware?"

Audacity jump-starts my larynx. "Gee, Antonia, I don't know. Though I do believe the larger question is, *why* is there no clean dishware? When here we have the modern miracle of hot and cold running water." I twist the tap to demonstrate. "Soap—and lo!—a sponge. Even"—a quick stride along the counter—

"the ingenious appliance known as the dish*washer*."

"Oh." She sends her glance askance.

"And while we're on the subject," Marsh chimes in, popping open the utility closet. "Here we have the mop, the broom, the dustpan—traditional tools I'm sure existed in seventeen hundred whenever."

I take it from there. "Ever so handy when it comes to spilled milk, cereal, just about anything that doesn't make it into your mouth, as you well know."

Flushing, Antonia's complexion deepens—it's like confronting an olive. "Alas, that is the problem," she creakily confesses. "I haven't the faintest notion how to use"—she flips useless digits toward the cleaning supplies—"such things."

With a soft snort, Marsh drops the dishwasher door. She, of course, has been doing chores since she could toddle and has often had cause for impatience when it comes to Swoon's idle rich. Naturally, she assumes she'll spend the next few hours applying serious elbow grease, but I shoot her a look: *Hold up.*

"You don't?" I'm full of mock chagrin. "Damn, Antonia, what sort of wife will you make Sin if you can't even keep house for him?"

The way she wrings her wrists and skitters her eyes, it's clear she's got a problem. "Gracious!" She touches the sticky counter, pulls back as if scorched. "Surely my Sinclair's the sort of man who likes everything just so."

Surely he's never brought her by the crummy crib he shares with Kurt Libo.

"What shall I do?"

Hooting louder now, Marsh doesn't bother to disguise her disgust.

"We could teach you." This could be fun, though I wonder at the source of the idea—a domestic goddess, or a mischievous one? "We'll tell you what to do, then inspect as you go along to make sure it gets done right."

The hope that enters Antonia's face, it's sort of sad. Does she really think I'd offer aid in any way? Didn't she hear my song last night, my reclaimed commitment to bouncing her butt? "What do you think, Marsh?" I say. "Start her with the bathroom? It's particularly gross in there."

Either Marsh fails to grasp the humor in this or she believes demonic ineptitude will just make matters worse. "Why bother?" she says. "Antonia, you have money; just get a maid."

Which of course makes sense. Yet Antonia's reaction is peculiar—to me, intriguingly so.

"A maid?" The prim way she latches her neckline, you'd think Marsh suggested she hire a hooker to accommodate Sin's manly needs. "I will have no maid in my home."

"Don't be silly, of course you will," I say dismissively, my precog engine revving, both barrels. "You can afford a full staff. A strong young girl for the heavy-duty stuff. A top-notch cook—Tosh knows this chick who trained in Paris; he'll hook you up. Oh, and a laundress to ensure Sin's T-shirts are starched and ironed precisely—"

"No!" the monstress almost shouts.

"But a lady of your breeding is naturally inclined to leisure." I cast my glance. "I mean, look at this place—you didn't even think to lift a finger." I turn to Marsh. "Okay, fine, *I'll* do the bathroom."

Antonia reaches for my arm. "Dice, please—do allow me, instruct me. I'm sure to enjoy humble duties, and even if I come to find them . . . tiresome, that would surely be preferable to having sneaky, skulking servants about."

I take back my arm, crossing it and its partner over my chest.

"You don't know what those people are like," she says. "Why, my father had to dismiss a cook once—some indelicate behavior with the butcher."

My unconvinced stare prompts her to continue.

"And the deceit, the skulduggery . . . oh, the very thought of that vile Mae Molly gives me the vapors."

"Ooh!" I nudge Marsh to feign interest.

"She must have been terrible," my girl plays. "Do tell, Antonia—did she steal?"

"Oh, indubitably, though I never caught her red-handed, vixen that she was, so cunning. Yet her treachery went beyond pilfering the silver; she'd snatch your very soul if she could."

A ripple of distaste courses through her. Marsh and I watch, rapt.

"Only no one would suspect; indeed I found her most congenial myself—at first. Her appearance abetted her knavery—some would call her pretty, I suppose, and she was . . . buxom. She had my mother wrapped around her finger, that's for certain. You see, Mae Molly was our lady's maid; ostensibly her duties included sewing, attending the toilette, assisting with the social schedule. Yet in truth it seemed she existed to amuse my mother. I would hear them laugh together, the Lady Anne often exclaiming over Mae Molly's wit. And of course she could sing . . ."

Antonia says it as if the talent were a curse, then attempts to correct herself with her forced excuse for a smile.

"I, however, had plenty of menial tasks for her, particularly once I began to sequester myself in the east wing." Here she seems to search for words. "There was a period—a phase—when I did not speak or venture much beyond my garden and was rather . . . dependent on the maid. I'd have her carry meals to my room and manage my chamber pot."

I've been back and forth from the east wing, a long walk with a loaded tray or bucket of you-know-what.

"I also relied on her to run errands: to the general store, the apothecary, the stationers—I'd become a prodigious lady of letters. Oh, she'd dash into town at the drop of a pin, that one."

In fact, I can envision her, sashaying around with her tiny

waist and switching hips, her cap so carelessly tied. I can also imagine the admiring glances she no doubt garnered from men and boys alike, one end of Swoon to the other.

"She did my bidding well enough," Antonia says. "But one day, after I'd cut myself pruning, I ran up to wash, when I heard Mae Molly in my room. Speaking aloud, some foolish game, I assumed. Rather than intrude and embarrass her, I decided to come upon her softly—that's when I spied what she was up to." A small shudder at the memory, and the young mistress goes on. "She'd littered all my dresses across the bed, and while holding one of my favorites against herself, assumed the role of my mother's confidante. 'Poor dear Lady Anne,' she said in a false cultured accent, 'my pity upon you—having such a sniveling, bumbling daughter. Perhaps if you were to send her away, some school that rigorously instills charm upon young ladies?'"

Okay, I'm beginning to see why Antonia's so servant abhorrent.

"She discarded the gown, chose another, and then began to pretend she entertained a suitor. Here, her manner changed very much!" Sensibilities sullied anew, Antonia again clutches her collar. "The things she said—the most salacious things! Acts she intended to . . . perform on the man. Deeds she desired him to do upon her. In the most deplorable detail. Even you would have found it obscene, Dice."

Even me, huh? She must've been something, that Mae Molly.

"Distraught, I ran in and threw myself at her. We tussled . . .

tangled. She was strong, and moreover terribly tricky. She gasped and pointed over my shoulder, and when I turned she got ahold of my hair, yanking out a skein."

A ho *and* a dirty fighter. Gracious!

"All the while she giggled, like this was jolly sport. How long it went on, I know not, but at one point she seemed to have had enough, shoving me down on the mountain of dresses, holding me fast with her knees and hands. ''Tis evil to peep, Miss Antonia,' she said in her own coarse brogue—if you can imagine *she* accusing *me* of wrongdoing! 'Ye shall burn in hell fer it!' Then she got up, turned on her heel, and left me there.

"Shocked though I was, I ran at once to my escritoire. A note to my mother was in order, exact without being indelicate, telling her what had transpired. Yet when I found the Lady Anne in the salon, Mae Molly was already there. I stormed in and presented my note, watched as my mother read it—and then the two of them fell to laughing, almost to the point of tears. Suffice it to say no action was taken against the foul creature. She was there in Forsythe Manor on my own dying day."

Catfights, subterfuge, hysteria—contemporary television has nothing on Swoon in the 1760s. A girl of Mae Molly's distinction has my psychic sense pinging, so much as I'd enjoy the spectacle of Antonia hunkered down with the toilet brush, I leave Marsh to supervise home ec and set out to dig up a little more data on the Forsythe lady's maid.

## LX

GAS IS IN FACT FOR SALE AT LIBO'S GAS & LUBE. THERE'S ALSO A mini-mart where you can purchase cookies and condoms in dusty packages dating back to 1987. Basic car maintenance (the as-advertised lube job, plus oil changes, tune-ups, and such) are less readily available since Kurt's father had a paralyzing stroke last winter; Kurt doesn't stoop to such tedium. For the most part, the garage is a front for Libo the younger's drug operation and a base for his true love and main means of support: auto restoration.

There's Kurt now—visible from the shins down, the rest of him cursing under the classic Cutlass I know well. Hopping off my bike, I try to slip past him, but even deep in mechanical concentration, Kurt can scent a female vibe. He rolls out on that wheeled contraption called, appropriately, a creeper and blocks my path.

"Heyyyy, Dice." Still prone, to afford himself that angle on my crotch.

I block his view with my handlebars. "Sin around?"

Kurt sits up. "Still sacked out like a rock star, probably. Me being a working stiff, I'm up and at 'em." He twiddles a ratchet around his thumb. "Trying to get this bitch up and running for the big day."

The big day. I'd like to ram that ratchet so far up his left nostril it comes out his right ear. "I'm going to go see him, if that's all right with you."

"Go ahead. Give him a big, wet, juicy one for me."

If only he'd creep back under the chassis where he belongs, but I know he'll be catching my rear-view stride. I make it wiggle free and take the iron stair. Firmly, I knock.

No answer, but the door's unlocked, so I go in. My boy's on the middle of his mattress, cross-legged, eyes shut, breathing long. Wonders really will never cease. First I dive off a cliff, and now Sin Powers practices meditation. It's more than rude to interrupt someone seeking inner peace; it's potentially disorienting, so I carefully lower to the edge of his bed and try to chill until he's done. Which isn't easy. Sin's in black socks, tightywhities and the slightest trace of smile. Shame on me! Here he's connecting to his higher self, and my mind's in the gutter.

A few minutes pass, and he finds me there. He says my name, I say his. We agree that it's good to see each other.

"To what do I owe the pleasure?" he asks.

"Can we take a walk or something? This place icks me out." It's true, the memory of my last and only visit is a grease stain on my consciousness, but apparently Sin laid down the law. I wouldn't want to lick the tiles or anything, but the apartment is clean, especially compared to conditions at 12 Daisy.

"Of course." He slides into jeans, buckles his belt, pulls on boots and PWT.

The Gas & Lube sags forlornly on the southern edge of town. Go straight and you're on the road less traveled to Norris; turn left—as we do—for a country lane to nowhere. Purposefully I keep just enough distance between Sin and me. It's our first occasion alone since he spoke of love on my front lawn, and much as I'd enjoy holding hands as we amble—much as I'd prefer to swap ambling entirely for kissing—I need to do this. Still, I stall, prolonging the precious just-us-ness.

"You seem different, Dice," he says, stroking his chin in appraisal.

Dare I share the journey gem, the deity throw-down, the surge it instilled when I sang? So tempting to tell the one I love, but what had Fracas cautioned: The more you divulge, the more you dilute. Not till I've put my skills into action, successfully or not, can I unveil their source, even to him.

"Amplified yet not louder," my boy goes on. "Magnified yet no larger . . . Enlightened, then?"

"Me?" I counter. "You've transformed Libo squalor into a zen den and I'm enlightened?"

A half smirk of acknowledgment. "Remarkable what a mantra and a can of Lysol can do. But truly, ever since Chester . . ." Maybe he senses my hesitance, and he respects that. "Perhaps it's just the haircut beginning to settle in."

I rake my fingers through it, an ideal segue. "So . . . Sin . . ." I bring it up casually, like she was a mutual friend from seventh grade. "Do you remember Mae Molly?"

"Mae Molly!" I thought I'd seen it all when I saw Sin Powers meditating—now I see Sin Powers blushing. "*The* Mae Molly? Mae Molly O'Rourke? Well, I . . . how do you . . . of course I remember Mae Molly," he finally spits out. "There wasn't a swain in Swoon she failed to impress."

Sin looks off to the copse of trees a few yards ahead; then he looks back at me. "Dice, when you and I first met, face-to-face, hands in hands, I told you of my life, what led me to this town."

It was late on the night of the Williams brothers' party. Sin and I under the fateful ash tree on the Swoon village green.

"At one point, I proposed to veer off on a tangent. 'Spare me the details,' you said. 'Just paint the picture in broad strokes.'"

That's right, I did, with a twinge that embarrassed me. After all, I didn't even know Sin—why the jealousy? Now, approaching the shade of the copse, following the questions as always, I suppose I ought to learn the answer to the one he so roguishly posed: "Shall I regale you with the tale of how I lost my virginity?"

He'd been headed west. Some hundred miles east, his home and business lay in ashes, but Sinclair Youngblood Powers was making peace with that and had set his sights on the frontier. A pipe dream, perhaps—for he was down to his last coin when he entered the tavern in a town called Swoon and met Elijah O'Rourke.

"You are a smithy, Sinclair? What luck!" Good fortune for the knacker—the fellow who made harnesses—for he'd recently lost his partner. "It has been a long month since Emmett Welsh keeled over at the forge, God rest his soul. But you would do well here, lad!" O'Rourke laid a fatherly hand on the young man's shoulder. "The farrier shop is all set up. You need only hang a shingle."

"An attractive offer, but I am headed west," Sinclair explained, firm of conviction if not finances. "I've heard well of Ohio."

The knacker nodded agreeably. "Aye, many horses need shoes out there." He drained his tankard and told the traveler, "But you must be tired and hungry this Sunday. Come have supper at my home, stay the night, and start fresh in the morning."

How generous of O'Rourke, who had a welcoming wife, a passel of boisterous offspring, a well-spread table, and a full keg

411

from the tavern. Most of all, O'Rourke had a niece—she just arrived from Ireland.

"I am most happy to know ye, Sinclair." A study in contrast she was: curvaceous of figure with small, childlike hands and feet. Jet tresses against fair skin. A heart-shaped face with round, wide, lash-lavished eyes, but the eyes were a cool celadon, a changeable, challenging color. Sculptured lips that looked demure when pressed, yet when parted, revealing many tiny, bright teeth, showed a mouth that knew pleasure.

"And I am most happy to know you, Mae Molly."

Had O'Rourke enacted connivance when he invited the stranger to dine? Or was it fate that brought the newcomers together? There is no answer save to say that by the time Mae Molly sang an old Gaelic tune while clearing the table, a deal was struck. Sinclair Youngblood Powers would stay awhile.

An enterprise flourished and a courtship kindled. The couple would meet in the blacksmith shop by night, the forge cooling, their passions flaring.

"Kiss me here," she would whisper, and he would obey. "Ah, like that—just like that."

She was his first kiss. He was her best kiss. Sometimes he would experiment. Sometimes she would direct. As long as they kept to kissing, they got along fine.

Trouble was, Mae Molly talked too much. For one thing, she schemed. Always about how Sinclair might improve his station—ingratiating himself to the town's founders, becoming active in the Congregationalist Church. She had her own sights set, as well—easy work in a wealthy house, inveigling her mistress.

For another thing, she promised. Mostly along the lines of "I shall make a man of ye, Sinclair." Allusions to a treasure between her legs, a secret honeypot that would be his alone. A treasure that would cause great pain to give, but pain she'd suffer gladly. A treasure that, once plundered, would forever renew—he could come, again and again, and find his strength there, his very reason for being.

"When?" he would ask, his mouth demanding, his eyes deep as mines.

"Soon," she would swear, her cool eyes glittering, her mouth a trophy cup.

Until came the night he took what she promised. She did not stop him. Rather, she clung and ground and bucked in wild, mad rhythm. With her throat arched and her eyes slit and her lips parted, indeed. Cooing and sighing and then crying out, then cooing and sighing again. Mae Molly hadn't exaggerated—this was a treasure!—and Sinclair so young to be the recipient. Yet when it was over, she slapped his face so hard he feared a tooth or two might have made it to Ohio without him.

"You have ruined me," Mae Molly said.

Still, on the next Sunday, when Sinclair came to O'Rourke's

for supper, Mae Molly seemed in fine form as she entertained another. Some pasty, paunch-bellied, chinless lad he recognized— the clerk at the general store. Stealing a moment by the hearth, he urged her to expound upon this guest.

"He is not but the clerk; he is nephew to the owner and possible heir." This she told him tightly, then adding a twist to her chiseled lips, "Not a half-breed savage nor bastard of ill repute!"

It was the last Sunday Sinclair would spend at O'Rourke's table.

And the last he saw of Mae Molly till his commission at Forsythe Manor—apparently she'd achieved her coveted position there. When Sinclair arrived to show the magistrate designs for the garden gate, she passed him in the foyer. He greeted her with subdued courtesy, but she bore through him with her glacial green stare as if they'd never tarried. Once his labors began in earnest, she bustled to his temporary forge.

The rendezvous was brief. "Ye don't know me, ye hear?" Mae Molly hissed. "Ye do not come up to the manor, front door nor back, for any reason—I don't care if ye torch yer fool head off! I'll not have the likes of ye meddle in the life I'm spinning. And if ye dare speak to me ever again, I'll cry rape—don't think I won't, by God!"

"Do not flatter yourself," he told her. "It is my fortune to have found true love—and to recognize it as such, compared to the besotted sickness you infected me with. I bid you luck with your avarice, and may you bid me same with my happiness."

He raised his chisel and returned to his work, and when the clump of damp earth she'd hurled hit his shoulders, he did not turn around.

There are various ways to retire virginity. It can slip away—the proverbial "it just happened!" You can exchange yours with a trusted friend's, find out together what the big deal is about. You can blast it to smithereens, as Sin did—infatuated, obsessed, madly in lust. Or if you're lucky, if you're in love, you don't "lose" anything but a tough scrap of skin a tampon no doubt already dispensed with and you gain so much in body, mind, and soul. I was lucky like that. Incredibly lucky. I think I still am. So after Sin finishes his tale, I very deliberately put my arms around him and lay my cheek to his chest. That's how lucky I am.

Then I slant my eyes at him. "So you never thought, not for a second, that your . . . acquaintance with Mae Molly and this craziness with Antonia might be, oh, I don't know . . . *connected*?"

"Connected?" He releases me to ponder this. "Why, no, not at all. Antonia was so young, and of high station, while Mae Molly was older—she must have been twenty at the time—and, well, in the terms of the day, a commoner. What connection could they possibly have?"

I shake my head. Of course he doesn't see it. He wouldn't, couldn't, him being male. Women comprehend the physics of life: for every action a reaction, a relation, a ramification. We come with internal stew pots, inner kitchen sinks—we know it all goes into the mix. Men are built with hatches, drawers, shelves—they separate, compartmentalize. In the summer of 1768, two women lived in the same house, with strong feelings for the same man. To that man's mind, they may as well have lived on different planets. To this woman's mind—psychic leanings totally irrelevant—they were involved, had to be. Now, by goddess, I've got to figure out how.

# LXI

NEXT STOP, THE LIBRARY, WHERE IT'S MORE LIKE THE MORTUARY—
the typical Swoonie's interest in literature must wane as summer progresses. Yet while I devote the next idle hours to how
a particular mistress-servant situation applies to our current
predicament, I come up empty. One recourse might be to
probe Antonia more about her maid—maybe she and Mae
Molly openly discussed Sin, and by openly discussed I mean
further hair-pulling fisticuffs. Tread with caution if I go that
route; Antonia won't appreciate me poking around—she's just
as likely to shut down or flat-out lie than supply any solid info.

I hardly expect her to greet me with much enthusiasm,
either, if she's been on cleaning detail all day. Yet as I turn
up the drive, someone's obviously glad to see me, chasing my
wheels in a tricolored collage. I toss the bike and call to her.
"Come here, you little furball!"

It's been days. Which isn't unusual. RubyCat appeared out of nowhere, a starving stray, and while she made herself right at home, she'd no way acclimate to full-time house-cat status. Believe me, I tried—all the animal websites advise against letting your pet roam free, but when R.C. wants out, she wants O-U-T, vociferously, destructively. Now she comes and goes through the flap—usually with clockwork regularity. Only whenever *I* take off (the rare weekend in the city, my recent sojourn to Chester), she'll disappear for the same stretch, like it's payback. Fortunately it's all good when we hook up again, frolicking on the lawn.

"Me! Me! Me!" she says.

And I'm like, "Huh?"

And she's all "Hey! Me! Ma! Pet me! Now! Ma! Pet me!"

This is bizarro. The feline brain being the size of a lima bean, it's easy enough to grasp its wants and needs, be that a sample of your turkey sandwich, a rub under the chin, or to be left alone, please. Only RubyCat actually addresses me, and here's what's weirder: It's funneling straight into my conscious. Never before have I experienced ESP in that government-secret-weapon kind of way (if I had I would've tailed certain teachers and notched more A's). Now this cat is coming in loud and clear—

"Maaaaa! Me! Pet meeeee!"

All right, all right!

"Not therrrrre! Here! Mmm. Mm-hmm! Prrrm-prmm-prmm . . ."

Guess I hit the spot since she lapses into purr mode and all I'm receiving are motorized murmurs of content. Just to ensure it's not some psychic hallucination, I ask, "So RubyCat, what you been up to?"

"Hmm? Me? Oh. Pop, Pea—hee-hee-hee!"

It takes a second, then I get it: Popcorn and Peanut are the Leonards' excitable dogs; R.C. gets off on tormenting them when they're tethered in the yard.

"Rabbit—fast, grrr," she continues her travelogue. "Mouse—snack, yum. Sleep. Repeat."

This is so cool! Useful, no—but definitely cool, definitely a goddess gift. As I send up appreciation to Arduinna/Diana/Whoever/I Forget, R.C. senses my wandering mind and, insulted, makes for the flap.

I wheel my bike to the shed and let myself in the back door. Washer and dryer both buzz industriously. The kitchen is spotless, as is our dining area. Here, by the telephone, a message in curly cursive: Pen, Bruise Blue, party, Wick. On to the living room, also picked up and slightly (irritatingly) rearranged, where I see Antonia in the bentwood rocker, bowed over my laptop.

"The house looks great," I tell her. "Thanks."

"You are most welcome. It isn't difficult, housekeeping. I

suppose that's why the lower classes so often do it."

Could she be more ignorant? "Actually, Antonia, the lower classes, as you deem them, are relegated to unskilled labor because they lack education and opportunity, largely due to efforts by your so-called upper classes." Just so she knows. Not that she cares.

"Oh . . . indubitably," she says, fixed on the monitor. "I didn't do the room you and Marsh sleep in, by the way."

The room we sleep in—how not subtle, like she already owns the place. I step behind her chair to scope her online viewing. More Tiffany bling? Uh-uh, the screen displays a stately hotel, whitewashed and columned, striped awnings on the windows.

"Lovely, is it not? Alas, it is fully occupied for the season." She sighs, clicks, and searches. "I simply must find something. The house won't be vacant till next month, and Sinclair and I certainly cannot live apart once we are husband and wife."

Vacant. I'd like to vacant her, with a vacuum cleaner. The power I felt post–journey gem is starting to deflate. So I can communicate with my cat—whoo-hoo. Antonia still seems to be getting everything she wants—my house, my man—and even has the nerve to trawl my Internet machine to reserve her honeymoon getaway. Trying my damnedest not to flounce, I exit for the porch, taking refuge in the glider's sway.

Yeah, except no peace for me, apparently, due to a noisy crow nearby. True, crows are typically loud enough to get your attention in a coma. Difference is, I understand the shrieking plain as day: "Casualty! Casualty!"

A second scream: "Location?"

"Catalpa! Catalpa!"

As the first crow replies, I spy him, perched high in the sugar maple that gives 12 Daisy Lane such vibrant curb appeal come fall.

Another caw, for: "Inspect and report!"

The first crow zooms across the road to the Leonard place, host to a massive catalpa (as a kid, I called it the string bean tree)—might an injured bird be lying underneath? I hurry to investigate and find two crows patrolling and, between them, a smaller one, toppled over and very still. Now, with a scream that's only a scream, a fourth bird dive-bombs his fallen comrade. Total ninja move. The other crows cheer as they, too, go on the attack.

Not on my watch. "Hey!" I'm flapping, I'm stomping, I'm yelling—basically making an ass of myself, interfering with the law of the jungle.

"Get lost, girlie!"

"Yeah, get out of here!"

"No! You get out. Shoo! Shoo, you sadistic dickheads!"

The trio departs, minimally—winging into the catalpa to observe from above. Either they're stone-cold killers, or the small bird is already dead and they're merely carrion cannibals.

On my knees I peer at the broken black blight on the otherwise pristine green. I don't see any blood. I don't see any breathing, either. Fortunately, I hear, faintly, "Don't . . . gape! Help . . ."

"You're . . . alive?"

An eye blinks open—a bright blue eye. "Not for long, at the rate you're going. Come on, gently—scoop from under . . . watch the wing, I think it's busted. Good, okay, now get me out of here before the big boys finish the job."

I rip into the Leonard house, hollering. Nobody home. What did I expect with no cars in the drive? Crap. The bird trembles against my chest.

"What's going on?" he wants to know.

"I'm thinking . . ."

"I know that. I hear you. What are you, some kind of witch?"

Not my favorite term, but never mind the semantics. "Yeah, I guess."

"Well, can't you heal me?"

"I conceded to witch, not orthopedic veterinarian." But I bet I know where I can find one. Cross the street, up the stairs, into my room. R.C., queen of the duvet. Great.

"There's a cat in here!" the crow croaks.

"Bird?" From guess who. "Ma . . . *bird*?!"

I yank a drawer and lay the winged wounded on a pile of tees, then stare down R.C., who can go from zero to pounce in six seconds. "Don't even think about it," I warn with a narrowed gaze. Then I hit another drawer for the huge paisley scarf Marsh has dubbed my tablecloth, and tie it into a sling.

I check the crow—respiration rapid, delicate breast heaving. "Does it hurt?"

"Only when I laugh," he says, and claps his blue eyes closed.

The harridan of Walden Haven may not recognize me when I burst into her office, but peering at my cargo, she approves my actions.

"The doc's on-site today," Alice Boyle says. "Follow me."

Once the vet takes the crow, I ask to wait for his diagnosis. Alice grunts (her version of pleasant), so I go outside, scoping Sin. Who's busy, I see, with one of the less appealing chores of the wildlife rescuer—but hey, shit happens . . . lots of it, apparently. So I wander on, hoping to say hi to . . . what had Sin named him, Luther?

At first the large, woodsy enclosure seems absent of animals. Makes sense—forest fauna probably lie low at midday. Still, I'm fiending for a peek at the baby deer, so I slip in, my tread and even my breath careful, quiet. To no avail, since the second I'm inside I make an unwitting leap from surreptitious to celebrity. Nests and burrows begin to rustle, flutter, buzz. One by one the denizens of this halfway house to the wild shyly show themselves.

Except for Luther. After all, we've met before. Bounding my way like a ballet ingenue, he hails me: "Dear lady!"

Of course I grin at the greeting—Sin's influence, clearly. "Deer boy!" I pun. As I lean forward, beckoning, the fawn . . . well, he *bows* to me, extending his reedy forelegs along the ground, placing his head humbly between them. It's a little disconcerting, actually. "Luther," I say, "cut that out," then try, "uh . . . please rise."

The fawn obeys and comes in for a nuzzle, his wet nose a peeled grape against my palm. Which encourages other creatures to venture closer, and soon I'm surrounded. Here a hare, there a skunk. A brick-red, barrel-chested robin alights on my shoulder. And hullo, what's that, a pineapple with its crown cut off? No, a turtle slowly yet boldly scaling my sneaker. Respectfully they inspect me, ebullient chatter bouncing in my brain. What a freak I must seem—a human with communion, simpatico, a beastie bond. All Arduinna et al's doing, and as I offer the goddess major gratitude, I hear another voice—this one outside my cranium.

*"Dice . . . ?!"*

The astonishment on my boy's face goes all the way to his hair follicles—scruffy whorls lift an inch off his head as he stares from the other side of the chain link. "Later, Luther," I say with a quick chuck under his chin. "See you, guys," I tell the rest. Then I let myself out and trot up to Sin.

For another beat he's simply agog. Then he says, "And I thought *I* was good with animals."

Again I debate giving details of my overnight in Chester. On one hand I want Sin to know me, everything about me, but on the flip wonder if certain enigmatic elements ought to exist between people in love. Stalling, I fill him in on the crumpled crow and, as I do, arrive at a compromise.

"I had a dream about you," I tell Sin. "Except he wasn't you. More like your twin, especially now." I stroke a knuckle along his bearded jaw. "You know . . . Pan?"

He does know, and knowingly he nods. "It was a pleasant dream, I presume."

"Uh-huh. Sort of like those dreams that aren't dreams we used to share."

"I see." His smirk is warm with mirth. "And did you and Pan do the sort of things you and I would do?"

Lifting my chin, I draw out the moment. "He wanted to, and I was curious. I mean, he's a god and all . . . but I—"

We're interrupted by a piercing whistle. Alice Boyle waves us toward the clinic. My escapade on pause, Sin and I sprint.

"This is one lucky fledgling," the veterinarian says.

*A baby!* I think. Must be why his eyes are blue.

"He's had a shock—probably flying low, crossing the road, got sideswiped by a car. That alone might have killed him if you hadn't acted quickly. But the wing isn't broken, only sprained. Couple of days he'll be good as new."

# LXII

WHICH IS HOW I CAME TO PLAY FLORENCE NIGHTINGALE TO *Corvus brachyrhynchos.* The vet affirmed that he's indeed male and, while still a fledgling, no baby—about eight months old, a teenager in bird years. I'll call him something romantic, like Romeo. Or, no, Cromeo. Or, no, is that too corny? Can you be too corny for crows—they love corn, right . . . hence scare-crows?

"I already have a name," the bird informs from his well-appointed cage—a necessary precaution (if he tried to fly too soon, he could reinjure himself, and of course there's RubyCat to consider). Walden Haven hooked me up, Alice Boyle driving Sin and me to 12 Daisy in her heap, drilling in the particulars of bird care and maintenance. Now, the following a.m., we sit together on the porch, me with my coffee mug, he with his seed cup.

"So what's the deal—are you always in my head?"

"Look, lady, I don't know how it works," he says with a caw. "I never communed with a human before. Or are witches human?"

"I'm human," I say. I don't add aloud: too human. "So what is it? Your name."

He screeches. It doesn't translate.

"That won't work. And forget Cromeo; total cheese. How about Edgar, as in Edgar Allan Poe? He wrote a poem about a crow . . . well, a raven, but same thing, right?"

"Wrong," he corrects, feathers ruffling. "But close enough— we're cousins. As to Edgar, it'll do."

We keep out of each other's skulls awhile, which has me reflecting on the previous evening. After getting the passerine patient settled in, it was time for dinner. So there I was, reluctantly demonstrating spaghetti sauce with basil and tomatoes from the patch while Antonia took notes and Sin sat in front of CNN, venting his frustration by yelling at the anchor dude. Good thing my cousin came by. If it had been just the three of us pushing down the pasta, I might've choked. Pen kept it all chipper and civilized, discussing Bruise Blue's premier paid gig at our kinda-sorta friend Caroline Chadwick's birthday party next week. Of course the convo crumpled when the significance of next week hit. Next week, maybe Crane Williams will be back on lead guitar. Next week, maybe Sin Powers will be out celebrating his recent nuptials in some seaside hotel.

Miserably, I sigh.

"What's eating you?" Edgar asks. "And speaking of eating, this seed sucks. How about digging me up a nice juicy grub or worm?"

"Since you asked, I'll tell you: My boyfriend's getting married in two days and guess what, not to me, so you might say I'm upset. Not that it isn't great having you here, gabbing away, but I was hoping my magical chops would go above and beyond this Doctor Doolittle routine."

The phone rings inside; I hear Antonia's tepid greeting.

"Oh, indubitably, Justice Rodgers. Yes, that is correct—the Williams estate . . ." Every nettlesome word seeps through the window screens as she finalizes the affair. "I believe a civil ceremony ought suffice." The judge must turn on the charm since Antonia next responds with her titter. "Yes, very well. A modest reception will follow—my intended and I do hope you'll be able to join us . . ."

Her intended. *Yeesh.* That mincing, persnickety manner really does nauseate me. Bet it bugged the crap out of Mae Molly, too. Not that I'm defending that sly, avaricious bit of bitchery; just wondering—no doubt she had ways of repaying Antonia for every trip down those east wing stairs with a full chamber pot.

"Yoo-hoo, lady!" Edgar taps his bill against the bars. "How's about some protein here?"

Exasperated, I glare at him. "I have a name too, Edgar. It's Dice. And you know what? I've come to the conclusion that crows aren't very nice." Articulate, yes—in fact, he makes R.C. seem positively Cro-Mag—but it's obvious why Morrigan has a corvid familiar; they are, pun intended, birds of a feather. "I mean, your own social group was about to peck you to pieces yesterday—what's up with that?" Chastising on, my voice ascends to the danger zone. "Then I rescue you, but do I get a single syllable of thanks? No! And now . . . now you order me around like a slave . . ." Oh, crap. I lose it—I do. I put my head on the wicker table and begin to blubber.

"Oh, stop that. Dice, will you please? I'm sorry, all right. And I am grateful, really."

I slide my teary face along my forearm to find Edgar eyeing me repentantly.

"It's just, us crows, we've got a reputation to uphold—we don't *do* nice. That doesn't mean we're bad," he goes on. "The thing with my brethren, when one of us is down, the rest will try to put him out of his misery—a mercy killing, really."

I lift my head. Maybe that's why the term for a flock of those mofos is "murder"—a murder of crows.

"And you know what, you're not in the mood to dig, don't

dig," he says. "Although for future reference, that rhododendron you got there is a gold mine for grubs."

I sniff, stow my tears. "You are incorrigible," I tell him. "The greediest, most self-interested little bugger I've ever met!"

"You think?" he says, his ruff bristled, one brilliant eye trained on me. "Well, then, you ought to get out more."

I stare back—and realize he's absolutely right. Mae Molly O'Rourke would make Edgar Allan Crow look like Mother Teresa. It's high time I got in her face—and I know just who to channel to make that happen. Of course, it will have to wait till tonight. Today's Thursday, and Tosh is off, so Bruise Blue practice is on—we've got another gig coming up. Besides, if I'm going to be tromping around a graveyard, I'm best off doing it in darkness.

The best part about today's rehearsal? Antonia Forsythe is absent. Pen dropped her at the Lovely Lady—despite a mostly grandmotherly demographic, it runs a bridal special: mani-pedi, eyebrow wax, and deep-pore facial. What a relief not having her here. We swing through the set in top form and actually have a blast.

Until Pen says, "Uh . . . Dice—is it in or out?"

And Tosh adds, "Just so you know, if we have a vote, we vote: in."

A fool who forgot ignorance is bliss, I ask what they're talking about.

Tosh glances at the rest of the guys. "Well, we've been calling it 'Let You Go.'"

Oh. That. *I can take her, I'm gonna make her, she gonna let you go.* The tune took a lot out of me, but put a lot into me too. I look at Sin, then check the rest of my bandmates, and then study the carpet.

Marsh comes over, a strong, slender arm around my shoulders. "We know you were freestyling . . ."

"But I recorded it on my phone," Pen pipes up. "In case you want a refresher . . ."

"Dice, it was so powerful," Duck reminds. "An anthem for the romantically disenfranchised—anyone who ever had a rival, or saw the one they love trapped in the wrong relationship . . ."

"True that." Tosh nods in affirmation. "An instant classic. That's why I'm saying we should share it with the world."

The world? Or at least Caroline Chadwick's birthday party? Assuming I make it to next week? "Of course," I say. "You're right—we should." I don't look at anyone when I add, "I can do it." Because I'm so not talking about the song.

# LXIII

ONE OF THOSE NIGHTS WHEN I WISH I DROVE. THE THREAT OF RAIN A psycho stalker, the clouds so low you can hear them huddle. I'm not even sure I know the way—I've visited the Grimley Parish Cemetery only once before, last Halloween, so I do peruse a few unnecessary hills till I find the place. But now I have. Some very old bones up in here.

As I train my flashlight, I get my bearings and head to the eighteenth century. Marker after marker after marker—none bears the name Mae Molly O'Rourke. More than halfway through it strikes me how upwardly mobile she'd been; maybe she found some jerk of a gentleman to marry her. Did I pass a Mae Molly Something Else? I'd hate to start over, since I'm taking a leap of assumption already. The Forsythes left town within a year of their daughter's death; Lady Anne easily could have brought her pretty, witty maid with her. Mae Molly may not have even made her ashes-to-ashes exit in Swoon.

Only whoa, ho, ho—what's this. A fancy monument inscribed MAEILI CHADWICK. Maeili. Gaelic to me, judging by my crash course in the Celtic tongue—Mae Molly a nimble conversion for a new life in the colonies. What's more, Caroline Chadwick's family goes way back around here, always in real estate, mega money—precisely the kind of clan an ambitious social climber would want to sink her hooks into. Maeili Chadwick, huh? Born: 1747. Died: 1809. I kneel at the grave. I feel at the grave. I'm still not sure, but it's worth a shot.

Flashlight: off. Summoning: on! "Morrigan! Persephone! Isis! Hel! Morrigan! Persephone! Isis! Hel! Morrigan! Persephone! Isis! Hel!" Thrice incant the goddess. "See me here in the black of night. Take my blood—an emblem of my devotion." With a razor I cut the meatiest part of my palm—no biggie, really—and squeeze a thin red line. "Know the great need in me and grant the dominion only your dark rule can provide."

Now comes the tough part, imploring the goddess within and without: "Hear this song in your honor and through it bring me the one known as Mae Molly O'Rourke, whose bones lie beneath this ground and whose spirit does not rest." No thunder, no lightning—the night still as a tomb. "Send forth Mae Molly O'Rourke so I may gain the knowledge I seek!"

It's called "Siúil a Rúin." A haunting melody in D minor. The lyrics I memorized phonetically off the Internet machine, but having read the English translation, aching with sorrow and loneliness for a lost love, it feels close to me.

And not me only . . .

"Memory fails, but me heart knows that tune!"

Yeah, I thought it might've been in her repertoire. An apparition shimmers before me, wealthy, elderly—Mae Molly on her burial day. Traces of the beauty that so beguiled my boy remain: the ebony tresses now polished silver, the skin still fair. Looking longer, though, I see the ravages unhappiness wrought—a mouth hard lined by perpetual frown, wattles of excess under her chin. Worst of all, flickers of dismal confusion in eyes that once so brutally assayed.

"You are Maeilli Chadwick, also known as Mae Molly O'Rourke," I say for confirmation.

"I am? Yes, of course I am." Her gaze bounces irritably. "Why am I here—'tis oh so cold. Where is me shawl? Bring it, girl."

She's not the boss of me—and we need to get that straight. "You're here because I summoned you. You're cold because you're dead and damned. But if you're honest with me, Mae Molly, the goddess of the underworld might release you, and you'd know peace, and no more would your soul be so easily called by this witch or any other."

A gasp from the ghost. "Witch!" Then she collects herself, says, "Honest?" in the huffy tone of liars. "What is it ye want, then—out with it!"

"I want to know about your former mistress Antonia Forsythe—"

"Mistress? I had no mistress! See my dress—is it not a lady's finery?"

"Think, Mae Molly. When you were young, you worked in a manor house."

"Did I? Oh, aye—yes." Drifting, drifting, then with fierce and sudden clarity says, "But I did not work for that oafish brat. The mother was me mistress, and she of royal blood . . . Lady . . ." She wrestles with it. "Lady Anne!"

"That's right, Lady Anne. But you served Antonia as well."

"So what?" the specter says with a snarl. "So what if I did?"

"So I want to know about her—and her relationship with Sinclair Youngblood Powers."

The sound of his name makes her clap her hands, those small, childish hands, so greedy and grasping. "Sinclair!" For a flash she's young again—lustful, insatiable. "My Sinclair! He loves me, ye know."

*Oh, no he doesn't,* I want to tell her. Never did. Never will.

"And I love him, truly—but we were not to be."

The first part of her statement throws me, since after all she spurned the boy. But maybe her hunger trumped her heart, so I question her on the second part. "Because he loved another?"

She cleaves those two hands together to squash the very idea. "That wasn't love! He simply wanted in with the Forsythes."

Harsh laughter, tinged with admiration. "How could I fault him for that? Take Antonia in marriage, he'd never sweat over the forge again."

Whoa—interesting. Mae Molly thought Sin as acquisitive as she. When he told her he'd found love, he spoke of Hannah Miles; only she got it twisted, presuming he meant Antonia, his access to the Forsythe fortune. Rapacious people must believe everyone is driven by bottomless want. And I thought love was the great motivator.

"Knocked me in the noggin, but Lady Anne might have conceded, despite Sinclair's low birth, so as to be rid of the sulky little nuisance." Again her palms rub, and with effort her lips creak upward. "But I put a fly in that ointment, by rights. Foiled them good and proper."

So the tarot proves true. Mae Molly O'Rourke, wielder of Five Swords, the spiteful, malicious cuts that bleed slow rather than kill quick. "You did? How?"

"How what?" she asks, expression occluded once more. "Oh, why do ye plague me, girl?"

"Because I need to know." Then, commandingly, or is it desperately, "And you *will* tell me!"

Mae Molly peers at me, cognizance returning, to foxily observe, "So ye love him too!"

"That's neither here nor there." I see no reason to contradict, but I'm trying to keep her focused. "How did you foil their plans?"

"It was the letters," Mae Molly reveals with sparkly satisfaction. "When Antonia wasn't with her roses, she was at her escritoire, that sphincter of a mouth screwed up all tight, quill poised as she composed her missives. Once whilst taking fresh linens to her room, I nicked a half-finished one from the desk—dripping emotion and metaphors likening his arms to tree boughs, that sort of rot. Ah, but even without peeking I could guess the contents, what with the moony way she acted whenever he'd come round. Well, of course she had no way to know Sinclair and I were lovers, so she had me deliver the epistles. Half daft and fully mute by then, she nonetheless made clear her plea—I saw the rapture in her eyes, his name across the envelopes."

"And . . . you didn't do it?"

"Do what? Oh, no . . . indeed I did not."

Could this be the secret to Sin's unuttered vow?

"I burned the bloody things. No . . . I thought to burn them, then thought otherwise, perchance they come in handy." She taps her temple to show her savvy, and with a chuckle adds, "Lest they be considered incriminating . . ."

Blackmail, she means. Why destroy evidence that someone of Antonia Forsythe's standing claimed love for a common man, a bastard, a half breed.

"Where did you put them?" I prod.

"I burned them, I told you!" she reneges angrily.

They didn't call it Alzheimer's back in the day, but clearly

Mae Molly was afflicted. "No, you didn't. You kept them. You *hid* them. Where?" I let her ruminate a moment more as my impatience percolates. "Tell me, and cleanse your soul. Tell me, and be set free."

Only Mae Molly brings her hands to her face and fills them with an anguished sob. When they fall away, I realize I'll be leaving this boneyard with one crucial question still unanswered.

"Have mercy, girl, I would tell ye—I would!—but a mouse has nibbled away at me mind like it were a hunk of cheese. The letters are in the manor, for certain. But I swear on my love for that man of mine I know not where I laid them."

I study her, a wretched crone in fancy clothes, cringing against her own gravestone. In her youth she plotted, seduced, and entrapped, only to wind up too bewildered to testify on her own evil. She got everything she wanted—just as Antonia believes *she* will—except, of course, for love. So I turn away from her.

"Wait!" Mae Molly cries. "What of the peace ye promised me?"

Wearily I turn back. "I didn't *promise*." The word is dirt in my mouth. "Your fate lies with my goddess now. Were you truthful, I trust that she'll free you in my good faith. Were you lying"—I level my eyes on her—"then suffer, bitch."

I'm drawn to Forsythe Manor like the spokes of my bike are magnetized. There's not much to see on a night so thick; it's more like I sense the house, its corridors, rooms, and closets, its myriad nooks and crannies. Somewhere inside, Antonia's love letters, unrequited and unread. Or not. In two centuries plus, any number of real estate agents, cleaning crews, or subsequent owners might have tossed them in the trash. Of course, everything I've ascertained about Mae Molly has me convinced that if she wanted the letters hidden, they'd stay that way till she was ready to retrieve them.

I think of the people in that house. Those who live there—Duck and his parents. Those who died there—Early and all those rootless spirits. Mostly, imprisoned there, the sweet, sensitive guy in love with my best friend—Crane. Are they counting on me to locate the letters that could unlock the puzzle?

I ought to head home. Instead I walk my bike up the curving drive and leave it at the top, then start across the lawn, following some masochistic mechanism toward Antonia's garden. Outside the stone fence, the perfume is so intense I'm surprised it's not visible as vapor. I don't know diddly about roses—when they're supposed to bloom, when they're supposed to die—but by scent alone can tell they're even more profuse now than on the day Crane vanished. You'd probably need a machete to move around in there—hardly conducive to a wedding.

"It's to take place right here." A sentry steps forward from the gate, his voice husky, hurting, yet still not resigned. Sin.

Why am I unsurprised to find him here, all alone in the

middle of the night? Because I know him—he's racking his brain, ransacking his memory, berating himself over some misinterpreted message he somehow must have sent. I suppose he simply aches to understand. Even if comprehension cannot keep him from the altar awaiting, he just wants to *know*.

Together we stand at the gate. His gate. Her gate.

With its stunning crux, that iron rose. Compelled closer, I find it in the dark, caress the petals just as Antonia did when she first set eyes on it. How thrilled she must have been—this work of art, rendered just for her, the poor little rich girl who had everything but nothing.

I pull back my hand and pivot, knowing my boy is near enough to kiss. And while my kiss might comfort him, it's the magic music inside me that rises up instead. *"Doesn't matter what you said . . . What you promised . . . What you did . . ."*

A groan comes from him unbidden. "Oh, my drowsy thrush . . ."

"Sin, I mean it! Pledge, promise, oath, vow—if there's one thing I figured out, it's that you can't *swear* to love." Speaking now, my pulse a rush and my words tumbling. "Love . . . happens to you; you don't make it happen. You damn well don't control it. Swear to love?" I shake my head. "That's not love; that's slavery."

Emotional slavery. Inflicted with expectations, executed with manipulations. It's putting chains around a heart, shutting something beautiful up in a box. That's what Antonia's done to Sin. Guess no one ever told her if you love someone, set him free.

"Love is a gift," I rant on. "We don't know what creates it and we don't know what sustains it. If we're smart, we revere it, treat it with the honor it fosters in us, but that's still no guarantee."

It's dark but I see his eyes shine; I see his smile. And I realize how, when I woke up alone that morning last fall, I wouldn't have been able to articulate any of this—I didn't understand our love till now.

A single step, and he closes the space between us. "What makes love so precious is its mystery," he says. "No one knows that better than we."

When he holds me, it's forever. When he holds me, it's for never. Then I look into his eyes again. "I don't care what happened at this garden gate two hundred years ago, and I don't care what goes down here tomorrow. All I care about is now. I love you, Sin. I love you now."

PART V

# THE GIFT

# LXIV

MY NAME FROM HIS MOUTH. SPOKEN AS ONLY HE CAN. THEN SIN proclaims his love and kisses me, a kiss that starts with lips and leads to his full-court press, our fingers fastened, against the gate. After which he sees me home—him pedaling and me doing my best to balance on the handlebars. Now here we are, about to part in front of 12 Daisy Lane, and he begins, shyly if you can believe: "Dice, do you think . . . would it be possible for you and I . . . to spend an evening—tomorrow evening . . . well, I suppose it's *this* evening by now—to simply . . . perhaps—"

"Sin." I have to interrupt. "Are you asking me out?"

"Yes. Yes, I am. Dear lady, won't you please come out with me, so that we may pursue, together, you and I, whatever our hearts desire, not to be denied?"

Any wonder I wake up this morning giggling aloud at the absurdity: I'm Sin's bachelor party.

In preparation, I while away much of the day imitating an odalisque. I know, I know—I ought to launch a cellar-to-attic search for Antonia's letters, only right now, in the throes of a potent, not unpleasant inertia, I could scarcely launch a search for toilet paper. I loll in my PJs, earbuds in, watching the ceiling fan spin. If only we had kumquats or bonbons—appropriate munchies for my mood.

The polar opposite of Antonia's mood. She's in a veritable tizzy. When I venture downstairs, I find her flitting from one piece of furniture to the next, trying not to nibble her freshly painted nails (a pukey pink that clashes with her gray-green skin). The TV remote has become an appendage as she spasms through soap operas, chat shows, gossip, golf. For the most part we avoid each other, despite the close quarters—the way you do when you're giving your mother the silent treatment. Though at one point the phone rings and we nearly butt heads.

"Hullo?" I listen, then extend the receiver. It's the Kendall Wynn Inn.

"This is Antonia Forsythe. Oh, what wonderful news. Yes, we shall see you tomorrow. Thank you kindly."

They must've had a cancellation. Antonia seems tickled (pukey) pink. She'd scowled at the computer when it looked like the Ramada off the highway would be the location of yonder bridal bed. Now she stares me down, her flat triumph rumpled by a bump of indecision. To wit: I'm still here, her great big loose end. Should she do me in or spare me, put me out permanently or force me to witness at the sidelines of her victory? I stand here—jaw jutted, hip thrust, spleen stalwartly filtering blood—and then sashay to yonder fridge.

No kumquats, no bonbons. Strawberries—that's kind of concubiney. I tote them to the porch, bite off a sweet bottom, and hold the cap to the bars of the birdcage. "Snack?" I say.

Peckish, Edgar investigates. "Not bad," he says. "Not worms, but not bad."

Heaving a grunt, I pop another berry, then flop to rummage under the rhododendron. Bird Boy wasn't kidding—it's a squishy smorgasbord down here. I'm back in a flash with a repulsive napkinful.

"All right!" Edgar gobbles, again and again. "You're spoiling me."

"Don't caw with your beak full," I tell him, grinning.

RubyCat, curled up on a chintz cushion, lifts her head to make sure she's not missing out. "Me? Meat?" she queries.

"No, my little furball," I assure. "Just bugs and berries."

Still, she rises to her toes, stretches a horseshoe, and leaps to pose in front of the cage. Edgar hops to his perch. A staring contest ensues, yet remarkably I sense no threat from either side. They just . . . regard each other. Somehow when I wasn't looking, those two established, if not a rapport, then a truce, a respect, no doubt in deference to me. Wiping my hands, I watch them watch each other, then park it in one of the wicker chairs. RubyCat claims my lap. Idly, I stroke her.

"So . . . ," Edgar says. "How's it going . . . with all your . . . everything?"

I cock my head his way. Confessing to the crow about my magical efforts wouldn't be a breach, would it? After all, he's part of them. And it's not like I'm making much progress, chatting up crotchety ghosts who've long lost their grip on reality. Maybe he'll have an insightful take on my encounter with Mae Molly. Maybe it would just feel good to vent, unload, divulge. So I do, spilling all I know about the summer of 1768: Antonia's mad crush, her maid's malicious meddling, the cache of letters still tucked away somewhere in Forsythe Manor, the wedding proceeding tomorrow as planned.

Edgar preens his ruff. Then he preens his chest. The cat leaves my lap for her cushion and begins to lick her coat fastidiously. Maybe grooming helps animals think, the way people will twirl a curl or gnaw a lip. Either that or I've bored the beasties.

At last, the crow says, "Sucks to be you, then."

Wow, such wisdom—I'm truly in awe. "Actually, no. Sin and I are in love, and in a few hours we're going on a date." So ridiculous, considering all we've been through—and by ridiculous I mean glorious. "After that, who knows—divine intervention?"

Edgar bobs his head with approval. "That's right, think positive. A wing and a prayer and all that." With a sudden flurry he tests out his own wings. "Speaking of which, I'm feeling A-OK and ready for takeoff. So why don't you snap the latch and let me out of here?"

Already? I was getting used to my acerbic feathered friend. But far be it from me to keep something beautiful in a box—or a cage. "You sure?" I say.

A few more mighty flaps in answer.

"You got it . . ." I swing the door and insert my forearm. Edgar climbs aboard, the pinch of his talons a scratchy caress. Carefully I bring him out until we're eyeball to eyeball. On impulse I kiss the top of his head.

He grabs a strand of my bangs, pulls it tight, lets it go.

The tip of RubyCat's tail twitches jealously—but just once.

"Okay, Dice, you take it easy," the bird says. "You're a good egg."

"A good egg? That's funny coming from—"

Before I can finish my sentence, the fledgling has flown.

Water roars into the claw-foot cauldron while I toss in feminine unguents and oils. Then I strip, the slopes and circumferences of my body growing dewy in the rising steam. Candles? Sure, why not; I spark up a few. Then compile implements on a tray: razor, pumice, pouf. All set to leisurely pamper myself, anoint and appoint myself. For him. Oh yeah, now I'm dewy on the inside too. Bubbles threaten to overflow—I shut the taps and

dip into the scalding brew. A gleeful pain, and gleefully I with-
stand it. Lower, lower, lower. Thighs waft wide. Breasts float
free. In a syllable: Ahhhh!

"Yo, rock star."

Ruby leans against the sink, her greeting piquant, her manner
mild, and her outfit . . . vaguely familiar. Which is very strange.
In life, she'd occasionally wear the same thing twice, but in death,
different story: She knows no sartorial budget or bounds and
constantly seeks to outdo herself. What's more, this dress—long-
sleeved, high-necked, basic not even black but beige—is so not
her taste. Funnily enough she looks awesome—elegant, languid,
even serene—like those frenetic fashion statements were kid stuff
and she's ascended to a whole new level. Just to mess with her, I
scoop some bubbles and blow in her direction.

She catches the froth on a fingertip, watches it fizzle to nothing. "I just wanted to check in," she says. "Make sure you're not
mad, the way I sent you into that party solo."

"You mean up in Chester?" It feels like eons ago. Warm bath
and fragranced atmosphere conspire, melting time and space
to a misty swirl. Or is it Ruby, her dress so simple, her voice so
soft, imbuing the room with tranquil entrancement. I sink to
my chin and tell her, "Don't be silly. I had the best time."

"I can tell," she says. "That makes me really happy, Dice.
Happy for you . . ."

I look at her, though she's blurry through the bubbles, in

that demure dress, the last dress she ever wore. Now her voice sounds fuzzy too, as if she's far away . . .

"Happy for me, too . . ."

Maybe that's because I've dunked all the way. Dimly, from underwater, I hear her call me Dice and say good-bye, and it strikes me—gently—that she never calls me Dice, and she never says good-bye. So when I emerge and find her gone, I know she's truly gone. Dissolved. Absolved. Bad influence turned guardian angel turned soul at peace. Everyone sensed a change in me after my night in the woods; Ruby understood it. When it comes to me, Ruby always knows . . . knew. I've found the goddess within—all of them—and by their guidance and their grace, I can go it alone. And Ruby can be free.

As to the demon in my house—it's still *my* house—I feel no fear. Is that her silent tread on the stair, come to hold me down, drown me dead? Let her try. Music is my aura, my amulet, my armor—music my sword and shield. So I finish my ablutions, deliberate and lazy, giving myself to the blues. Sing low, sing strong. Know it, mean it, make it my own. *"Just a little spoon of your precious love satisfies my soul . . ."*

# LXV

Date details? Sorry, no. Suffice it to say it starts with an equine whinny at my door and ends at the same place a little after dawn. A final kiss and then I tra-la-la traipse inside. My house. My stuff. Too bad the redolence of roses lingers, even with an early breeze and every window wide. Fortunately, I catch a whiff of something else and follow it. Mmm . . . much better . . . butter.

Marsh in the kitchen, making toast. At one point last night, Sin and I showed up at the Double K and she fixed us a caloric peccadillo that's not on the menu and probably illegal in several states.

"Hey . . . ," I whisper.

The knife clangs against the plate. "Dice!"

I hold a finger to my lips.

"You were gone all night!" She takes it to a hush. She doesn't ask if I'm okay—she sees me beaming.

"Don't be freaked if Black Jack seems a little out of it. We put some miles on that bad boy."

Marsh grins. "I'll give him a lump of sugar. Did you guys have fun?"

"Yeah." I crick my neck as the fun catches up to me. "Lots of it. Now I've got to crash."

She considers her toast, then me, struggles to keep her voice steady. "What about later? Are you planning to . . . you know . . . attend?"

"The Swoon social event of the year? I wouldn't miss it."

"Oh, Dice." Marsh nibbles her lip. "How can you be so . . . so . . ."

What is it that I am? Insouciant? Fatalistic? Wasted on after-glow? This afternoon at four, my absolute worst-case scenario is set to kick in, and I won't be doing a damn thing to stop it. Which is actually all right with me. Because sometimes you can follow the questions till you hit a brick wall—or a stone wall with an iron gate in the middle. Sometimes you can be up to your eyeballs in blessings and still blunder around like a babe in the woods. Sometimes you have to let hope and faith and trust do their thing, relinquish the control you never had in the first place, and accept what's going to happen like a wave coming in from the sea. Pure love is stronger than promised love. I believe that, and belief is all I need. It's all anybody needs. "I don't know," I finally reply. "The universe is a whacky place."

"The Universe." Capital implied. "Like the tarot card."

"That's right. The end is the end, and whoever's left standing dusts off and starts again." Which probably sounds more ominous that I want it to. Really, I'm good. "Look, I'll see you there." Then I add, "Crane, too."

The alarm goes off. The shades are drawn and the house is silent. The bride and her attendants must all be across the road, primping at Pen's. Flower girls Charlotte and Willa chattering excitedly, my cousin painting brave faces with the magic of her makeup kit, Antonia . . . whatever she's feeling, if she feels at all.

With a stretch, I decide to revel in Sin all day—his essence, his taste, all over me. I fling back the summer blanket; drink in my naked self. Fresh and tender, throbbing before I can trace it with a fingertip—it's back, my blue bruise. I marvel at it for a minute. Then I force myself to break the daze, get dressed, and dash.

The first thing that hits me at Forsythe Manor is the Cutlass parked in the drive. Guess Kurt got it fixed just in time; threw in a wax job, his gift to the groom. At least he didn't attach tin cans and a JUST MARRIED! banner to the rear bumper. Here's Pen's ride, of course, and the Pinch Me Round van. An unfamiliar vehicle that must belong to the justice of the peace; who else would drive a Buick sedan? I'm not late, but clearly everyone's here. I dump my bike—better hustle.

Except for the JOTP in pinstripes and Marsh's sisters, clad to be cute, everyone else is beyond causal, like we got together for a Bruise Blue rehearsal and came outside for a break. Pen defiant in shapeless black; Tosh still sporting cook pants. Kurt, the unlikely best man, oleaginous as ever. Me in comfort clothes—ancient cargos, skinny-ribbed tank. And the groom? The groom is the groom. The groom is in jeans-boots-PWT, mirrored shades and shaggy hair and that scruffy, silky beard (that does tickle . . . divinely). In other words, the groom is gorgeous.

The sight of him stuns me. A few hours ago we were together, in every definition of the term. Now some old guy in a suit will drone mumbo jumbo and by the powers vested in him by the great state of Connecticut pronounce Sinclair Youngblood Powers and Antonia Forsythe Powers husband and wife.

I beseech Sin's shades; he removes them and sends his gaze into me.

Do I make the sound of timber falling? I don't know, but Pen and Tosh trot up.

"Hey . . ." My cousin administers a quick hug. Then she and her boy each take a flank and link arms through mine.

The judge starts to sneeze. And sneeze and sneeze. The breeze has picked up, scattering pollen like talcum powder—poor geezer must be allergic to roses. He pulls a linen square from his breast pocket and blows.

Marsh steers her sisters our way. Another bout of wind swirls up, stealing the petals from their baskets, lofting them like paper scraps, letters torn up in a rage.

"Heyyy!" cries Willa.

"Noooo!" cries Charlotte.

"Girls, please don't fuss," Marsh scolds. Then she gasps and nudges me.

Duck resplendent in twin tails, ruffled shirt, cummerbund like a satin hammock, pointy patent-leather loafers. Did I mention the hue? Baby blue. On his arm, the bride wears white. The bouquet gargantuan, every flower on earth must represent. The gown is a full-on fairy-tale parody that falls unevenly across her body and jerks rather than billows with her gaffe of a gait. The hair—though Pen was no doubt tempted to botch it—is sleek, upswept, and amply sprayed, but no amount of bronzer-blush combo could correct the atrocious tint to her complexion. She totally should have gone for the veil. Antonia is every inch a zombie bride. I can't suppress my giggle.

Then the judge sneezes six more times in succession, honks into his hankie, and opens his book, which is clearly a prop. He could deliver this no-frills oration in his sleep. Then he begins. "Dear friends . . ."

The JOTP is a professional; he officiates as such. Yet this has got to be the weirdest wedding of his entire career. The bride is gruesome, the fellow giving her away far too young for the fatherly role, the best man anything but, and the groom, by all appearances, is entering martyrdom, not matrimony. Still, he carries on, sallies forth—till he reaches the "forever hold your peace" part, and it's clear that the preceding weirdness was merely a warm-up.

Stopping midsentence, the JOTP removes and wipes his glasses, replaces them, and continues to stand there agape. We turn and see why. A patch of taupe, like a bald spot on the lawn, scurrying toward the garden gate. Closer it comes, and I realize the rapidly moving swatch of landscape is . . . furry? That's right, furry. An infantry of field mice, four-legged foot soldiers, and running alongside, leading the charge, the field-mice field marshal, is a cat. A calico cat. *My* calico cat. Who must, in some way, deliver a command, since the mice—dozens and dozens of them—split formation to make a semicircle around us, and then stand fast.

Someone cries, "Eek!"

I think it's Willa. Or maybe Duck.

Now, from above, a terrible scream, along with a whirring dense as a military helicopter. The airborne squadron is a murder of many, blue-black iridescent wings battering the sun. Crows wheel and swoop in unison, then all at once swerve away, leaving just one of their ranks—small but feisty—to drop something from his beak between the judge and the nuptial pair.

Sin says, "What's this?"

Everyone wonders the same thing. Me included—and then all at once I know. A little bird didn't have to tell me. My psychic sense didn't have to tell me either. This is faith, hope, and trust in action, made manifest, come to our rescue.

A fragile, yellowed bundle, tied with ribbon, once red, now the palest blush. As Sin bends to retrieve it, the crow roosts on the uppermost bar of the gate. In my head he hails me, and when I meet his eye, he winks.

"It's . . . they're letters," Sin tells our small assembly. "Letters addressed to me."

Recognizing her own calligraphy, Antonia says, "Why . . . indeed they are—my letters to you. Sinclair, my dearest, had you mislaid them?"

"Mislaid them?" Sin riffles the envelopes. "What are you talking about? I've never seen these letters."

"But of course you have—I had my maid deliver each one."

A flare of anger in Sin's eyes—he remembers that maid, all too well.

"You mustn't pretend, Sinclair." Antonia scans the faces around her, then returns to his. "After all, when first we wooed, I did not speak." That titter. Thin, cracked. "If you hadn't read my letters, we'd not be exchanging vows this day."

Pushing the aviators to the crown of his head, groom regards bride with absolute earnestness. "Antonia," he says, "I never received these letters. Nor did I read them. Look here: the seals are all intact."

Antonia drops her mammoth bouquet to examine, one after the other, where her wax monogram remains. "But . . . but, Sinclair—this is a mistake . . . a cruel prank . . ." She presses the envelopes against his chest. "You . . . I . . . after all . . . the gate!" Reels toward his masterpiece. "Right here in the center, my iron rose!" Pets the metal madly. "In my very last letter, I implored you to give me a sign of your sworn love, and here it is!" Tinny and shrill, her voice scales several octaves into hysterics. "Here it is! Here it is!"

Now Sin passes the letters to his grease-monkey groomsman and with one purposeful stride faces the ashen abomination. With sadness. With sympathy. With, at long last, comprehension. "Antonia, I'm truly sorry," he says. "This gate was built to your father's specifications. I drew several plans; the one with the rose centerpiece is the one he commissioned. This is the gate I was set to create all along, before you and I ever met."

For several frozen seconds she is silent, the gray eyes spent bullets, the mouth a grommet. Then she begins to keen—a frightful wail of refusal. The promise she'd clung to through centuries, through incarnations, falls away, proving false, and all that's left is the grain of doubt. The simple sorcery that aided Antonia once fails her now. What comes from the earth belongs there in the end. So her bouquet withers where she let it drop.

Then her hands—so adroit with the trowel, so secure in the soil—shrivel like autumn leaves. The malnourished rosebud lips release their final epithet and are sucked inside, her entire visage a sinkhole now. Flesh peels back from limbs; breasts and belly reduce to peanuts; bones go brittle as twigs. Then there is just a white dress on green grass, fluttering in the dying breeze.

Sin gazes at it, dazed, then hunkers down. He means to gather it up but can't seem to complete the task; the gown across his knee, he turns to me. I go to him, picking up an end, and together we fold the garment like a flag draped on a soldier's casket. He takes the dress, together with the envelopes, and lays them on the altar. The crow flies from his post on the gate to land on the stack, observing Sin and me with an unblinking stare. At that, relief begins to beacon from my boy's eyes.

The briefest glance at his left wrist and then, "We're free," Sin says in front of everyone, and only to me. "Dice . . . we're free."

Not just us. From the house we can hear shouting. A bit weak, but utterly joyous. We hear, "Marsh!" And we hear, "Duck!" Dozens and dozens of field mice scatter as Crane Williams comes tearing up the lawn toward the garden gate.

## LXVI

New England beach communities are beyond busy at the peak of summer. Even a remote island off the coast, the kind of craggy rock with one hotel and two restaurants, will be popping. Yet with persistence, if one trawls the Internet machine, one can sometimes find the rare, last-minute reservation.

Sin and I stay a week. The most glorious week of our lives.

When the sun is out, we swim far beyond the breakers—as natural as breathing to me now. We lie in the sand, walk on the shore. He gets so brown; I get a few freckles.

When the moon is out, we have a meal on the veranda at one restaurant or the other, and then it's back to the beach. Me riffing whatever trips off my tongue, him answering on blues harp. Waves are our audience, crashing approval, or just crashing, since that's what waves do. Occasionally, we catch a falling star. We don't wish on it, though.

And when it storms—as it will, with unpredictable regularity come summer in New England—we make thunder and lightning of our own.

Until we return to the real world. In three days, the house at 12 Daisy Lane will officially belong to Sinclair Youngblood Powers. He's going through with the sale, since after all, real estate is a solid investment. Not as solid as gold, maybe, but Antonia's dowry weighed nearly eighty pounds (translating to some 1.3 mil in cold hard cash), so Sin's pretty much established for a while. He didn't want to leave my parents in the lurch. Besides, to him and to me, 12 Daisy Lane is our house now. These last few days and nights, as we putter in the yard, play with the cat, pounce on each other in bed—normal, ordinary acts—mean more than our idyllic island escape. Even boxing up my crap has the special bittersweet flavor of dark-roast coffee.

"You want to keep these?" Garnet-colored cordial glasses my mother flipped for at a flea market. "I doubt Momster remembers buying them. She's an impulse-purchase person."

Sin's up on a stepladder, taking down my Nana Lena's "old" set of "good" china, used at this address exactly twice. "A bit dainty for my needs," he says.

Shrugging, I swathe them in Bubble Wrap. "What about these?" A pair of champagne flutes.

"Those stay," he says decisively. "For your visits."

"Oh, okay—that ought to give me incentive."

He makes me a face—half-up, half-down. Then I hear someone call my name. Inside my head. Out on the porch. If it isn't Edgar Allan Crow on the wicker table, behind a stack of woebegone letters.

"Special delivery," he says. "In all the hubbub, you forgot them."

Yeah—accidentally on purpose. I fiddle with the edge of an envelope. "Thanks . . ."

"Don't mention it. They were in the nursery, by the way. A slotted panel under the dormer window. Hermetically sealed, practically. But you know mice."

"Actually," I say, "I don't know mice."

"For future reference, then: As rodents go, they're completely single-minded and can get in anywhere. No chink too small, that's their motto."

"But how—"

"R.C. recruited them." He anticipates me. "Guaranteed feline protection across her territory."

"But how—"

"I told her the plan and she was all, 'Ooh! Yay! Good bird!'" the little mastermind explains. "She'd been going bonkers wondering how to help you. Not exactly bright, that one—but she loves you."

She does. And I love her. That's why she won't be relocating. This country cat would climb the walls of an Upper West Side apartment—literally, on Momster's drapes. I look at her, a-snooze on her cushion; then I look back at Edgar. "So anyway,"

I tell him, "I'm pretty much out of here. College . . . in the city."

He gives a shriek, beats his wings, cocks his head at me. "You'll be back," he says, and then takes off. Not big on mushy farewells, apparently.

But I don't sweat it. Since he's right, I will be back, and I will see him. I did my research. Crows live about seven years, assuming they avoid oncoming SUVs. One thing I envy about other animals: They have no concept of their own mortality. Humans are the only creatures that know we're going to die.

I flip through the letters. Seven in all. This must be the first one, formally addressed to Mr. Sinclair Y. Powers, Swoon, CT. This must be the last, to My Darling—.

*Sorry, Antonia,* I think. He's *my* darling.

I swivel to see him standing in the doorway. Lofting the letters, I say, "Mail's in."

Sin shudders. "I don't want them."

I don't either, really. Yet I can't see torching them, after all we've been through. Plus, they probably have some historical significance. Maybe tonight, when we head to the Williams place—our last Bruise Blue jam for a while—I'll excuse myself. Slip up to the nursery, find the panel under the dormer, put the letters where they belong.

The Williams place. That's what it is—forget Forsythe Manor. With Duck and his parents heading to London and then Madagascar next month, Crane will be squire and Marsh—already halfway moved in—his lady. They're officially engaged, Crane pulling out the ring within minutes of his reappearance that fateful Saturday. A spontaneous betrothal blowout ensued, so the goodies Tosh brought for the "modest reception" didn't go to waste.

If I can't accustom to calling it the Williams place, maybe Swoon Sounds will catch on. That's the school Crane's starting up—a rock 'n' roll conservatory for Connecticut rich kids. He'll be headmaster, Pen will manage, and Tosh will drive himself nuts between cooking and teaching. Marsh will stay out of it—vet tech training will have her up to her eyeballs in anatomy. Maybe she'll go all the way and become a veterinarian. Hell, maybe I'll be an animal behaviorist, and we'll partner up someday. Anything's possible. This we know.

But I'm spacing. "What's up?" I say to Sin, heading back into the house.

"I found this clattering around in the clothes dryer." He dangles a silver charm by its chain.

The archangel. The demon slayer. Collateral for the journey gem. After Fracas and I made our exchange, I tucked Saint Michael in the pocket of my skirt—damn, that load of laundry was way past due. "No worse for wear," I say. "I'll return it tonight."

Maybe Tosh will give the amulet to Pen. A nice present, a sweet sentiment, but hardly necessary. My cousin is proving she can take care of herself. Hear that, all you demons?

Excuse my psychic shout-out, but this is Swoon, C-T. Even on a peaceful summer afternoon, doing mundane chores with the boy I love, I'm well aware of that. Here and there I sense stuff, in the spaces between our sentences, the stillness around our gestures. Positive sparks, negative charges. Whispers in shadows, omens in the wind. Specifically, there's still that gaping spectral fissure at Forsythe Manor—I mean the Williams place, a.k.a. Swoon Sounds. The notion seizes me—all those inquisitive, talented kids roaming the old house, all those tortured spirits roaming too . . .

Abruptly I sit down, gaze off.

In half a breath, Sin kneels before me. "My lady?"

A perfunctory peck assures him I'm fine, but he wants further confirmation, taking a deeper kiss. After a moment, he parts my thighs to trace the blue cascade that spills down my leg. It's fading, almost gone, a plain old regular black-and-blue.

Inevitably he asks, "As to your first visit?"

Swoon in autumn. The hay rides. The corn maze. The foliage a riot of hues and the crisp air rife with apples, spice, wood smoke, and definitely not roses. "How about Halloween?"

"Halloween! That's eons away," Sin complains, a gentle growl. "Perhaps I shall come see you in the city before then. I believe I'll like New York."

I smile at him. I say, "You may."

Sort of permission. Kind of invitation.

"Very well, then," he banters back. "I may."

It's a possibility. Not a promise. Never, between us, anything so foolish as a promise.

# POSTSCRIPT

My Sinclair—

Whilst you have spoken to me sweetly, and I
have penned you many missives in kind, our
love transcends vulgar verbalism. It is with
our sighs, our glances, and our gestures that we
convey our true passion. Soon—soon!—we shall
add kisses and caresses to our vocabulary. But
first, before I agree to be yours forever, I must
ask that you give me an irrefutable symbol of
your devotion. Trust your imagination, my
darling—it will reveal to you the most sincere
sign by which to swear your troth to me. Trust,
too, that when I see it I shall know. I shall
write you no more, for this final letter tells all.
Eagerly, I await your promise, and remain,
faithfully, adoringly . . .

Yours—
Antonia

## ABOUT THE AUTHOR

Nina Malkin is the author of four other novels, one novella, and a memoir. She's also an award-winning journalist specializing in pop culture and lifestyles, whose work has appeared in the *New York Times*, *Entertainment Weekly*, *Real Simple*, and numerous other publications. Nina lives in her native Brooklyn with her musician husband and assorted felines. Find out more at ninamalkin.com.